The Midnight Queen

By Sylvia Hunter

The Midnight Queen
Lady of Magick
Season of Spells

a&b

The Midnight Queen

SYLVIA HUNTER

Allison & Busby Limited
12 Fitzroy Mews
London W1T 6DW
allisonandbusby.com

First published in 2014.
This edition published in Great Britain by Allison & Busby in 2016.

A CIP catalogue record for this book is available from the British Library.

10 9 8 7 6 5 4 3 2 1

ISBN 978-0-7490-2036-1

Typeset in 11/16 pt Adobe Garamond Pro by
Allison & Busby Ltd.

The paper used for this Allison & Busby publication has been pro[illegible] legally sourced from well managed and credibly certified forests.

Printed and bound by
CP[illegible] CR0 4YY

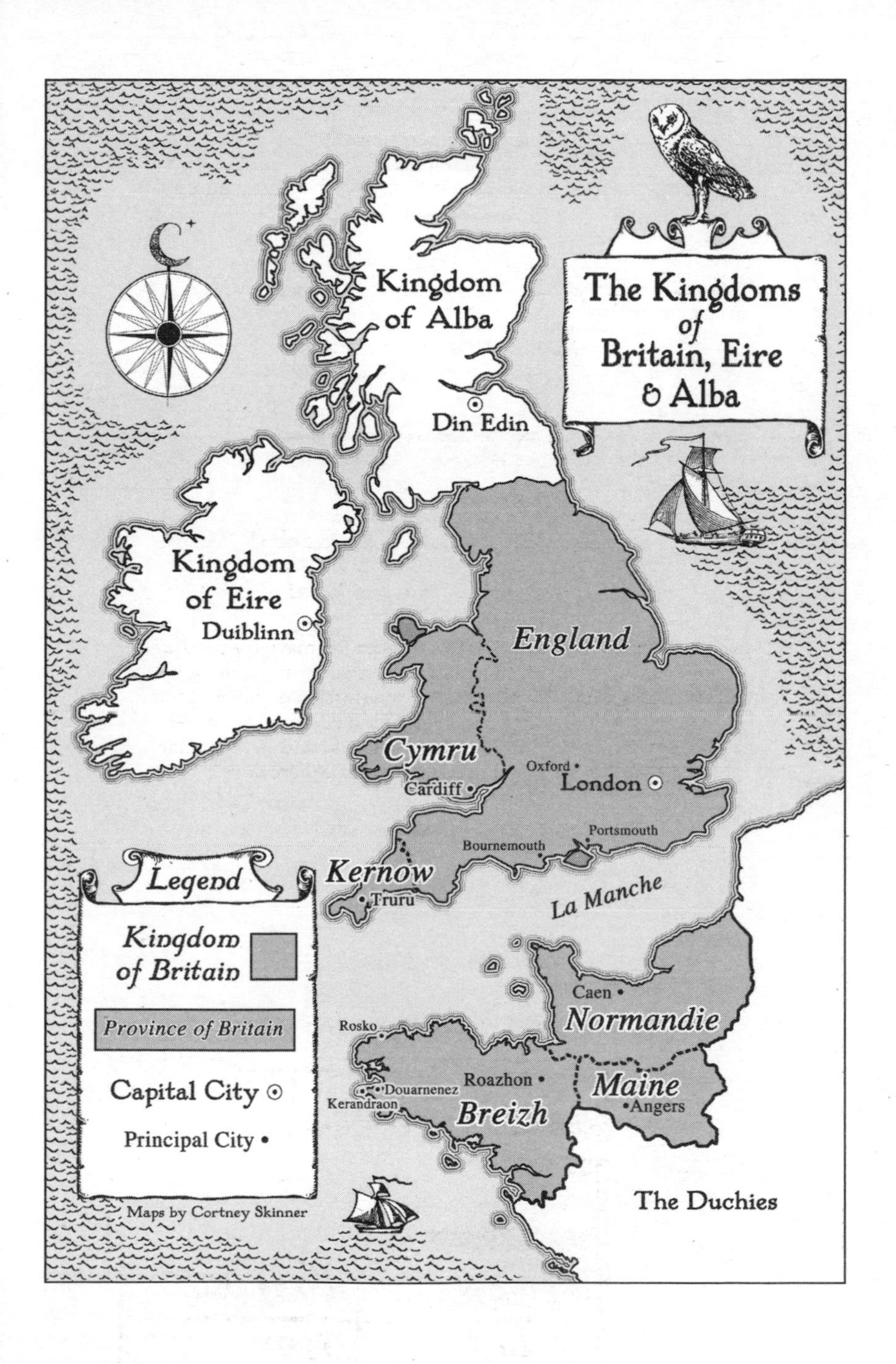

The Kingdoms of Britain, Eire & Alba
Kingdom of Alba
Din Edin
Kingdom of Eire
Duiblinn
England
Cymru
Oxford
London
Cardiff
Portsmouth
Bournemouth
Kernow
Truru
La Manche
Legend
Kingdom of Britain
Province of Britain
Capital City
Principal City
Caen
Normandie
Rosko
Roazhon
Maine
Douarnenez
Kerandraon
Angers
Breizh
The Duchies
Maps by Cortney Skinner

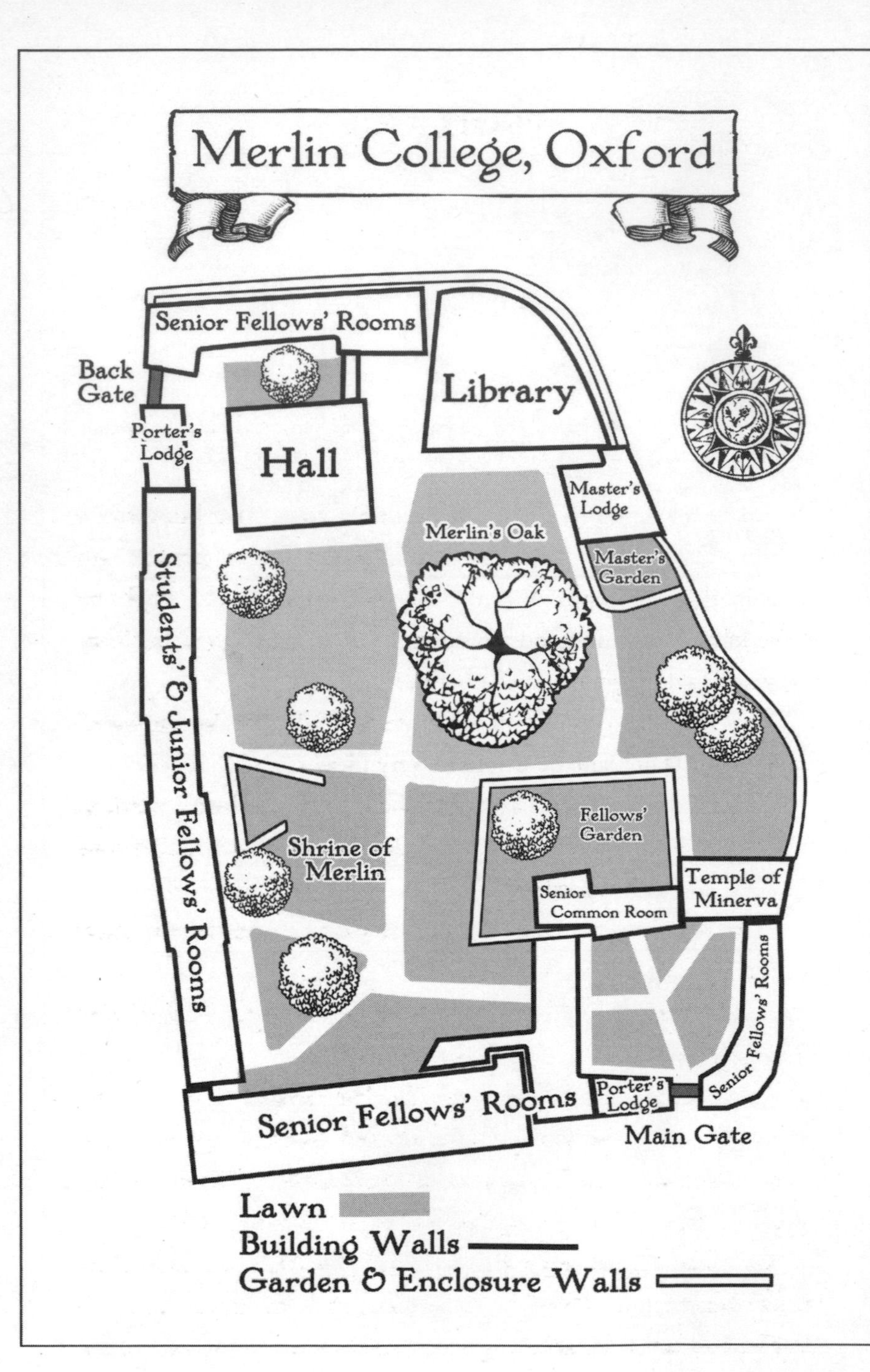

Merlin College, Oxford
Senior Fellows' Rooms
Library
Back Gate
Porter's Lodge
Hall
Master's Lodge
Merlin's Oak
Master's Garden
Students' & Junior Fellows' Rooms
Fellows' Garden
Shrine of Merlin
Temple of Minerva
Senior Common Room
Senior Fellows' Rooms
Porter's Lodge
Senior Fellows' Rooms
Main Gate
Lawn
Building Walls
Garden & Enclosure Walls

PROLOGUE

It was his own fault entirely, Gray reflected later. That morning in Merlin's South Quad, when Taylor and Woodville had pressed him to join them in some not-quite-specified excursion, he ought to have known that no good would come of it; what good had ever come of Taylor and Woodville before?

'It is a special commission of Professor Callender in the town,' said Taylor. 'I am sure he would be very pleased . . .'

'It would do you no harm, Marshall, to render him a service,' said Woodville. 'And,' he added delicately, 'there may be some coin in it for you, if we speed well.'

A hit below the belt, indeed, but that was only what one expected of Alfric Woodville.

'I have run afoul of the P-proctors b-before,' Gray pointed out. 'I am not very eager to do so again.'

'Nonsense!' said Taylor bracingly. He clapped Gray on the shoulder, with some force; Gray stumbled, half in reaction to the blow, half startled by Taylor's sudden camaraderie. 'What can the Proctors do, when we are commissioned by a Senior Fellow?'

Gray had wished very much to know why, if this was indeed his tutor's business, the Professor could not simply discharge it himself, but he had not been able to get the words out. Having now some inkling of the circumstances, he doubted that Taylor or Woodville would have told him in any case.

'Give me t-t-time to think,' he had said instead.

In the end, however, he had agreed to be of the party. Crowther and Evans-Hughes – good, solid, trustworthy men, though perhaps rather easily led, and the latter in particular always rather short of coin, since (like Gray) he spent too much of his scholarship income in the bookshops of the High-street – had been talked round by Taylor, or perhaps Woodville. They in turn had recruited Gautier, who always seemed to Gray to be in need of looking after, and these three earnestly represented to Gray the advantages to all of having with them the most powerful mage of the Middle Common Room.

After a year's almost constant disparagement by Professor Callender, Gray dismissed this as patent flattery, but the participation of Evans-Hughes and Crowther did lend a more respectable air to the proceedings.

Finally young Gautier had said, with perfect gravity, 'Please, Marshall, do come with us; we should all feel safer, you know.' And Gray – perhaps feeling the effect of having grown up with three younger siblings – had let himself be persuaded.

Thus it was that, in the depths of a murky June night, six Merlin men came to be stealing along Oxford's New Road in the general direction of their College. The street being otherwise dark and still, their black gowns and subfusc formed a dense creeping shadow against the night.

Taylor and Woodville were cautiously triumphant; the others, knowing themselves by now to be embroiled in something at best equivocal, had long ceased to enjoy themselves and thought only of returning to the safe haven of the College walls.

'What's the hour?' whispered Crowther.

Evans-Hughes replied, 'Nearly one past midnight.'

'Apollo, Pan, and Hecate!' said Gautier. 'We shall all be killed on sight!'

'Shut it, you fools,' hissed Woodville.

They were about to round a corner when from over the road came the sound of heavy footsteps.

A moment later a crowd of townsmen was upon them, in drink and in vicious mood. The historic tendency to mistrust University mages, who shut themselves up in book-rooms instead of putting their talents to good honest work in field or pasture or sick-room, was suddenly of very much more than academic import to the Merlin men.

'Look at 'em, sneaking about the streets when decent folk are abed!'

'Aye, and working nasty magicks, I'll wager.'

The angry mutters crescendoed into shouts: 'Have at 'em, mates! Knock 'em down!'

Though few of the townsmen were armed, and none heavily, their advantages in size, strength, and numbers were quickly felt. The air was chill and heavy with dew, and Gray succeeded in drawing down a fall of hailstones, then another and another, which drove back several of their attackers but, alas, only enraged the rest. One flung something at his head; he tried to dodge it but succeeded only in changing the angle of impact. To his left, Woodville had summoned a deadfall tree-limb from someone's garden and was wielding it, inexpertly, as a sort of flail; to his right, Evans-Hughes bloodied the nose of a young man nearly twice as wide as himself, grinned in fleeting triumph, and then was borne back against Crowther by an answering blow to his temple and fell insensible upon the cobbles.

Taylor, alone of the students, did not fight at all; he was entirely occupied with the teakwood box cradled in his arms, hunching and twisting his body to shield it both from sight and from harm. When the tide of the fight pushed Gray near him, all the hairs stood up on the back of his neck.

Young Gautier darted between two staggering townsmen, caught Gray's arm, and pressed a handkerchief to his bloodied mouth. 'Go and get help, if you can,' he urged, his voice low and urgent. 'Get the Professor – get anyone – even if it must be Proctors.'

A moment later, Gray's gown fluttered down to rest atop a heap of now-outsized garments, and Gautier tossed a large grey owl into the air, to take desperate flight in the direction of the College.

A few lights still burned in upper windows at Merlin, among them that of Appius Callender, Regius Professor of Magickal Theory – tonight playing the expansive host to a party of distinguished and influential guests. The Professor was calling fire to light his pipe when something outside the window caught his eye, and the fire streaked past the pipe-bowl to set his robe alight. Distracted by this embarrassing contretemps, he did not recognise the owl.

The great bird approached the open window and – instead of sailing neatly through it – crashed headfirst into the barrier of a reinforced double ward, fell two storeys, and landed in a heap on the cobblestones.

There it struggled briefly to right itself, then quivered and shimmered and grew into Gray Marshall, sprawling dazed and naked in the street.

Gray staggered to his feet and looked up at the window. 'Professor!' he shouted. 'Professor, trouble! Help!' There was no answer from above.

With an effort, Gray raised his voice to maximum volume and bellowed, 'Help! Help, anyone! Proctor! Porter! A fight in the New Road – Merlin men in danger!'

Heads began to emerge from windows; Gray turned with profound relief towards the usually menacing sound of the Proctors' men erupting from the Porter's Lodge near Merlin's back gate. 'The New Road,' he repeated.

Then he swayed on his feet, reached out for support, and, failing to find it, collapsed, striking his head hard upon the cobbles.

Gray woke, groggy and with pounding head, in utterly strange surroundings – not in the Infirmary, nor in his own rooms overlooking the Garden Quad, but (he eventually discovered) lying on a pallet in what seemed a windowless box-room, and covered only by a rough blanket, long unlaundered.

His head ached so that he could scarcely think. His first efforts to sit up and look about him proving spectacularly unsuccessful, he subsided, retching and gasping for breath, to his original supine posture.

Eyes closed, he lay still, sorting out the half-familiar smells. Pipe tobacco was among them, he decided at last; bergamot, juniper, mace; a nose-wrinkling undertone of asafoetida.

'Mother Goddess!' Gray whispered suddenly. The smell was very like his tutor's study.

The room was dark; no door was visible. Stretching out his hand, he tried to call light – as he had done thousands of times since first learning to use his magick as a child – the better to investigate his surroundings.

It was when the effort failed, and left him dizzy and seeing spots, that he began to see what trouble he was in.

Approaching footsteps warned Gray an instant before the door opened. Instinctively he closed his eyes and relaxed his limbs, breathing deeply to feign sleep.

'Well?' A bass voice, impatient.

'There; do you see?' he heard the Professor say. 'The boy fancies himself a master shape-shifter and has drained his magick down with that idiotic stunt. He will sleep for hours yet.'

More footsteps.

'Very well,' said the basso. 'He will give thanks for a lucky escape, I should hope.'

'And you are certain the wards on the outer walls will hold?' said another voice – this one higher and faintly nasal.

'What do you take us for?'

'Leave the boy, then; we have not finished.'

The door closed, the footsteps retreated; but Gray, now listening hard, could still – just barely – hear the voices, though their words came to him only in disjointed phrases.

'We dare not act before the Samhain term,' said the nasal voice. '. . . too much groundwork left to lay . . . afterwards we shall have little time to prepare . . .'

'. . . great pity that your students failed you so badly, Professor,' said the basso; his tone rode the knife's edge between commiseration and mockery. 'I know . . . counting on them to provide—'

'We do not know yet that they have failed,' the Professor retorted, louder. 'All we do know is that they were waylaid on their return. I shall see tomorrow how they have sped.'

'And can another such attempt be made . . . seek it elsewhere?' This was the nasal voice, which Gray was finding more and more unnerving.

'Leave all of it to me.' The Professor's tone grew louder yet, impatient. 'What would you have me do? If your involvement is revealed, then all our efforts here will have been for naught. You must let me work in my own way.'

'But of course,' his companion replied, soothing now. 'You must . . . think best.' Then his voice sharpened, and Gray heard him clearly: 'Only make very certain that no one can draw any connexion to you, or to any of this night's doings, when the Master is gone. Do not give me cause to regret granting you the choice of subjects to test your method.'

At this Gray, who had been sitting upright, one ear pressed to the box-room door, fell back with a little gasp. *I am dreaming, surely. Have I just now overheard a plot to do away with the Master of Merlin? No – surely this is only some academic contretemps? Mother Goddess, bountiful and kind, wake me from this nightmare . . .*

'Marshall!'

Gray woke again, slowly and painfully, to the Professor's impatient voice. Sleep had not helped him; on the contrary, the blinding headache and general malaise had been joined by a wide assortment of very specific aches and pains.

Worst, he was still stark naked in his tutor's box-room – and desperately needing the privy.

'I am awake now, sir,' he managed to say. June sunlight streamed in the open doorway; he screwed his eyes shut against the pain. 'S-sir, are – the others, are they—'

'Nothing you need worry about, my boy,' the Professor replied, with the heartiness Gray had come to dread. 'Taylor and Evans-Hughes are in the Infirmary, but the healers tell me they will be themselves again in no time at all.'

He did not address the obvious questions: what of the rest? Why was Gray here, and not in the Infirmary with Evans-Hughes and Taylor? How long had he been here?

A scout loomed behind him in the doorway, carrying a stack of folded clothes, a basin and ewer, a towel, Gray's shaving kit. He looked about him impassively for some surface on which to place them.

'Now, Marshall,' the Professor went on, 'I have sent for some things from your rooms, and when you have washed and dressed I shall take you to the Infirmary. Though there is very little the matter with you, I expect.'

Gray was about to blurt out that something was very wrong indeed, but it had become a matter of instinct with him by now never to offer his tutor any unnecessary advantage over him. 'Y-y-yes, sir,' he said instead.

'Good, good. On you go, then.' And the Professor was gone, leaving Gray alone with the scout.

'You may as well put all of it on the floor,' Gray said, wearily. 'What can it matter? Here – let me take that.' He relieved the man of the basin and ewer. 'And I thank you. I am much obliged to you.'

'Sir.' The scout, looking faintly surprised, nodded at him, then began dusting off a trunk to serve as a dressing-table.

Gray set down the basin and ewer and looked through the pile of clothes. There was a handkerchief that was not his – a minuscule *AG* was embroidered in one corner – and something else vital was missing. 'Do you—?' He stopped. 'I b-beg pardon; I do not know your name . . .'

'Baker, sir,' said the scout, without looking up.

'Baker, I wonder – do you know what became of my gown?'

'I am sorry, sir,' Baker replied. 'I couldn't rightly say.'

Once in the Infirmary, Gray contrived to escape, briefly, from the Professor and the chief healer, and found Taylor and Evans-Hughes in adjacent beds, both looking battered and miserable. This was not unexpected – very probably he looked the same himself – but he was shocked by their reaction to his arrival.

Taylor, whose fault all of this was, if anyone's, narrowed his eyes and turned his bandaged head away; gentle, bookish Evans-Hughes greeted him with curses.

'What—?' Gray began, then stopped, bewildered.

'How *dare* you!' Evans-Hughes growled. 'How dare you show your face, after—'

'Don't talk to him,' said Taylor.

'What is it you suppose me to have done?' Gray demanded. 'What happened, after Gautier sent me for help—?'

'Sent you for help!' Taylor scoffed, ignoring his own advice. 'How easy to make such a claim, now he cannot speak against you.'

'Cannot – why not? And where is he?'

The other two exchanged a look that Gray could not interpret.

'The Proctors brought him in,' said Evans-Hughes.

'Dead,' said Taylor.

Gray's stomach lurched, and he sat down, hard – on the floor, there being nothing else within reach. He felt the blood drain from his face. Only last Beltane-time they had all drunk to Arzhur Gautier on his eighteenth birthday . . .

'But the Professor . . . the P-professor said . . .'

Before he could finish his sentence, two strapping healer-assistants, dispatched by their master, came to haul him up by the arms and march him away to a hot bath, and thence to bed.

The Professor was waiting for him there, wearing his heartiest and most insincere smile. 'Marshall,' he said at once, 'I have decided that you shall accompany me to my country home, and remain there for the Long Vacation. It will do you good to spend time in different surroundings. And, of course, I should otherwise be forced to agree with Proctor Morris that your actions in abandoning young Gautier to his fate cast into grave doubt whether you merit a place at Merlin – much less the continuance of your fellowship. You will much prefer to consider your situation at some distance, I am sure.'

It was a command and a warning – not an invitation – and there was only one possible response. 'I thank you, sir,' Gray said miserably.

All along their journey – to Portsmouth and across the Manche to the province of Petite-Bretagne, at the eastern edge of the kingdom – Professor Callender kept Gray closely leashed. At one posting-inn, some way inland from the port of Aleth, Gray contrived a few unwatched moments in the taproom, where a silver coin he could ill afford to part with secured him a bottle of ink and a sheet of rough note-paper, and wrote a brief and anxious note to Henry Crowther. The barmaid accepted it from him, and promised to see it safely into the next post-bag bound for England; on running him to earth, however, the Professor scolded him so caustically and publicly for leaving his rooms that Gray fully expected her to think him a lunatic and drop it into the midden-heap instead, and could not summon the necessary resolve to try again at their next halt.

In every idle moment, his mind reverted to that half-overheard conversation in the Professor's rooms. Unquestionably there was a conspiracy of some kind, and the Professor deeply involved in it. Who had those two men been, whose voices now seemed burnt into his mind's ear? That they meant ill to Lord Halifax, Master of Merlin College, was plain. But ill of what sort? What did they hope to gain by his removal, and how did they mean to achieve it?

Had Woodville known of this? Had Taylor? What of the others? *Not Evans-Hughes, surely. Not Crowther. Mother Goddess, not Gautier!*

What did the Professor believe Gray to have done, or heard, or seen, that they had not, that he should keep Gray – alone of the more than half-dozen men conscripted to that ill-starred errand – so close at hand?

And, supposing that he attempted to tell someone the little he had overheard – if it had not been only the product of magick-shocked delirium – who would believe him?

If there was a way out of this tangle, Gray could not see it, try as he might. *I know what I am running from. What am I running towards?*

PART ONE

Breizh

CHAPTER I

In Which Gray Meets Sophie

Gray toiled in the midsummer sun, on his knees among the rhododendrons, through an afternoon that seemed to last a month. Beautiful, Callender Hall's gardens might be, but after only half a day he had already conceived a passionate hatred of them, and of flowering shrubs in particular. What was he doing in this distant corner of the kingdom, so far from all he knew? Why condemned to this sweaty, thirsty, apparently pointless labour? His eyes stung; his knees ached; his hands were scratched and sore. He missed his cramped, chaotic rooms at Merlin College with an unexpected intensity – and had even begun, in spite of everything, to miss the home of his childhood.

He had just begun to think, implausibly, how much pleasanter returning to that home for the Long Vacation might have been – as though any such course had been open to him – when he saw the girl striding across the lawn.

She was of middle height, straight and slim; she wore a plain gown, sturdy boots, and a man's straw sunhat, large and ragged in outline, whose shadow hid her face. From a distance, her determined gait reminded Gray forcefully of his sister Jenny.

The girl stopped in front of Gray. After a moment, during which he stared blearily at her skirts, she dropped to her knees in the grass, bringing her face level with his. A faint breath of lavender and rosemary briefly displaced the overpowering scent of compost.

'You look dreadfully tired,' she said, and he blinked at her; was this the manner of this country, then, for young girls to speak so forwardly to strangers? Well, and he had often enough heard his tutor call it backwards and uncivilised . . .

'Will you come indoors and have a drink?' the girl went on. Her Français had a perceptible, and rather appealing, local accent. 'Otherwise you shall certainly collapse into the shrubbery. And the Professor, you know, is *most* particular about his rhododendrons.'

She stretched out a slim brown hand, and Gray, bemused, took it. She heaved him up, with little apparent effort, and helped him out of the rhododendron bed. Slowly unfolding to his full six feet and three inches, he went on blinking and wiped a grubby forearm across his brow. The girl looked up at him, one hand on the crown of her preposterous hat to stop it from falling backwards, but if she found his appearance in any way unusual, she gave no sign.

'I cannot think why he should try to grow them here, in all of this sun,' she said, as she led him towards the house. 'Every summer without fail, three or four of them fall dead; no one else would be so obtuse as to lay all the blame on his gardeners, instead of having the poor things moved to a shadier spot. And I suppose he treats his students no better.'

Though harbouring his own seditious views about his tutor, Gray had not thought to hear a renowned Senior Fellow of Merlin College discussed in such flippant terms in his own garden; the experience rather unnerved him. Worse, the longer the girl spoke, the more conscious he became of the very ungentleman-like appearance he must be presenting – stripped of coat, collar, and neck-cloth, his shirtsleeves rolled up above his elbows, dappled all over with flecks of loam.

'I – I am very sorry,' he said; 'I do not seem to have c-caught your name.'

The girl sighed and shook her head. 'Shall I never learn? I suppose Amelia is quite right to call me a barbarian.'

She stopped, turned and made him a little bow, saying, 'My name is Sophie Callender. It is a great pleasure to make your acquaintance, Mr . . . ?'

Had she meant to put him at ease, she could not have chosen a worse tactic.

Gray had been unnerved already, but to find himself conversing so familiarly with what must surely be one of Professor Callender's own daughters . . .

He began to stammer: 'I really – I have not finished in the garden – I ought not—'

'Nonsense,' said Miss Callender firmly, taking him by the elbow before he could make an escape. 'There's no evading the shouting, whether you would or no; and you still have not told me your name.'

'M-m-my apologies, Miss C-c-callender.' Gray kicked himself in the ankle, hard, in an effort to get his tongue under control. 'It is Marshall; Graham Marshall, of Merlin College.'

But am I? He clung to it nonetheless, for if he was not Marshall of Merlin, what other place had he in the world?

'A pleasure to meet you,' she repeated, tugging him by the arm towards the house. 'And I beg of you, *not* "Miss Callender" – that is my elder sister. *I* am Sophie.'

Gray wondered again whether such an unexpected mode of address might be quite usual here; after a moment he said, 'My sisters call me Gray.'

'I shall call you that also, then,' said Sophie. 'I should have liked to have a brother. Gray. But you are not very grey, are you? You must wear a hat, if you are to slave in the garden all day.'

She smiled as they turned into the kitchen garden and approached the back door. Inside the welcoming cool of the dark entry, she planted Gray in front of an enormous hat-stand-cum-mirror, and, with an inward groan, he saw what she must have meant: wherever his skin was not covered by clothing or layers of dirt, the sun had burnt it bright red.

In the kitchen, Sophie bustled about in the cold-room while Gray scrubbed his hands and face in the huge stone sink. Sophie handed him a clean linen towel, and took it away again when he had finished; then she presented him with a silver cup, worn thin with age and polishing.

'My welcome to this house, Graham Marshall,' she said.

Gray took the cup from her hands and raised it. 'I thank you for this welcome,' he said, 'and may the gods smile on you and on this house.'

The little wine in the cup was rich and sweet, and Sophie smiled up at him as he drank it.

The flagstoned kitchen was by far the pleasantest room Gray had seen in this house since his arrival late the previous evening. The sun streamed cheerfully in at high, narrow windows. The table at which they now sat, drinking chilled lemon-and-water poured by Sophie from an earthenware pitcher, was scrubbed and shining; along the whitewashed walls, about the level of Gray's shoulders, copper and brass utensils hung gleaming at measured intervals. Sophie looked so much at home here that Gray had difficulty picturing her in any room that would suit the Professor.

How typical of the Professor to have dropped him into this mystery with no preparation whatsoever.

I must sink or swim, he reflected, *and if the Professor has his way, I shall sink like a stone.*

Sophie, trying her best to make conversation, began to despair of her efforts. Amelia would have flirted, as easily as breathing; flirting did not come naturally to Sophie, however, and in any event to flirt with Gray – having claimed him, however jestingly, as a brother – was beyond her.

Though he did not seem much like other students of the Professor's, she reminded herself that they had scarcely met, and she might well be mistaken. She was tempted to ask his opinion of a puzzling passage in the book of magickal theory that she had most lately (and secretly) borrowed from the Professor's library – but what if he too should take the traditional view of the female mind's suitability for magickal study? Sophie had been read lectures enough over the years that she had no wish to provoke another.

'Where is your home?' she asked instead.

Staring down at the table, he said, 'I was born in Kernow.'

'It's said to be a beautiful country,' offered Sophie, who had never travelled more than a few miles from Callender Hall.

'It is that,' said Gray.

There was a silence then, until Sophie thought to say, 'Have you sisters or brothers, at home in Kernow?'

'I have t-t-two of each,' he said, looking up. For a moment Sophie saw a sharp, raw pain in his eyes; then it was gone, and a carefully neutral expression took its place. 'You have an elder sister, I b-believe you said?'

'Amelia, yes. Joanna, my younger sister, is away at school.'

I should like to know why you looked like that when you spoke of your brothers and sisters. But she could think of no way to ask such an impertinent question without giving offence.

The conversation limped along until Sophie hit on the happy expedient of the weather, from which they progressed to the Professor's gardens and the pleasure of a cool drink when one is very thirsty. Sophie had refilled their glasses three times before she noticed that the light had changed – and a moment later, there was Mrs Wallis, bustling in with the kitchen-maid on her heels to set in motion the preparations for dinner, and to scold Sophie (though in an affectionate tone that robbed her disparaging words of any real force) for cluttering up her worktable.

'Out with you, Miss Sophia,' she said firmly, by way of peroration. 'Dinner at 'alf past, and five courses, orders of 'Erself. I can't be doing with you lot underfoot.'

'Oh, *gods and priestesses*,' said Sophie, under her breath.

'Who is "Herself", then?' Gray asked, when they had made their escape. He was back in the rhododendron bed, digging; Sophie sat on the path a few feet away, heedless of the damage to her gown, fanning her face with her appalling hat.

She glanced heavenwards. 'Mrs Wallis will get herself into trouble one day, talking in such a way before those who ought not to hear it,' she said. 'She means my sister Amelia. The *real* Miss Callender, you know.'

'You are not on the b-best of terms?' Gray hazarded, his mind straying to his long, fractious history with his brother George.

'An infamous suggestion!' said Sophie. 'Certainly we are on good terms. As hedgehogs and carriage-wheels are, or geese and foxes.'

Despite himself, Gray smiled. 'If I am to meet this p-paragon,' he said, 'I ought to be prepared. I beg you will tell me all about her.'

Miss Amelia Callender was precisely as advertised: a very pretty girl, everything about her most elegant – and not for a moment was anyone at her dinner-table permitted to forget it.

Gray received exactly as much notice and attention from her as her assessment of his station required; he could almost see her mental abacus at work, assigning appropriate value to his speech (a gentleman's), his family (unknown, and therefore suspect), his status as her father's student, his dress (respectable but dull), and his person (too tall, too plain, and decidedly too much sunburnt). Conversing with her proved easier than he had feared, for she had clearly no interest in any topic of importance outside her own sphere, nor did she seem likely to remember, for more than a few moments, anything he said.

The Professor – pink-faced and blustering as ever, his grey eyes half hidden under sprouting, tufted brows – introduced Gray to his daughters. Gray was about to mention Sophie's having welcomed him already, but she caught his eye and silenced him with a minute shake of her head.

'I – I hope my c-coming has occasioned no inconvenience to you, Miss C-callender, Miss Sophia,' he said instead, discomfited.

Miss Callender cast him a suspicious glance; the Professor, however, seemed oblivious, saying only, 'Amelia, my dear, you will remember, I hope, that you are to call tomorrow on Lady Guischard?'

The dinner was a good one, and Gray, after his exertions in the garden, very hungry. He ate heartily and managed to reply when spoken to, but his mind was elsewhere – studying the interaction of the Professor with his daughters, of the sisters with one another, and the behaviour of each. Had he first met Sophie here, he might scarcely have noticed her; in the company of her father and sister she was silent and dull, unremarkable and colourless. Even her eyes seemed to have lost their spark; in fact – Gray squinted briefly across the table, and the hairs rose on the back of his neck, as though someone were working magick nearby – not only their spark but much of their colour. Her gown was much grander than the one she had worn to wander about the garden earlier in the day, but it too had a sort of drabness, as though, when dressing for dinner, Sophie had carefully chosen those of her garments best suited to blending into the woodwork. Through the whole of the meal, she spoke scarcely a dozen words.

It was very odd, for his first impression of Sophie had been that, though no great beauty, she was at any rate worth looking at and had interesting things to say.

But this was not the first puzzle presented by Professor Callender's household and Gray's own peculiar status there, and would surely not be the last.

* * *

Dinner was followed by an uncomfortable quarter-hour's tête-à-tête with the Professor, Sophie having meekly followed Miss Callender from the dining-room, during which Gray was asked his opinions of the house, the garden, the neighbourhood, and Mrs Wallis's cookery. Beyond an earnest commendation of the last, he was not at all sure how he replied; by now, exhausted and sun-touched, he was in constant danger of falling asleep where he sat. But he knew the Professor well enough to understand that the questions were asked pro forma; Gray's true role was – as it had been for the past three terms – to listen and nod politely while his tutor held forth. In any other company he would long ago have excused himself, pleading some indisposition or simple fatigue, and sought his bed; but being still so uncertain of his standing here, he dared not risk insult to his host.

Finally Professor Callender tapped the ash from the bowl of his pipe and rose from the table. Gray trailed him apprehensively into the large drawing-room, where Miss Callender sat in state on a rose-coloured sofa, presiding over an ornate silver tea-service. Her father smiled fondly at her, seated himself in an armchair before the hearth, and took up a book.

Miss Callender looked up with a dimpled smile.

'Will you take tea, Mr Marshall?' she enquired.

Gray nodded absently and looked about for Sophie, whom he spotted at last in a distant corner of the room, in a small circle of lamplight, her head bent over some piece of fancy-work. He was studying her, and contemplating various means of attracting her attention, when Miss Callender said loudly, at his elbow, 'Your tea, Mr Marshall.'

Gray started violently, causing his hostess to spill hot tea all over her elaborately beaded gown.

Sophie looked up at Amelia's squeak of outrage, just in time to see her sister drop a teacup and saucer; their guest put out one hand, not to catch them but to *summon* them, and set them gently on the tea-tray.

Sophie rose, grinning, and tried to catch his eye, but he was entirely occupied in stammering apologies to Amelia and mopping up tea from the carpet with his handkerchief.

'I beg you will not trouble yourself, Mr Marshall,' said Amelia stiffly, and rang the bell. She left off fussing with her gown to pour out another cup of tea, into which she dropped two lumps of sugar before holding it out to Sophie. 'Take Papa his tea, if you please.'

Sophie stepped carefully around Gray and approached her father's armchair.

'I thank you, Amelia dear,' the Professor said.

Then he glanced up from his book, frowned in surprise to see Sophie, and looked past her at Amelia and at Gray, still on his knees by the tea-table, handkerchief in hand.

'Mr Marshall!'

Gray's sunburnt face flushed redder, and he dropped the handkerchief. 'I am s-s-sorry, sir,' he said.

The Professor shook his head. 'When a man cannot drink his tea in peace in his own drawing room—'

'Certainly you may drink your tea in peace, Papa,' said Amelia crisply. 'We should not dream of disturbing you with so slight a matter.'

'It is all very well to say so, Amelia, but have I not been disturbed already? Am I not beset by noise and upset and inconsequential chatter, everywhere I turn?' The Professor half rose from his chair and cast a baleful eye at Gray. '*Mr* Marshall! Have you been so long at Oxford as to forget what is due to a lady's drawing-room?'

'Now, Papa,' said Amelia soothingly, 'you are tired from your journey, and fatigue has made you cross. Should you like a little music?'

There was this to be said for Amelia, that she could manage the

Professor better than anyone else could. He subsided, grumbling; Amelia directed at her sister a tight-lipped smile that Sophie interpreted without difficulty: *You will play your part civilly*, it said, *or I shall make you very sorry.*

Mrs Wallis came in, observed Amelia's trouble, and, hiding a smile, bustled away again to fetch the means of repairing it; Sophie put down the Professor's tea and went into the smaller drawing-room to open the pianoforte.

She wondered at her own irritation of spirits. How many of the Professor's students had lost their heads over Amelia, and done foolish things as a result? Small wonder if this Gray Marshall should do likewise – and small reason for Sophie to be vexed with him, if he did. *If I were one of Gray's sisters*, she told herself, by way of excuse, *I should not wish him to fall into Amelia's clutches.*

But when, in the midst of a long, melancholy *pavane*, she glanced back over her shoulder, she saw Amelia drinking her tea alone, wearing a sour expression, and Gray in the chair Sophie had abandoned, concealed behind a book.

The *pavane* freshened into a triumphant little *bourrée.*

'Sophia, *must* you play so loud?' said Amelia, after only a few measures. 'You make my head ache.'

'Indeed, Sophia,' the Professor added peevishly, 'there is no call for such *boisterous* music, so late in the evening.'

Sophie rolled her eyes and said without turning round, 'I beg your pardon, Amelia. Sir.'

At the end of the phrase she stopped, shook out her fingers, and took up the *pavane* where she had left off. Though the Professor had returned from Oxford only yesterday evening, the Long Vac had already begun to seem very long indeed.

CHAPTER II

In Which a Prediction of Sophie's Comes True, and Sophie and Gray Discuss Magick

As Sophie had predicted, the following day began for Gray with a dressing-down from the Professor, beginning with rhododendrons and progressing in quick succession to Gray's shameful clumsiness, his idiocy in the matter of sunhats, his lack of intellect, and his general inadequacy. After a full year under the Professor's tutelage, and three before that as a mildly troublesome Merlin undergraduate, Gray knew better than to protest that he had neither asked to work in the garden (or, for that matter, to be here at all) nor claimed any horticultural expertise whatsoever. Instead he assumed an attentive and chastened expression perfected during his second university term, murmured 'Yes, sir' and 'No, indeed, sir' at the appropriate moments, and waited patiently for the torrent to abate. While so doing, he calculated the likely distance from Callender Hall to the home of his sister Jenny, and whether he might soon expect a letter from her in answer to his own.

He once or twice felt, as he had last night at dinner, the familiar little prickling sensation that meant someone was using magick nearby, and pondered what the Professor might be up to, deciding eventually that the source must be an ambient spell – a protection, an amplification . . .

For a moment, then, he went cold with fear: what if there should be some sort of listening-spell in place here? Sophie's guileless derision of yesterday, which he had thought safe enough because they were out of doors, might well have consequences she could not have foreseen. With this in mind – his attentive expression never wavering – Gray summoned what magick he could to cast his inner eye and ear on his surroundings. Certainly there was *something* there, but if a listening-spell, it was none that he had ever encountered before.

'Remember where you might now find yourself, boy,' said the Professor, reaching his peroration at last, 'were it not for my intervention.'

Sent down in disgrace, thought Gray, *or dead in the street like poor Arzhur Gautier – or safe in my rooms at Merlin, had your bully-boys left me out of their gods-accursèd schemes to begin with.*

'Y-yes, sir,' he said aloud. 'I th-thank you, sir.' He gazed down at his toes, lest his face betray him.

The Professor had stalked away to resequester himself in his study, and Gray was arming himself for a renewed assault on the hated rhododendron bed, when Sophie emerged from the shrubbery, carrying a sunhat even larger and more tattered than her own. This, with a diffident smile, she presented to Gray. 'I found this hat for you,' she said.

Gray took it, rather startled, and turned it over in his hands. 'I thank you,' he said. 'That was k-kind.' Absent-mindedly murmuring a mending-spell, he traced a finger along a rent in the hat's crown, knitting the edges back together. He was pleased to discover that the effort this required was much less than it would have been a fortnight ago, in the aftermath of his accident with the Professor's wards at Merlin.

Sophie seemed disproportionately impressed. 'How clever!' she said, scratching the bridge of her nose. 'Could you mend mine, also? That is, if . . .'

'Of course.' Gray reached for it. Sophie watched, apparently fascinated by this simple trick, as he repaired each hole and rent.

When he handed the hat back to her, she admired it for a moment, turning it this way and that, before putting it back on her head.

'I do wish I had magick,' she said.

'Have you not?' Gray looked up, surprised. He felt rather light-headed now, and knew too late that he had overreached. 'B-but—'

'Not a flicker,' she said wistfully. 'The Professor tested all of us when we were small, he says. People do think it odd that two talented parents should have *three* talentless children; but there it is.'

'Then your mother—'

'Her talent was a minor one, by all accounts. And of course, being female, she had little training, for she was not a healer. And then . . .' There was a pause, and Gray waited for Sophie to elaborate; instead she said, 'Still, I should think it must have been better to have it than not.'

'Well,' said Gray, 'magickal talent is sometimes less helpful than you might suppose.'

She tilted her head, politely sceptical, but made him no reply.

Pellan, the Professor's head gardener, emerged from the potting-shed and directed Gray to the thinning and weeding of a floral border on the far side of the house. Sophie, instead of retreating indoors, fell into step beside him.

Which were plants, and which weeds, Gray could not reliably determine, and the floral border seemed interminable. Sophie observed his efforts with every appearance of interest, and from time to time she reached out a slim brown hand to pluck up some small green thing; he wondered how much she must detest her sister's company to prefer his, and made Herculean efforts not to utter ill-bred imprecations with every other breath.

'I fear I am quite out of my depth,' he confessed at last.

Sophie's brown eyes danced, but she refrained from smiling. 'I had begun to suspect it,' she said kindly. 'You had only to ask. Look: this one is hawkweed, you know, and *that* is calendula. Can you not – that is – *magick* the weeds away?'

'No, indeed,' said Gray. 'Living, growing things . . . their magick is like healing – a very specialised one. Which is not where my talent lies.' *Assuming that I have still any real talent to speak of. Am I doomed now to spend my existence summoning teacups and mending hats?*

'Which explains, of course, why the Professor has put you to work in the garden.' Sophie cast up her eyes. 'He means to show you that he has the whip hand of you, and can exercise it as he likes.'

So precisely did this assessment echo Gray's own that he cast a sidelong glance at her, wondering whether, after all, she did have some magickal talent – of the sort, which he had once read of but never seen, that can be used to hear other people's thoughts.

Catching his glance, she further startled him by saying, 'That was no magick. Only, I have known the Professor all my life, you see. It is not only you and I who know what he is, but most people have not the temerity to say it.'

'But you have?'

'That,' said Sophie quietly, appearing to scrutinise her fingernails, 'depends very much on who might be listening.'

There was a pause, in which only the sound of Gray's mattock could be heard.

'And what do *you* think of him?' asked Sophie.

Gray snorted. 'It is not my place to think anything. He is my tutor; I follow his advice on what I ought to be reading, and how to pass my examinations for Mastery. And at the moment I am beholden to his hospitality. Hence the gardening.'

Sophie frowned. 'You must have an opinion,' she said. 'Being so very much cleverer than he is.'

She spoke with perfect gravity, and appeared surprised by Gray's hoot of derisive laughter.

'It is quite true,' she said. 'The Professor is an old fraud. Only so blessed *distinguished* and *well connected*, and so full of sage aphorisms and pronouncements, that nobody thinks to ask whether he really knows what he is talking of, or can *do* anything at all. But you' – she nodded slowly, eyes narrowed – '*you* can do things. I'm sure of it.'

Gray put down the mattock and sat up straight, stretching out his arms above his head. 'Nonsense,' he said. 'I am a hopeless ignoramus of no learning and very little talent. Has not your father told you?'

Sophie made a most unladylike noise.

'Sophie, take care,' Gray said then, his voice low and urgent. 'Whatever he may lack, he has influence and ambition – mind you do not underestimate him. He is not kind to his opponents.'

Then, recognising how much he had nearly revealed, and to whom, he set his teeth and grimly picked up his mattock. Bending his head to his work, he nearly missed Sophie's sharp, appraising look.

For the next se'nnight Sophie applied her mind with some energy to the problem of Graham Marshall.

Gray was unlike any student the Professor had previously brought home; not only was he not pompous, superior, or condescending, he also very obviously (did he know how obviously?) disliked the Professor – who equally obviously despised him. When Appius Callender invited a student to stay for the Long Vacation, that student was invariably as much like the Professor himself as a man of eighteen or twenty could well be – well born, well dressed, and generally well looking, more interested in the University for the influence, advancement, and connexions it could afford him than for what he might learn there – and was accompanied by a servant or so and an assortment of well-appointed luggage.

Alasdair Wickliff, for example, who had been the Professor's guest for the Long Vac when Sophie was fourteen, and Amelia just seventeen – a senior undergraduate of nineteen or twenty, middling tall and handsome, with vivid blue eyes and fair hair. Like most young men, on first encountering Amelia he had exerted himself to impress her; Amelia, for the first time, had become so besotted as to begin daydreaming of marriage proposals in her sisters' hearing.

Sophie had taken a more than usually strong dislike to Wickliff. Ten-year-old Joanna found him desperately dull, he having little interest in horses and none whatsoever in flying kites or catching frogs. Sophie soon remarked that he flirted not only with Amelia but also with nearly every other young woman, whatever her station, who crossed his path. This she mentioned, cautiously, thinking to put Amelia on her guard, but Amelia only tossed her head and said accusingly, 'I ought to have known you would be jealous!'

In the end, Sophie remembered Wickliff so vividly because he had vanished abruptly from Callender Hall after coming to grief over a pretty Breizhek kitchen-maid. Neither Amelia nor the Professor had ever again mentioned his name, and there had been a coolness between Amelia and Sophie since that summer.

Gray, unlike Wickliff and all his fellows, had arrived quite alone, with one battered trunk, which apparently was half filled with books; and even Sophie, though growing to like him very much, could not honestly describe him as other than plain.

The Professor, moreover, issued such invitations with only two purposes in mind: to provide sycophantic company for himself, or eligible suitors for Amelia. Gray was self-evidently neither – and, indeed, it appeared to Sophie that her father was not only avoiding Gray's company himself but attempting to discourage any closer acquaintance with Amelia.

Yet here was Gray, and here he remained, in a condition that – though he shared their meals, as a guest ought – was very like servitude.

Further, he spoke and behaved like a gentleman, if an awkward and diffident one, yet his coat-sleeves were an inch too short for his arms, his boots worn down at the heels. Those of his possessions which Sophie had had occasion to see were in a similar state – sturdy goods long used, well kept but often mended. Was he a fraud? An interloper? A gentleman fallen on hard times?

'I do think it very kind of Papa to attempt to improve Mr Marshall,' said Amelia one morning, when Sophie and she were working together in the morning-room. 'But I fear his efforts are quite wasted.'

'Indeed?' Sophie kept her eyes on her crewel-work, lest her expression reveal how much this subject interested her. 'How so?'

'Oh! I do not think Mr Marshall improves at all,' said Amelia. 'I begin to believe he is not worth the trouble. *I* certainly do not intend to take any further trouble about him; a young man who does not so much as remark when one wears a new gown . . . !'

'But, Amelia,' said Sophie, with as much gravity as she could muster, 'young men cannot be expected—'

'Oh! As to knowing the difference between one gown and another, certainly not. But a man ought to take notice of one's appearance, Sophia, even when he does not understand what it is he is taking notice of.'

Indeed, his behaviour on that first evening notwithstanding, Gray had quite failed to offer Amelia the abject admiration she considered her due. Sophie could not be certain whether Gray's indifference to her sister's charms indicated (as she rather hoped) unusual perspicacity, or whether it was mere absence of mind; its result, however, was that Amelia had quit the field altogether, giving Sophie, for almost the first time, both opportunity and leisure to study the ways of young men – at any rate, of one young man. What manner of life had he led, that she so often saw him look fearful or unhappy? What made his stammer come and go? Why should the Professor bring him here, only to disdain him, and why should he bear so meekly the Professor's ill-natured, often ill-deserved rebukes?

Sophie found this philosophickal study an absorbing one; Gray, she concluded, was a far more interesting person than either he or the Professor wished her to believe.

* * *

'Sophie! So-phieeee!'

Gray, dressing himself for dinner in his bedroom, wondered at the cheerful cry. The voice was one not known to him, and, of all the household, only he himself used the name Sophie preferred, and then only when no one else was present. As he tugged a comb through his thick sandy hair, still damp from washing – trying as he always did to force it into some semblance of respectable neatness – he listened closely for a reply.

It came soon enough, in Sophie's familiar voice: 'Joanna, do be quiet! Come in, come upstairs. If the Professor hears you screeching like a fishwife, we shall be read lectures for a month.'

Joanna. This, then, was the youngest Callender daughter, home at last from school in Kemper. Heedless of her sister's admonition, she chattered eagerly all the way up the stairs.

'If only you would walk as quickly as you speak,' Sophie said. She sounded harassed, yet there was an affection in her tone that Gray had never heard when she spoke to her father or Miss Callender.

He abandoned his hair as a bad job and stepped out of his room just as Sophie was shepherding the newcomer, and a stableboy laden with valises, across the landing. Joanna – a stocky, open-faced girl of perhaps thirteen, who bore no evident resemblance to either of her sisters – stopped short at the sight of him, looking him up and down with candid grey eyes.

'Who are you?' she asked.

'*Joanna!*' Gray came very near to laughing at Sophie's outraged tone but restrained himself to spare her dignity. 'Mr Marshall, may I introduce my sister Joanna? Joanna, Mr Marshall is one of Father's students, and our guest for the summer.'

Joanna curtseyed haphazardly, revealing to Gray that her petticoats were edged in mud and her scuffed boots half unlaced.

Gray bowed gravely in return. 'I am delighted to make your acquaintance, Miss Joanna.'

'You have the most enormous boots I have ever seen,' said Joanna.

Joanna's presence enlivened that evening's dinner conversation considerably. She seemed to have made a project of provoking her father and eldest sister; in the face of her continual efforts in this direction, and Sophie's to school her to silence, Gray could think of almost nothing to say that would not make matters worse.

Over the second course Joanna announced her intention to seek a university place on leaving her school. Sophie frowned and muttered, 'Do be quiet!' Miss Callender, displaying a most uncharacteristic want of poise, choked on her wine. The Professor, to Gray's surprise, said only, 'You will find that you think very differently in a few years' time, Joanna.'

'Indeed I shall not,' she retorted, with the sort of defiance Gray wished he himself could bring to bear against his tutor. 'It is quite absurd that only boys are allowed to do anything interesting, when everyone knows that girls are *much* cleverer.'

From Sophie, Gray had learnt that Joanna, far from being a keen scholar, was in fact much despaired of by the headmistress of her school, being prone to gaze out of the window during lessons that bored her and to involve her fellow pupils in nocturnal escapades of various sorts. He wondered whether this apparent shift of interests was genuine or whether, as he very much suspected, it was simply the latest in a series of calculated attempts to shock her father.

'Some girls may indeed be very clever,' said the Professor, still uncharacteristically calm, 'though I must say that, alas, those present at this table are all uncommonly silly.'

Even Miss Callender looked mildly annoyed at this. Gray bristled, silently, on Sophie's behalf, and shot her a sympathetic look across the table; she would not meet his eye, but gazed without expression at the silver epergne in the middle of the table.

'No matter how clever a woman may be, her mind and temperament remain ill suited to such advanced study as must be undertaken by a university undergraduate.' He turned to Gray, smiling the smile that always portended something unpleasant for its recipient, and added, 'I am sure you will agree, Mr Marshall?'

'As you say, sir,' Gray muttered through clenched teeth, looking at his plate.

'You told me he was clever,' Joanna said accusingly, when the sisters had removed to the drawing-room after dinner.

'I beg your pardon?' said Sophie.

'Your Mr Marshall,' said Joanna, scowling ferociously up at her. 'You said he was clever, and kind, and interesting, but he is exactly like Father.'

'You are mistaken, Jo,' Sophie said. 'I have known Gray far longer than you have, and I am sure you—'

'What is there to mistake?' said Joanna, impatient. 'When one man professes an opinion, and another man replies with *As you say*, what are we to think but that his opinion is the same?'

'I cannot think any such thing,' Sophie replied staunchly, thinking of Gray's gritted teeth and downcast gaze; but as she was equally unable to explain his apparent endorsement of the Professor's views, Joanna remained unpersuaded.

The next morning Sophie set out immediately after breakfast and searched the gardens until at last she ran Gray to earth.

'Joanna believes that you agree with the Professor,' she told him without preamble, lying prone at the edge of a gravel path in order to peer at him through the box hedge. She had lain awake half the night fretting over her quarrel with her sister; never before had their opinions of any person been so much at odds.

'I imagine it possible that such a thing might occur,' Gray said.

His head was bent to his work, so that she could not see his face. 'In theory.'

'That women's minds are not suited to advanced study, I mean,' she said impatiently. 'Do not be obtuse. I told her that she was quite wrong, of course, but . . .'

Gray at last put down his trowel and looked at her. 'But . . . ?'

'But . . . if you do not agree, why not *say* so?' She paused again, biting her lip. Amelia would call this sort of enquiry *prying*, but Sophie felt that she must have an answer. 'And not only that. It is perfectly clear that he loathes you, and you loathe him. I do understand that you must put up with him during term time, but I *cannot* any way see why you should come here and let him treat you as he does, as though the laws of welcome meant nothing. Mother Goddess, Gray! He treats you with more thorough contempt than he has ever shown even to *me*.'

Gray looked angry – but not, she thought, at her – and perhaps a little ashamed.

'I came here,' he said quietly, looking down at his filthy hands again, 'because your father gave me no choice; and I hold my tongue because if he were to throw me out, I should have nowhere else to go.'

Sophie could not at once think how to reply. She sat up, wrapping her arms about her knees, and considered. After a moment, she heard again the soft *chunk* of the trowel.

Very quietly she said, '*I* am glad you are here.'

The sound of trowelling stopped. Sophie lay down again and peered through the hedge. Gray looked at her with a sort of astonishment in his face; then he smiled slowly, tentatively, and said, 'So am I.'

Sophie dreamed that night, as she often did, of blood and fire and broken limbs, and of death falling from the sky.

On such occasions, it was her habit upon waking to creep down the servants' staircase to the library, where for some years now she had been systematically working her way through the Professor's collection of basic works on magickal theory. Most lately she had begun on the *Elementa magicœ* of Gaius Aegidius; it was very slow going, for although notionally meant for novices, it was written in a style so ornate that Sophie found she must read each individual period at least three times before she could parse out its meaning.

She persevered, however, until the words began to swim before her eyes. Then she climbed the library stairs and from the top shelf over the door retrieved another book. This one was smaller, old and worn, with the marks of small fingers upon it; the title stamped on its spine – it was a book of minstrel-tales for children – was in Brezhoneg, and on the flyleaf was written, in a child's uncertain hand, *Laora.*

The name notwithstanding, the book had belonged to Sophie's mother, who had used to read to the girls from it when they were small.

Sophie chose a page at random and began to read, intending only to refresh her eyes and her mind for a renewed assault upon Gaius Aegidius, who appeared to be working himself up to an interesting discussion of spells relating to water. Instead, however, she found herself leaning her chin upon her hand and considering her mother.

Sophie had been three years old, or thereabouts, when, escaping from the nursery one summer night to look at a beautiful full moon, she first overheard one of her parents' ugly arguments. The words eluded her – they were too distant, and spoken in a language imperfectly understood – but the voices, chill and venomous, sent her fleeing back to her bed, where she lay long awake before succumbing to a sleep beset with nightmares.

The next day she had watched them carefully. But all seemed as usual: Papa kept to his study, except when walking the gardens with Pellan, and patted the girls' heads absent-mindedly when they passed by him in the shrubbery; Mama heard Amelia's lessons, spoke with Mrs

Wallis, watched Sophie and Amelia play in the garden with their dolls. Sophie splashed Amelia with water from the fountain, and Amelia cried; it seemed to Sophie now that Mama had moved more carefully and spoken more sharply than was her wont, but at the time she had been outraged by the unfairness of being scolded for such a trifle.

Soon enough the summer was over, and the Professor back to Merlin College for the Samhain term. The house, as always, had worn a more cheerful air when he had gone, but this time Mama seemed not to share it. She had begun to grow round, and had dark smudges under her eyes.

'Mama, why are you sad?' Sophie remembered asking one day. She had escaped from the nursery-maid again and found Mama weeping silently over her fancy-work: a tiny white bonnet, like the ones Amelia sewed for their dolls.

Mama had smiled sadly and stroked Sophie's hair. 'You shall understand one day, dear heart,' she said, which meant – Sophie had known this much already – that no more answers would be forthcoming, however many questions she might ask.

A few days before Beltane, the nursery-maid had brought Sophie and Amelia to see Mama in her bedroom, where Mrs Wallis showed them, not a doll, but a tiny, pink-faced baby girl with wide-open slate-blue eyes. 'This is your new sister, my dears,' she said, smiling.

The servants exclaimed and cooed at the baby, but Sophie saw that Mama was weeping quietly.

'The gods withhold their gifts from me,' she muttered, as though to herself. 'I was so certain, and yet it is another girl-child, the poor thing. He will be back again, and again, the brute, as long as he has no son . . .'

Mrs Wallis's smile had vanished as Mama spoke, and Sophie had heard no more, for the nursery-maid was hurrying her and Amelia out of the room.

* * *

Sophie could not recall exactly when, or how, she had discovered herself to be her mother's favourite child. But certainly by the age of seven, she had come to understand this truth and was beginning to grasp the unfairness of it. If Mama should love her better than Amelia, that was only just, since Amelia was Father's favourite; but it was too bad of Mama (and Father, too) to spare no love for Joanna – who, besides, was not much more than a baby and could scarcely have done anything to deserve it.

Sophie could not pretend that she had not adored her mother, but from the beginning of Joanna's life she had also loved her small sister fiercely – and not only for the sake of Joanna's answering devotion. Not that Joanna was difficult to love. All the servants, and Mrs Wallis in particular, found her round, solemn face and disconcertingly astute questions rather endearing than not, and tended to spoil her, and even Amelia, in those days, had been, if not precisely doting, at any rate very fond of her. So it was not that Joanna lacked for love, exactly, and Mama had never been unkind to her; only . . . Joanna followed Mama with her wide grey eyes, candid and sad in her stoic little face, so happy to receive even an absent half smile, and Mama might have made her so happy with a kiss or a caress, or by admiring her adorably wobbly little dances – but Mama never had. Joanna had never *cried*, of course – Joanna was known even then for never crying.

Sophie had said to Amelia one day, 'When I am grown up, I shall have *six* children; and I shall love them all alike, and play with them as much as they wish, and never lose my temper or scold them.'

'You will have to get a husband first,' replied Amelia, tossing her head. 'It is a great pity that you are not pretty. Still, Papa will find someone to marry you, I suppose.'

And Sophie had snorted derisively, and said, 'I shall find someone myself, I thank you.'

* * *

Then Mama had died, when Sophie was eight and Joanna only four. Joanna had seemed to go on very much as before; she did not mope and weep as Amelia and Sophie did. But Sophie had much more dreadful nightmares now, and was often enough awake o' nights to know that Joanna suffered likewise; she knew, if no one else did, that there had been a hurt, bewildered child hidden behind that stoic facade. But she could find no opportunity to kiss and comfort Joanna, who would not, except in sleep, admit to feeling anything.

Instead, taking advantage of the disorder into which Mama's absence had temporarily thrown the household, Sophie had taken Joanna with her when she fled the melancholy house to ramble around the park. They searched for frogs and water-snakes; they picked flowers and wove daisy-chains; they sang together (Sophie tunefully, Joanna in her small, earnest monotone); and Joanna seemed to feel happier. Sophie, after a time, had begun to feel happier also.

Sophie blinked, stretched, and rolled her cramped shoulders with a sigh. It was a relief to have Joanna back again, however uncomfortable she might make things with the Professor and Amelia. Joanna did not mock her interest in magickal theory and, unlike Amelia, could be relied upon not to reveal her reading habits to the Professor. Unfortunately, Joanna was also unlikely to be helpful in her quest to decipher Gaius Aegidius. Now, Gray, on the other hand . . .

The sound of footsteps in the corridor outside warned Sophie that dawn was approaching, and with the ease of long practice she replaced the codex on its shelf, slipped out of the door, and crept back up the stairs to her bed.

CHAPTER III

In Which Gray Writes a Letter and Makes a Pilgrimage

My dear Jenny, Gray wrote, *I hope this finds you very well.* Sighing, he put down his pen and raised his face to the window. It was late evening, and all over the grounds of Callender Hall darkness was absolute. At the moment Gray wanted nothing more than to be out in that darkness, flying. He knew very well that he was not yet recovered enough to execute a shape-shift and would only tumble to his death on the flagstones below. But he yearned towards his broad wings and round owl eyes, the loft of an updraught, the tiny night sounds – despite the disastrous ending of his last such flight. Grim-faced, he picked up the pen.

> *You may have heard distressing tidings of my doings, Jenny. I hope you have not been anxious on my account. Be easy: I am well and mostly whole, and I believe no permanent damage has been done.*
>
> *As I wrote from Oxford, my tutor has invited me to be his guest in the country – your country, I should rather say – until the next term begins. His house and gardens are situated in a most beautiful part of the country, as tranquil as one could wish – a charming prospect all in all. I am as well occupied here as I could possibly be elsewhere.*

Gray looked up again, chewing the end of his pen. The number of things he could safely write about was pitifully small compared to the many more interesting subjects which he should have liked to discuss with Jenny – with any friendly and sympathetic person, for that matter. If only such a person were to hand!

He longed to confide more fully in Sophie. But of what use – beyond relieving his feelings – could such a confidence be to either of them? A poverty-stricken student mage, estranged from his parents, who (so ran the Professor's tale) had had to be rescued through the kind offices of his tutor from rustication – or worse – was no suitable acquaintance, still less a suitable friend, for the daughter of any respectable man. Sophie would wish to help him, he knew, but he saw no means for her to do so – only myriad opportunities to antagonise her father, which would do Gray no good, and might do Sophie harm.

There was nothing to be done, then, but write to Jenny and wait to see what came of it.

> *I have told you before of my tutor, Professor Callender. Also in his household are his three daughters, among whom is one at least whose acquaintance I think you might very much enjoy.*

After another long moment's window-gazing, he added,

> *I understand, too, that the library is very fine, though I have yet to see it.*

This was the broadest hint he dared drop that he was prisoner and not guest.

What else was there to say? It would all depend, he supposed, on how Jenny replied; if it was not safe to write openly, if his letter had been tampered with either before or after its arrival, she would discover it and let him know.

Please give my love to all.
Your affectionate brother,
G

Gray made a second copy of the letter, then folded and sealed both copies and scrawled directions on their outsides, first to Jenny at Kergabet, her husband's country seat, and next to their London lodgings, having, to his chagrin, no very clear idea of her present whereabouts. Then leaving them on the desk, he rose and went to the window, where he stood for a long time, yearning for wings.

From the beginning of his magickal education, what Gray had most desired to learn was the art of shape-shifting, and the warnings of his undergraduate tutor, Master Alcuin – 'This is a difficult and exacting magick, Marshall, one that most who attempt it will never master' – had only fuelled his determination to succeed.

The first step – he had learnt by now that this was always the first step – was to study: the anatomy and habits of a wide variety of animals, the histories of other successful shape-shifters, the means by which such transformations may be accomplished.

The second was to choose a shape. For Gray the choice was half made already: his desire to learn this magick had begun as a dream of flight, of soaring out of reach of boyhood tormentors. He pored over drawings of birds and spent hours – both by day and by night – observing the avian species that haunted the College grounds. Finally, on a rare visit to London, he spent a day in the city's famous Menagerie, and there a marvellous bird caught his eye: a large owl – round yellow eyes framed by rings of white and dark grey, long grey wing and tail feathers crossed with pale mottled bands – blinking solemnly on a tree-limb. As Gray watched, fascinated, the owl spread huge wings and dropped off into space, gliding silently across the aviary to alight on another perch. Then its head revolved almost completely, so that it seemed to look directly at him.

'Please, what bird is that?' he asked a passing menagerie-keeper.

Smiling at his enthusiasm, the old man replied, 'The Great Grey Owl.'

After months of repeated attempts, Gray's first successful shift lasted only moments; the second, less than half an hour. But within a fortnight of that first success, he had taken to owl-shape as if born to it.

Only now, when it was lost to him perhaps for ever, did he recognise how profoundly he had come to depend upon his ability to escape into the sky.

Jenny's answer, when it came several days later, eased Gray's mind, at least on one subject. Her husband, she wrote, despite disapproving of her disobedient brother and her continued correspondence with the same, was an honourable man who would never dream of opening or reading her personal letters; nor had her scrying detected the interference of any other person, so that Gray might safely write whatever he wished.

And I hope you will take the earliest opportunity to do so, as I have heard much about you this past month that requires explanation.

'I should imagine so,' Gray said aloud, ruefully, as he sat down to answer Jenny's letter.

The following week, seizing his moment whilst both the Professor and Joanna were temporarily silenced by mouthfuls of rabbit with onions, Gray took the unprecedented step of asking leave to go sight-seeing – largely as a means to test the length of his tether.

'I have heard, sir,' he began, 'that the Temple of Neptune at Kerandraon is very fine. I wondered whether I might have leave to pay a visit there.'

When the Professor, despite ostentatious raising of eyebrows at this description of the local *pèlerinage*, did not immediately refuse, Gray, emboldened, went on: 'Perhaps Miss Callender and S—and Miss Sophia might be persuaded to accompany me—'

'I should be pleased to act as your guide to our beautiful country,' Miss Callender said, 'but unfortunately my duties as mistress of this house keep me far too busy.'

Gray hid his relief behind a look of polite regret.

'However,' she went on, briskly, 'I am sure my younger sisters would derive great benefit from such an edifying excursion. Papa, you will of course send them in the barouche, and Mrs Wallis can easily spare Katell or Gwenaëlle to attend them?'

Gray sighed inwardly. However – supposing that the still-silent Professor consented at all – a Breton maidservant would be vastly preferable to Miss Callender herself, whose chill civility was almost more wearing than her father's open disdain.

Appius Callender began to look thoughtful.

'Very well,' he said at last, and pursed his lips. 'Sophia, you and Joanna may go, and Morvan shall drive the barouche. Amelia, you will speak to Mrs Wallis about the arrangements . . .'

Gray looked up, astonished at his success, into Sophie's wide eyes.

The Professor went out alone after luncheon the next day, driving himself in the phaeton, and returned as the rest were dressing for dinner. Conversation at table, such as it was, gave place to a long lecture on the original construction and the more recent renovation of the temple they were to visit, which might better have held the listeners' attention had it contained more of history and less of the politics and arithmetic of patronage.

'Had matters been left to the architect,' said he, when Sophie ventured to ask whether it was known who had built the original structure, 'there would be no temple to visit. It is men of substance who build temples, Sophia, not architects and stonemasons. Now, the temple at Kerandraon, as I have said, was to have been refurbished by Sieur Guion de Cournouaille; but, however, he was killed by – killed, that is, in an affair of honour, and his heirs refused to support the project . . .'

There was more in this vein, to which Sophie could not attend. She did succeed in collecting that the work on the temple had at length been paid for by the then Duke of Breizh, to whom a memorial stone had afterwards been erected, on the seaward colonnade. This the Professor particularly commended to Gray's attention as being of great historical interest.

'Yes, sir,' said Gray, in the tone Sophie had come to recognise as indicating thorough absence of mind.

The following morning, the five of them – Sophie and Joanna facing Gray in the barouche, with the luncheon hamper on the floor between them, and Gwenaëlle perched beside Morvan on the box behind the horses – departed early for Kerandraon, a market town along the coast.

The moment the carriage moved beyond sight of Callender Hall, Joanna left her seat beside Sophie to slide in next to Gray, and Gwenaëlle clambered down from the barouche box into the space thus vacated.

'We are leaving the park now, and see – here is the first of our farms,' said Joanna to Gray, a little farther on.

As she spoke, and as his eye fell on the white and green of sheep and meadow, Gray's heart lifted strangely, as though freed from some oppressive weight; the three girls grew cheerful and voluble, chattering in Breton and occasionally glancing sidelong at their male companion amidst flurries of laughter.

The whole undertaking had assumed a glad and carefree air, and Gray smiled, at first, to see Sophie for once looking like any girl of seventeen, enjoying an outing with her contemporaries. As he could now understand only one word in ten of their conversation, however, he soon felt distinctly left out, and – as they had perhaps intended – turned from them to study the passing landscape.

He had wondered often that the Professor should choose to spend his holidays in such an out-of-the-way place, fond as he was of rich food, influential society, and the sort of entertainments more easily found in Oxford or London than on an isolated estate in Petite-Bretagne. With such income as the Callender estate must supply, surely one need not live halfway to Cape Finis Terra, unless by choice.

On the other hand, Gray could easily imagine living here himself. The country was so beautiful – richly green to the south, with the wild scent of the sea gusting from the cliffs to the north – and so like his native Kernow, even to the half-familiar sounds of the local language, that a wave of homesickness assailed him, such as he had not felt in many years. The few people they passed in the fields and pastures were hale and deeply tanned; they paused in their work, first to study the approaching conveyance and then, once it drew near, to greet 'Dim'zell Zophie' and her entourage with every appearance of friendliness. Sophie, Joanna, and the servants returned these salutes with smiles and cheerful greetings of their own.

The Temple of Neptune, aptly enough, perched at the cliff's edge on the southern side of the cove in which nestled the town of Kerandraon. Originally built in the *style greco-romain* of so many centuries past, with a broad, gently pitched roof supported by Doric columns on two sides and (in deference to the local climate) thick stone walls on the other two, it had gradually acquired decorative additions of a more local bent, so that now it might just as well have been dedicated to the Breton sea-queen Dahut as to Neptune. This Gray supposed to be the reason the Professor had described Duke Gaël's refurbishments as insufficiently ambitious; a man more convinced of the superiority of Roman worship, law, and custom he had never yet encountered.

'This is a chancy place,' said a quiet voice at Gray's elbow, speaking in strongly accented Français; Gray turned to see Morvan, the Callenders' coachman, nodding his grizzled head. 'The old magicks are strong here. Some can feel them – if they know what to look for.'

Gray studied the old man – Breton born and bred, thrice his own age at least, but lean and spry and strong, with a glint of sharp intelligence in his dark eyes. 'Oh?' he said, in an encouraging tone.

'They say,' Morvan continued, lowering his voice still further, 'they say as Lady Laora made pilgrimage here, to try if the Lady Dahut would save her from being sent away to marry the Saozneg King.'

Gray blinked. *Lady Laora?* Yes, the second bride of King Henry the Twelfth had been the daughter of the Duke of Petite-Bretagne, he recalled – very likely a distant descendant of Duke Gaël. Perhaps it was only natural that she should seek the gods' help in a place with such a connexion to her family. Though everyone knew of her mysterious disappearance, Gray had never before heard it said that she had gone unwilling to her marriage-bed; might that explain – if not excuse – what she had later done?

'But then, they likely say that of every temple along this coast,' Morvan went on; he grinned briefly, his air of mystery quite vanished. 'Draws the pilgrims, y'see.'

Gray thought he did see; the Breton queen's notoriety had faded in England since his childhood, but perhaps here her fame persisted. Joanna had scampered away up the steps; Sophie and Gwenaëlle were filling their arms with the dahlias and lilies for which they had begged the head gardener before setting out that morning. Before Gray could collect himself to pursue this interesting topic, Morvan had thrust an armload of flowers at him and moved away, trailing the girls up the temple steps with the rest. Gray followed more slowly, pausing to admire the elaborate knotwork carved into the temple's supporting pillars.

He reached the entrance well behind the others and lingered there, listening to their footsteps and letting his eyes adjust to the relative darkness within, striped slantwise by the bars of sunlight admitted by the seaward-facing colonnade. It was here that he began to hear the voices.

What first came to his ears as a single blurred muttering soon resolved into several distinct voices – one deep, slow and resonant; another higher, a sad repeated keening; others that ranged the octaves between, rising, cresting and falling like the waves of the sea. And, indeed, what he heard might have been merely the crash of surf against the cliffs below, magnified through the temple, whose sea-ward wall was open to the elements. But Gray, who had lived near the sea for much of his life, was not long in recognising these voices as something other – something *more.*

The old magicks are strong here . . .

Stepping cautiously forward into the temple proper, he at once beheld the great altar to Neptune but found it deserted. Farther in, and at length he discovered Sophie, Gwenaëlle, and Morvan, kneeling to present their offerings at a smaller, humbler shrine set into the left-hand wall. Gray tried to recall what he had read about Breton gods and goddesses of the sea, but by now the voices were so loud, so urgent, that he had little attention to spare. He could hear just well enough to be sure that some of them spoke or sang words – but not words he understood, though he could hear their kinship to the local language and to the Kernowek and Cymric he had heard spoken all his life. He shut his eyes and concentrated intently, bending both mind and magick to the task of understanding *just one word, just one, just one . . .*

But just as he felt he was about to catch hold of something, Joanna screamed.

A priest and two acolytes came running as Joanna's single shriek, abruptly stifled, echoed around the great stone hall, confounding Gray's efforts to locate its source. The flowers fell unheeded, scattering across the stones, as he looked about, frantic, for some sign of her. Finding none with his unaided eyes, he drew on his talent to seek her, never stopping to think that the magick might not answer his call.

The words of the finding, as familiar as his own name, flew out in all directions and sank into the stones, setting the very air humming with his magick. He recalled them, focusing all his being on the mental image of Joanna's round, defiant face, and the magick pointed the way for him, just as it always had. He followed its urging at a run, his long legs covering the length of the temple in a few strides – only barely registering Sophie, Morvan, and Gwenaëlle following in his wake, or the priest shouting at them to come away.

Joanna teetered at the seaward edge of the temple floor, one foot suspended over empty air where there had so lately been solid stone, her body pressed back against one of the supporting columns. Her face was ashen, her lips pressed together in a vain effort to quell the chattering of her teeth. Gray gestured to Morvan, who braced him firmly as he leant out towards her, caught her arm, and slid his own about her waist to pull her back.

When Joanna had collapsed, mute and shivering, into Sophie's arms at the foot of the altar to Neptune, Gray and the priest returned to the scene of the near-catastrophe and lay prone to examine the place where a segment of the ancient, weathered stone had given way.

The priest was not much older than Gray, and his face nearly as white as Joanna's. 'I cannot understand it,' he said, over and over.

And, indeed, it did seem inconceivable that this structure, which had stood here – so the Professor said – for some fifteen centuries, should so suddenly crumble under the weight of a thirteen-year-old girl.

Gray muttered brief prayers to Neptune, Dahut, and anyone else who might be listening, lest the incident represent some manifestation of divine displeasure.

This ought not to have happened, surely.

It was not until their much-subdued party had nearly reached Callender Hall that he remembered what else ought not to have happened as it had. If Gray could not set wards, could not shift, could only just call light enough to see by . . . then how had he so effortlessly produced that powerful finding-spell?

Amelia blanched at their tale, her blue eyes round, and rang for shawls and hot toddies. The Professor, who had looked aghast at their bedraggled return, grew increasingly dour.

'Mr Marshall has exposed you both to unconscionable dangers,' he declared. 'You may be sure he shall not be permitted to do so again.'

'But, Father!' Joanna exclaimed. 'Did you not hear me? It was Mr Marshall who found me and came to my rescue!'

'From a predicament, Joanna, in which he himself had placed you.'

'But—'

The door of the sitting-room opened to admit Mrs Wallis, bearing a tray of steaming cups, and Katell with an armful of winter shawls. Sophie accepted a cup of hot toddy, grateful both for its warmth and for Mrs Wallis's timely interruption. The Professor was quite capable of confining them both to the house for the remainder of the summer, simply to punish Joanna's insolence; to be forced to circumvent such a restriction, as she knew from past experience, would be tedious in the extreme.

'Sophia!'

'Sir?'

The Professor regarded her with narrowed eyes. 'Have you anything to add to your sister's tale?'

Sophie considered pretending that she had had Gray under her eyes all the time and could swear to his innocence. But the Professor would question Morvan and Gwenaëlle, and though either would lie without hesitation to protect her or Joanna, she could not trust that they would do the same for Gray. She could point out again that Joanna had ventured so near the colonnade only to look at the memorial stone, which yesterday the Professor had told Gray was so much worth examining—

Sophie shut her lips tight on that disquieting thought. Surely she was imagining things – and the Professor would not thank her for making such a suggestion.

'Nothing, sir,' she said instead. 'I can attest that Joanna's rescue was just as she tells it, but no more.'

The moment the Professor looked away, she cast a pleading glance at Mrs Wallis.

'Professor, sir,' said the latter. ''Ad not Miss Sophia and Miss Joanna best be put to bed? They 'ave 'ad a dreadful fright and are not themselves.'

'Indeed, Papa,' said Amelia, 'I think Mrs Wallis is quite right.'

The Professor's gaze swept over them again, suspicious, but he allowed Mrs Wallis to bundle them off upstairs.

Joanna was put firmly to bed, over vigorous protests, and left to her own devices. Mrs Wallis lingered with Sophie, however, tidying needlessly and asking unaccountable questions.

'I was very frightened indeed,' said Sophie, in answer to one such, 'and Joanna I am sure was quite terrified. But we are perfectly recovered now, Mrs Wallis, I promise you.'

'Yes, dearie, I see you are; and you are quite sure there was nothing – this Mr Marshall 'as not been making a nuisance of 'imself . . . ?'

Sophie could not at once make sense of this remark; when at length she divined its meaning, she half wondered whether Mrs Wallis had not been sampling the Professor's brandy to steady her nerves. Had it been anyone else, she might have said so, but Mrs Wallis had known her and her sisters from the cradle and had looked after them since their mother's sudden death – if she was occasionally a trifle zealous in guarding them from harm, it was hardly to be wondered at.

'I have not the least complaint to make of Mr Marshall,' she said firmly. 'I believe I am quite safe from unwanted advances on his part.' A less happy thought occurred to her, and she caught Mrs Wallis's sleeve. 'I hope you will not put any such idea into the Professor's head?'

'I should think not, Miss Sophia!'

She stayed a few moments more, pottering about Sophie's bedroom and humming quietly to herself; Sophie began to feel terribly sleepy, and only just glimpsed the silent closing of the door before sliding headlong into oblivion.

CHAPTER IV

In Which Sophie Shows Talents of a Nonmagickal Sort

If Joanna's near-accident at Kerandraon was indeed a sign of divine displeasure, Gray saw no further evidence of it. Nor, fortunately, did the Professor again call him to account for endangering Joanna's and Sophie's lives, as he had on that first afternoon, but Gray's comings and goings grew more circumscribed and more closely watched, and Sophie more cautious in her excursions into the garden.

The success of his finding-spell in the temple had given Gray hope that his magick might be soon restored. Throughout his many experiments in the ensuing weeks, however, it remained at such a low ebb as to prevent his warding his bedroom against listening-spells – or transforming so much as a fingertip into a feather.

One blazing August morning, having gained the farthest reaches of the garden before recognising the absence of his now-familiar sun-hat, Gray returned to the house to look for it, irritated and already sweating in the heat. Upon his return, he cursed under his breath; the hat was not in its place on the hatstand. Where in Hades had he left the thing?

With an exasperated sigh, he ducked through the doorway and started towards the back staircase, whereby he could reach his bedroom without risk of encountering the Professor or Miss Callender. Halfway to the first floor he paused, listening; somewhere in the house, someone was singing.

The voice was at once familiar and strange, and Gray instantly recognised the song:

Ae fond kiss, and then we sever!
Ae fareweel, and then for ever!

He shivered. He and his sisters had often played that music and sung those words, before their mother – who disdained the Border Country dialect of her childhood home, and who did not wish to encourage romantic notions in her daughters – declared it unsuitable for their tender years. Though Cecelia, a cynic even in childhood, considered its sentiments amusingly histrionic, Gray and Jenny had always found it affecting and had been genuinely grieved when it was forbidden to them.

Deep in heart-wrung tears I'll pledge thee,
Warring sighs and groans I'll wage thee . . .

Now, listening, Gray could no more have stopped climbing than if strong chains had been dragging him forward. As though bespelled, and dismayed at his inability to resist, he ascended the staircase and softly trod the passage on the first floor, through the baize door and out towards the drawing-rooms. The music came from the smaller of these, which Gray had not previously had occasion to enter.

He entered it now, and – hairs rising like an angry cat's – halted on the threshold in amazement.

The singer, of course, was Sophie. This was not amazing; Joanna he knew to be quite tone-deaf, and Miss Callender – no, the notion was absurd. Although the voice did sound *remarkably* like Jenny's, he knew that Sophie it must be. But that Sophie could look like this . . .

Her hair was dark and shining, her cheeks glowed pink; she

wore, he thought, the same blue gown as at breakfast, but there the resemblance ceased. Hearing Gray, she looked up at him but went on singing; her dark eyes sparkled so that he could not restrain a grin. How could he have thought her dull and listless at table that very morning? She was radiant now, joyful – beautiful, in fact. It was difficult to know how the same person could present such a different appearance, unless by some magickal transformation.

Her song ended, Sophie rested her hands lightly on the keyboard and smiled up at him.

'I thought myself alone in the house,' she said. 'Amelia has gone visiting in the carriage and taken Joanna with her, and the Professor is out walking. This is not the sort of music they would approve of, you see.'

She paused.

'They do not much like me to sing,' she said. Which explained, presumably, why he had never heard her do so before.

'I have not heard that song in – in years,' said Gray. He became vaguely aware that he was staring, and with an effort he turned his gaze to the window. 'It is not one my mother approves of, either.'

'So you know it? How wonderful!' Sophie clapped her hands like a delighted child. 'Will you sing it with me, then?'

In the warm room Gray shivered. 'I – I only came in to look for my – my hat—'

'Please, Gray.' Her tone was quite serious now. 'I shall not keep you long from your work. Just once.'

There is nothing I should like more, thought Gray – *only I fear the consequences.*

'I should be honoured,' he said at last.

Sophie smiled.

Singing with Sophie, Gray discovered, was very different from singing with Jenny or Cecelia.

To begin with, she was a better musician than either; hearing her play the pretty, capricious music that pleased her father and Amelia, Gray had often pondered how many thousands of hours she must have spent in practising, to attain such consummate skill as made even the most difficult piece sound natural and unstudied. Though they had never before sung together, she followed his lead perfectly and without apparent effort; a glance from her told him to carry the melody, and her clear soprano wove bewitchingly about it, her fingers never stumbling in the rippling accompaniment.

There was something else, too – some indefinable sense that, despite all Sophie's protests, this room had magick in it.

Had we never lov'd sae kindly,
Had we never lov'd sae blindly,
Never met – or never parted . . .

In the middle of the second verse, Gray's knees went weak and he clutched at the lid of the pianoforte to stop himself from falling. Sophie's voice faltered, and the instrument fell silent.

'Gray?' she said softly. 'Gray, are you not well?'

Gray's vision blurred, and the room began to turn about him. Gentle hands caught his elbows; an arm round his waist supported him to a sofa, where he sat, head in hands, trying to regain his equilibrium. He was vaguely aware of someone kneeling at his feet.

'Out,' he managed to say. He felt trapped, stifled; blinking desperately in an attempt to clear his vision, he was assailed by a sense of despair, of cold black dread, and he staggered to his feet, frantic for air. 'Out – I must get out – please, outside—'

There was a flurry of movement and the sound of window-sashes flung open. Gray felt a breeze, smelt a hint of trees and sun, and lurched towards the source of these salvifics. Hands on the windowsill, head and shoulders as far out into the air as he could manage, he drew deep, ragged breaths. Slowly the panic receded.

'Gray,' Sophie whispered, behind him. 'Gray, come back to me.'

He turned to look down at her. Her face was pale, her eyes large, and – no, it must be his own bleary eyes that made the rest of her look pale as well. 'I felt—' he began. Remembering what he had felt, he began to shiver.

'You are ill,' said Sophie. The gently scolding tone he knew was creeping back into her voice. 'Going out without a hat again, as though you knew no better. Very likely you are sun-struck. You ought to be abed. Can you walk, or . . . ?'

'Certainly I can walk,' Gray said, rather crossly, though in fact he was far from certain.

As Sophie slipped an arm about his waist to support him, he considered protesting that he was not ill, had in fact been feeling very fit until a few moments ago. In the end, he said nothing: Something undoubtedly was the matter with him now.

But it had, he was equally certain, nothing to do with being out in the sun.

Mrs Wallis brought him a tray at noon: tea, toasted bread, and strong beef broth, an invalid's meal. Gray glowered at it. 'I am not ill, Mrs Wallis,' he said.

'Miss Sophia tells me you 'ad a touch of the sun this morning,' Mrs Wallis replied calmly. Gray knew Sophie well enough by now to suspect that she had not put the matter so politely.

'It was not the sun; it was—'

It had felt, in fact, rather like magick shock – the dragging, hollowed-out aftermath of too much magick used too quickly – though magick shock had never so terrified him. But *could* one be magick-shocked who had used no magick?

Sophie. The thought assailed him as he drifted into sleep, full of toasted bread and beef broth. *I used none – but I am sure that Sophie did.*

At dinner that evening, Gray – feeling much more himself after sleeping nearly all day – watched Sophie as steadily as he dared. Once or twice he caught her eye and chanced a smile. But his vigilance was of no use; the eager, vivid Sophie of the morning was gone, replaced again by a shadow of herself who seemed bent on escaping notice.

It is *magick*, Gray thought; *magick this morning, and magick now. There can be no other explanation. Sophie's own magick, whatever her father may believe. But what manner of magick is this?*

He had an unwelcome sense that someone was waiting for him to speak.

Professor Callender said, in the tone of one ill-pleased to be repeating himself, 'We shall soon be welcoming another guest, Mr Marshall – rather a distinguished one, I am happy to say. I am sure we shall all enjoy his company; do you not agree?'

Had the Professor ever in his life asked a question that really *was* a question? 'Yes, sir,' said Gray. 'Of course, sir.'

Gray stood in the centre of his bedroom late that evening, in the light of a single candle on the desk, and prepared to speak a warding-spell.

This has gone on long enough, he admonished himself. *The magick was there at Kerandraon; it is there still, if only you will have faith in it. Magick cannot simply disappear.*

He drew a deep breath, set his shoulders, and straightened his back. Closing his eyes, he reached down into the core of his magick, the words of the warding ready on his lips.

At the first syllable, his stomach began to churn. Swallowing hard, he went on; the Latin words that ought to have slipped fluidly out into the air had to be forced out, painfully, through his clenched teeth.

His vision blurred. Before he had finished even half the spell, he collapsed.

When he woke – disoriented, with queasy stomach and pounding head – his first thought was that, somehow, he had returned to Merlin while he slept, to begin his waking nightmare all over. Soon enough he recognised his surroundings, but his relief was short-lived, for with it came the remembrance of what he had tried, and failed, to do.

Was it possible that his magick *had* simply vanished? That his violent encounter with the wards on the Professor's Oxford rooms, in bringing on the worst case of magick shock he had hitherto suffered, had also done him some more permanent damage?

One need not – as the Professor himself gave daily proof – possess any extraordinary practical talent in order to master the most arcane minutiae of magickal theory; indeed, the Professor was not alone among the Senior Fellows in disdaining what he termed 'vulgar and unnecessary display'. Even limited, as he now appeared to be, to the smallest of magicks – calling light and fire, summoning small objects from close at hand – Gray might yet have spent many happy years as a Fellow of Merlin, teaching magickal theory to eager young men.

And what choice had he, with no abode but his College rooms and no income but his College scholarship?

But never again to fly! To pass another year, or more, under the Professor's stultifying tutelage, deprived of that escape! And even this prospect, he suspected, was unduly optimistic; he had only the Professor's word (and not so much his word as an oblique threat to the contrary) that his name would be cleared in return for his compliance.

On the other hand . . .

On the other hand were the comforts of home and family, the more appealing for being so long denied him. Perhaps even now, if he gave in – if he begged forgiveness and submitted himself to his father's wishes – he might once again be welcomed there.

Tomorrow I shall tell the Professor that I intend giving up my Mastery and taking up the commission my father wishes to purchase for me, he decided. *And then perhaps he will let me go home.*

So saying, he betook himself to bed, only to be denied for many hours the relief of sleep.

CHAPTER V

In Which Professor Callender Welcomes a Visitor

Gray began the next morning by searching the house for his tutor, intending to carry out his resolve of the night before. This quest proving fruitless, he sighed in resignation and fetched his gardening hat.

Before the day was ended, he had undergone a change of heart.

Still wanting an early glimpse of the Professor's 'distinguished guest', he contrived to find work that placed him within sight of the front of the house. This was bound to irritate Pellan, who did not like anyone else – even the Professor, who paid his wages – to decide things about *his* gardens, but a dressing-down from Pellan would by now be nothing unusual, and the events of the summer had given Gray a strong distaste for surprises.

The visitor was due to appear in the course of the morning, but when Joanna came out to summon Gray to luncheon, there had still been no sign of any new arrival.

'Do you know who this mysterious visitor is to be?' he asked her as they trailed towards the kitchen garden. Although Joanna lacked Sophie's gift for blending in unseen, she was, through continual gossiping in Breton with the house servants, often in possession of useful information.

This time, however, she only shrugged. 'I have not the least idea,' she said, plucking a leaf from a stand of bee-balm in passing. 'But he must be terribly rich or terribly important, for Father to make such a to-do.'

The same thought had occurred to Gray.

'And if Father admires him so,' Joanna continued, 'he will be dreadfully dull and probably very stupid, and we shall all be expected to flatter him and agree with everything he says. I have been considering,' she said, her round, freckled face screwed up in thought, 'whether I ought to fall down the stairs and sprain my ankle, or simply take to my bed with a chill.'

Despite himself, Gray had to stifle a snort of laughter. 'Never the stairs,' he said. 'You should not like your injuries to be *too* real. And a chill is difficult. A headache is what you want: very easily feigned – no outward signs – and should a healer be sent for, you can say it has gone away.'

Joanna looked reluctantly impressed. 'Sophie was right,' she said; 'you *are* rather clever.' Then, her face resuming its more customary expression of pugnacious suspicion, she demanded, 'How did you come to be studying with *Father*? Had you done something to make the College angry with you?'

Gray had largely overcome his resentment at being expected to work outdoors in all weather, amidst clay and compost and thorns, yet still look the gentleman at meals. But today, as he hurried into the dining-room to join the others at table – his hair hastily slicked down and, under his coat and waistcoat, a clean shirt sticking to still-damp skin – the Professor's disapproving glare forced him to swallow back a hot, unreasonable rage.

'M-m-my apologies, sir,' he stammered, trying to slip gracefully into the empty place opposite Sophie and Joanna. He might have spared himself the effort; the chair he drew out from the table scraped horribly along the floor, his legs tangled with the cloth, and, attempting to keep his balance, he put his elbow down in a clatter of silver.

Amelia and the Professor glared; Joanna for once had the grace to muffle her giggles. Sophie looked across at him with sympathy in her dark eyes.

'Now that Mr Marshall has had the goodness to join us,' said Professor Callender, with one last disparaging look at Gray, 'let us begin our meal.' He offered the ritual words of thanks to Jove and Juno, to the All-Father and the Mother Goddess; Gray had never once heard his host invoke any local deity. Gray – raised on Kernowek servants' tales – was of a different habit; under his breath he murmured his own thanks to Cerridwen, Rosmerta, and Dahut before lifting his knife and fork.

They were still at table when young Katell, smoothing her skirts with trembling fingers, opened the door of the dining-room.

'Begging your pardon, m'sieu',' she said in hesitant Français, 'the coach 'as brought your guest. Shall I show 'im in, m'sieu'? I told 'im I'd show 'im to 'is rooms if 'e wanted, but—'

'That will do, Katell,' said the Professor, in the same language; 'that will do. Show him in.'

Katell curtseyed again and fled; the Professor and Amelia looked after her, shaking their heads.

Then the door opened again and Gray heard Katell's voice again: 'M'sieu' le Vicomte Carteret,' it said, as a dark-haired, slightly stooped man of perhaps forty or fifty sidled into the room.

The Professor was on his feet, ushering in the newcomer while his flustered housemaid brought another chair to place beside Gray's. 'I beg you will allow me to present my eldest daughter, Amelia,' he said; the stranger bowed. 'My daughter Sophia; my daughter Joanna.'

Gray fancied that the stranger studied Sophie's face just a trifle longer than was polite.

'And this,' said the Professor, turning to indicate Gray, 'is a student of mine, Mr Marshall.'

Viscount Carteret – *where have I heard that name before?* wondered Gray – also turned, and nodded to Gray. 'A pleasure to make your acquaintance, Mr Marshall,' he said.

Gray bowed silently in return. His mind was racing, and he was grateful that the obligatory gesture of respect hid his face, however briefly. For, if he could not recall where he had heard this man's name, he had not forgotten that insinuating nasal voice.

'Will you not take some refreshment with us, my lord?' said Amelia.

Lord Carteret turned to her with a smile. 'I beg you will excuse me, Miss Callender,' he said; 'I fear I should be at best indifferent company.'

I did not mistake the voice, thought Gray; *it is he, indeed.*

'My journey has been long,' their guest continued, 'and I am presently more in need of repose than of refreshment.'

So saying, he allowed Katell to lead him away to Callender Hall's best-appointed guest-room.

Gray's relief at this departure was considerable. Though not unpractised in the art of concealing his state of mind from others, he feared that this shock, combined with the previous evening's disastrous experiment, might be too much for him. He needed time to think, and certainly, if the Professor's co-conspirators had begun to pay him private visits, Gray could no longer consider simply running away home.

He sat silent, thinking furiously, while the Professor lectured his daughters on the honour bestowed by Viscount Carteret in deigning to visit them. The oration was a long one, suiting Joanna's prediction that the honoured visitor would be 'desperately dull'. It was also a masterful exercise in saying much while revealing little.

'Father,' Joanna interrupted, drawing an ominous beetling of the paternal brows, 'I wish you will tell us who this Lord Carteret is.'

After a pause, during which even she seemed to recognise that perhaps she had gone too far, she added, 'If you please.'

Professor Callender drew himself up in his chair. 'I had forgotten,' he said icily, 'the boundless ignorance of the world in which my offspring choose to bury themselves.' He looked down his large pink nose at Joanna.

This seemed hardly fair. Across the table, Joanna was bristling again, and Gray sent her a silent plea to keep her temper. Perhaps Sophie was at the same time exercising some more concrete form of restraint, for, though visibly fuming, the younger girl held her tongue.

The Professor was still speaking, but his student could hardly credit what he said: '. . . Lord President of the Privy Council, King Henry's closest advisor.'

The chief Privy Counsellor? Here, *in this house?* Gray fought to keep his jaw from dropping open. His next coherent thought – harking back to that dreadful night in Oxford – was, *Why should such a man interest himself in the affairs of Merlin College?* But that voice . . .

If I have not mistaken his identity, then his loyalties are suspect – more than that! – and this is surely no mere social visit. I must discover what he has come here for.

In the salver on the hall table was a thick letter directed to Gray in Jenny's hand. He picked it up and made to take it with him, up to his bedroom to resume his working clothes. Before he had reached the staircase, however, he found himself cornered by his tutor, who wore his bluff and hearty air.

'Well, Marshall,' the Professor huffed, 'and what think you of our distinguished guest?'

'I – I hardly know, sir,' said Gray. 'I have not yet had leisure to form any opinion of His Lordship.'

'Ah! You have never before been in company with him, then.'

Had Gray had any respect for his tutor's intellect, it must have sunk under the weight of this clumsy attempt to trap him.

'No, indeed, sir,' he said, with perfect truth. 'I have never seen His Lordship before in the whole of my life. My family, you know, is in Town very little.'

Please, All-Father and Great Mother, let him not ask whether I've heard *him.*

Those deities for once answered his prayer fully and promptly: the Professor nodded, apparently satisfied, and Gray made his escape up the front staircase, Jenny's letter in hand.

A quarter-hour later, he descended by way of the back stairs, having no longer any reason to haunt the front drive. Pellan was waiting for him, grim-faced as ever, with buckets of compost and two spades. That afternoon, under Pellan's direction, Gray and the undergardener shovelled compost onto the roots of every tree in the vast grounds – or so it seemed to Gray.

At last Pellan deemed their task complete, and Gray was left to his own devices for the hour before dinner. Idly fingering a long scratch left on his wrist by a rose-tree, he let himself in at the garden door, hung up his hat, and wearily climbed the back staircase.

As soon as he entered his bedroom, he saw that it had been searched. Though the physical signs were subtle – not the neatness imposed by a housemaid's labours, but a disorder just perceptibly different from that which he had himself created – the air was thick with upheaval.

At once he crouched down to retrieve, from beneath the overbearing wardrobe that filled one corner of the room, the spell-locked case, brought from his College rooms, in which he had been keeping the more revealing of Jenny's letters. Scratches about the keyhole showed that the lock had been tried, but the searcher had not forced it. Gray breathed a sigh of relief; nowhere else in this room was there anything to show that he was not a voluntary and perfectly contented guest in this house. And the latest letter, by purest happenstance, he had still in his trouser-pocket. He took it out and broke the seal.

Gray dear, he read in Jenny's confident hand, *I hope you are well. I wish that you would write to my mother; she tells me often that she has heard nothing of you these many weeks, and is anxious for news of you. Of course I have assured her that you are safe and well, but she would be easier in her mind could she read the same in your own hand.*

Gray snorted; how like Jenny to put such a complexion on things, to attempt some sort of reconciliation, when in fact she herself had for some time been the only member of their family to spare him a kind thought.

He folded the letter away with the others and tripped the lock with something like relief; though his rooms had been searched, surely there had been nothing much to learn from the exercise. But though the incident had shaken him, it had also given him an idea. *Two can play at that game, my Lord President.*

For some days no opportunity offered itself for discreet investigation of Lord Carteret or the Professor; Gray was kept always at work, and under supervision, by Pellan or by the Professor himself. At last, however, having done his best to present an appearance of blithe innocence (not to say bovine stupidity), and having seen the Professor and his guest exit the house and pass by him in the general direction of the stables, he waited until Pellan's back was turned and his attention occupied by a molehill, then stole back into the house, via the kitchen, to put their absence to some use.

He crept as silently as he could down the dim, wood-panelled corridor that led past the Professor's study. Pausing outside the door, he pressed his ear against the polished oak just above the uppermost hinge, listening. He heard nothing but the thump of blood in his own ears, however, and so judged it safe to turn the door-handle.

Here Gray met his first check, for – not surprisingly – the door was locked and warded.

The lock first, he decided. He knew a number of spells for unlocking doors, as a result of his own unfortunate habit of losing keys; he had one hand on the door-handle and was preparing to spread the other over the lock when someone behind him said, 'Mr Marshall!'

Gray started guiltily and turned to look; one of the housemaids – Gwenaëlle, who had gone with them to Kerandraon – was coming up the corridor towards him, wearing a linen apron and an expression of surprise. Mrs Wallis's bristling key-ring was in her hand, and Gray had a sudden idea.

'Gwenaëlle, perhaps you help me?' he said, speaking in halting Breton with what he hoped was a winning smile. 'The Professor sends me to fetch something from his room, and says the door is open, but I find it locked. But if you have got another key . . .'

Gwenaëlle looked up him, her fine dark brows drawn together. Gray prayed to Janus, god of gates and doors and decisions, that she might see nothing to decide her against him. At last she said, 'No one but Professor Callender has the key to this room, Mr Marshall. *Mantret on.*' *I am sorry.*

Gray shrugged and let his smile twist sidewise, rueful. 'No harm,' he said. '*Trugarez deoc'h.*' *Thank you.*

He could not now linger there without her finding his behaviour suspicious; unfortunately, nor could he, as he had planned, climb the stairs to try the door of Lord Carteret's bedroom. Instead, therefore, he put his hands in his pockets and trudged away in the direction of the kitchen, as though returning empty-handed to the Professor.

Gray had intended only to avoid arousing suspicion; it appeared, however, that his dejection had instead evoked Gwenaëlle's sympathy for a fellow sufferer from her employer's caprices, for she said quietly, 'Mr Marshall, wait.'

Gray turned; she gave him a small smile and held up a key. 'Mrs Wallis's master key opens most of the doors in the house. This one too, it may be.'

Gwenaëlle looked carefully up and down the corridor before trying the key in the lock. For a moment it stuck fast, and she frowned; then she wiggled it gently, and with a soft click it turned.

Gray thanked her, and to his great relief she withdrew the key and went away about her business, leaving him to deal in solitude with the Professor's wards. This he had expected to present the more difficult challenge; releasing another mage's wards was always a tricky business, and Gray's present limits did not encourage optimism. To his surprise, however, the wards proved to be of the most basic kind, sufficient probably to protect the room against eavesdropping but, despite his very questionable intentions, offering no resistance to his crossing the threshold.

Gray had never been invited to enter this room, but it reminded him strongly of the Professor's study at Merlin: well stocked with claret, port, and brandy, a small selection of books tidily arrayed in glass-fronted cases, busts of Pythagoras and Apuleius. He had not time for a thorough search – even if he were fortunate and the Professor did not soon return to the house, Gwenaëlle might pass by again at any moment and hear him rummaging in drawers and pigeonholes – but he cast his eye over the contents of the desk and opened each of the drawers. The exercise was rendered less efficient by not knowing what it was he sought. There might have been a letter half written, a book open for consultation, some object concealed in a pigeonhole that resisted easy explanation, but there was not. There were, however, several codices stacked on one corner of the desk, and at the top of one stack a small leather-bound codex with a title in Breton stamped upon the cover, which surprised him a little, for he had never heard the Professor speak so much as a single word of that language. There was also a broken pen, one anomalous brown-and-tawny feather tossed carelessly in among the white goose-quills that were recognisably the Professor's. Might this have been abandoned by Lord Carteret? Gray pocketed it on the chance.

His hurried but systematic rummage concluded with the pockets of the powdering-gown that hung from a hook on the back of the door. Here at last he found something, or what might be something: a folded sheet of note-paper, at the top of which was written, in the Professor's careful hand, the words *lightly the gods' gifts*, and below it, in a different hand altogether, a long series of figures. Gray frowned at it. Could it possibly be of any significance? Surely, if it were, the Professor would not have been so careless with it? But he kept his study locked, and no doubt considered this a sufficient precaution.

Gray could not, he decided, take the chance of missing what might be a clue to the Professor's intentions. Stealing it would draw too much attention; was there time to make a new copy for himself? Quickly he collected pen, ink, and writing-paper from the desk and began copying the document. When he had finished – his copy scrawled so quickly as to be only just legible, but as accurate and complete as he could make it – he tucked the original back into the pocket where he had found it, and the copy into the front of his shirt.

After closing the door behind him, he spent an anxious few moments standing in the corridor with one hand spread over the lock, leaning his forehead against the oak and muttering first another prayer to Janus, then a locking-spell that he had read in the *Acta Societatis Magicam*, a few months and a lifetime ago. Though it was a small spell, he could not at first catch the trick of it, the shaping of his magick to persuade the tumblers to turn – the point was not to lock the door by magick, as he had planned to unlock it, but to induce it to lock itself as if with a key. On the third repetition, however, just as his hands were beginning to shake and his ears to imagine footsteps approaching behind him, the lock yielded with another soft click.

Gray exhaled raggedly, scrubbed his sleeve across the keyhole, and hastened away to the back stairs.

The guest-rooms allotted to Viscount Carteret were neither locked nor warded. It would have looked suspicious, Gray supposed, to lock one's door in a house in which one had been welcomed as a guest; did the lack of wards – even against listeners – suggest that Lord Carteret had not sufficient talent to set them?

Given the lack of such precautions, it was not to be supposed that Gray would find any incriminating object or document lying about in plain view. Having shut the door behind himself, therefore, he began his search with the sorts of hiding-places he might have used himself. There was nothing interesting on the top of the wardrobe, beneath the bed with the necessary, under the washbasin, or tucked between the dressing-table and the wall; nothing in the pockets of any of Lord Carteret's coats or concealed among his linens. There were no stacks of books that might have concealed papers; the small escritoire had but one drawer, which proved to contain only perfectly innocuous writing-paper, ink-bottle, and pounce-box.

Gray carefully avoided passing before the window, which faced backwards, lest he be seen from without, but suspended his search periodically to cast an eye down into the park. To do so he approached the window from the side, on his knees, and peered through the pane in the bottom corner. He was glad of this precaution when he spied the Professor and his guest, still some distance away, walking unhurriedly back towards the house; in his hasty retreat from the window, his glance fell upon a lacquered dispatch-box which had been secreted in the narrow space between the wardrobe and the outer wall, on the far side of the window.

Gray scuttled across the gap and drew the box from its hiding-place.

It was locked, of course, but as he had managed to relock the door of the Professor's study . . .

The small lock yielded without protest to one of his collection of unlocking-spells. Inside were what appeared to be a letter, folded but unaddressed and still unsealed, and a small leather-bound codex. Gray extracted the letter and studied the close, crabbed script. His heart beat faster; it was another inexplicable series of figures, written, he was almost certain, in the same hand as those he had found in the Professor's dressing-gown pocket.

He crept back to the window and, seeing Lord Carteret and the Professor still strolling about the gardens, apparently absorbed in conversation, took pen and ink and added this new series of figures to his copy of the first set. When he had finished, returned the original to the dispatch-box, and tucked the copy back into the breast of his shirt, he turned his attention to the codex.

It appeared to be a diary; dates and engagements were recorded in the same crabbed hand, with occasional names but a preponderance of initials. Gray's pulse quickened as he found the date of his expedition with Taylor and the others noted together with the initials *AC* and *M*, though in fact it left him none the wiser – *AC* must be the Professor, but *M* might be anyone in the kingdom. Gray was unshakably persuaded, however, that whoever *M* was, he would speak in an imposing basso.

He turned the pages eagerly but found nothing that, even to his mistrustful eye, presented the least appearance of suspicion, nor the least clue to the identity of *M*. It was immediately evident, however, that any passage longer than a few words was written in some private cipher – not the same one used in the letter, for rather than figures it consisted of roughly word-sized groups of Greek characters.

Gray knew an agonised moment of indecision. Nearly every page of the diary was filled with cryptic or enciphered notations, which at present he could make nothing of. He had certainly not time to copy the whole of it and did not dare take it away with him, but still less could he see any way to determine which passages, even should he succeed in deciphering them, might be of use to him. The entire exercise, moreover, had begun to make him uneasy, for the gods knew what state secrets might be quite properly concealed in the papers of a man with responsibilities such as Lord Carteret's. Gray had no business here that he could defend. Still, Lord Carteret had been in the Professor's Oxford rooms, had certainly spoken of some plan to harm the Master of Merlin in some way, whether bodily or not. And so Gray, despite his misgivings, found the most recent additions to the diary, one of them dated to the previous day, and transcribed them onto another sheet of the Professor's writing-paper before carefully replacing the book in the dispatch-box. The box was locked by the same expedient as the Professor's study – the spell was easier to work this time, whether because of that prior success or because this much smaller lock required a proportionally smaller expenditure of magick – and restored to its place of concealment, and Gray was half out of the room before, with a stifled 'Horns of Herne!' he turned back, retrieved the dispatch-box, and polished away the handprints from its glossy surface with the tail of his shirt.

It was a matter of moments to traverse the corridor to the servants' staircase and ascend to his own bedroom. Once there, Gray retrieved his writing-case from beneath a stack of grimoires on his desk and spoke the words to suspend the spell that locked it. Then he began patting his pockets for the key.

It was not until he had exhausted all possible pockets and resorted to a further trial of the unlocking-spell that left him dizzy and gasping – *I have found my limit, then*, he reflected sourly – that, raising a hand to tug at his collar, he remembered that he had hung the key on a length of twine about his neck.

The pen and the papers safely locked away alongside Jenny's

letters and Arzhur Gautier's handkerchief, he crept down the stairs again and made his way back to the spadework he had abandoned in the kitchen garden.

Lord Carteret departed a few days later, having given no visible sign that Gray's incursion into his private papers had been remarked upon – unless it were some little added contempt in his gaze. The contempt was certainly justified; Gray had sat up late every evening since, poring over the purloined documents until his eyes swam and his head ached, but they remained as cryptic as ever, and Gray as much in the dark as before. He felt slow and stupid, as though he had drunk too much wine, and no amount of sleep or fresh air seemed to clear his head.

The fog slowly lifted over the ensuing days, until Gray regained sufficient self-command to recognise that what had seemed an ordinary lock on Lord Carteret's dispatch-case must have had some defensive spell upon it, designed to befuddle intruders.

He had yet to break Lord Carteret's ciphers, however. He felt sure that if he could only have had the help of his friend Evans-Hughes – who delighted in puzzles and ciphers of all sorts, and was gifted at scrying besides – the documents must have rendered up their secrets in short order, but given the circumstances of their last meeting, he could not imagine that Evans-Hughes would be at all disposed to help him, even if they had not been separated by nearly the width of the kingdom.

Might Master Alcuin be of some assistance in this? Gray had written his former tutor several letters – in the same cautious vein as his first letter to Jenny – but he had as yet received no reply, which made him suspect something amiss. The Professor had certainly had the Proctors on his side, and the gods alone knew how many of the other Fellows; the Porters too, it might be. If that were so, it would be foolhardy to make such an inflammatory request in a letter that might be opened and read by any of these. Though the cipher in the diary might perhaps be couched as merely a puzzling passage of Greek . . .

Gray took the pages out yet again and laid them flat on his desk to peer at them by candlelight. Whatever the language was, it was certainly not Greek; the passages he had copied filled both sides of one sheet and one side of a second, yet in all that text there was not a single word he recognised, and there were too many letter combinations that ought not to occur in that language. Nor had Lord Carteret simply used Greek characters to render text in some other tongue – or, at any rate, not Latin, English, Français, Cymric, Kernowek, or Brezhoneg. Most probable, then, that the text had been first enciphered in its original language, then transliterated into the Greek alphabet. Gray supposed vaguely that the original language might also be Erse or the Gaidhlig of Alba, but he had no particular reason to suppose that Lord Carteret spoke either one.

He turned back to the ciphered letters, if letters they were, and tried to recall everything he had ever heard from Evans-Hughes on the subject of cryptography. He had run through what he was sure must be every possible simple substitution of figures for letters, to no avail. But there were other types of ciphers that used figures, if only he could remember what they were.

And why did that almost nonsensical phrase in plain Latin – *lightly the gods' gifts* – seem so familiar?

Sleep overtook him before he arrived at an answer to this question, and when, some hours later, he awoke, woolly-headed and stiff from sleeping at his desk, his bleary eyes opened upon the same few words. *Lightly the gods' gifts . . .*

The candle at his elbow flared, guttered, and died. In the sudden darkness, a period crystallised in Gray's mind, and he sat up so abruptly that his head swam. *The gods' gifts are lightly given, and as lightly reclaimed.* It was a line from the *Sapientia Delphi.*

A codex cipher. It is a codex cipher, and all I need in order to read it is a copy of the Sapientia Delphi.

CHAPTER VI

In Which Jenny Makes an Important Discovery

A fortnight after Lord Carteret's departure, on an August morning when the fickle Breton sun shone with unaccustomed ferocity, Gray looked up from the tree-stump he was digging out to see an unfamiliar carriage – small, but very grand indeed – sweeping up the broad drive of Callender Hall. He stiffened, alarmed. As the carriage rattled past, he saw on its door the arms of his brother-in-law, Sieur Germain de Kergabet.

His first, irrational thought was, *Something dreadful has happened to Jenny.* He dismissed it immediately, however; Gray was the last person in Jenny's family to whom Sieur Germain was likely to pay a personal visit in such a case. It then occurred to him that Sieur Germain might be an acquaintance of the Professor, and the idea made him groan aloud. He put down his spade and loped towards the house.

The truth, as he learnt from Mrs Wallis on his way through the kitchen – he could scarcely appear before potential guests of the Professor in his stump-pulling attire – was stranger yet: chancing to visit the neighbourhood, Mr Marshall's sister had, most naturally, decided to call upon her brother's friends.

Jenny sat with the Miss Callenders and Gray in the large drawing-room, slim and upright on a velvet-covered settee, and accepted a cup of tea but declined her hostess's stiff, almost ungracious, offer of further refreshment. Miss Callender seemed disinclined to conversation; Jenny did her best, but Gray thought she looked more tired and anxious than her day's journey alone could account for.

'What a lovely pianoforte you have there, Miss Callender,' said Jenny, nodding at it through the open doors. 'You must play and sing a great deal, I suppose?'

'Oh!' Miss Callender gave a dismissive little laugh. 'No, indeed, Lady Kergabet. It is my sister Sophia's property now. One must put away such amusements, you know, when one has the running of a household. In any case, my father does not much care for singing.'

'I am sorry for it,' said Jenny. 'It must be a grief to you. I know that I should miss my playing and singing very much, were I made to give it up.'

Gray was sure Jenny had meant this remark kindly; it seemed Miss Callender did not take it so, however, for she flushed a little, and looked put out, and made no reply. Sophie, watching from the corner to which she had retreated with her interminable fancy-work, gave a grim little smile.

After nearly a quarter-hour of such limping conversation, a gleam of inspiration lit Jenny's face.

'Miss Callender,' she said, 'my brother has told me so much about your father's gardens. Might I be permitted . . .'

Miss Callender jumped – almost literally, thought Gray – at this suggestion.

'My sister is very knowledgeable about the gardens, Lady Kergabet. I am certain that she would be delighted to show them to you – would you not, Sophia?'

And Sophie, rising from her seat as though she had been included in the conversation all along, smiled warmly at Jenny. 'Certainly,' she said, and added, as though casually, 'and perhaps Mr Marshall will join us also?'

Jenny's answering smile radiated profound relief.

Gray, seated on a stone bench in the kitchen garden, extracted a small bundle from his pocket and handed it to his sister. Sophie watched, puzzled, as Lady Kergabet carefully unfolded the object – a perfectly ordinary handkerchief, rather the worse for wear – and turned it slowly in her hands, her pale, delicate eyebrows drawing together in concentration.

'What is she doing?' Sophie whispered to Gray.

'Scrying is Jenny's magickal talent,' he said softly. 'Watch and see.'

Lady Kergabet had closed her eyes and was frowning a little, murmuring steadily under her breath. Finally she raised her head on a long sigh and opened her eyes, blinking at Sophie and Gray.

'You were right,' she said bleakly. 'I am very sorry.'

'Mother Goddess.' Gray did not stammer, but his voice shook. Sophie turned to him, startled, and saw him clasp trembling hands between his knees. 'Poor Gautier. How did it happen? Did you see?'

Lady Kergabet shook her head. 'I have tried my best,' she said, 'but you know the things I see are often quite incomprehensible.'

Sophie tried to recall what she had read about scrying – the art of reading from an object the emotions, thoughts, or actions of its owner. It was a not uncommon skill, but one that – like healing – must begin with inborn talent; some of the authors she had studied set great store by it, while others wrote of scry-mages only in the most disparaging terms, conceding that they could not easily lie about what they saw, but insisting that they were very apt to be deluded or mistaken. The same object, she knew, would not necessarily produce the same fragments of understanding for every scry-mage who examined it; the echoes of ownership could fade or grow warped with time, and spells existed which could be used to create false echoes, or to alter or obscure genuine ones.

'Gray, who is Gautier?' said Sophie. 'What—?'

But Gray seemed not to hear her.

'If your friend was the owner of this handkerchief, however,' Lady Kergabet continued, 'then he is certainly dead.'

'Dead? One of Gray's friends is *dead*?' Sophie looked from one of them to the other.

Gray stared at her as though just now reminded of her presence. He looked back at his sister; she shook her head. 'It is . . . I asked Jenny for tidings of my friend Gautier; I had had ill news of him, and I hoped it might be . . . mistaken, but . . .'

Hesitantly, Sophie laid a hand on his arm as his voice trailed off. 'I am very sorry,' she said.

They walked for some time, apparently at random but drifting gradually farther and farther from the house. When they had reached a point sufficiently distant, Sophie melted tactfully away into the shrubbery, leaving Gray and Jenny alone together for the first time since the latter's marriage more than a year before. The moment their hostess was out of sight, Jenny flung herself at her brother, reaching up her arms to encircle his neck; startled and pleased, he lifted her off her feet and embraced her fiercely. She was heavier than he remembered.

'I have been so *worried*, Gray,' Jenny whispered. 'And now your friend—'

He set her down gently and clasped her hands in his. 'Some dreadful thing is happening,' he said earnestly. 'Here, and at Merlin. Gautier is dead, and others than myself have been injured; his death was not meant, I think, but I fear there may be worse to come, though I do not know just what—'

'Gray.' Under her bonnet and the mass of wheat-coloured curls,

Jenny's pale face was drawn tight with confusion and alarm. 'Gray, dear, please tell me what you do know – you frighten me terribly. Whatever it is, you know you have only to ask, and I shall do all I can to help . . .'

Gray sighed. He and Jenny, only a year his junior, had been confidants and confederates almost from the cradle; he knew her, none better, a woman of courage and good sense. Still, alone she was no match for the Professor's coven and their plot – whatever it might be; he ought not to involve her, knowing that there might be danger to her, but . . .

'Jenny,' he said abruptly. 'Will you scry something else for me? Now, quickly?'

'Of course. Whose is it?'

He hesitated. 'I am not altogether sure,' he said. 'But I hope it may tell us something that I want very much to know.'

'Well, then?' She held out her right hand.

Gray fumbled in the pockets of his coat; after a moment he produced the broken pen he had abstracted from the Professor's study, which together with Gautier's handkerchief he had retrieved from his writing-case upon hearing of Jenny's arrival. Had he already made this choice, even then?

He dropped the bent quill into her open palm.

When Jenny opened her eyes again, she was ashen-faced and trembling.

'You must not stay here,' she implored him. 'Come home with me now, Gray, please!'

Shaking his head, Gray steered her gently to a seat in the shade of a little rose-tree and sat beside her, clasping her chilled hands in his. 'Tell me what you saw,' he urged her, his voice pitched low lest, even here, they might be overheard.

Jenny took a deep breath, then let it out again; the trembling eased a little, and the colour began to creep back into her cheeks.

'It was quite clear,' she said at last. 'Much more so than before. Your Professor – he told you, I suppose, that he is protecting you?'

Gray nodded, already disappointed – this he had always known to be at least half a lie, and Jenny's words proved the pen to have belonged to the Professor and not, as he had hoped, to Viscount Carteret – but determined not to show it.

'Gray, he intends no such thing,' said Jenny. 'He may not have meant your friend to die – I cannot tell – but he certainly means that you should.'

Gray's first thought was neither shock nor, strangely enough, alarm, but rather, *Now I know why he let me go to Kerandraon, and what he hoped might happen if I sought out old Duke Gaël's memorial stone.* The second was that the Professor had evidently no very great care for his daughters' safety, and the third, a fervent hope that his own attentions to Sophie and Joanna had not already exposed them both to further danger from their father.

'You do not seem surprised.' Jenny's voice – low but tense, almost angry – interrupted his thought.

'I did not need to be told that the Professor wishes me ill fortune,' Gray said bitterly. But this new knowledge solidified in his mind that he had overheard a plot aimed not merely at the ouster of Lord Halifax, Master of Merlin, but at his death.

Sophie and Joanna found them, nearly half an hour later, still arguing in heated undertones.

'I *will not* leave them here to fend for themselves,' Sophie heard Gray whisper, as she emerged into the clearing around the rose-tree. She was about to clear her throat or cough to announce their presence when Joanna – predictably – forestalled her: 'Leave who?' she demanded, careless of grammar, planting herself before Gray and his sister with hands on hips.

Both of them whirled to face her, Gray looking appalled and Lady Kergabet guilty.

'Be quiet, Joanna,' Sophie scolded, as though she were not herself wild to know the answer to her sister's question. 'This is not your affair.'

Gray, recovering as much poise as he had ever had, crouched down to speak to Joanna face-to-face. What he said Sophie never discovered, but when he stood up again, her younger sister was unusually silent.

'We ought to go back,' Sophie said, and added, 'Amelia will worry.'

The others all nodded their agreement with this transparent falsehood.

Jenny had gone back to Kergabet, and Gray remained. Unable as yet to face the Professor, he had asked Morvan to say that he was ill, and eaten his dinner from a tray; now, alone in his bedroom, he sat before the open window, pretending to study.

Just before taking her leave, Jenny had tucked a letter into the pocket of his coat and whispered, 'I could not find the book you wanted, but I have brought you this,' as he bent to kiss her cheek in farewell. Now he drew the letter out and turned it over in his hands. No direction was written on the outside, but the seal was familiar – an owl of Minerva, superimposed upon Merlin's Oak. Gray's pulse quickened. What was this?

He broke the seal and unfolded the letter. It was disappointingly brief, but the hand was more than familiar. 'Magister,' Gray breathed. At long last, he had an answer from Master Alcuin at Merlin.

My dear Marshall, the letter ran,

I was grieved by your letter, and very much hope that you are well. I must urge that you send no reply; I strongly suspect that continued correspondence will put us both in further danger. Since receiving your first letter I have been followed and spied upon; I cannot be certain by whom, but I have recognised at least one protégé of your host. I am sorry to say that the tale you were told of your friend is indeed perfectly true, and moreover, that the blame is almost universally ascribed to you.

Gray stared in a sort of dull horror, his eyes stinging with tears as though he were hearing anew of Gautier's death. He could not go back, then; another home was lost to him, unless he could somehow prove his innocence, nor could Master Alcuin now help him in unravelling Lord Carteret's ciphers.

He could not claim to feel surprised by the news that all of Merlin believed him guilty: the Professor's threat *qua* invitation had all but promised it. He could not even be astonished to learn that he had unwittingly thrust Master Alcuin into difficulty, if not outright danger – but he could curse the thoughtlessness that had led him to do so.

Ought he to have gone away with Jenny? Did he put Sophie and Joanna in greater danger by remaining here than he might have done by leaving them?

In truth, he was more confused now than ever; he hardly knew which idea was the more preposterous – that the Professor, of all people, should be contemplating murder, or that he himself should be the target thereof.

What, after all, had he done that the Professor could object to? He had been on the man's own accursèd errand when all this began; he had not volunteered for the task but been recruited, under some protest, by the Professor's two favourites, Taylor and Woodville. Still he might have resisted, Taylor and Woodville being what they were, had other men he trusted – Evans-Hughes, and Crowther, and Gautier – not been of the party.

He scrubbed angrily at his stinging eyes and tried to think. He had overheard that strange conversation in the Professor's rooms, true; but the Professor surely did not, *could* not, know that he had done so. And what in Hades had Gray been doing there, when he ought to have been in the Infirmary with Taylor and Evans-Hughes?

Well, somewhere there must be answers to all of these questions, and he would – he must – find them out.

Gray shook his head. The world had gone awry; times were bad indeed if the gods' attempt to restore order to the Kingdom of Britain could find no better instrument than Graham Marshall.

Unable to sleep, Gray rose from his bed an hour or so past midnight and wandered about the house, trying to feel thankful at having called enough light to guide his way. So lost in thought that he paid little heed to where his feet were taking him, he blinked in surprise to find himself standing before the doors of the Professor's library. With a shrug, he turned the handle on the left-hand door and pushed it open. Once inside, however, he was stopped in his tracks by the scene within.

Seated at the oaken table – clad in a velveteen dressing-gown, a candle at her elbow, poring over a rather battered codex and humming softly to herself – was Sophie.

At his approach she looked up; the humming ceased, and for a moment naked terror immobilised her features. Then, seeing by whom she was discovered, she relaxed, eventually producing a smile.

'You have found me out at last,' she said softly. 'You did not imagine, surely, that he *allowed* me to read these things?' When Gray remained where he was, staring, she waved a hand at him. 'Come in, then, and shut the door.'

So began perhaps the happiest, and certainly the most interesting, period of Sophie's life to date. Gray, it appeared, not only was prepared to tolerate an unending stream of questions beginning, 'What does Gaius Aegidius mean by . . . ?' but seemed actually to enjoy helping her to unravel the overwrought Latin of the *Elementa magicae*, and they passed many a midnight hour in this pleasant pursuit.

It was perhaps a little disconcerting that he had appeared at the door of the library just when she had been fervently wishing for someone to help her with Gaius Aegidius, but Sophie did not receive so many gift horses as to be in the habit of looking them in the mouth.

'You are very patient,' she said to him, on a night when they had spent the best part of an hour parsing through a single page on the subject of the heritability of magickal talents.

'I have always liked teaching,' Gray replied, smiling at her; it was a smile with a good deal of regret in it, but still a world away from the desolated expression she had momentarily seen on that first night when he had opened the library door. 'I had in mind to become a teaching Fellow, and make it my living. Though I do not suppose I shall be permitted to do so now,' he added ruefully, half under his breath.

'Why not?' Sophie asked. 'You must know that you have a decided gift for it. Oh! Do you mean, because you are having such trouble with your own magick?'

'No, because—' But whatever Gray had begun to reveal, he evidently thought better of finishing, and merely said, 'That among other things, yes. Now: this passage is the key to understanding Gaius Aegidius. What do you make of *nihil in hominum genere rarius praedito magnis viribus et magna sapienta inveniri potest*?'

Sophie parsed it carefully out, and after some thought suggested, '"Nothing is more rarely found among men than one endowed with great strength and great wisdom"?' She considered: if Gray had asked for her interpretation of the passage, it could only be because there was something in it besides its plain meaning. What else might it mean, then? 'I suppose it might mean that Gaius Aegidius had met many strong fools and many wise weaklings, and . . . and thought the whole world must match his own experience.'

Gray rewarded her with a more genuine smile. 'And there you have the essence of the man,' he said, 'and the reason that one must regard his pronouncements with some degree of caution. Though the spells themselves are perfectly sound, in my experience.'

Sophie nodded and made a mental note. Not, she reflected sadly, that she was ever likely to have occasion to use any of Gaius's spells, or of anyone else's.

Some half-dozen of Gray's own books found their way into Sophie's possession over the course of these midnight meetings: his own copy of the *Elementa magicae* – its pages closely covered with annotations variously informative, exasperated and amusing – together with Sir Ivor Newton's *Principia alchemica* and the first two of the six-volume *De Ratio Magicis* of Junius Quintus Gratianus, among others. He asked her on several occasions whether she was quite sure that she had no magick herself, but gave it up when, instead of turning the conversation, she let him see that the question distressed her.

Sophie in turn undertook to improve Gray's command of Brezhoneg, beginning with a book of adventure tales of which Joanna was particularly fond. He was quicker at it than she had expected; Brezhoneg, he explained, was related to two languages with which he was already familiar – Kernowek and Cymric – which made his task easier.

'Who is Laora?' Gray asked one night, tracing the inscription on the book's flyleaf – *ex libris Laora* – with one finger.

'She was a cousin of my mother's, I believe,' said Sophie. 'Many of her books are inscribed so, instead of with her own name; she inherited them, she told me.'

'It was the name of the last queen, the Breton queen; the one who – who had rather a unfortunate end,' he said. 'Morvan mentioned her to me, in Kerandraon.'

'Breizhek,' Sophie corrected with a smile; 'in Brezhoneg we say *Breizhek*, not *Breton.* It is a common enough name here – perhaps all the little Laoras were named for the Queen? My mother's was Rozenn, and there are at least a dozen little Rozenns among the Professor's tenants.'

It was late, and Sophie was very tired; it must have been for that reason that her eyes suddenly burned with tears.

Gray looked tactfully away and opened the codex to the story they had begun a few nights earlier – the tale of the wasp, the dragonfly, and the spider. 'I cannot make out this phrase,' he said, pointing. 'It looks like "winged needle".'

By now Sophie had had time to dab at her eyes with the sleeve of her dressing-gown, and her voice was perfectly steady when she said, 'That is another name for a dragonfly.'

CHAPTER VII

In Which Sophie Loses Her Temper

If the library of Callender Hall contained any clue to the Professor's intentions, or to Lord Carteret's ciphers or the identity of the *M* mentioned in the latter's diary, Gray had not succeeded in finding it; nor, so far as his numerous and fervent searches could determine, did the library contain a copy of the *Sapientia Delphi.* Having, at some risk of discovery by Mrs Wallis and the housemaids, returned to rifle the Professor's study once more and, finding no further evidence of wrongdoing, dared his bedchamber as well with exactly the same result, Gray had not held out much hope of the library in any case.

He had, however, discovered a quick and enthusiastic pupil in Sophie, and there was some small consolation in knowing that for the first time since his arrival at Callender Hall, he could be of genuine use to someone.

One morning after breakfast, when the Professor and Amelia were gone to call upon a neighbour and Gray was balancing on a milking-stool, doing battle with some especially vicious species of beetle for dominion over Pellan's beloved climbing roses, Sophie emerged from the house, carrying in her arms a large codex bound in faded green leather, and took up a station on the bench beneath the rose-arbour.

Gray winced as a dead beetle fell onto a verso page; Sophie, unperturbed, brushed it away.

'Listen to this passage, Gray,' she said. 'Gaius Aegidius was rather tiresome in life, I suspect, but this fellow must have been perfectly insufferable!'

Gray granted himself a momentary respite from the beetles to listen. Alas, he recognised the style before she had read a dozen words. 'I see you have discovered Xanthus Marinus,' he said.

The beetles, he decided, were much to be preferred; Xanthus Marinus called to mind subjects he had rather not dwell upon.

Gray had received his first-class degree amidst the proud families of his year-mates – Convocation being one of the few days in the year when even female guests are welcomed indiscriminately into the closely guarded preserve of Merlin College – and the resounding absence of his own. In the pocket of his new MagB gown reposed a letter from his sisters, which he had read and reread, taking some comfort from their evident pride in his achievements, but troubled by Jenny's news that she was soon to be married to a wealthy Breton nobleman more than a dozen years her senior. *It is a good match*, she assured him, but Gray, reading between the lines, could see that, thus far at least, the affection was all on one side.

He had begged leave to return home for part of the Long Vac, and received from his father, via his mother, grudging assent to a fortnight's visit. He had been eager to see Jenny and Celia, relieved to learn that George would be from home nearly all the summer; he had pretended quite successfully, he thought, that his father's refusal to speak to him caused him no pain.

Master Alcuin – who, having no wife or children to call him elsewhere, spent most of his time in College, among his books – had called on Gray in his rooms the week after Midsummer. A full circle of the College grounds at last brought him to the point: that Gray, if he was to continue his studies, must do so with some other, more senior tutor.

'You have already learnt much of what I can teach you,' he said.

'Have you a recommendation, then, Magister?' Gray enquired.

'I have several,' said Master Alcuin. 'But it does not signify; such decisions are taken by the Registrar, as you well know. You are to study with Appius Callender.'

'That p-p-pompous old—'

'Guard your tongue,' the older man hissed fiercely.

This, as it turned out, was wise counsel indeed, and Gray now rather wished he had better heeded it.

He had approached the first meeting with his graduate tutor with trepidation. With Master Alcuin he had achieved a happy sort of harmony, but while Everard Alcuin was the sort to let the tea kettle boil dry or miss dinner in hall because he had become involved in translating some obscure text and lost track of time, Appius Callender's reputation was of an influential man, well connected outside the University.

Their acquaintance did not begin well. Gray, anxious to make a good impression, took care to put on a fresh neck-cloth, straighten his hair, and mend an unaccountable rent in his gown; as a result, however, he was late in presenting himself – by less than a quarter-hour, which Master Alcuin would scarcely have remarked upon – and the Professor greeted his arrival with a disapproving glare.

'Marshall, is it?' he said, and, consulting a notice from the Registrar, 'A student of that reprobate Alcuin's. Of course. Well, Mr Marshall, you will find that we do things differently here. At the *very* least, a student at your level might be expected to understand the importance of punctuality – do you not agree?'

'Y-y-yes, sir,' said Gray miserably. 'I am sorry, sir.'

The two other graduates already seated in the Professor's study were introduced as Henry Taylor and Alfric Woodville. Both were well known to Gray by reputation – Woodville being much in demand as a forger of extraordinary furloughs and letters lamenting the imminent deaths of elderly relatives, and Taylor renowned as a special protégé of Professor Callender's. And both, it transpired, had studied with the Professor since matriculating to Merlin. As the session proceeded, Gray wondered how the latter could endure their sycophantic replies to his every utterance; he soon learnt, however, that such was exactly what the Professor expected – nay, required – of his students.

He had never thereafter, perhaps unfortunately, learnt to march quite in step with Taylor and Woodville.

At a second meeting, Gray had been strenuously interviewed and thoroughly dressed down by his new tutor; despite having recently sat a rigorous set of examinations and passed them with the highest possible honours, he was made to feel inadequately trained and insufficiently well read.

'You have not studied Xanthus Marinus?' the Professor repeated, incredulous.

'X-x-xanthus Marinus?' Gray stammered, riffling through the closely written pages of his memory. What he found, at last, might better have been left unsaid: 'D-do not most modern thinkers b-b-believe his ideas to have been superseded by—'

'Ha!' Professor Callender cut him off with a scathing bark of laughter. In a tone Gray later came to know all too well, he said, 'You must learn to walk, Mr Marshall, before you aspire to run.'

Gray had briefly demonstrated his proudest achievement – the flawless and nearly effortless shape-shift – and ventured to note that he could now sustain it for half a day without ill effects. The working which had so impressed his Baccalaureate examiners that, to a man, they rose to their feet and applauded its astonished author, the Professor had at once pronounced *a foolish, frivolous waste of magick.*

'I shall tell you,' Gray said to Sophie, shaking his head irritably as though he could thus erase Appius Callender's contempt, 'what there is to be learnt from Xanthus Marinus: that a man of little talent may deprecate in another, achievements which he cannot match himself.'

And Sophie, turning on him that sharply appraising gaze by means of which both she and Joanna occasionally made him feel thoroughly so wrong-footed, said, 'The Professor thinks very highly of Xanthus Marinus, I suppose?'

Gray sighed. 'If you will come to the library tonight,' he said, 'I shall bring you something more worth your trouble.'

Not a se'nnight later, Gray was descending the staircase, bound for his afternoon's labours, when the sound of raised voices drew him to the large drawing-room. He ducked in through the door at the south end of the room just in time to hear Sophie say, 'Yes, Father, I did read them. And not only those.'

Father and daughter faced each other squarely at the drawing-room's north end; Sophie's expression was mutinous, the Professor's verging on apoplectic.

'Sophia, these books are deeply unsuitable reading for a young woman,' said the Professor.

'My mother read such books.'

'So she did. You would do well to remember what became of her.' *And what* did *become of her?* wondered Gray.

'I am most surprised at this underhanded behaviour, Sophia,' the Professor went on – and looked it. Evidently he knew his own daughters no better than he knew his students. 'Whatever did you mean by it?'

'I meant to *learn* something,' Sophie said, impatient. 'Something else than embroidery or dancing, or playing pretty tunes on the pianoforte. I am not a decorative object, Father. I have an intellect, also, and I wish to make good use of it.'

Gray had seldom seen the Professor look more outraged.

'That you should undertake to decide such a matter – I should not have thought it possible for a daughter of mine to be so insolent – and to *me*!' He paused for breath; the codex with which he had been gesticulating also came momentarily to rest, and Gray, dismayed, saw that it was the copy of *De Consolatione Magicae* that he had given Sophie to restore her faith in scholarship after her encounter with Xanthus Marinus. Had she forgotten it in the library? Or been reckless enough to carry it about the house with her when her father was at home?

'And the *foolishness* . . .' the Professor continued. 'Well: I have been too trusting. Henceforth, Sophia, the library doors will be locked at all times, and the keys in my own care, and you shall not speak to Mr Marshall unless I or one of your sisters is present.'

'*Father!*'

The Professor gave a great sigh. 'I must accept the responsibility,' he said, with exaggerated patience. 'I have allowed you unreasonable freedom, and have let a Breton peasant have the raising of you, and this is the consequence. Perhaps it was unwise to allow a person of Marshall's character into my home—'

'I will thank you to leave Mr Marshall's character out of this!' Sophie cut him off. 'I had been reading *unsuitable* books for years before ever I met him. The worst that can be said of Gray is that he has some respect for my intellect.'

For shame! said a voice in Gray's mind. *Will you let her defend you, and stand silent?* He started forward, determined to say something – anything – in Sophie's defence, but she was speaking again, dark eyes narrowed in her pale face. 'What is it you imagine will become of me, if—?'

This time the Professor cut her off. 'This is all done for your good, Sophia,' he said, 'as you will appreciate one day. If you hope ever to quit my home for one of your own, you would do well to learn womanly submission.' He turned sharply and strode out of the drawing-room by the north door, calling for Gwenaëlle to fetch Miss Callender, Mrs Wallis, and his hat and gloves.

'Amelia!' he was heard to demand. 'Where is Morvan with the carriage?' And a moment later, 'Mrs Wallis, Miss Sophia is to be confined to her room until I decide otherwise, and on no account is to be permitted to communicate with Mr Marshall. I shall deal with both of them tomorrow.'

Gray heard, but did not catch, the housekeeper's murmured reply; he was watching Sophie, who clearly – far from having learnt submission, womanly or otherwise – was consumed with fury. Her hands were clenched into white-knuckled fists; her hair seemed to crackle with energy. Gray could hear her rapid breathing. His every hair rose on end; he struggled for breath in the suddenly airless room, feeling dizzy and sick; there was a roaring in his ears, and dark blots swam before his eyes.

He heard a sort of shimmering, shattering sound; then small sharp pains freckled the right side of his face and neck, his arm, his ribs. Something trickled down his face; he put a hand to his temple and brought it away wet with blood. A breeze, briefly gentle but growing more savage, jostled the potted plants and curios that cluttered the room. The sound came again, and again, louder and louder; at last Gray saw that the drawing-room windows were bursting inward, each more violently than the one before. Sophie, oblivious and rigid with fury, was perfectly aligned with the last, northernmost window when a horrified Gray hurled himself at her, knocking her to the floor. Abruptly the noise ceased and the breeze died away.

In the vast stillness that followed, Gray and Sophie stared at each other in horror.

'You said you had no magick!' he exclaimed. He pulled her against him, clasping her so tightly that he could scarcely breathe.

After a moment he loosed his hold to look down into her face.

Her brown eyes were pale and huge with shock, her face the colour of tallow; even her hair looked faded and dull. What manner of magick was this?

'What happened?' she whispered. She touched Gray's cheek, where blood was already drying. 'Gray, your face is bleeding. What—?'

'Horns of Herne, Sophie, you blew the windows in! If *that* was not magick—'

She blinked up at him. Her gaze followed the sweep of his arm about the room, taking in the windblown furnishings, the shattered glass. She shook her head.

'*You did this*,' he said. 'Or your magick did. Has nothing like this ever happened before?'

'Of *course* not!' said Sophie – her voice a little stronger now. 'Only in – never when – *no*! My father has always said I have no magick. Surely – surely, if I had, even *he* would—'

Gray looked about him, eyebrows raised.

It was at this moment, of course, that Miss Callender came into the drawing-room.

Gray sprang away from Sophie as if from a hot stove, blushing scarlet. 'M-m-miss Callender,' he stammered. 'I fear—' But her expression stopped his tongue.

Sophie began to shiver.

For once Miss Callender seemed at a loss for words. She opened her mouth as if to speak, then shut it again, and stood, for what might have been hours, gazing in silence about her ruined drawing-room. Finally she appeared to notice her sister's waxen face and chattering teeth. 'Sophia,' she said reprovingly, 'you had best go up to bed. You are unwell – perhaps you have taken a chill. Mr Marshall, *what* have you done to the drawing-room windows?'

Sophie looked from her sister to Gray, and Gray found his voice again. 'She has not c-c-caught cold, Miss C-callender,' he said, ignoring the question of the windows. 'She is m-magick-shocked. She needs a hot drink and something to eat – cheese, or cold beef, or—'

'My dear Mr Marshall, my sister has no more magick than I have,' said Miss Callender, with her father's exaggerated patience.

Gray rather wished that she had witnessed Sophie's display; it might have saved argument. 'Miss C-callender, I assure you—'

A small sound from Sophie made him turn round. She was trembling more violently than ever, and – Gray knelt to look more closely, and breathed a few choice curses – a line of bright blood trickled from each of her nostrils.

Apollo, Pan, and Hecate! She will be very ill indeed unless I do something at once.

Sophie touched her upper lip, looked at her reddened fingertips, flinched, and swallowed hard. Her eyes met Gray's, frightened and pleading. Under their gaze, something in him roused itself and shook off the last vestige of concern with propriety.

'Come with me,' he said. Sliding one arm around Sophie's shoulders and the other under her bent knees, he straightened, towering over the protesting Miss Callender. 'Rest easy, Sophie. We shall soon have you set to rights.'

In the kitchen Mrs Wallis and Gray plied Sophie with strong cheese, new bread, ham, and hot, sweet tea. She ate eagerly; soon the colour began to return to her cheeks, and her trembling ceased.

Gray had forgotten his own injuries in his fear for her, but with her visible recovery this effect of mind over flesh began to ebb. Using his right hand to pour her a third cup of tea, he winced as each small splinter of glass made itself felt.

'Gray, your arm – your *face*,' said Sophie, repentant. 'I am so very sorry. Mrs Wallis – could you—?'

'Of course, dearie,' said the latter – who seemed remarkably unperturbed by the situation. 'Whatever was I thinking of? Come 'ere, young man. Let's 'ave a look at you.'

Gray submitted meekly, expecting simply to have his wounds bathed and bandaged. But after rinsing away the blood, the Callenders' cook-housekeeper calmly laid strong, callused fingers against his temple and began drawing out the glass and sealing the cuts with a healer's magick. Gray swallowed astonishment; servant or no, how had such a talent slipped the leash of the College of Healers?

Sophie, scratching at the bridge of her nose, caught his eye and produced a shadow of her usual pert grin.

'One finds magick in the most unexpected places in this house,' she said.

'Sophie,' Gray began, 'I owe you an apology.'

'I very nearly put out both your eyes,' said Sophie. 'Surely it is not *you* who ought to apologise.'

'Certainly I ought. I ought to have defended you.' Sophie frowned at this, but he went on: 'At the very least, I ought to have warned you what might happen.'

She sat up straighter. 'Warned me? Do you mean that all the time you were asking me whether I was sure I had no magick, you *knew*?'

'Well,' said Gray. 'Not *knew*, as such. In fact, were it not for the excellent Mrs Wallis, I should have the scars to prove the contrary. But I ought to have done. I have certainly suspected for some time that you were talented – thought you must be – only I did not like to distress you by speaking of it. And I had never guessed that you might be so powerful. I shan't underestimate your capacities again.'

'Gray, stop it,' said Sophie, shifting in her seat. 'You make me feel quite frightened.'

'I am sorry for it; but you must understand the implications.

Not least, what the Professor may think to do about it. Sophie, in your reading of magickal theory—'

'Wait. Stop. You said you had suspected. What made you suspect?'

'Have you . . . have you never a peculiar feeling, when someone around you is using magick?'

Sophie looked puzzled. 'What sort of feeling?'

'I feel it as though all my hairs were standing on end. But others feel it in different ways, and I have met talented people who feel nothing at all. Your father, I think, does not.'

Understanding dawned on her face as he spoke. 'I know what you mean now,' she said. 'At least . . . you'll think it silly.'

'Indeed I shan't. Wait—' Gray smiled suddenly. 'Is it – does your nose itch, just *there*?'

She stared at him, at the finger that touched the bridge of his nose. 'However did you know?'

'I've just remembered,' he said. 'You were scratching it this morning, when Mrs Wallis was healing my cuts – and the same that day just after I came here, when I was mending the hats. But the point is that I have *felt* magick being done dozens of times since meeting you, and there was sometimes no other way to account for it, though I could not think at first what magick it was you might be doing. So I ought really to have known that *something* would happen, and warned you.'

'That is unfair,' Sophie protested. 'How should you guess that my father would provoke me into breaking windows?'

'And what of this morning? Ought I to have stood there like a stuffed dodo while the Professor—'

'I can fight my own battles, Gray,' she said firmly. 'I have done so all my life.'

And when Gray moved to speak, she glared at him. 'If you intended to say that they ought to be fought for me because of my sex, you had much better hold your tongue. I should not like to hear you echo the Professor.'

Gray hastened to change the subject. 'What did he mean by his ominous hints about your mother?'

'She died when I was eight years old,' Sophie said. 'She tried a spell that got out of hand, and it drained her talent and killed her. At least—' She paused, looking thoughtful. 'At least, that is the tale the Professor has always told. I begin to wonder, now, how much of it is true.'

'Is there anyone else who might know?' Gray asked. 'Miss Callender, or Mrs Wallis, or . . .'

'Amelia!' Sophie snorted derisively. 'And I have asked Mrs Wallis, and she tells the same tale, but of course with Mrs Wallis one never knows.'

She was silent for a long moment, apparently lost in thought. Then her brows drew together and she looked up at Gray, dark eyes narrowed. 'You said just now – you said you could not think *at first* what magick I might be doing. Does that not mean that today was not the first time? And that you know *now* what it was?' She stopped, still frowning. 'Not that I *was* doing magick. I have not the least idea *how*.'

'But you have,' said Gray. He stood, annoyed to find that his legs still trembled, and crossed the room to stand by the large cheval-glass in the corner. 'Come – I shall show you.'

Sophie folded her arms. 'Show me? Show me what? How?'

'Come,' he repeated, and held out a hand.

With visible reluctance she obeyed. Taking her hand, Gray drew her in front of the mirror, which he tilted so that both of them could see their faces. The part of his mind not focused on conquering Sophie's scepticism appreciated the cool, firm touch of her fingers, and recorded that her hair smelt pleasantly of lavender and rosemary. Then he stepped back to stand behind her, his hands on her shoulders.

Their two faces looked out at them, one scant inches from the top of the glass, the other nearer its centre. Sophie's reflection showed dark eyebrows drawn together above large brown eyes; a face pale and tight-lipped, framed by chestnut-brown curls. 'What is it?' the face said, twisting up and around to stare into Gray's.

'Close your eyes,' he said. She did not. He pressed her shoulders very gently. 'Trust me, Sophie. For a few moments, no more. I should never ask you to do anything . . . anything *wrong*. You have my word.'

Her eyes closed.

'Now,' said Gray, 'think about . . . imagine you were with the Professor now, you and your sister Amelia, all going to dine at the Courtenays', with all their friends. Picture it in your mind, and think how you might feel as you went into the dining-room.'

He knew that she was following his instructions when, in the mirror, her reflection began to change. 'Now open your eyes,' he prompted, and she did so.

Now the Sophie in the glass had limp, dun-coloured hair, pale lips, thin and sallow cheeks. Dull eyes blinked in puzzlement. 'But that is only *me*,' she said.

'Of course.' Gray nodded. 'But bear with me a moment. Think about something that makes you happy – think about singing! – and go on looking in the glass.'

In an eyeblink the reflection changed again: cheeks plumped and warmed, hair darkened and grew glossy and thick, lips blushed and curved into a smile. The dull eyes grew deep and wide and sparkling.

'Do you see?' Gray asked.

'But,' Sophie said, 'anyone's face may change when her . . . her feelings change. Is that not so . . . ?'

'Not as yours does, Sophie,' he said gently. 'It is one thing to smile or frown, or blush, or grow pale. This . . . this is altogether different. Do you not see that your very eyes and hair change colours?'

She shook her head.

'I have never seen the like. When it suits you not to be noticed, you blend in. When you are happy . . . Like a human chameleon – you have read of the chameleon? Shape-shifting is one thing, but to do it without the least effort or thought, as you do . . .'

'This is not *shape-shifting*!' Sophie protested, turning to look up at him. 'Shape-shifting is powerful magick, difficult magick. I am no chameleon. What you speak of is only . . . it is only . . .'

'I think,' said Gray quietly, 'that it is a very rare magick, and a great deal more powerful than mine.'

'But . . .' Sophie turned from him, and from the mirror, and sank down upon the sofa. 'Gray, the Professor – he told me – how could he not know of this?'

Of course he knew. He must have known. And it followed, did it not, that he must have had some strong motivation for keeping that knowledge from the person most concerned. He had kept her so close, in such isolation: why?

Gray had never wished to drag Sophie or her sisters into this whole sordid business. But . . . *I will deal with them both tomorrow*, the Professor had told Mrs Wallis, in a voice of grim resolve. What had he meant by that? Certainly nothing to Gray's benefit, or, he was reasonably certain, to Sophie's either.

But Gray could say none of this here. Bad enough that he had said so much already; he could not risk discussing such matters where the Professor might have listening-spells in place. *The garden. We shall say she needed some fresh air.*

Leaning down to her ear, he spoke low and urgently. 'Sophie, come out to the garden with me. There are things I must tell you.'

CHAPTER VIII

In Which Mrs Wallis Comes to a Decision

'*Sophie! Mr Marshall!*' Joanna's voice, shrill with an anxiety not natural to her, rang out among the shrubberies and floral borders.

'*So-phieeee!*'

Gray and Sophie, out of sight in the little-tended corner they had judged safest from listeners, looked at one another and wondered what to do.

They had spent the past hour seated upon the grass in anxious, whispered conference, Sophie's eyes growing wider and her face paler as Gray related the circumstances and events that had led to his presence in her father's house and the discoveries he had made since his arrival. He wondered that she could so easily credit the bizarre tale he was spinning; Sophie had never struck him as credulous – rather the reverse. But perhaps she heard the desperation of truth in his voice, or perhaps the discovery of her magickal talent had made her more inclined to believe the unbelievable, for she questioned his recital of strange facts and half-proved fancies scarcely at all.

At last he had said, 'He has done his best to make it impossible for me to return to Oxford, but now I believe I must; and now he has threatened both of us – I cannot think it safe for you to remain here, certainly not once he discovers what has happened.'

And Sophie had not looked revolted, or even surprised; she had only looked at him gravely and said, 'I should like to see this College of yours.'

Then they had fallen to discussing ways and means.

'There is one of the Professor's riding horses that would be tall enough for you, I think,' Sophie had said, 'and only one of the grooms sleeps in the stables at night, and the dogs know me. Do you think, if we were very quiet – and if you were to help me with the tack – might we take two horses without raising the alarm?

'But we must say nothing to Joanna,' she added urgently, as though Gray had been suggesting that they should.

'You cannot be afraid that she would betray you?'

'No,' said Sophie. 'That is not what I am afraid of, at all.'

Hearing Joanna calling them ever more frantically, they exchanged a nod of resignation. Gray clambered stiffly to his feet, then reached down to help Sophie; they slowly made their way towards the house.

'What if he is come back already?' she asked suddenly, though they both knew the Professor to be dining at the Courtenays', and likely to return very late or perhaps, as on two previous occasions, not until the morning. 'Amelia will have told him everything . . .'

Cautiously, diffidently, Gray put an arm about her shoulders, as he might have done to comfort Jenny or Celia. 'You were not frightened of him this morning,' he reminded her.

'I knew so little this morning,' Sophie said. She shivered as they passed the central fountain, with its statuettes of Venus and Adonis. 'This morning I thought him only a pompous, petty-minded fool. Now—'

'*Soooooo-phie!*' Joanna sounded close to tears.

'Joanna!' Sophie called, pulling away. 'Joanna, it's all right – we are here, safe. By the fountain.'

There was a sound, as of running feet and bending branches; after a moment, Joanna's flushed, freckled countenance appeared in a gap between two box hedges, and in another moment she was standing before them, hands on hips, eyes narrowed indignantly.

'No one knew where you had gone,' she said accusingly. 'I called and *called.* I thought you had been kidnapped, or—' Stopping abruptly, she turned that indignant gaze full on Gray. 'Mr Marshall, you are not *courting* Sophie, are you?'

Gray stared.

At his side, Sophie began to laugh – a muffled, half-manic giggle. He turned slowly to look at her; by now she was gasping for breath, her face pink, her eyes watering. 'Sophie,' he said quietly; and then, when she reacted not at all, '*Sophie!*'

She drew a deep, ragged breath and choked back one last giggle. 'I am sorry,' she said, hanging her head. Then, after a moment, she calmly extended a hand to her sister. 'Come along, Jo, dear. We had best show ourselves before someone else thinks to miss us.'

Miss Callender waited in the hall, in loco parentis, to greet her wayward sisters, and had evidently been marshalling her arguments at leisure for some time.

'Sophia,' she began composedly, her ire evident only in the fingers clenched among the folds of her gown, 'Mrs Wallis tells me that indeed it was *you* and not Mr Marshall who was responsible for destroying the large drawing-room. She has, however, *refused* to tell me how or, more importantly, *why* you have seen fit to behave in so destructive a fashion. You, I trust, can offer some explanation?'

Sophie fetched a sigh. 'It *was* magick,' she said at once, folding her arms. 'Father made me extraordinarily angry, and what you saw was the result. Mr Marshall assures me that once I have learnt a measure of control, I shall be able to prevent such unfortunate accidents in future.'

For a moment Miss Callender gaped at her sister. Then, as gracefully as if she had rehearsed the motion, she turned to glare at Gray, contriving somehow to look down her elegant nose at him despite her inferior stature.

'Mr Marshall,' she said – the four syllables carrying a

hundredweight of disparagement and scorn – 'My father will be *most* displeased that you have encouraged my sister in this *unfortunate delusion.*'

Gray, exasperated by her wilful stupidity, drew breath to retort, but before he could speak, both he and Sophie were shouldered aside by a furious Joanna.

Goddess grant she has not her sister's magick, or we shall all be incinerated where we stand.

'You know *nothing,* Amelia!' Joanna declared. 'Nothing about anything! You would not know magick if it slapped your face – you've nothing in your head but frippery and flirtations. You believe every idiotic lie Father tells you, and what's more—'

Miss Callender, pale with rage, raised her hand to strike her youngest sister – Gray heard Sophie's indrawn breath – and, each of them taking one of Joanna's elbows, they half dragged her away towards the relative safety of the kitchen.

'How dare you!' Miss Callender shouted after them, all composure gone. 'I shall tell Papa! He will—'

Joanna struggled wildly. 'Do as you like!' she cried. 'It will not make you one jot less stupid!'

She succeeded in freeing herself of Sophie's grip and made as if to fly at Miss Callender again. 'I think not,' said Gray, catching her about the waist with his free arm and slinging her, kicking furiously, over one shoulder. Abruptly she went limp, as though defeated, but Gray's brother Alan had long ago taught him that trick, and he merely tightened his grip about her knees.

Gray deposited Joanna, red-faced with outrage at being carried topside-to, on the flagstones of the kitchen floor, where Mrs Wallis regarded her with an expression mingling amusement and dismay.

'Now then, Miss Joanna,' she said. 'And what 'ave you been and done this time?'

Joanna ceased glowering at Sophie and Gray, the better to glare at Mrs Wallis. 'I *cannot* understand why you must all protect Amelia,' she said. 'You know quite well that she would never lift a finger for any of us, and she has always been Father's favourite; it is not as though she needs anyone else on her side. Herne's horns, Sophie! If—'

'Jo*an*na!' Sophie tried valiantly to look disapproving whilst struggling against laughter. 'Wherever can you have learnt such language?'

Out of the corner of her eye, she saw a deep flush creeping up Gray's face.

Mrs Wallis looked hard at Sophie, with an odd abstracted look upon her face. Then she straightened decisively in her chair and cleared her throat.

'We appear to be straying from the matter at hand,' she said crisply. 'What have you told Miss Amelia?'

'The truth,' said Gray. 'As far as we know it.' He seemed not to notice how little she sounded like herself.

Mrs Wallis sighed. 'Unfortunate,' she said. 'I had hoped . . . Well. And what did she make of it?'

'An "unfortunate delusion", I believe she said.'

'Amelia has never been particularly adept at irony,' said Mrs Wallis, with another weary sigh, 'but this time I believe she has surpassed herself.'

'You *knew*,' Sophie choked. 'You knew that I was capable of this.' Both girls looked thunderstruck, as though a mainstay of their existence had been violently struck away – as, perhaps, it had.

'I suspected,' Mrs Wallis amended, still infuriatingly calm. 'Something must have happened sooner or later, with so much magick and no training at all. The – that is, your father put all his trust in the interdiction, but—'

'Of course!' The crash of Gray's fist on the tabletop made all of them jump. 'An interdiction! First that confounded box-room, and now this house. How *could* I be so stupid? I ought to have recognised it at once.'

'What is an *interdiction*?' Joanna demanded.

'An ambient spell,' recited Sophie, 'designed to impede or prevent certain uses of magick.'

'So,' said Mrs Wallis, nodding in what looked very like satisfaction, 'you have made good use of your nights in the library. Well done, Miss Sophia. And what else might you know about interdictions?'

'*That* is why he brought you here,' Sophie said to Gray, ignoring this interruption. 'It must be. So as to cripple you, and prevent your telling anyone what you know. An interdiction is not like a protective working – it cannot be attached to a movable object, or imposed on a person without his consent. So he brought you here, and then interdicted the house and grounds—'

'But it was not for *me*, Sophie,' Gray protested. If she had not collected thus much from Mrs Wallis's earlier assertions, could he convince her? 'The Professor may well have interdicted the box-room in his College rooms on my account, but the interdiction here was already in place when I arrived. It was for you.'

'Then,' Sophie began after a long moment, her voice pitched scarcely above a whisper, 'then he *did* know. You were right, Gray; he knew all along, and hid it from me. But' – for a moment as imperious as Amelia, she rounded on Mrs Wallis – 'but not from you.'

'I knew you were talented long before he did, Miss Sophia,' said Mrs Wallis, meeting her gaze with perfect calm. 'Your mother told me, when you were only a babe in arms.'

'My *mother*?' Sophie's face was ashen now, as starkly white as the kitchen walls. Joanna's rapt gaze moved from one of them to the other, as though she watched a duel or a game of tennis. 'When I was a babe in arms? But how . . . ?' Her voice trailed away.

'The present interdiction on this house is the Professor's work,' Mrs Wallis explained, 'but it was meant to replace one worked by your mother, when you were very small. She suspected that you should grow into considerable power; she meant to teach you the use of it, when you reached the proper age, and worked the interdiction to guard against . . . accidents. Accidents of the sort that occurred this morning. Alas, after her death, the Professor . . .' Mrs Wallis paused delicately. 'His talent was never as great as your mother's – an affront on her part which he has never forgiven – and he did not take seriously her predictions with respect to you. And of course, as you know, he does not consider higher magickal teaching appropriate to the female sex.'

Here Joanna made an impolite noise; Sophie seemed about to question some part of what she had heard, but Gray, wishing the tale to continue uninterrupted, laid a hand on her arm.

'He seems to have decided,' Mrs Wallis said, 'that, rather than put himself to the trouble and expense of educating you and teaching you the use of your talent, it would be easiest simply to continue the interdiction, maintain the fiction that you are as untalented as your sisters, and trust that no happenstance should result in the discovery of the truth.'

Again Sophie began to laugh, the sound quickly taking on a manic edge. She controlled herself, however, sufficiently to gasp, 'Perhaps he will enjoy the irony – I should never have known, had he not made me so *furious* . . .'

'On the contrary,' said Mrs Wallis, 'I planned to explain all of this to you when you came of age, when the Professor had no longer any standing to prevent it. In the meantime, you have had the library, and a measure of safety in your innocence, and now' – she nodded at Gray – 'it appears that you have also a teacher.'

If she had intended this last as a diversionary tactic, it was extraordinarily effective, for Sophie turned at once to Gray, her eyes widening, and said eagerly, 'You will teach me, will you not? I shall have so much to learn. Oh! Shall I be able to call light?'

'I should expect so,' said Gray, answering the second question first, 'and I shall do my best, of course, but—'

'But you have just said,' Joanna interrupted him, 'that there is a spell upon this house to prevent people from working magick.'

'Evidently,' Gray said, 'this interdiction is a selective one, affecting only those acts requiring a very significant expenditure of magick.' Somewhat abashed to find that he had reverted to the formality of the lecture hall, he glanced to Mrs Wallis for confirmation.

'It is meant to interdict only very powerful spells, yes,' she nodded. 'Else it would interfere with the running of the household.'

This was only natural, of course; had the interdiction been worked to affect all magicks, he should not have seen the Professor call fire to light his pipe, could not himself have called light for nocturnal excursions or worked his small spells to unlock doors, should at this moment have been swathed in linen bandages to protect the morning's injuries from infection. And no mage could live comfortably under a total interdiction, as three mages – four, if one included Sophie's mother – had quite evidently done in this house for many years.

'But what happened earlier today, then? *That* was a significant expenditure of magick, certainly . . .'

As soon as he had said it, however, the answer came to him: 'It was *stronger* than the interdiction,' he said, awed. 'It – broke through the Professor's spell. Not a deliberate channelling of magick, but . . . a dam bursting. A conflagration.'

He shuddered, imagining how that conflagration might have ended.

'Do you mean—?' This from Joanna. 'Do you mean that Sophie has *stronger* magick than Father's?'

Gray nodded. 'Considerably stronger than his, and almost certainly stronger than mine.'

'Small wonder that he does not like either of you, then,' said Joanna.

Into the thoughtful silence that followed this pronouncement came the jangle of the bell from the large drawing-room, shockingly loud. Sophie jumped, and Joanna clapped her hands over her ears.

'Miss Amelia's drawing-room must be put to rights,' said Mrs Wallis, as if to herself, rising from her chair with a sigh.

At the kitchen door she turned and spoke again. 'You put yourself in great danger this morning, Miss Sophia. I should advise you to retire to your room – and to sleep, if you can. I shall send your dinner up to you. As for *you*—'

The drawing-room bell rang once more, a long impatient peal.

'I shall go up to my room and stay there, Mrs Wallis,' said Joanna meekly.

Mrs Wallis paused to fix her with a penetrating stare. 'See that you do,' she said.

When she had gone, the three of them regarded one another in consternation.

'What has become of our Mrs Wallis?' said Sophie. 'And who, in the name of all the gods, was *that*?'

The locked doorknob rattled softly; someone was turning it from the outside.

'Sophie?' Joanna called softly. 'Sophie, may I come in?'

Sophie waited in silence, hoping that Joanna would think her asleep and go away. Instead, the knock and the call were repeated.

Grimacing, Sophie unlocked the door and opened it an inch.

'I had rather be alone, just at the moment,' she said.

'Why?' Joanna demanded. 'What are you about?'

'Nothing. I only – Go *away*, Jo. Please.'

Joanna slid her boot-toe into the gap between door and jamb. 'I shan't,' she said. 'Not until you have told me *why*. You know I can keep a secret if I must, Sophie.'

Sophie tried to shut the door, but her sister was too quick for her. The booted toe kept door and frame apart just long enough for Joanna to lean her full weight hard against the door; Sophie was knocked off balance, so that Joanna half fell through the doorway and fetched up rather violently against a bedpost. Sophie leant on the edge of her dressing-table, flushed and breathing hard.

'Are you all right, Joanna?' Gray's anxious baritone enquired.

At the sound of his voice Joanna whirled to face him, looking astounded and incensed.

'I *told* you to go away!' Sophie hissed. It was now too late to exclude Joanna from this conference, but still vital to preserve its secrets from other ears; hastily she shut the door and locked it again.

'But you – you—' Joanna began.

There was a certain satisfaction, Sophie thought grimly, in having rendered both of her sisters speechless in the course of a single day. 'Yes, Joanna, I am indeed aware of that there is a male person in my bedroom,' she said. 'I should be grateful not to have the whole household's attention drawn to the fact, however.'

Joanna opened her mouth again but quickly clamped both hands over it. Having drawn several deep breaths, she lowered her hands and said, very quietly, 'What is Mr Marshall doing here?'

Sophie looked at Gray, who returned her gaze with a barely perceptible lift of brow and shoulder. Then turning to her sister, she said fiercely, 'Swear on the bones of our mother that you'll tell no one.'

Joanna's grey eyes grew wide. 'I swear,' she whispered.

'We intend to run away.'

For a moment Joanna stared at her, and then at Gray. Sophie held her breath for the inevitable outburst, but when it came it took a most unexpected form.

'Horns of Herne!' Joanna exclaimed. 'This is *dreadful.* I shall owe Katell ten copper coins.'

'*What?*' Sophie's incredulous exclamation was doubled in her ears by Gray's.

'We had a wager,' Joanna explained, impatient, 'and Katell has won it. She heard him call you "Sophie" in the garden last week and wagered me ten coppers that you and Mr Marshall would be away to the Sisters of Sirona before summer's end. *I* said that you would never be so foolish.'

The manic laughter rose to Sophie's lips again – would there never be an end to this day's absurdities?

'I am not running off to be made handfast to Gray, Joanna,' she said, as patiently as she could manage. 'I do not want – that is, I am not ready to marry just yet, and if I *were* to marry, I hope I should do it properly, and not by eloping to the Sisters of Sirona in the middle of the night. But you must see that I cannot stay here, in the Professor's house, after what has happened today – nor can Gray, either.'

Joanna frowned. Sophie ought to have known, she told herself, that her sister would not be so easily put off. But the rest of the story was Gray's secret, not her own, and he had not authorised her to repeat it.

'Where *are* you going, then?' Joanna demanded. 'And how did you intend getting there? I hope you did not mean to steal one of Father's carriages; you would be found out and dragged back here within the hour.'

'I have at least *that* much wit left to me, thank you,' Sophie retorted, at last goaded beyond caution. 'We thought to take two of the riding horses. They will not be missed so quickly. As for our destination—'

Her near indiscretion was stopped by her sister's laughter. 'You meant to go on horseback, with that valise?' Joanna pointed to the large case open upon the bed, filled haphazardly with Sophie's belongings. 'And if Father should come after you, in the carriage-and-four? How did you think to get away unseen? And how much coin have you? What will you live on, until you reach wherever-it-is?'

The justice of all these criticisms struck Sophie of a sudden, deflating at a stroke her furious anger at her father, her determination to remove herself from his influence, and her confidence in the plan she and Gray had concocted. They had neither of them enough experience with subterfuge – not even so much as Joanna had gained, from an addiction to minstrel-tales and servants' gossip; their entire scheme was at once revealed to be jury-rigged, ludicrously ill planned, and amateur in the extreme, and Sophie felt all the absurdity of having believed they might succeed.

'Joanna is right,' she said, turning to Gray with a heavy heart and seeing her own melancholy state reflected in his face. 'We shall have to stay and take what comes.'

'I did not say you ought not to go,' Joanna protested. 'I only said that your plan was stupid. Now that I know what you are about, we shall be able to think of a better one. For if we are to leave, it must be tonight, while he is not here to stop us!'

'If *we*—?'

There was a knock at the door. Startled, they turned to look; the door opened – though Sophie knew she had locked it – and in the doorway stood Mrs Wallis, wearing a lawn apron and a determined expression. Over her right arm hung several heavy leathern bags. 'Fortunately for all of us,' she said, as she distributed these to her astonished audience, 'Miss Sophia's safety does not depend on Miss Joanna's inventiveness alone.'

She surveyed Sophie's ransacked bedroom, marking Gray's presence only with a slightly lifted eyebrow. 'Pack your things, all of you,' she said. 'Only what you can carry. We shall take our leave an hour past midnight.'

CHAPTER IX

In Which a Journey Begins

Already growing stiff and sore after less than an hour on horseback, Gray peered over his shoulder, looking back the way they had come. Callender Hall lay still and dark, and all about its nest of gardens and follies, fields and woods, men slept.

As they passed the limit of the Hall's grounds, Gray had felt the upwelling of magick as the interdiction lost its hold on him and marvelled that he had not recognised it on their last departure. Having never been deprived of his magick before this summer, he was unprepared for the elation attendant on its renewal, for the sense of wholeness that he only now understood to have been lacking. He fancied that Sophie, too, ahead of him on her placid brown mare, sat a little straighter now.

They had spent the time between Mrs Wallis's dramatic pronouncement and the hour after midnight in a quiet, covert flurry of activity. Thinking over the day's events as he hastily stowed his belongings in one of the proffered saddle-bags, Gray could not help but wonder at the extraordinary good fortune that had juxtaposed Sophie's outburst with the Professor's absence from home. Perhaps it was only natural that after such an extended run of ill luck, they (and he, in particular) should be blessed by the Fates through the removal of one obstacle, but even if the cause were nothing more than the chance turning of Fortune's wheel, the effect was cheering. It was an inexpressible relief to Gray merely to know that his captor – for such the Professor must be called – was not in the house with him; the thought of leaving this prison behind made him nearly dizzy with hope. Further than the leaving, however, he would not yet allow himself to think, so many things were there that might still arise to prevent even this from taking place.

It had not occurred to him then to question how Mrs Wallis came to have such a comprehensive plan of escape at the ready. He did so now. Certainly she was not the ordinary cook-housekeeper he had once thought her, but for what reason had she been so well prepared for flight?

For so she had certainly been – for how long, Gray could scarcely guess. Before their astonished eyes parcels of food, pouches of coin, and dark cloaks were produced from hidden recesses in the kitchen and offices; arriving, at the appointed hour, in the stables, they had found a groom waiting – Gray did not like to think what threat or inducement had been offered him – with Joanna's pony and three of the Professor's best riding horses, their hooves wrapped in rags to muffle the sound of iron shoes striking the cobbles of the forecourt.

One might almost think that Mrs Wallis had done this sort of thing before.

Though they were riding at a walk, when the sun rose their small party was already well away from Callender Hall, bearing north-east towards the coastal road that connected Kerandraon with the port of Douarnenez to the east and with the Pointe du Raz far to the west. At Mrs Wallis's direction, they stopped shortly after dawn where their path crossed a stream, dismounting and leading their horses into the trees, where they could drink and graze without attracting notice.

Joanna looked about her with evident interest. Despite the

loveliness of their surroundings, however, Sophie's gaze lingered on Gray.

It was not that he had grown larger or taller (being already – Sophie chuckled silently – rather taller than necessary). Certainly he could not be said to have improved in looks, being still sandy-haired and suntanned, with a crooked nose and, to make matters worse, a day's growth of beard, at which he scratched absent-mindedly with one long hand. Still, she could not help staring. Perhaps he stood straighter, or perhaps his gaze was more direct and confident, or perhaps . . .

'He looks different,' remarked Joanna, who had approached unseen and unheard, so deep was her sister's concentration. 'And so do you. Even Mrs Wallis does.'

Startled, Sophie at last withdrew her gaze, turning instead to frown at Joanna – who certainly looked just the same. 'What do you mean?' she demanded, sotto voce, hoping that she did not look as dreadfully fatigued as she felt. 'Different . . . how?'

Joanna shrugged. 'Not *bigger*, exactly,' she said. 'But . . . *more*.'

She trailed away and began to forage in Mrs Wallis's saddle-bags.

Sophie turned again towards Gray, to find him gazing back at her with a speculative expression. He smiled and took a step towards her.

She had been used to consider Gray as a boy of about her own age, earnest and anxious and apt to need looking after. Now however, she looked at him and saw a man.

'Did you feel it, too?' he asked her. 'When we passed the limit of the Professor's spell?'

Exhausted, saddle-sore, and hungry – recklessly fleeing the only home she knew, in quite inappropriate company – uncertain where they were bound, or what awaited them there – Sophie nonetheless felt that at last her luck had turned.

* * *

Mrs Wallis appeared to consider their journey as being under her direction. This was only natural, as she had made all of the useful arrangements; still, Gray disliked not knowing where she was leading them, and it had become clear that her plans, whatever they might be, conflicted with his own. About mid-morning, therefore, he abandoned his place at the rear of their little column to pull his mount alongside hers, noting as he did so that she rode remarkably – suspiciously – well for a female servant.

The time had come for Gray to test some of those suspicions.

'Mrs Wallis,' he began, pitching his voice to reach her ears alone. 'I should like you to answer me a question or two.'

She turned her head briefly to look at him, then returned her gaze to the path ahead, so that the brim of her capote hid her face. 'You are most welcome to ask, young man,' she said. 'I cannot promise to answer so fully as you may wish.'

Quashing the urge to demand an explanation of this statement, Gray reminded himself to tread carefully. 'Our destination has not been discussed,' he said.

'That is not a question.' Her tone held a trace of amusement. 'But I shall answer it nevertheless. You intended to travel southward, to make for your brother-in-law's estate – an excellent plan, had not your sister so lately visited Callender Hall and made your connexion to Kergabet known there. The servant girls may gossip about your sweeping Dim'zell Zophie away to the priestesses of Sirona, but their master will expect you to take refuge with the most powerful friends at your disposal.'

'You believe the Professor will seek us there?'

Gray saw at once the likelihood that she was right, and his heart pounded at the narrowness of Sophie's escape – and Jenny's. How could he have been so stupid?

'Where do we ride, then?' he enquired. 'I see that we skirt the road, and that we bear east . . .'

Mrs Wallis now turned again and fixed on him a penetrating stare which made him squirm within, though he met her eyes steadily enough. He could not seem to keep hold of all the questions he had meant to ask, but at least he should persist in asking this one.

'Your scheme was to deliver Miss Sophia into your sister's hands,' said Mrs Wallis, 'and yourself ride hard for the nearest seaport, for some urgent purpose of your own.' By her expression, she saw Gray's astonishment at her knowledge of intentions he had not revealed even to Sophie. 'You have some good reason for this, I am sure?'

'I—'

'You could not have persuaded her to remain behind, Mr Marshall – not without violence – and young Joanna still less. Were I you' – here Mrs Wallis smiled thinly – 'I should not mention to either of them that ever you entertained such a thought.'

'Mrs Wallis—'

At last she seemed to remember his question: 'We ride for the port of Douarnenez.'

'Douarnenez!' For a moment Gray's dismay overcame his discretion. At Mrs Wallis's raised eyebrows, he lowered his voice: 'Is it not . . . ill-advised . . . to take ship so close to home? Shall we not be followed?'

'I am sure we shall eventually be followed, Mr Marshall, wherever we may choose to go.' She turned away again. 'In Douarnenez there are friends who will conceal the evidence of our passage. Elsewhere we may not be so fortunate.'

Gray nodded slowly, beginning to see the outline of her plan.

He slowed his tall bay gelding, meaning to let the others overtake him and resume his rearguard post, and glanced back along the path to reassure himself that their party remained intact. Some dozen yards behind and below him, Joanna sat her pony with stolid determination, her gaze fixed on the way ahead. Catching Gray's eye, she smiled grimly. Gray returned her look, wondering idly whether a lady's side-saddle was as uncomfortable as the ordinary sort; then he raised his eyes to look behind her.

Sophie swayed with her mare's gentle gait and closed her eyes; and then, appallingly slowly, she toppled forward and down, head first over the mare's off shoulder, to fall to the ground in a crumpled heap.

'*Sophie!*' Horrified, Gray wrenched his mount around and kicked it into a canter, covering the fifty yards between himself and Sophie in a moment. He dismounted in a slithering rush and knelt beside her, scarcely aware of anyone or anything else.

Close to, fumbling with Sophie's bonnet-strings, he could see the marks of utter exhaustion on her face. He bent his face to hers; feeling against his cheek the phantom touch of her breath, he exhaled on a long sigh of relief, discovering only now that he had been holding his breath in fear. Little wonder that after yesterday's ordeal, their nuit blanche, and today's long ride, she was at the end of her strength. They were all of them fatigued, but the rest had not borne the burden of a recent brush with magick shock.

Carefully – little as he knew of healing, he had better have left this task to Mrs Wallis, but he felt that it was his – Gray felt along Sophie's hands and arms for any sign of injury. Finding none, he turned his attention to her head, dreading to find that it had struck a stone in her fall, and was relieved to see no evidence of harm. He murmured thanks to the horse goddess Epona that Sophie had avoided tangling her foot in the stirrup and her skirts in the pommels of her saddle, shuddering as he imagined her dragged limp behind a bolting horse.

'Sophie,' he said again, chafing her icy hands. 'Sophie, come back to me.'

He remembered, suddenly, the time eight years ago when, during one of the family's rare visits to London, his sister Cecelia had nearly died of a fever. Their frantic mother had sent Gray, Jenny, and their brother George to temple after temple with offerings of wine, candles, and coin – and Gray himself had felt as frightened and almost as helpless as he felt now.

'She must have let her foot slip out of the stirrup,' said Joanna, startlingly close behind him. 'She *will* do it. She is a *dreadful* horsewoman.'

It reassured him to hear Joanna thus disparaging her sister, despite the trembling voice in which she did so.

At last Sophie's eyelids fluttered; the hands Gray held gripped his fingers in return. '*Petra . . . ?* she murmured, blinking drowsily, as though she merely woke from a deep sleep. '*Pelec'h emaon?*'

Despite his summer's haphazard tutelage in the language, it took a moment for Gray to parse the Breton for *What?* and *Where am I?*

He and Joanna helped Sophie to sit up. Mrs Wallis had by now taken charge of all the horses; she passed four sets of reins to Joanna and knelt at Sophie's side, producing from some pocket a copper flask. 'Drink,' she urged. Sophie did so and gave a choking gasp.

'Aquavit,' Mrs Wallis explained to the others. 'Now, then, Miss Sophia: can you ride? We had best not linger here.'

Sophie looked bemused. 'I . . . I am not sure,' she said, reverting to English. 'I do feel tired. So *sleepy.* I should be afraid of falling off again . . .'

'You shall ride with me,' said Gray at once, 'and we shall put your mare on a leading rein.'

The others looked doubtful, Sophie most of all. 'Or,' he added, 'perhaps Mrs Wallis has brought some rope.'

Sophie only seemed more bewildered, but Joanna had heard him aright: 'He means, you shall ride with him or he will *tie* you into your saddle,' she translated in a reverent whisper.

'I shall try,' Sophie said, looking up rather doubtfully at Gray's leggy gelding. 'If you think I ought.'

* * *

Most of Gray's many questions remained unanswered – even unasked – and his every conversation with Mrs Wallis seemed to raise more puzzles than it solved. He thought he might trust her to act in the best interest of Sophie and Joanna, as she saw it; so far their paths converged. But who *was* Mrs Wallis, and what other schemes might she have afoot?

For the moment, he was forced to concentrate on the task – much less easy than he had first supposed – of directing his mount while preventing Sophie, now slumbering more or less in his arms, from taking another tumble. She had already slept several hours, and Gray was relieved to see a more natural colour creeping back into her cheeks; he had never known anyone to die of magick shock, but neither was it usual to possess so much magick unawares. For all her study of grimoires and spells, Sophie had very little idea what she might be capable of – or how to bend her talent to useful pursuits. He had promised to teach her, it was true, but he would have been happy to see her in more able hands.

Perhaps Master Alcuin might teach her. He has not the prejudices of so many of the others – and Sophie would like him, I think.

An earlier conference with Mrs Wallis had determined – or had she simply decreed? – that they must halt before nightfall at whatever inn or wayhouse offered, though they would not yet have reached Douarnenez – Sophie's accident having delayed them some considerable time.

'We shall need a disguise,' said Joanna, startling Gray from his reverie.

'A disguise?' Again that hint of amusement in Mrs Wallis's tone. 'What manner of disguise had you in mind?'

'Well, *something*,' Joanna retorted. 'False names, at any rate. We are far too close to home to risk announcing ourselves at an inn *as* ourselves.'

'Joanna is quite right,' said Gray, who had given up any pretence of addressing either Sophie or Joanna as etiquette demanded. 'Our plan – Sophie's and mine – was to travel as brother and sister. Could we not . . . ?'

'That is not such a very bad plan, after all,' Joanna said. 'We both can be your sisters, Mr Marshall, and Mrs Wallis can be . . .'

'Your widowed aunt,' said Mrs Wallis promptly, confirming Gray's suspicion that Joanna was not the first of their party to consider the question of disguise. 'We have been on a tour of Breizh; we have been called home urgently and must take ship for England as soon as may be. You and I, Joanna, as well as your sister, have been travelling here some time and learnt something of the country – but *not* the language,' she added severely. 'Your brother is but lately come from our home in England, to fetch us there.'

'I see,' said Joanna. Her grey eyes gleamed. 'That way we need not explain why Mr Marshall knows the country so little. But—' Her face took on a worried cast. 'What if we should be asked questions about our home? Sophie and I know nothing at all of England, Mrs Wallis. And no more do you.'

Mrs Wallis turned to her with a maddening smile: 'That's as may be, Miss Joanna.'

'Trevelyan,' Gray said absently, his mind running by instinct to the names of his childhood acquaintance. 'Chickering. Howell. Sophie, should you not like to stop a while and rest?'

Sophie shook her head and produced an expression that must have been meant for a smile.

'But Father knows you come from Kernow,' Joanna objected, from the back of her piebald pony. 'We should be found out in no time.'

Gray doubted this, but one never knew. 'Hughes, then,' he said. 'Morgan. Richards. Dunstan—'

'Dunstan,' Joanna repeated. 'What sort of name is that?'

'Saxon as ever was,' said Mrs Wallis. 'Dunstan will do very well for the three of you, I think. And Richards for me. You may call me Aunt . . .' She thought a moment. 'Aunt Ida.'

Again they looked to Sophie for some comment, but she appeared to have none to contribute. On waking she had resumed her former seat, and Gray found, to his surprise, that he rather missed her presence. Though less pale than before, and better controlled, she yet looked tired and drained, and her air of not caring what befell her alarmed him.

'I shall be Harriet,' said Joanna, 'after all those kings, and, Sophie, you could be . . . what about Elinor? That's a pretty name.'

Sophie shrugged.

'And *you* ought to be Edward, Mr Marshall,' Joanna went on, 'after the Crown Prince, and all those *other* kings.'

'On one condition,' said Gray, managing a half smile in response to her enthusiasm. 'You must stop calling me "Mr Marshall".'

'Why, I shall call you "Ned", of course, dear brother,' said Joanna primly.

She would, Gray suspected, have expanded indefinitely on the fictitious Dunstans, had anyone given her the least encouragement. None being forthcoming, however, she soon subsided into a thoughtful silence, and the four of them rode on, hardly speaking but for the others' enquiries after Sophie's health, until at length they reined in their mounts before a half-timbered wayhouse, well covered in ivy, along the coastal road.

CHAPTER X

In Which the Travellers Seek Shelter, and Joanna Enjoys Herself

Suspicious as he was of Mrs Wallis's motivations, and irritating as he found her evasions, Gray continually had cause to be grateful for her participation in this venture.

Just now, in the wayhouse courtyard, she was explaining their circumstances to a stout, red-faced Breton innkeeper.

'Two rooms,' she said in English, rather more loudly than necessary. '*Two*, do you understand? *Deux chambres*.'

The innkeeper replied in Brezhoneg – Breton – and at some length.

'*Two* rooms.' Mrs Wallis held up two fingers, and raised her voice still more. 'A large one – *une grande, et une petite*. One for him' – she gestured at Gray – 'and one *pour nous trois. Oui?*'

A small crowd had gathered to watch the fun, and a chuckle rippled through it as the innkeeper repeated his Brezhoneg inventory of the available guest-rooms and their tariffs.

'*Vous n'avez aucun français?*' Mrs Wallis broke in, with a gesture of despair so convincing that even Gray half sympathised with her invented difficulties.

Feeling in the pocket of his coat for the purse she had given him, he stepped forward and laid an authoritative hand on her arm. 'Please, Aunt Ida,' he said. On cue, Mrs Wallis ceased gesticulating and, with a nicely judged show of exasperation, turned her back on the business to take Gray's place with Sophie, Joanna, and the horses.

As expected, a lack of bluster and the appearance of a coin or two were of considerable benefit in concluding the negotiations for a large room for the three ladies and a smaller one for Gray, as well as baths and a hot dinner for all of them, and feed and shelter for their mounts. A hostler was summoned to take the horses to the stables; the inn-keeper took charge of the travellers' saddle-bags, and his wife, attracted by the commotion, appeared behind him, white-capped and plump, to cluck sympathetically over the white-faced Sophie and hurry them all upstairs to their rooms.

Within, the wayhouse gave Gray a pleasant sense of concealment. Its corridors and staircases were dimly lit by candles in sconces along the walls, sometimes perilously near the blackened cross-beams that threatened his head as he trailed the others past the public rooms and up the stairs. From a few doorways faces turned in their direction as they passed, but none seemed to evince more than the usual interest in the arrival of a party of strangers.

Gray's room, though so tiny that it might once have been a clothes cupboard, was well supplied with the matériel for shaving, and he set about this task as soon as he had removed his coat and boots. He expected to be facing the curious stares of the inn's other guests over dinner, and felt he would carry it off better if he looked less like a travelling mendicant. Before he had finished, however, he was interrupted by a timid knock at the door; on opening it he found Joanna – *Harriet*, he reminded himself sternly – standing on the threshold, wearing a clean gown and anxious look.

'Aunt Ida has put Elinor to bed,' she said loudly. 'Elinor is a great deal too ill to be moved, she says. She asks me to say that—'

'Come in out of the corridor, Harriet.' Gray took hold of Joanna's arm and tugged her into the room, closing the door behind her.

'What do you mean, ill?' he demanded in a low voice.

Joanna folded her arms. 'We are travelling *incognito*, you know,' she said. 'She is not ill, exactly. Not fevered, or spotted, or coughing. But she has gone to sleep again, straight to sleep with all of her clothes on. And' – this in unbelieving tones – 'she said she did not want a bath, or even any dinner.'

Gray frowned as he again set razor to cheek, trying to recall everything he had ever learnt about magick shock. Again he was brought up short by the recognition that Sophie's was a more powerful talent than he had ever encountered before – and drained almost completely in one mad, abandoned burst of rage. He could only guess at the effects of such an accident.

'What was it M—Aunt Ida wished you to tell me?' he asked Joanna, who was watching him with narrowed eyes.

'That one of us ought to sit with Elinor, while the others go down to dinner,' she said. And, lowering her voice, 'She has not exactly said so, but I think she would prefer you to stay, as you are quite the most conspicuous.'

Gray was immediately struck by the impropriety of this suggestion. Yet just as they had agreed to keep their use of magick to the barest minimum, it was in other respects the most prudent course. He was certainly the most recognisable of the party; the country might be full of young girls travelling with respectable matrons, but few of them would be accompanied by an unusually tall young man whose clothes did not quite fit him. Then, too, this was just the sort of office that an affectionate elder brother might well perform for his sister, and thus perhaps would serve to reinforce their disguise.

He ran a hand through his hair, undoing at a stroke all his careful work in front of the glass.

'I shall ask them to send up something to eat, of course,' said Joanna, as though mere hunger had made him hesitate.

'Mind you don't ask in Brezhoneg,' he admonished her in a low voice; despite everything, she grinned.

There was a sound from the corridor. 'I shall tell Aunt Ida to expect you at once, then, Ned,' Joanna said, in a prim voice quite unlike her own.

'I thank you, Harriet,' said Gray.

Sophie slept unquietly. At times she cried out some half-intelligible protest; at others, sobbed or moaned as though in pain. Try as he might, Gray could not wake her from her nightmares. If this was indeed only magick shock, it was the worst he had ever seen. He was again reminded of his sister's frightening illness and delirium, and more than one prayer for Sophie's safety escaped his lips while he watched by her bedside, smoothing the damp hair from her forehead or – when the noise from the public rooms below was such as he thought must prevent anyone's hearing – singing to her the half-remembered lullabies of his childhood.

Perhaps half an hour after Joanna and Mrs Wallis had gone down to their dinner, a knock on the door heralded the arrival of one of the innkeeper's daughters, a dark-eyed, sweet-faced girl of fourteen or fifteen, bearing an enormous wooden tray on which reposed a covered dish of bouillabaisse, bowls and spoons, glasses, a decanter of wine, and several warm loaves. The aroma of the stew made Gray's mouth water but seemed to have no effect on Sophie.

The girl cast a frightened eye at her as she set down the tray. 'Does she need an 'ealer, m'sieu'?' she asked timidly.

Gray smiled at her. 'I thank you,' he said, 'but my aunt is a healer herself. What my sister most needs is rest and good food, and both seem in excellent supply here.'

She curtseyed, dark curls bobbing with the motion of her head, and left them alone again.

Another quarter-hour, and Sophie abruptly sat bolt upright, her eyes flying open in a face white as the linen bedclothes. One hand reached towards Gray; he took it in both of his, and her fingers clutched his so tightly that he bit his lip to stifle a yelp.

'Gray, what is happening?' Sophie whispered. 'I have had such *ghastly* dreams, worse even than . . . Is *this* how it feels to have magick? Can I not – give it back, or—?'

Gray smiled grimly. 'Remember we may have listeners,' he said, leaning closer. 'You must be Elinor, and I am Ned. What you feel now will pass,' he continued, a little more loudly. 'It is only the after-effect of yesterday's . . . accident. The nightmares are not a usual symptom, but I think . . .' He lowered his voice again and said, 'You have so *much* magick, you see, and you must have used nearly all of it. You must never do so again,' he added severely. 'You might have died.'

Sophie's eyes grew wider still.

'Do you remember what you told me about your mother? What your father claims may not be the truth, but it has happened, more often than you may think.' Gray paused, considering. 'I've no great expertise in treating magick shock, you understand, but ordinarily, with rest and good food, the effects vanish within a day or so – less, in general. You recovered so quickly, at first, that I thought all would be well . . . but your nose bled, which I cannot explain, and then you have had almost no rest . . .'

'Gr—Ned,' Sophie began, her expression conveying how absurd the name felt on her lips, 'is this what happened to you, that day, when we were singing?'

Having tried to forget that experience, Gray was reluctant to bring it up again.

'I am not altogether certain,' he said at last. 'There are definite parallels. But it cannot have been any ordinary sort of magick shock, of course.'

'Why not?'

'Because I had not used any magick,' he said patiently. He was still holding Sophie's hand; he made to let it go, but she prevented him by laying her other hand over his.

'I have one theory,' he admitted.

Sophie looked up at him expectantly. To his relief, the colour was again creeping back to her face, and she looked less haunted than before, as though this odd conversation cheered her.

'I shall tell you whilst you eat,' he said pointedly, freeing his hands; he fetched his dinner tray from the top of the wardrobe and handed her one of the small loaves. Obediently she broke a piece off one end and put it into her mouth.

'It has to do with the interdiction,' Gray began, still keeping his voice low. 'You know that an ambient spell, poorly cast, can have unintended effects – its effects may even be reversed, or reflected, in certain circumstances. The *Codex of Aled ap Bedwyr* gives the example of a flawed warding-spell that trapped the caster of it in his workroom until he died of hunger.'

Sophie gasped.

She has not read that one, then, Gray thought with grim amusement. 'When I tried to ward my own bedroom – after Kerandraon – the result was very much the same,' he said. 'It is possible that on the occasion you mention, you worked the magick, while I felt the effects.'

'But—' Sophie looked horrified. 'What magick? I didn't – I *couldn't* – I don't understand . . .'

Gray shook his head. 'There was magick in that room,' he said. 'I felt it – it called me there. Have you never thought that the Professor might have a *reason* for forbidding you to sing?'

The look of horror deepened. Sophie opened her mouth, but whatever she had intended to say was banished by a knock at the door.

The same young girl had come to retrieve the emptied dishes; Gray thanked her politely and promised to leave the tray outside when they had finished. The discussion interrupted by her arrival had started an idea in his mind. While Sophie sat up in bed, applying herself to the bouillabaisse, he left her long enough to venture down the corridor to his own room, whence he returned bearing a small stack of codices.

Sophie looked up at the sound of the door closing. Seeing Gray and his armful of books, she laughed aloud – a small, incredulous, choking sound. 'You have not brought all your books?' she demanded in a whisper.

Gray shrugged, a little affronted. 'I am a scholar, after all,' he said. 'I should not feel properly equipped without a few useful works of reference. Had you rather I left them for the edification of your father?'

'I – no, of course not.' Looking chastened, she took up her spoon again.

Gray resumed his seat, absently picked up a piece of bread, and opened the topmost codex.

'What is it you are looking for?' said Sophie, when she had finished the soup. 'Might I be of help?'

It had grown darker, and the candles Mrs Wallis had lit guttered irritably in the breeze that crept between the shutters. Gray called enough light to read by, sending the small, cheerful orb gently upwards to float above both their heads, then blew the candles out.

Sophie was momentarily distracted. 'You promised to teach me how to do that,' she reminded him.

'Tomorrow,' said Gray, without raising his head. 'Or perhaps the day after. Not now, when you are half dead with magick shock.'

'Then let me help you with . . . whatever it is you are doing.'

'As you like.' Still mentally parsing the florid Latin of Gaius Aegidius, he handed her the next volume in the stack. 'You gave me an idea just now; I am looking for references to *magia musicae*.' Then he helped himself to another piece of bread and returned to his search.

At first he heard Sophie turning pages; soon, however, even this small noise ceased. 'Have you found something?' he asked eagerly, looking up.

But she had not. 'What language is this?' she said, holding out the codex. 'It is nothing like Latin; a little like Brezhoneg, but . . .'

Gray took it from her and shook his head. 'That is the Lesser Mabinogion,' he explained. 'The language is Old Cymric, more or less. There are a great many archaisms, naturally . . .'

He hunted through the codices and found a small, rather battered one also written in Latin, with marginalia in English. 'This one will be easier going,' he said, handing it to Sophie.

She took it, but instead of opening it continued to stare at him. 'Are all the men at your college like you?' she enquired.

Gray chuckled. 'Not at all,' he said. 'Some are admirably earnest scholars, and some of us are utter reprobates always a hair's breadth from being sent down. Why do you ask?'

'I only wondered,' said Sophie, looking thoughtful, 'whether I should like it there.'

When Mrs Wallis and Joanna returned, they had made little headway in their researches; Gray had found one glancing reference, and Sophie another, but both, said Gray, too vague to be useful. *The singer may work various magicks, even as the Sirens of Homer*, read one marginal gloss in Sophie's text, which, she reflected, was of as much use as the statement she had once read in an antique scroll of her father's, that *Magick is the gods' gift to mankind, and their curse.* True enough – but what good did it do to say so?

'You will never guess what we heard at table,' Joanna said, almost before the door had closed behind her.

'Wait.' Closing his eyes, Gray murmured a long Latin phrase that Sophie vaguely recognised as a warding-spell. A brief, warm whisper seemed to pass over and through her, and the bridge of her nose itched fiercely. 'There,' Gray said. He seemed pleased with himself. 'I quite understand, Mrs Wallis, that we agreed to use as little magick as possible, but we do need a few moments' open conversation.'

'You look much better, Sophie,' Joanna said. She perched at the foot of the bed.

'I feel better,' Sophie admitted. 'But I am rather afraid to sleep again. Gray believes that I am still suffering from magick shock, and ought to be quite well again in another day, but if I am to have such nightmares . . .'

'You hadn't any nightmares on the journey,' said her sister. Mrs Wallis frowned, speculative; Sophie flushed at the memory of waking with her ear against Gray's heart. It was true enough that she had slept more soundly perched on his saddle-bow than in the inn's warm, soft bed.

'Never mind that,' she scolded, hoping to direct attention elsewhere. 'Tell us your news.'

Joanna's round face grew positively gleeful. 'It seems,' she said, 'that a certain local gentleman has lost his housekeeper, and two daughters, and a particularly wayward student.'

'So the news has travelled as quickly as we have,' said Gray. 'That bodes ill.'

'Not at all.' Mrs Wallis spoke for the first time. 'The elder daughter, you see, has run off with the student to be married, and the housekeeper has taken the younger, who appears to have been in their confidence, to seek them and bring them back. She does not yet know where they were bound, but the younger sister did let slip a hint that they might be gone southward, to the Temple of Sirona in Kemper, or even as far as Karnak—'

'What in Hades are you playing at?' Gray's voice was tight with fury. 'Her reputation will be in shreds before another day has passed – and her sisters' as well. Have you not thought what such a tale will mean for—?'

'Stop it, Gray,' Sophie said, laying a hand on his arm. What he said of Amelia and Joanna was perfectly true, but had not his sisters married very well indeed, despite his own misconduct?

'The same would have been said had I left no evidence,' Mrs Wallis was saying now. 'As it is, we may hope that when we are sought, it will be too late, and in the wrong direction entirely.'

'But,' said Joanna, suddenly frowning, 'where, exactly, *are* we going?'

It was high time, Sophie decided, to stop playing at Mrs Wallis's game of mysteries. 'We are going to England,' she said, 'to stop Father and his friends from committing a murder.'

Joanna's stunned disbelief, when Sophie and Gray had finished explaining themselves, was something to behold. '*Father*, plotting to kill the Master of his College?' she exclaimed. 'With that horrid Lord Carteret? What can it be to him? And *that* is why you wanted to run away?'

Gray and Sophie nodded solemnly.

Joanna looked outraged. Had she, despite everything, believed herself to be merely abetting an elopement?

Ignoring her expostulating sister, Sophie levelled a cool stare at Mrs Wallis. 'Nothing surprises you, it seems,' she said. 'Now, why should that be?'

'I did raise you and your sisters, Miss Sophia,' Mrs Wallis replied mildly. 'I am no longer so easily astonished as I once was.'

Sophie folded her arms and looked down her nose, Amelia-like. 'That will not do, I'm afraid,' she said. 'Surely you cannot expect it. *How* is it you seem to know everything before it happens? Are you a foreteller, as well as a healer? Have you put listening-spells on Gray's gardening-tools, or—?'

Gray put a hand on Sophie's shoulder. Her mouth snapped shut, but she continued to glare; from the foot of the bed, Joanna was glaring too.

'It is my duty to know these things, Sophia,' said Mrs Wallis. 'I am your guardian; your mother left you to my care, and, whatever you may believe, no charge could be of greater weight to me, or of more value.'

Her companions gaped at her.

'But,' said Sophie, 'why . . . why *my* guardian, and not Joanna's? And what need have we of a guardian, when we have a father living?'

'Each of you has a father living, yes,' said Mrs Wallis. Gray frowned at this peculiar expression of the facts and waited for her to elaborate, but she did not.

For the next quarter-hour Mrs Wallis's impassive calm met Sophie's and Joanna's increasingly importunate questions. Gray's own suspicions, growing all the while, at last produced an ultimatum.

'We go no farther,' he declared, coldly furious, 'until you have explained to us whence came all the coin, and why you had all in readiness for flight before we thought to flee, and what was your purpose – and, above all, Mrs Wallis, *who you are*.'

Mrs Wallis presented an appearance of dignity in defeat, but Gray thought he detected a contradictory gleam of satisfaction in her dark eyes.

'Tell me, children,' she said softly. 'Has any of you heard the tale of the Midnight Queen?'

Joanna's grey eyes lit with recognition, but Sophie frowned, puzzled, and asked, 'Who?'

'Queen Laora,' Mrs Wallis told her. 'Second wife of King Henry, and eldest daughter of the last Duke of Breizh . . .'

'Oh!' said Gray. 'She who eloped with a Breton nobleman – or perhaps was a spy in the pay of the Alban king? And I once heard it said, I believe, that she had smothered the little Princess, and fled when . . .'

His voice trailed off as he saw that Joanna was looking at him in astonishment, and Mrs Wallis in what might almost have been dislike.

'No, no,' cried Joanna; 'she ran away because—'

'Listen,' said Mrs Wallis quellingly, 'and you shall hear the *true* tale, from one who knows the whole of it.'

'I was there, when Queen Laora made her choice,' Mrs Wallis said. 'I have heard that the servants in the Royal Palace in London spoke of it in whispers for years thereafter, that final confrontation between King Henry and herself.'

'*You* were there?' Joanna demanded. 'How came that to be?'

Sophie expected a reprimand, but Mrs Wallis only smiled – a tight and mirthless smile – and said, 'Listen.'

Joanna subsided, listening tensely; her hand crept into Sophie's, and Sophie squeezed it gratefully.

'His Majesty,' Mrs Wallis went on, 'had only one living child, the little Princess Edith Augusta, for his first wife, Niamh of Eire, was barren; but he had high hopes of more. A son, of course, like any man,' she added bitterly, with an unreadable glance aside at Gray.

Gray looked as though such an idea had never crossed his mind.

'*Needed* a son, surely,' Sophie said; 'Princess Edith Augusta could not have inherited the throne.'

'Women did, in Breizh, before the Saozneg conquest,' said Joanna.

'In any event,' said Mrs Wallis, 'His Majesty was pleased with himself, and with his Queen and his child and the sons he was certain would follow, and in this optimistic humour he sent an embassy to the Iberian Court.'

This meant nothing in particular to Sophie – that the great Iberian Empire existed, in splendid isolation away to the south, was the sum total of her knowledge thereof – but Joanna and Gray both sat up straighter.

'The Iberians were not greatly interested in an alliance of any sort with Britain,' Mrs Wallis continued, 'but they were, as ever, eager to bring new and valuable magickal talents into their bloodlines, and for that purpose were prepared to make unusual concessions – to grant us, in fact, some limited access to the extraordinarily varied commodities produced in the far reaches of their empire.'

Sophie frowned, puzzling this out.

'Queen Laora knew, of course, that her daughter must one day marry out of her family and her home, as she had been – as she had done herself. The prospect of sending the Princess away to Iberia when she reached the age for marriage did not please her, but it was not unexpected; the prince to whom she was betrothed was more than twenty years her senior, and though this, too, was not a pleasing prospect, such betrothals often come to naught. She therefore made no objection. The Iberian Empress, however, demanded that the Princess be sent there within the year, to be raised in her household, and this Laora could not bear.'

'What did the Iberians want her for?' Sophie asked. 'What talent had she, that they considered so valuable?'

'Can you not guess?' Mrs Wallis said softly. And, when Sophie shook her head, she continued, 'Well. The Queen wept and begged and raged at her husband; she demanded to know what could have possessed him. He was patient with her, for he loved her, in his way, but she was desperate in her fury, and his patience had its limits.

'"The Princess has a duty to her kingdom," he finally said. "She is too young to understand this, but it is no less true for that. Think, too, how much less difficult it will be for her to leave us now than in two years, or five, or ten—"

'"And if I refuse to let her go?" Laora demanded. I could have shaken her for such reckless idiocy; but it would have done no good.

'In any case, the King only looked perplexed. "I am her father," he said, "and you do not rule me, Laora, nor this kingdom. Your consent is not required." I believe he was no happier than she, at sending his child away so young; but he would not break his word. And, of course, he believed they would have other children.'

Mrs Wallis drew one hand across her eyes – a weary gesture, as though the telling of this tale exhausted her.

'He did not hear what she said to him as he left her chamber; but I heard it. *There will be no other children, my lord.*'

There was a long, tense silence. Sophie became aware that her grip on Joanna's hand was painfully tight, and made an effort to relax her fingers.

'The King did not yet know it,' said Mrs Wallis, 'but that was the last he was to see of his wife and daughter. That evening Laora kept her room, feigning illness – it cannot have been difficult, for she was utterly wretched – and made her plans; or, rather, she made plans, and her cousin, her best-beloved handmaiden, attempted to dissuade her, and succeeded not at all.

'They collected together all the coin and jewellery they possessed, and anything else that might possibly be sold for coin. They chose their plainest clothing and altered it as much as time permitted, to render it less conspicuous, and at the second hour after midnight, when the household slept as much as it ever does, they bundled up the infant Princess and took their leave.'

'And no one saw them, and stopped them?' said Joanna, voicing the disbelief that Sophie also felt.

'No one stopped them,' Mrs Wallis replied. 'Many must have seen them, but without remarking their passing, or remembering it afterwards as worthy of remark. Mr Marshall, what does this fact suggest to you?'

Gray frowned fiercely – an expression not of anger but of furious concentration – but said nothing.

'Queen Laora was determined to return to her home country; she had some mad idea of throwing herself on the mercy of her father, but was at last persuaded that no good could come of such a course. Her handmaiden was for directing their flight to Eire or Alba, or into the Duchies, where they should not be known, but she loved her mistress too well to stand forever against her dearest wish.

'At length they found a small, modest house to let in a small, modest market town in the province of Kernev, and established themselves as a young widow, of modest fortune and modest talent, and her faithful servant, and began to look about them. It was clear, of course, that Laora must marry—'

'What?' Sophie exclaimed, before she could stop herself. 'Why?'

Mrs Wallis gave her a pitying look. 'How else were they to live? For a time they might subsist upon the proceeds of their clothing and jewellery, but even carefully husbanded, these resources could not last for ever.'

'But she was still married to the King,' said Joanna.

'Indeed,' said Mrs Wallis, 'but her suitors had no means of knowing it. And as for the King, if he could not find her, and she would make sure that he could not, he must marry again, for he still had no son. If he were not persuaded that she and her daughter had drowned while crossing the Manche, as the rumour then was in Breizh, then he must eventually have divorced her in absentia.'

'But they did die,' Sophie said. 'Did they not?' A creeping dread had begun to take hold of her, though what she dreaded, and why, she could not have told. The beating of her heart threatened to choke her; she remembered her mother's books, the name *Laora* carefully inscribed in so many of them instead of Mama's name, Rozenn; *I inherited those books*, Mama had said, when Sophie had asked why.

'Laora died, yes,' said Mrs Wallis, 'but not then. Though in some ways . . . but no.' She gave Joanna a long, sad look. 'It was not such a very bad plan,' she said, with a sigh. 'Its downfall was that the most eligible of Laora's suitors was a wealthy widower with a young daughter – a Fellow of Merlin College, by the name of Appius Callender.'

CHAPTER XI

In Which Mrs Wallis Is Asked Difficult Questions

'Impossible,' Sophie said flatly.

'Sophie is a *princess*?' said Joanna.

'How do we know that you speak truth?' Gray demanded. So bizarre and unexpected was Mrs Wallis's tale that it would not strike him until much later how far – once again – she had managed to evade his questions. Had all the tales been false, then? The version of events current in England in his boyhood had painted a very different picture of Queen Laora's actions. *The Breton harlot*, he had heard her called, *the false queen, la traîtresse* . . .

'Has Sophie a crown-shaped birthmark somewhere?' said Joanna eagerly. 'Or a locket with her parents' portraits? Or a royal signet-ring? Or—?'

'You, miss, pay too much heed to minstrel-tales,' Mrs Wallis interrupted, her tone severe.

Joanna's chin rose, her brows drew down, and she was drawing breath to protest this judgement when Mrs Wallis went on: 'Think, child. Had the truth been discovered, the Iberian marriage might yet have been carried through.' The colour drained from Sophie's face, and she clasped her trembling hands together. 'The last thing your mother wished was any visible sign that Sophia Callender was in fact Edith Augusta Sophia, Princess Royal of the House of Tudor.'

Sophie's throat worked; her face, already pale, began to look a little green.

'The magick,' said Gray. 'Of course, her mother's magick is the sign. It was there all along, had anyone been by to see it.' Then he dropped to one knee beside the bed and bent his head over Sophie's hand. 'Your devoted servant, Your Royal Highness,' he said softly.

With an inarticulate cry, Sophie snatched her hand away. When Gray looked up at her, she drew back and slapped him, so violently that he nearly lost his balance. Then, turning her back on them all, she burst into tears.

Sophie would not have either Gray or Mrs Wallis near her, and Joanna's glares could have frozen Tartarus itself. They retired, therefore, to Gray's tiny chamber, where Gray set his wards against eavesdroppers and perched on the end of the bed, and Mrs Wallis settled herself in the only chair. For some time they sat in silence, considering their respective positions.

'You were the faithful handmaiden,' Gray said at last.

Mrs Wallis inclined her head.

'Who *are* you?' he asked her, for at least the fifth time since their departure.

'My name would mean nothing to you,' she said.

Gray frowned at her; she met his gaze steadily, her face expressionless, until at length he tacitly conceded the field.

'Tell me,' he said instead, 'what is it Sophie does when she sings, that triggered the interdiction and gave me hallucinations?' There seemed no use in concealing this aspect of his 'illness' now. 'Was that her mother's magick, also?'

'No,' said Mrs Wallis, thoughtful. '*That* talent she has from her grandmother – her father's mother.'

There was a silence as Gray recalled the book of Breton tales in the library at Callender Hall, the faded *ex libris Laora* inscribed on the flyleaf, and wondered what other volumes of hers he might have found there, had he known how useful it might be to look.

'It strikes me,' he said, changing the subject, 'that it would be wise to make a survey of the neighbourhood – to know whether we are pursued.'

'An excellent plan.' Mrs Wallis raised her eyebrows. 'How exactly do you propose to carry it out?'

Recklessly cheerful at the thought of what he was about to do, Gray beamed at her. 'You may have the use of my room as long as you like, Aunt Ida,' he said brightly. 'You shall have a full report when I return.'

Enjoying her bemused stare – *So there is one secret of mine that she has not penetrated, after all!* – he ducked behind the dressing-screen that hid one corner of the room; he was forced to bend almost double to make the barrier do its office, as its upper edge scarcely reached his ribs. After a few moments, feeling at once foolish and exhilarated, he crouched down, the ancient oaken floorboards smooth under his bare feet, and closed his eyes, breathing deeply and slowly, willing his body to relax.

Slowly he focused all his thoughts, all his magick, and the pent-up energy of his long summer's yearning to fly, into the process of the shift. The more his body shed its human aspect, the lighter and more compact his crouched form became, the more he had to steady himself against a tide of joy. That he was weary and stiff and saddle-sore no longer mattered, now that he had his wings again.

At last, blinking round eyes, he emerged from behind the screen: nearly two feet and a half of soft, grey-barred feathers, sidling awkwardly on splayed-out talons.

Mrs Wallis, for the first time in Gray's memory, looked nonplussed. She stared at his owl self for a long moment, and then, slowly, she began to chuckle. 'A Great Grey,' she said at last. 'Very fitting, indeed – though a native bird would be less conspicuous.' She drew something from her reticule.

Then, to his surprise, she leant down and lifted him in her arms. 'For safety,' she said, looping something round his left leg. 'A charm left me by Queen Laora, to shield the wearer from unwelcome notice. Good hunting, young man. And *keep well clear of the interdict*.'

Then Mrs Wallis carried him to the window and tossed him out.

The inn's upper storey was not so high as the window of Gray's college rooms, and he had a nervous moment before instinct took over and he surged aloft. His blocky, compact body hung suspended between his outspread wings, more than four feet from tip to tip. He must not fritter away all the effort of this magickal working, he knew; he must do what he had promised, and reconnoitre the path they had taken. But in those first moments he could not resist simply circling, borne along on pillowing updraughts.

This, he thought, half giddy with the joy of it – *this is how it feels to be properly alive.*

The Great Grey Owl is not built for majestic soaring, but such a bird can coast on the breeze as well as any other with large, strong wings. Gray flew as high as he dared, attempting, with little success, to spy Callender Hall in the distance without coming near enough to run afoul of the interdiction; then, coming down to a more owl-like elevation, he explored the path their party had taken, gliding silently from tree to tree in search of any sign of pursuit. He found none, which did not surprise him, but he was puzzled to discover that even their own passage had left almost no visible traces. He had not thought to use any means of obscuring their trail – but evidently someone else had done so.

And there could be no doubt, surely, who that someone was.

At breakfast the next morning, Sophie could scarcely bring herself to meet Gray's eyes. She felt ashamed of herself – though her anger at him remained. Had she struck him because she believed him to be mocking her, or because she knew that he did not? And how was she to justify to him, or to anyone else, what she could not explain even to herself?

Joanna and she had lain awake into the night, discussing in whispers Mrs Wallis's more than incredible tale. Joanna seemed less perturbed by her mother's not having been properly wedded to her father than vexed to find the Professor her father in truth – having, it transpired, long fancied herself a changeling-child. Sophie herself was so overwhelmed by these latest revelations that she could scarcely manage to order her thoughts coherently.

'I cannot bear it,' she had sobbed into her pillow, shrugging off Joanna's attempts at comfort. 'I do not *want* to be a princess, Jo. Nor to be Elinor Dunstan. Mama was right to run away! Imagine, an Iberian prince – an *old* Iberian prince – and I should never have known Mama at all, or Breizh, or England. Or *you*, Jo. I want . . . I want to go back, back to the – to *Father* – and Amelia. I want to be *myself* again.'

'You *are* yourself,' said Joanna. 'What other choice is there? And Mama had better have stayed, and done her duty, and let you do yours; I cannot see that her marrying Father did the least good to either of you.'

'But, Jo! Only think, if Mama had not married the Professor—'

'It will all come right in the end.' Joanna overrode Sophie's protest, heartlessly cheerful. 'You know very well you were miserable with Father and Amelia; now you need never answer to them again. You have always wished for magick, have you not? Well, here's your wish granted, and your very tall beau to teach you the use of it—'

'Gray is not my beau, Joanna,' Sophie interrupted. 'You are a silly girl, and your imagination has got the best of you.'

In the darkness, Joanna's silence managed to seem both knowing and smug.

'Will he teach me still, do you suppose?' Sophie asked, after a long moment. 'After what I . . .'

'He would follow you to the four corners of the world, I should think,' said her sister.

Recalling Joanna's words as she raised her teacup to her lips, Sophie cast a sidelong glance at Gray. His hazel eyes were fixed on her; when her gaze met his, he reddened – abashed, she supposed, at being caught staring – and assumed a deep interest in his bread-and-butter. When their breakfast had been eaten, and its remains cleared away by another of the innkeeper's pretty daughters, Sophie rose from the table first, intending to flee upstairs and busy herself with preparations for the day's journey. But Gray laid a gentle hand along her arm, and she subsided, still avoiding his eyes.

'Elinor,' he murmured, 'I had thought today, perhaps – as we ride, you know – I might teach you a few useful magicks . . .'

Sophie looked up at him then, and saw her own hurt and embarrassment mirrored in his face – and something else, too, at sight of which her lingering anger evaporated. 'I should like that very much indeed,' she whispered.

They rode through a fine drizzle, scarcely felt but for the increasing heaviness of their dampened cloaks. Sophie's bonnet fell down her back, and droplets beaded her dark hair until she resembled some sort of rain-spirit – perhaps, Gray mused, such as might attend on Thor, northern son of the All-Father, to scatter rain in the wake of the god's thunderbolts.

The thought made him smile a little; the smile widened into a yawn, aftermath of the previous night's surveillance.

'You are tired,' said Sophie; she wore a guilty look. 'I am very sorry to have kept you from the use of your room—'

'It is not that,' Gray said hastily, stifling another yawn. 'I was out last night long after everyone else was abed – scouting, to see whether we had been followed.'

Far from being reassured, she now looked horrified. 'But what if we had been? You might have been caught – or hurt – or—'

'Nothing of the kind!' he retorted cheerfully. 'I am not such a fool as to go on foot. I flew.'

'I should have liked to see that.'

'So you shall. But not in broad daylight, and not—' Gray paused. 'I expect the horses would be very much put out. Now: shall we begin your lessons?'

They began with the first thing every talented child learns: how to call light. 'As you may remember, the usual spell is *adeste luces*,' said Gray, suiting the action to the words; a little burst of light sprang from his open hand and wafted upwards, hanging in mid-air until he snapped his fingers to vanish it. 'But the spell is only an *aide-mémoire*, a means to—'

'To ensure that the magickal energy is focused on the correct object or outcome, yes,' Sophie nodded, impatient.

Gray smiled. 'Very well, then: try.' He pondered briefly whether, given the power she possessed, it were safe to set her such a lesson; the custom was to teach the calling of light to the very young, and of fire to the not much older, that they might learn control while their talent was not yet strong. But Sophie's magick was by no means fully restored; she ought to be safe enough.

The object of these ruminations frowned in concentration and, clutching the reins with one hand, held out the other stiffly. '*Adeste luces!*' she commanded.

Nothing happened.

Sophie turned to Gray with an accusing look. 'It took me the best part of a week to learn to call light,' he reminded her.

'But you were a child of four!'

'And as experienced in the conscious, deliberate use of my talent as you are now.'

She fetched a deep sigh.

'Teach me, then,' she said grimly.

It was such a simple task, a trifle, done without thought; yet he had struggled to learn it once, and someone had taught him.

'Close your eyes,' he directed, 'and breathe slowly and deeply.'

Sophie obeyed; he sidled his mount closer to hers, so as to catch her if she lost her balance, mentally calling down Epona's blessing on the patient beasts, and the stablemen who must have trained them.

'Now,' he continued, when he judged that she had attained the correct state of calm reflection, 'to use your magick consciously and deliberately – to *wield* it – you must first summon it, and you cannot summon it unless you know how to find it.'

'But—' Sophie protested, her eyes still closed.

'That was different.' He answered the question she had not asked. 'It was unconscious and – need I remind you? – utterly uncontrolled. Magick is – magick is like fire: controlled, an invaluable tool; uncontrolled, a catastrophe.'

'Yes, I see,' said Sophie, low.

'Now, attend. You can *see* your own magick, and hear it, but the looking and listening are of a different sort.' Gray thought for a moment: how had his mother taught him this, all those years ago?

'Listen to the beating of your heart.' Gray's voice was low and patient. 'And when you can hear it, shut out all the other noises around us, until my voice and your own pulse are the only sounds you hear.'

Sophie obeyed, and the doubled thump – a louder beat, then its echo – seemed to grow until it thundered in her ears. By comparison, Gray spoke in a distant whisper: 'Now follow that sound to the centre of yourself – if you listen in the right way, it will lead you aright.'

She listened; she tried to follow.

What must I look for? she wondered bemusedly; she could not tell whether she spoke aloud, but was only half surprised when Gray's voice answered, 'Something like this.'

Opening her eyes, she saw hovering in the air before them the faint image of a bloom – like a huge, half-opened rose, but made all of a deep blue-green flame. With the image came a sort of music, like the deep resonant drone of a bass viol. She knew, without being able to explain how she knew it, that he had made for her a seeming of his own magick, and shivered at the open-hearted trust demonstrated by this gesture.

For what seemed a very long time Sophie let her mind roam while she listened, trance-like, to the beating of her heart. Just as she began to fear that she was doomed to failure, her inner vision shifted imperceptibly, and before her mind's eye, in her mind's ear, blazed a blue-white flame-flower, small but dazzlingly bright – like but not like one of Pellan's vivid dahlias – and each petal singing, high and clear.

'Good,' said Gray; at the same time, from far ahead came Mrs Wallis's voice: 'Are we to ride all day, you two?' Startled, Sophie opened her eyes and nearly fell off her horse.

'Did you see it, too? Or hear it?' she demanded of her companion; then, remembering, she said, 'Were you reading my thoughts?'

Gray chuckled. '*That* is a rare talent indeed,' he said. 'No: I answered the question you asked, and made a picture for you, and then I saw your expression change and knew you had found it. You had the same look as my brother Alan.'

'Are all your family talented, then?' Sophie could not resist this opportunity to enquire, albeit obliquely, about the brothers whom Gray almost never mentioned.

'Strictly speaking, yes,' he said. 'All of us can do the ordinary things – calling light and fire, small summonings. Jenny, as you know, is gifted at scrying, and—' He frowned, seeming to recollect that she had distracted him in mid-lesson.

'Close your eyes,' he said firmly, 'and find it again.'

It was so much easier this time that she could scarcely credit her own struggles of a few moments ago. 'Now,' said Gray, 'keep hold of *where* it is, and how it feels, and try whether you can maintain your hold on it when you open your eyes.'

Sophie concentrated hard – too hard, it seemed, for the sense of her magick slipped away from her. The next time, too, and the next, but at last she succeeded in grasping some phantastickal thread – a petal of that strange, singing bloom, perhaps – and keeping her awareness of it with her.

Gray smiled at her, his expression mingling pride and satisfaction. 'You are very quick,' he observed. 'Now, try the spell again.'

'*Adeste luces*,' Sophie whispered, concentrating all her will on kindling that thread of magick into a little orb of light like Gray's.

And, for just a moment, a light hovered and flickered above her outstretched hand.

'I have done it!' she squeaked, thunderstruck, delighted – forgetting temporarily the many and varied worries that pressed in on her mind. 'Joanna!' she called, and from twenty feet ahead her sister turned to look – though there was no longer anything to see.

The next effort lasted some thirty heartbeats, and the next twice as long.

Thus passed the journey, so rapidly that Sophie was surprised and dismayed when, just after noon, the roofs, walls, and crowded ship-masts of Douarnenez came into view.

CHAPTER XII

In Which Joanna Is Disappointed

In Douarnenez Sophie, Gray, and Joanna passed some hours' enforced inactivity at an upstairs window of an inn – rather more prosperous-looking than the last – on the rue des Marsouins, facing east across the wide, gentle curve of the bay. The water glowed a deep blue-green, patterned with the white triangular sails of fishing-boats. Half hypnotised by the ever-shifting blue-white lines of breakers rolling in to shore, Gray could easily believe that, as the old tales had it, somewhere beneath these waters rested Dahut's drowned city of Ys.

Mrs Wallis had gone in search of an acquaintance who might, she said, help them on their way.

'The captain of the *Brav Avel* will give us passage to the port of Brest,' she announced, when she returned towards mid afternoon, 'but he draws the line at three horses and a pony. Mr Marshall, you shall have to sell them before tomorrow's high tide.'

'*Sell* Gwenn-ha-du?' Joanna's voice wavered between outrage and tears; Gray was doubly glad of his wards upon the room. 'You cannot sell him, he is my *friend* – I have had him since I was a little girl—'

'Jo.' Sophie rose to put an arm about her sister's shoulders. Joanna glared at her.

'Come down to the stables with me, Joanna,' said Gray, gently.

He had intended only to give Joanna the opportunity of a private farewell, but the result proved better still. They had not been long in the stables before the stableboy, Ewen, struck up a conversation with the tearful Joanna, on the subject of Gwenn-ha-du. No more than an hour later, Ewen had pointed Gray in the direction of a likely buyer for the two mares and expressed such affection for Joanna's beloved pony that when, on the following morning, Gray ventured to suggest leaving Gwenn-ha-du in Ewen's care, Joanna acquiesced with many tears but very little real protest.

From Douarnenez they sailed round the Crozon peninsula to the large, bustling port of Brest, where, feeling safely anonymous, they sought their rest at the sign of the Midnight Queen.

The painting on the inn's signboard, though clearly meant to represent Queen Laora, looked no more like any living woman than inns' signboards generally do, and rather less than some. In the dimness within, however, the travellers at once confronted a hanging portrait – an apprentice's copy, perhaps, of his master's work – at sight of which Mrs Wallis fell abruptly silent, and Sophie paled and clutched at Joanna's arm.

'What—?' said Joanna. Then her grey eyes widened, and she looked from Sophie to the portrait and back again.

The young Queen Laora – perhaps not yet a queen, when this likeness was taken – had indeed been a great beauty. There was just enough of Sophie in the spare, exquisite features to make their kinship plain, but this woman knew herself beautiful and was accustomed to drawing all eyes. Gray saw Sophie in her frank, challenging gaze, her lifted chin and long white hands, and Joanna, distantly, in the set of her unsmiling lips.

'Mama,' Sophie whispered, and raised a hand, as though against her will.

Mrs Wallis was first to recover her composure, and contrived to shepherd the girls upstairs, almost as though nothing untoward had occurred.

Gray followed them, forcing a reassuring smile at the innkeeper's wife.

'You are wrong, Sophie,' he heard Joanna say as he reached the top of the stairs. When he opened the door to the third-floor sitting-room that was to be theirs, Mrs Wallis was shushing her irritably, and without reference to any of them Gray solved the immediate problem by means of a warding-spell.

'You may say whatever you like now, Joanna,' he said.

'I am *not* wrong,' said Sophie, ignoring him altogether.

'You are. I don't deny it may be meant for Mama, but Mama never looked like *that*.'

Abruptly Sophie ceased bristling and subsided into a chair. 'I saw her look so, once,' she said, low, 'when she thought no one observed her; I have remembered it always. But I had forgot that you were not yet born.'

Her words seemed to strike some chord with Joanna, which Gray could not divine, for her round face grew still and closed, and she turned brusquely away to gaze out of the window.

It occurred to him that Mrs Wallis must know the truth, if anyone did, for if her tale was true, she must have seen the original of that portrait – had even, perhaps, witnessed the taking of it. But when he turned to look at her, his questions died on his lips.

Could anyone be so white and still, and yet breathe?

After a moment Mrs Wallis raised her eyes to his and by a look beseeched his silence. How young she looked, in her distress! Gray averted his gaze, feeling that he had seen what he ought not.

Then turning to Sophie, Mrs Wallis said, 'It is your mother, indeed, though I know not how that copy came here. The likeness was done at her father's wish, before we sailed for England.'

'She prayed that she need not go.' The words were out before Gray could think better of them.

Sophie was staring at Mrs Wallis now, as if hypnotised, and Joanna had turned again from the window, regarding Sophie with eyes suspiciously bright.

'Her father stood firm so long that at last she had no choice but to consent to the marriage, and do her duty,' said Mrs Wallis to Gray. 'But neither he, nor anyone, could force her to go gladly, and her vengeance was that he should be daily reminded that she did not.'

There was a long silence.

'Yet when she chose for herself,' said Sophie at last, 'she chose the Professor.'

'There is a world of difference, Miss Sophia,' said Mrs Wallis, beginning to sound like herself again, 'between a maiden of nineteen and a mother of four-and-twenty.'

By now Gray was growing comfortably familiar with the persona of Ned Dunstan and, at times, rather fonder of Ned than of himself. Ned was confident in his business dealings and always had sufficient coin to tip for services rendered; his clothes (purchased in Douarnenez with a little of that same coin) were of good quality and fit him perfectly. Ned stood tall and straight (whereas Gray Marshall, embarrassed by his height and gangling limbs, had tended to stoop a little), and his confidence was surely justified, his parents reposing such trust in him as to charge him with the safe conduct of his sisters and their aunt.

Joanna, once reconciled to the loss of Gwenn-ha-du, seemed equally happy in the character of Harriet Dunstan, and Mrs Wallis – though she had been play-acting for so many years that the exercise ought surely to have lost its charms – positively delighted by Aunt Ida. But Sophie, it appeared, took no more pleasure in Elinor than in anything else.

From Brest, on the proceeds from the Professor's horses, they travelled post across the broad plain of Leon, keeping at their own request to the less-used roads and passing through, or around, Guipavas, Landerneau and Landivisiau, Trievin, Kervren and Kersaliou. They were three days on the road, and passed two nights at rather unprepossessing inns, making their way towards the northern tip of the province of Finisterre, and the port of Rosko. Here Mrs Wallis took possession of another upstairs sitting-room in another Breton inn, whence she sent the inn's servants scurrying with letters to all her acquaintance in the town.

Always the story of their flight followed them, embroidered with ever more preposterous detail. But thus far it did not seem to have occurred to anyone they met to connect that highly entertaining tale with four ordinary, respectable, rather dull travellers. For, since discovering the truth of the young ladies' ancestry, they had all – and Sophie especially – taken pains to present to the world as unremarkable an appearance as possible. Gray heard one day, while waiting for a change of horses, a version that described the villainous student as unusually tall (though also, helpfully, as dark-haired and strikingly handsome); he took to wearing Mrs Wallis's concealing charm tied round his wrist at all times, and thus went unremarked in many a crowded street and dining-room.

Though he did his best to hide it, Gray fretted. He wondered anxiously whether his letter to Jenny from Douarnenez had reached her, and, if so, whether it had done so in time to stop her writing to him again at Callender Hall. He pondered the various possible consequences if the Professor should seek him and Sophie at Kergabet, and the worrying import of the letter Jenny had brought him from Master Alcuin. As September waned and the time neared when, presumably, the Professor must also be journeying towards Oxford, he worried that they would cross his path and be discovered, or worse.

When no more specific anxiety presented itself, he fell back to worrying about Sophie, who remained withdrawn and melancholy, whose face, relaxed in sleep during their long hours on the road, showed clearly the dark shadows under her eyes.

Joanna, when questioned, said merely, 'She has always had nightmares. Perhaps being so far from home has made them worse?' And Sophie herself denied that anything was amiss.

One thing, however, could still draw out the quick and vivid Sophie of their nights in the Professor's library.

'Will you teach me that?' she asked Gray eagerly one evening, when – lethargic after a long day's journey, and disinclined to rise from his chair – he summoned the cup of tea Mrs Wallis had just poured out for him and balanced it on his knee.

Weary though he was, Gray could not help smiling at her enthusiasm. This lesson, too, began with a series of failures, but by the time Mrs Wallis ordered the girls to bed, Sophie was in high spirits, having succeeded in summoning both Joanna's gloves and her own hus-wife and thimble from Gray's hand across the tea-table to her own.

Such rapid successes inspired Gray to tease her, gently, about their roles being very soon reversed. He had remarked before that though her prior education had been so haphazard and eclectic, she asked perceptive questions, and her thirst for knowledge easily matched his own; it had wanted only this last shared endeavour to cast him back, for those hours, to his happiest days at Merlin.

In Kervren he at last gave in to her persuasion and demonstrated a shape-shift, allowing her to disentangle his wings, feet, and tail from the shirt and trousers that collapsed around his owl body, and to perform the useful offices of tossing him out of the window and letting him in again. She was more enthralled by the reality of this magick even than by the idea of it, and he was sure that, could he have read her thoughts, he should have seen in them a burning determination to master it herself. That she could do so he had no doubt; *but surely*, he told himself, *she needs a teacher more skilled and experienced than I.*

The closer they came to reaching England, still unimpeded and apparently unpursued, the more Gray feared that some dire setback awaited them, some ambush of the Fates.

When they reached Rosko, whence they would take ship for Portsmouth, Gray made a decision. For some time he had been struggling with conflicting impulses. On the one hand, each passing day made it the more urgent to decipher the documents he had copied from Lord Carteret's dispatch-case, and clearly the sensible approach was to make use of every resource available to him; Mrs Wallis was one such. On the other hand, he neither understood nor entirely trusted her motivations. It had become plain, however, that the problem was not to be solved by his own unaided efforts, and so on the evening of their arrival in Rosko he closed the door firmly on his doubts and brought out his ciphered messages – now sadly the worse for their journey – to show to his companions.

'Mrs Wallis,' he said, 'what do you make of this?'

Sophie gave the grubby papers a heavy-lidded glance and returned to drowsing before the fire. Joanna, however, jumped up from her chair, and Mrs Wallis looked sharply up from the letters to Gray's face and demanded, 'What are they, and how came you by them?'

'I have not the least idea what they are,' said Gray, 'but the originals belonged to Professor Callender and Lord Carteret; I copied them in the hope that they might prove useful.'

Joanna vented an admiring *Ooh!* which drew Mrs Wallis's frown in her direction – but only for a moment.

'And it seemed advisable to you to violate Professor Callender's hospitality by rifling the possessions of a fellow guest?' Mrs Wallis asked Gray.

Wrong-footed by the conversational tone in which she delivered this accusation, Gray spoke without thought: 'What hospitality? The Professor never welcomed me to his house; it was Sophie who did that. And,' he added, as three pairs of eyes turned towards him in astonishment, 'I suspected him of plotting murder, which I think must be some excuse, if my actions required one.'

Sophie's dark eyes were round as soup-plates. 'Why did you stay?' she asked him. 'If he did not welcome you, you must have known that he meant you ill.'

Gray gave her a sort of half shrug. 'I thought he merely wished to treat me as a servant,' he explained – which had been true enough, to begin with. Her troubled expression did not fade, but she said nothing more.

Joanna had stationed herself just behind Gray's chair, the better to peer over his shoulder. 'That looks like Greek,' she said now, tapping one finger on the extract copied from Lord Carteret's diary.

'It is not Greek,' said Gray, and began to explain his theory, but Joanna's attention had already passed on to the other document.

'Does that come from a book?' she demanded after a moment. '*Lightly the gods' gifts*?'

Gray looked up sharply. 'It *echoes* a book,' he said. 'The *Sapientia Delphi*. "The gods' gifts are lightly given, and as lightly reclaimed." This, below the gap, is copied from another document, which had no such notation. If I am not mistaken, it uses a codex cipher—'

'Of course!' Joanna said.

'A codex cipher?' From her seat before the hearth, Sophie looked up again with a flicker of interest.

'A cipher that relies on a codex that both parties own,' said Gray. 'The figures will be in pairs – the first is the folio, the second the word itself.'

'It is an excellent code,' Joanna added, 'because no one can break it who does not know which book to use.'

'But you believe he has given us the book,' said Mrs Wallis, in a sceptical tone. 'Why—?'

'This notation,' said Gray, pointing, 'was on the message I found in the Professor's study, written in his hand – an *aide-mémoire*, I expect. Of course he did not mean anyone else to see it. Had I been able to find a copy of the *Sapientia Delphi*—'

'But the Professor has got a copy,' said Sophie. She had curled herself tight in her chair, her arms wrapped round her drawn-up knees. 'It was in the library until he came home for the Long Vacation, and then it disappeared. Things often do, you know,' she added, defensively. 'He takes them into his study, and they do not find their way back until he has gone away again. I should not have remarked it at all, if it had not been one of those I was reading at the time.'

'It was not in his study,' said Gray, and steadfastly ignored Joanna's narrow-eyed stare. 'Nor in his bedroom. Was he carrying it about with him? In any case, finding another copy must be our first order of business, when we come to Oxford.'

Mrs Wallis nodded grimly.

On a brilliantly sunny morning, at sea between Rosko and Portsmouth, the travellers perched on water-casks and coils of rope in the prow of their ship, which ran before a fresh breeze that whipped the ladies' skirts and shawl-ends about their bodies and threatened to carry slender Sophie off entirely. The ship was neither more nor less than a Flemish smuggler's craft, rigged fore and aft like a fishing yawl, and its crew ignored their passengers as studiously as they ignored its cargo. The rough deck under their feet rolled with the motion of the sea.

They had spent the voyage discussing, in low voices and from every possible angle, the sum of their knowledge of the crime they sought to prevent. It was little enough: the Professor's mysterious errand and the strange behaviour of Henry Taylor; the snatches of conversation Gray had overheard in the Professor's rooms at Merlin;

Lord Carteret's inexplicable visit; the near-accident at Kerandraon, which all agreed had been intended for Gray; the testimony of Master Alcuin, that he had been watched and followed since receiving Gray's first letter from Breizh, and of Sophie, that the Professor's copy of the *Sapientia Delphi* had been removed from the library, which suggested – to Joanna's inventive mind, at any rate – that he had been in the habit of exchanging ciphered letters with Lord Carteret and other co-conspirators unknown.

'It is Lord Carteret's involvement that disturbs me,' said Gray 'Professor Callender has no love for Lord Halifax, and College politics are meat and drink to him; but what can it possibly profit the President of His Majesty's Council to involve himself in such an affair, when he must have so many more pressing matters to attend to?'

'You said,' began Sophie, her fine dark brows drawing together in troubled thought, 'you said that Lord Carteret mentioned giving the Professor *his choice of subjects to test his method.* Surely . . . surely that can only mean that there is someone else they mean to attack?'

Gray felt as though a truth he had long been suppressing had risen up to stare him in the face. 'Someone more important to Lord Carteret,' he agreed.

'Someone at Court, then?' said Joanna, sitting up straighter on her water-cask. 'A political rival, perhaps!'

'Perhaps,' said Mrs Wallis pensively. 'He must have many such, I suppose.'

'But you have another hypothesis, I think,' said Gray.

'Perhaps,' Mrs Wallis repeated. Her fingers tightened on her reticule; she turned and gazed back over the waves towards Breizh.

As Gray was just beginning to make out the distant shore, Sophie abruptly turned round. 'I have been thinking,' she said, in an oddly distant tone, 'what would happen if we changed our minds.'

'Changed our minds about what?' Joanna enquired.

Gray's stomach churned in a way that had nothing to do with the rolling of the deck.

'About *this*.' Sophie waved one arm at the ship, the waves, the crying gulls. 'No one knows where we are. We might go almost anywhere from Portsmouth – even to Eire, or Alba—'

'Sophie, a man's life is at stake,' said Gray. 'Most probably more than one.'

'I wish no one ill,' she said. 'But my mother risked all to protect me, and the nearer we come to Court, the nearer I am to falling again into my father's power. You have told us, ma'am, that Lord Carteret was among His Majesty's closest advisors even before I was born. If he knew who I am, he would not take my part, or yours, or Joanna's; and if he has allied himself with the Professor, then he is no friend to Gray. Suppose that we do succeed in thwarting their plans at Merlin; we shall have made a dangerous enemy. And if we do not succeed—'

'We must succeed,' said Gray. He had Gautier's death on his conscience already; he tried not even to consider the consequences of failure here.

'But if we do not?' Sophie insisted. 'We are known to Lord Carteret, and whether or not we succeed, whether or not he discovers who I am in truth, he will know us to be his enemies. *All* of us,' she repeated, with a meaningful glance at Joanna. 'And if they intend next to target some member of the King's Court—'

Then some other thought seemed to occur to her, and she broke off, scowling. She drew a deep breath and said, with the air of one facing a repellent and long-avoided task, 'Mrs Wallis, does the Professor know who it is he married?'

Mrs Wallis sighed. 'She would tell him,' she said. 'I could not prevent her.'

CHAPTER XIII

In Which Sophie and Gray Learn Something to the Purpose

'*How long has* he known?' Sophie's voice was flat, emotionless.

Mrs Wallis smiled thinly. 'Fifteen years, more or less. She trusted him, at first, more than he deserved; by the time she understood his character, it was too late to undo what she had done. He used it against her more than once.' She glanced at Joanna – a moment, no more, but her look was troubled. 'She came to fear that he would use it against you also. Has none of you wondered why I should have enough coin at the ready to bring us this far?'

Gray darted his eyes at Joanna, then at Sophie. 'You brought it with you,' the latter faltered. 'You and Mama. When . . . when you ran away.'

'Some of it,' Mrs Wallis agreed. 'Your mother, as it happens, did have the wit to conceal one important matter – the extent of the coin and the . . . saleable property with which we managed to escape. Only a small portion of it passed to your father' – she nodded at Joanna – 'on their marriage; the rest we hid, or distributed for safe-keeping to a few trusted friends. I was charged with retrieving it at need, for use in removing you both, should anything . . . untoward occur.'

'Removing us, where?' Drawing herself up, Sophie glared down at her guardian with an expression that could only be described as imperious. 'For how long, and to what end? For what could he do to us,' she added scornfully, 'that he has not already done?'

Mrs Wallis's face darkened. 'You underestimate his capacity for malice,' she said. Looking at Sophie, then at Gray, she went on: 'Together you are far more powerful than he, and either of you could best him in a battle of wits, fought fairly. But—'

'It never would be fought fairly,' Joanna interrupted. 'Father can scarcely manage not to cheat at chess, if he sees any possibility of losing; what might he do in a contest whose outcome truly mattered?'

There was a grim silence.

'We cannot let them succeed,' said Sophie at last, 'whatever their aim. But' – she looked pleadingly at Mrs Wallis – 'you will not send me back to him? To the King? Mama would not have wished—'

'We shall do what we must,' said Mrs Wallis. The chill in her eyes sent a shiver down Gray's spine.

Sophie evidently read in those eyes the futility of her pleading. 'My choice, then,' she said grimly, 'is between Scylla and Charybdis. Between the father who would use me for political ends and the one who would use me for personal gain.'

'Between one who has made your life a misery and one who may yet prove to wish you well,' Gray suggested.

'Yours is a generous nature, indeed,' she retorted. 'But perhaps it will not come to that.'

Portsmouth after the Equinox was the scene of much activity. To the usual hectic comings and goings of a busy commercial port – the fishing vessels offloading their catch, the merchant ships bringing Flemish cloth, Breton cider, wine from Bourgogne or tea from the Indies, or weighing anchor with cargoes of china clay or tin – was added the traffic of the season: gentlemen and ladies returning from their pleasure tours across the Manche, along with the first of those who had spent the summer on their country estates and would pass the winter in London. Ships of the Royal Fleet were putting in for repair, and the town was at once recovering from its Equinoctial celebrations and beginning to make ready for the great festival of Samhain.

And at the sign of the Black Horse, in the Old Town, behind the strongest wards Gray could set, an energetic dispute was in progress. Though begun on fairly level terms, it was now a contest of three disputants against one, and quickly becoming a rout.

'What proof have you that other Fellows of Merlin are not involved as well?' Mrs Wallis folded her arms.

'None whatsoever,' Gray said. 'Indeed, I doubt not there are others. But there is one man at least of whose loyalties we may be absolutely certain. Have you any such acquaintance still in England, after sixteen years? Any who can be counted upon to put our interests above Lord Carteret's?'

Mrs Wallis's expression made clear that this shot had struck home. 'Who is this trusted friend of yours, then?' she enquired. 'Your former tutor, who has spent the summer months dodging the Professor's spies?'

'The same,' Gray said. 'It will not be easy, but Master Alcuin will help us, if he can. And he is as likely to betray me as . . . as I am to betray Sophie.'

'*That* ought to settle the matter,' said Joanna; Sophie looked at her crossly, but smiled at Gray.

Mrs Wallis nodded, her expression resigned.

'I have been thinking,' said Gray, 'that if they wish to test the effectiveness of their method, as we believe, then it must be one they are not altogether sure of. Not a knife to the heart, or a sword-thrust; not hemlock in the Master's wine. Lord Carteret was very clear that the Professor must be careful to let no one connect him to the death. If their aim is to avoid the appearance of foul play—'

'Then an "accident" is most likely,' Joanna interrupted him. 'A fall from a horse, or a fall down the stairs, or . . .'

'Or some more obscure poison,' said Mrs Wallis.

'Obscure poison.' Struck by a thought, Gray leapt up and begun to rummage through the trunk that held his books.

A quarter-hour later, he gave up the search; like the elusive *magia musicae*, the object of his quest was not to be found in any of the texts he had brought with him. But Master Alcuin would know, if anyone did.

'May I show you something?' Sophie asked, suddenly shy.

Gray smiled up at her. 'Of course,' he said. He put down the book he had been reading, marking his place with a strip of linen, and sat back in his chair to give Sophie his full attention.

She drew a deep breath and shut her eyes; it seemed to work better this way, though she had given up drawing on the magick directly. Instead, she called up in her mind an image of herself, of a Sophie whose hair was fair and straight, whose eyes were blue, whose small, straight nose was sprinkled with freckles beneath a high, smooth brow. When she opened her eyes again, Gray's awestruck expression told her more clearly than any words that the transformation had been perfectly done, but she could not resist crossing the room to examine her reflection in the glass.

Gazing intently into the blue eyes that were and were not her own, she heard soft footfalls approach, and after a moment Gray's hands descended to envelop her shoulders. 'Extraordinary,' he said. 'If I knew your character less well, Your Royal Highness, I think I should be quite frightened of you.'

Sophie pulled away from his hands, irritated at this reminder of her larger predicament, and went to the window, letting the mental image go.

'I am sorry,' Gray said. 'I spoke thoughtlessly.'

When, reluctantly, she turned back to face him, he began again: 'Tell me, was that a face you've practised, or was it improvised for the occasion?'

'I did practise a little,' she admitted. 'I should like – I ought to be able to . . . to masquerade as someone else, if I try, do you not think? Someone in particular, I mean. That might be useful.'

'I can think of no reason why not,' Gray said. 'But it would not be easy. There is so much more than the face to be considered – form, and height, and voice, and gestures . . .'

'I shall begin with Joanna, then,' Sophie declared, 'and you shall judge how well I succeed.'

But perhaps, again, her approach to the task was flawed, for by the time Joanna herself came to summon them to dinner they were weary of the exercise, and – apart from a pounding headache – Sophie had nothing to show for her efforts.

Perhaps, she thought, *I shall try again after everyone is abed. It will be more restful than sleeping.*

To arrive at an inn at twilight, and remain shut up, unseen, until one's departure the following morning, is to invite all manner of speculation among one's fellow guests. In the course of their journey, therefore, the travellers had made a habit of taking either dinner or breakfast in the common dining-room, and sometimes of appearing, severally or together, in the common room in the evening. At the Seven Sisters at Crookham near Newbury, Mrs Wallis retired to her room after dinner, pleading exhaustion, while Joanna wandered off for a look at a very fine black saddle-horse rumoured to be stabled below. It was Gray and Sophie, therefore, who re-emerged from their rooms at twilight, to prove themselves unremarkable travellers and to gather what news they could from their fellow guests.

Pausing before the door of the inn's common room, Gray looked down once more at his companion's dark eyes, sparkling in the face framed by her glossy chestnut hair; he felt as proud of her as though she had truly been the young sister whom he was escorting home. She must have taken pains, both physical and magickal, with her appearance; Elinor Dunstan bid fair to be the loveliest young woman most of those within had seen in some time.

This thought led to another, far less welcome.

'You look very lovely,' he told Sophie, quietly. 'But would it not be best to draw as little attention as possible?'

Blushing, she dropped her gaze, and Gray instantly regretted having spoilt her innocent pleasure in her appearance. 'Of course,' she said. 'I apologise; I had not thought. Perhaps if I looked more like . . .'

She bent her head a little and closed her eyes. As he straightened, still watching her, Gray became conscious of an odd sensation, a mental stirring that he could not quite identify. Just as he began to grasp what it was, and to be astounded by it, she raised her head so that he could see her face.

Or, rather, the face that she now wore.

It was Jenny's.

Gray's stomach lurched. 'Stop that!' he exclaimed, turning away from her.

'Gr—Ned?' Sophie said. 'What is it? What have I done?'

'I . . .' Feeling ill, Gray groped frantically after some rational explanation for his reaction; he could hardly say to Sophie, and still less to Elinor Dunstan, *I wished very much to kiss you just now, until you looked at me with my sister's face.* 'I am sorry if I frightened you. I have not seen you imitate so perfectly before – you were the very spit of Jenny – it was . . . it was a shock.'

All of which was true, in its way – Sophie had met Jenny only once; how in Hades had she produced so accurate a copy? – though not at all the whole truth; he hoped it would be sufficient excuse for his behaviour.

'I ask your pardon,' said Sophie. Gray turned back to her; she looked up at him – now very much herself again – and he breathed a prayer of thanks. 'I only thought . . . I thought we should be less conspicuous if we looked more alike.'

'And you were right, I am sure.' He smiled down at her as reassuringly – and fraternally – as he could manage. 'I do apologise for frightening you. You will do very well now, I think.'

Sophie's expression was doubtful, but she squared her shoulders and slipped her hand through the crook of his arm, an innocent, sisterly gesture. Now dreadfully conscious of her touch, Gray hoped, absurdly, that she would ascribe his trembling to anxiety over the task at hand.

'Shall we go, then?' he asked.

In the common room of the Seven Sisters, two young ladies whispered together on a velveteen settee, under the watchful eye of an elderly matron; some half-dozen gentlemen of widely differing ages and varied appearance sat or stood about the room, some engaged in conversation, another reading a news-sheet, a pair idly playing at draughts.

On hearing the door close behind Sophie and Gray, all fell silent, the better to scrutinise the newcomers.

Sophie's face grew warm under the gaze of so many strangers. She clung to Gray's arm – the more because she could not understand what had passed between them, only that she had tried to produce some family resemblance, and perhaps succeeded too well – and needed no artifice to appear young and diffident. His smile of encouragement failed to reach his eyes.

Despite the season, the evening was chilly, and a fire had been lit; they crossed the room to sit by it, where they might be best placed to overhear any useful fragments of conversation. Gray's arm trembled a little beneath Sophie's hand.

Then, as had happened once or twice before, the eyes turned away, the strangers' gaze slipping over Sophie and Gray as though they were – if not invisible – so unremarkable as not to be worth looking at. Gray's quick, appraising glance confirmed that her devout wish not to be noticed had made it so.

He found her a seat near the hearth and took up a station facing her, one elbow on the high mantelshelf, his back to the crackling fire. Sophie gazed pensively into the flames, trying to look as though she were not paying the least attention to anything else.

For some time she heard nothing of any interest; weary and drowsy, she had half slipped into the embrace of Morpheus when a few unguarded words made her ears prick up.

'What news from Town, Tregear?' The speaker had a deep voice and spoke in an oddly accented English. 'One hears the most confounded odd rumours . . .'

'Softly, Dallyell!' Tregear's accent echoed Gray's, Kernow overlaid with Oxford, and his voice was strained and anxious. 'The rumours come nearer the truth than their authors know. The old man grows quite mad; for sixteen years he's sought that Breton harlot and her child, and 'tis worse now than ever, as though those three bonny Princes were no more than dogs or horses.' His voice dropped to a murmur: 'I wonder that the Queen can bear the insult to her sons.'

Sophie's hands clenched in her lap. *It is my father and mother he speaks of. My father mad, and my mother a harlot.* If she willed it strongly enough, might she simply disappear?

'And the tales of . . . unhealthy magicks?' Dallyell persisted. 'Of calling on strange gods?'

'I wish 'twere in my power to deny it.'

Dallyell gave a low whistle; when he spoke again, his voice was scarcely above a whisper. 'Hades and Proserpina keep such tales from the ambassadors at Court . . .'

'From your lips to the gods' ears,' Tregear murmured.

Out of the corner of her eye, Sophie saw the two men clasp hands and move away to refill their glasses. For some time she went on listening, picking out bits and pieces of the conversations taking place around her, but – unless it were of value to know that the barque *Julia Augusta* had survived an attack by pirates off the Iberian coast, or that the Duchess of Norfolk had started a fashion for sea-green velvet – to no further purpose.

Was this Britain's vision of her King – mad, deluded, obsessed?

And if it was also Lord Carteret's view, what might he intend?

Sophie looked up, and her eyes met Gray's; his face had paled under its sunburnt brown. 'I feel a little unwell, Ned,' she said, as clearly as she could manage. 'I should like to return to my room, I think.'

'Of course, Elinor dear,' said Gray, offering his arm again as she rose from her seat.

PART TWO

Oxford

CHAPTER XIV

In Which Oxford Is Not Quite as Sophie Expects

Rain fell steadily as September wandered into October and the four travellers wandered into the town of Oxford.

Since first discovering the existence of such a place – a city of temples and libraries, a city whose very purpose was to support the pursuit of knowledge and wisdom – Sophie had yearned to see it. Expecting that after another unquiet night, she would nod off during the journey, she had made Gray promise to wake her when the town came into view. From engravings and sketches seen at Callender Hall she recognised at a distance the great temples of Minerva and Apollo, the Great Library, the towers and gates of the outermost Colleges: King's, Marlowe, Bairstow. As they skirted the town, bound northward to a wayhouse on the Cherwell, Gray pointed out the newly built Museum of the History of Magick and the roof of the Infirmary. Certainly the place did not appear to best advantage under the burden of the day's steady drizzle, but Sophie was captivated.

They had nearly reached their destination when she spotted the small dome, the green of aged copper, at the centre of a group of derelict buildings – windows empty and dark, ivied walls half overgrown with weeds – on the far bank of the Cherwell. For no reason she could discern, the scene was oddly familiar. 'What place is that?' she enquired, pointing.

'Those are the buildings of Lady Morgan College,' Gray said, with a thoughtful glance back at her. 'Not used these past two hundred years perhaps. The green dome is a shrine to Minerva, as Sophia, personification of wisdom.'

Lady Morgan College. Sophie remembered reading of this place in one of her mother's books: a college for women, founded by a Cymric noblewoman in an earlier age; once a great centre of learning, the equal, if not of Merlin, certainly of many of the newer colleges. Abandoned, now, since the time of the Princesses Regent. This Sophie had never understood: Princess Edith Augusta – her own namesake, as she now knew – was said to have been a woman of great erudition, and to have possessed powerful magick; she herself had studied at Lady Morgan College, and yet it was in her time that the University had once again become the domain of men alone.

As those desolate, forsaken buildings – once a living, breathing community dedicated to the pursuit of wisdom and protected by the goddess Minerva, now an empty stone shell half reclaimed by the dedicates of Gaia and Hegemone – disappeared around a bend in the road, Sophie was gripped by a sudden, overwhelming sorrow. 'I wish,' she said, in a voice half choked with tears, 'I wish that I could bring it back to life.'

'Perhaps you could,' said Joanna, 'if you were to become a princess again.'

The wave of loss and foreboding ebbed a little; Sophie swallowed and pulled a wry face at her sister. 'You overestimate my influence, I think.'

'But if *you* cannot do it, Sophie,' Gray said, 'then I can scarcely imagine who could.'

Leda and the Swan was, as its garish and rather suggestive signboard intimated, not in the habit of receiving respectable ladies. While Mrs Wallis contrived, as always, to appear perfectly at ease, Sophie and Joanna looked about them with barely concealed apprehension, and Gray squirmed under the innkeeper's knowing gaze. He knew very well what the fellow must think, and could not help feeling that a more capable man would not suffer such impertinence – nor would a more sensible one have brought three gentlewomen here to begin with. But if they were to avoid meeting any of Gray's acquaintance – and all had agreed that this was vital – they had no good alternative.

Though the innkeeper at first was prone to delighted leering, a stern look and a few quiet words from Mrs Wallis produced in him a remarkable civility and (she assured the others) perfect discretion. The business of negotiating for their rooms was mercifully brief, and they were soon safely ensconced in the chamber – cramped, unpleasantly furnished, but passably clean – that would be the ladies' abode whilst they remained in Oxford, discussing strategy as Mrs Wallis unpacked their things.

'The first order of business,' said Gray when he had warded the room, 'is to explain matters to Master Alcuin, and seek his help. Sophie and I shall go – incognito, of course. Then—'

'How,' Joanna objected, 'can Sophie possibly go into Merlin College incognito? You have got that charm of Aunt Ida's, I know, but no matter how clever Sophie may be at not being noticed, she is a *girl* . . .'

Gray looked at Sophie, who returned his gaze with a pleased half smile.

'You have not told Joanna of your newest discovery, then?' he enquired. Joanna glowered, ill pleased at being left out of a secret.

'I did mean to show you, Jo,' Sophie said. 'Watch, now, and you shall see.' She closed her eyes and bent her head.

Though he had observed variations of this process so many times by now, Gray remained fascinated. Though Sophie's face was hidden, he could see her hair blur and shift, her slender neck change shape. Hairpins clattered to the floor as long, dark locks grew lighter and shorter; head and neck shifted in curve and heft, and when at last Sophie raised her face again to look at the other three, it was with the wide blue eyes, straight brows, strong cheekbones, and tow-coloured curls of a young man. Perhaps rather a *pretty* man; Sophie's prior experience with young men was not extensive.

The effect was jarring, and Gray looked away for a moment, enjoying Joanna's gobsmacked expression instead.

'Ladies,' he said, 'allow me to introduce my friend . . . shall we call him Arthur?'

The name had come to him unbidden; an echo of the lost Gautier, perhaps.

Sophie laughed and let the magick go, shaking out of her eyes her own long, chestnut-coloured hair. Gray had a sudden, mad urge to run his fingers through those glossy waves; he stifled it by reciting to himself, in Old Cymric, the first five Descents of the Greater Mabinogion.

'We shall go into the College,' he continued, when he had recovered his equilibrium, 'and to Master Alcuin's rooms, and explain to him what we are about. Lord Halifax – the Master of Merlin, that is – could scarcely do otherwise than have me clapped in irons if I approached him as myself, and is unlikely to agree to see us even as strangers, but Master Alcuin will be able to gain us an audience.'

'But he wrote you word of his being watched.' Mrs Wallis had not appeared to be listening, but Gray knew her ways too well by now to have been misled.

'Yes,' said Joanna, 'Gray did say that. Will you not be seen, both going and returning?' she demanded, looking from Sophie to Gray and back again. 'What if you are recognised – will the Proctors not lock you up, for what happened to your friend?'

Only a few weeks ago such an objection might have reduced

Gray to stammering counterarguments – but no longer. 'We shall not be there as ourselves,' he pointed out, 'and we shall have Sophie's magick. And, once we have warned him of the danger that threatens him, our own danger will be at an end.'

Out of the corner of his eye he saw Sophie nodding agreement as she finished pinning up her hair. But Joanna had not yet done. 'And if this Lord Halifax refuses to believe your tale?'

'We shall cross that bridge when we come to it, Joanna,' Sophie replied severely. '*If* we come to it.'

'Be *careful*, Sophie,' said Joanna, anxious. Then, turning to Gray, she tilted her head back to glare up at him and went on, sternly, 'If anything should happen to my sister, I shall make you *very* sorry.'

Sophie shifted restlessly from foot to foot, feeling out-of-sorts and awkward in the trousers, shirt, and coat which Mrs Wallis had paid an uninquisitive seamstress in Market-street to make for her as Samhain-night masquerade wear. Keeping her boy's face on, and her voice in a range suited to a youth of her own age, required considerable mental effort – she had not known how much, for such things had never much mattered before – and she was increasingly nervous about the whole scheme. And Gray had given her a most peculiar look, on first beholding her in her mummer's garb, which had not helped matters at all.

'I shall be perfectly all right, Jo,' she said, rather more impatiently than she had intended. 'Gray knows what he is about, you know, and I shall have nothing to do but look like this and . . . and talk a little with Master Alcuin.' She turned to Gray. 'Have you the—?'

Forestalling her, he shot back the cuff of his coat so that she could see her mother's obsidian charm on its black silk cord about his wrist. 'I shall be as inconspicuous as anyone could wish,' he said. Had Sophie known him less well, she might have missed the undertone of worry in his voice. Possibly he regretted having yielded to her insistence on accompanying him. So be it; not for any consideration would she allow him to run such a risk alone.

They followed the Cherwell down to the unassuming wooden bridge that, on the opposite bank, joined their path to the South Road into the town. At first Gray strode along in silence, apparently lost in thought, and Sophie was forced into a half trot to keep pace with him; after a time, however, he slowed his pace to ease her way. There was nothing much to discuss, Sophie supposed, their plan having been thoroughly hashed out already, but the silence unnerved her, and at last, half unconsciously, she began to sing.

She stopped when, on turning southward, into the Mansfield road, they first began to encounter other foot traffic. She had not supposed Gray to be listening to her half-whispered song, but when it ceased, he turned back to her, looking surprisingly cheerful, and said, 'I thank you – that was a clever thought, to sing a cheery walking song!'

Sophie considered asking him what in the world he meant – she had in fact been singing a Brezhoneg lullaby under her breath – but thought better of it. 'Are we nearly there?' she enquired instead. She had not enjoyed the walk; her trousers chafed the skin of her legs, the starched collar cut into her neck, the coat was too warm, and the new boots pinched her feet most unpleasantly.

'Nearly,' said Gray happily, as they turned into Wellspring-street.

In less than a quarter-hour they had reached what Gray called, with a sweep of his hand, 'the Broad', and were passing the imposing frontage of Plato College; then, abruptly, Sophie found herself standing before the Porter's Lodge of Merlin.

This was the first test; if a shielding-charm, a false name, and a new suit of clothes could enable Gray to pass unchallenged through the front gate of his own college, then, surely, there was every chance that the rest of their mad scheme might succeed. As Sophie held her breath, Gray lifted a hand and knocked smartly on the heavy oaken gate.

After a moment a stolid, pudding-faced Porter put his head out of the square hatch six inches above Sophie's head. 'Names?' he enquired.

'Edward Dunstan,' said Gray, 'and Arthur Randal.'

'Merlin men?'

They had decided the previous evening that it would be best, at this stage of the journey, *not* to be Merlin men. 'Marlowe,' Gray said. 'I am a Marlowe man. Young Randal' – with a careless gesture at Sophie – 'has not matriculated as yet.'

'And what do ye here, then?' The Porter raised his eyebrows at them.

'We are paying a few calls,' said Gray, and then, in a display of recklessness that made Sophie's heart leap into her throat, 'Is Professor Callender in College at present?'

'Aye, just yesterday arrived.' The Porter opened the gate for them, no longer seeming much interested in their doings. 'Ye'll find his rooms yonder,' he said, with a gesture so vague as, had they been genuinely in need of guidance, would have been worse than useless.

'I thank you,' Gray said cheerfully. 'Come along, then, Randal. Look alive.'

Sophie followed Gray through the gate and into the broad green quadrangle of Merlin College. Had they had leisure, she might have spent the next hour gazing about her at the weathered stone buildings with their mullioned windows, the statuary scattered about the walls, the few capped and gowned students crossing the velvet lawn – some with their arms already full of scrolls, or their faces buried in books – and revelling in the atmosphere of the place, heavy with magick, with a hunger for knowledge and discovery.

As it was, however, she scurried across the quad at Gray's heels, scarcely able to glance at all these wonders before they were past and gone. On the other side of the quad Gray led her through a long, arched tunnel and, opening a door in one of its walls, plunged them into a rabbit-warren of corridors and staircases. Though Sophie lost her sense of direction almost at once, Gray strode confidently forward, obviously in his element – as well he might be, having spent nearly four full years of his life within these walls.

'We shan't really be anywhere near—' she began.

'Of course not. But we know now that he is here, and we must be on our guard. Now, wait—'

Suddenly Gray disappeared through a door marked (in English, Français, Latin, and what Sophie supposed must be Cymric) *Junior Common Room*, emerging a moment or two later with his arms full of some dark, heavy stuff.

'Here.' He thrust half the bundle at her. 'Put this on.' As he spoke he was shrugging into what Sophie at last recognised as a commoner's gown: short and open-fronted, with two long black streamers to each shoulder in place of sleeves. Belatedly she tried to follow his example, only to become tangled in this second layer of unfamiliar haberdashery. Gray came to her rescue and lent his handkerchief to mop the perspiration from her face and neck, and before long two counterfeit Merlin undergraduates made their way along the corridors towards Master Alcuin's staircase.

This – their first goal – seemed to Gray almost anticlimactic: only the heavy oaken door of his tutor's rooms, before which he had stood, through which he had passed, a thousand times at least. Though never in quite the same circumstances, it was true.

He lifted a hand and rapped once, then three times in quick succession, then once again. He held his breath, waiting, sensing that Sophie, beside him, was doing the same. Would Master Alcuin help them? Would he – Gray experienced a moment of gut-twisting horror at his own stupidity – would he be in College to be asked?

There came muffled footsteps, then Master Alcuin's familiar voice: '*Quo vadis?* Have you no respect, whoever you are, for the sported oak?'

Gray put his face close to the aged wood and said, 'It's I, Magister – your scapegrace student. With a friend. May we come in?'

What might have been a gasp of surprise was followed by the familiar soft creak of the inner door; at last, ponderously, the oaken door began to open towards them, and they stepped back to avoid being knocked flat.

Master Alcuin saw Sophie-as-Arthur first, and looked puzzled; this was no student of his, no student, in fact, that he had ever seen before. 'Magister,' said Gray softly, and his former tutor looked up – for he was no more than two inches taller than Sophie – and saw him. This time Gray knew he had not imagined the gasp of shock he heard.

'*Marshall?*' the older man whispered. 'And who is this?'

'A friend,' Gray said, as quietly as he could. 'One you shall enjoy meeting, I assure you. But I think—'

'Of course, of course!' Master Alcuin's tone was the one he used when he was angry with himself for forgetting something very important – the name of one of the sons of Don, say, or an obscure Erse foretelling-spell. It transported Gray briefly to an era of his life which, by comparison, seemed idyllic.

Sophie tugged at his sleeve, bringing him back to reality; Master Alcuin was waving them through the door, glancing furtively about the landing outside his rooms. Gray sighed and followed them in. His mentor locked both doors behind them and at once filled the familiar enamelled welcome-cup.

CHAPTER XV

In Which Gray Encounters Surprise and Disbelief

Gray warded the room. Master Alcuin, in an apologetic murmur, warded it again, then, with the suddenness of a summer cloudburst, demanded, 'What, Marshall, in the name of Merlin himself, do you mean by coming here?'

Gray blanched, and for a moment Sophie was certain – despite their welcome – that they had made a dreadful mistake. 'I am constantly watched,' the don continued furiously. 'You might have called on almost anyone else without danger, but I—And *he* is here – here in Oxford, though not living in College, for he has brought a daughter with him, it appears – you are mad to come here, Marshall, you shall be discovered and—'

Gray and Sophie exchanged a look of mingled horror and relief: Master Alcuin was not concerned for his own safety, then, but for Gray's. Sophie's heart warmed towards this odd little man, to whom Gray had told her he already owed so much. *But Amelia is here,* she thought – not without wonder, for the Professor had always maintained the strictest separation between his family and the sacred groves of Oxford. *We might have run against her at any time yesterday, and been altogether undone . . .*

Master Alcuin now appeared to remark once again that Gray was not alone; his expostulations continued, not allowing either

Gray or Sophie, supposing her to be so inclined, any opportunity for reply. 'I should not have thought *you,* Marshall, foolish enough – inconsiderate enough – to involve an innocent bystander—'

Here, finally, Gray cut him off. 'Magister,' he said, 'I fear that Sophie is hardly an innocent bystander.'

Sophie elbowed him sharply; Master Alcuin at once turned to her, pale-blue eyes narrowed in suspicion.

'We are wasting time. Show him,' Gray ordered, and Sophie, with some relief, unbuttoned her waistcoat and relaxed into her natural shape. Her hair, long again and uncontrolled, tumbled wildly over her shoulders and into her eyes. As she shook it impatiently back from her face, Gray stared at her, his lips moving rapidly but silently, as though he were working some spell, and it struck her that this was almost the first time he had looked her in the eye since their leaving the inn.

Their host was almost hopping up and down in his excitement, questions tumbling from his lips faster than any human being could have answered them.

'Magister.' Sophie had heard Gray use the same kind but quelling tone on Joanna. 'Magister, please; there is much to tell you, and little time. If you will sit down, we shall explain everything.'

The elderly don did as he was bid, sinking slowly into a wing chair upholstered in threadbare blue velveteen; Gray and Sophie took two of the room's other three seats. 'Perhaps, Marshall,' said Master Alcuin after a moment, still staring at Sophie with a sort of awe, 'you will begin by introducing me to your friend.'

Gray looked at Sophie, who at once took matters into her own hands. 'My name is Sophie Callender,' she said.

The effect was immediate; had she chosen to tell the whole truth, Gray thought, Master Alcuin could hardly have been more shocked. 'It is true, then,' he said, shaking his white head. 'I had dismissed the tales as common-room gossip, yet here you are, together . . .'

'Not *quite* true,' Gray interposed. What exactly had the common-room gossip been? Some of the variations of themselves that they had collected during their journey had been positively scurrilous. 'Both of us fled the Professor's . . . *hospitality*, yes, but not alone, and not . . . this is not any sort of elopement. Our purpose, I fear, is a far less pleasant one.'

The tale, it seemed to him, grew more phantastickal and less plausible with every telling; by the time they had finished explaining their purpose (leaving aside, for the moment, the matter of Sophie's true identity), it would be astounding indeed if his mentor did not instantly throw them out. Master Alcuin listened intently, however, and seemed – though increasingly astonished – never to doubt their words.

'It is an almost incredible tale,' he said at last. 'In other circumstances, Marshall, I should be most disinclined to believe it. But there have been . . . peculiar doings here of late. Since receiving that letter of yours I have myself been under constant watch; there seem to be listening-spells everywhere I go, and out of doors I am followed. It is difficult to know why this should be, unless something very sinister be afoot.'

'You do believe us, then?' cried Sophie. 'You will help us?'

Master Alcuin smiled at her exactly as, on their first meeting some four years ago, he had smiled at a young and eager Gray.

'With all my heart, young lady,' he said, with rusty gallantry. 'I am at your service.'

Master Alcuin, as Gray had predicted, possessed his own copy of the *Sapientia Delphi*, so that they need not venture forth to the Library. It fell to Sophie – who could not read Greek – to unravel the codex cipher, while the others worked on Lord Carteret's diary, which Master Alcuin, hinting at a wealth of past experience with codes and ciphers, had pronounced to be a double substitution cipher. It was tedious work, and she often lost her count of the lines on a folio and had to begin again, but it pleased her to be doing something practical to thwart her stepfather.

The words came slowly – for such a small book, it had a great many pages – and it was not until she had deciphered the last of them that she set the *Sapientia Delphi* aside and looked at the whole of the translated message.

The first half of it – the half taken from the Professor's study – read,

Expect visit
Require proof that method prepared for test
Query girl as promised
Proof necessary to persuade old man

The second read,

He has the girl
Test will occur as planned
Make all necessary preparations
Upon his return be watchful
Send no answer

'Gray,' she said. 'Look.'

Both Gray and Master Alcuin left their work to examine her transcription.

'*He has the girl*?' said Master Alcuin in a puzzled tone. '*Query girl as promised*? *He* I suppose is Callender, given the circumstances, but who is the girl?'

Sophie and Gray exchanged a look. 'We cannot know,' said Gray after a moment, 'but it seems likely that the girl is Sophie.'

Master Alcuin frowned up at him, then down at Sophie.

'And what should Lord Carteret want with you, my dear?'

'I have not the least idea,' said Sophie, not altogether truthfully. She read over the messages again. '*Query girl as promised?*'

'A weakness of codex ciphers is the difficulty of punctuation,' said Master Alcuin.

And Gray: 'It is not *Query girl as promised* but *Girl as promised?*' His hand gripped Sophie's shoulder for just a breath. 'He came to Breizh to inspect you, I fear, as well as to satisfy himself that the Professor's *method*, whatever it is, was well in hand. It was a risk, that visit, but not the greatest he might have taken; anyone might reasonably choose that part of the kingdom for a holiday, and we may presume that he did not dispatch his message until he was safely away from Callender Hall.'

Sophie shivered. '*Proof necessary to persuade old man*,' she read. She could guess who was meant, and surely Gray could guess also; she hoped Master Alcuin would not. 'Whatever proofs he needed, we must suppose from the second message that he found them. And if the test is to *take place as planned . . .*'

'Then Lord Halifax is still their first target.' Gray's voice was grim.

Lord Carteret's diary, when at length Master Alcuin hit upon the correct combination of substitutions to decipher it, proved equally interesting. They had not rationally supposed that he would set down the details of a murderous conspiracy in pen and ink – it would be dangerous to risk anyone else's reading them, and he himself presumably did not need reminding – but he had done what was, for their purposes, the next best thing: the entries Gray had copied contained, interspersed with dyspeptic complaints about his journey and disparaging comments on the conduct of Breizhek servants and the tedium of country living, a number of brief self-directed memoranda:

Boy less stupid than C believes; girl perhaps even more so.
Biddable and dull. Mother?
C wavering? Not to be trusted. Direct M to watch.

Gray glanced from the transcript in his hand to Sophie's on the table. 'Lord Carteret's second message was directed to this *M*, then,' he said. 'And *M* must be someone here in Oxford, if he is charged with watching the Professor.'

W reports HM visiting Temple of Taranis.
W reports HM entertaining priestess of Arawn and E distressed.
HM et al. to Caernarfon Sept. Direct W to follow.
Girl remains doubtful but evidence satisfactory.
C insists method prepared. Direct M test to proceed as planned.

'This is proof, surely!' Sophie exclaimed.

'It is proof of something,' Master Alcuin said cautiously. 'It does little to enlighten us as to the nature of the threat, or its ultimate target, but it is indeed suggestive. Without the original document, however, it is not much better than hearsay. We might easily have fabricated these messages, and, as they are copies, scrying can tell us nothing.'

'*E is distressed*,' said Gray, 'as anyone might be by a priestess of Dread Arawn – he or she is connected to *HM*. And if *W* is following to Caernarfon—'

'But who is HM?' Sophie said. Then understanding dawned in her dark eyes as she added up the clues. 'Lord Carteret has set this *W* whoever he is, to spy upon the *King*?'

They stared at Gray's transcription, absorbing the implications of this, and of the words *Proof necessary to persuade old man*, and of the rumours they had heard at the Seven Sisters in Crookham. At last Sophie said, hesitatingly, 'You do not think that *he* is their next target?'

Gray felt like a terrier who has grasped the tail of a rat and found a rabid bear at the other end of it. 'I fear we can draw no other conclusion,' he said.

It was a testament to Master Alcuin's appreciation of the gravity of the circumstances, Gray reflected with a wry smile, that he did not spend the whole length of their journey to the Master's Lodge conducting a detailed enquiry into the precise workings of Sophie's magick. His former student could see very well that he was aching to do so, but instead he kept up the sort of inconsequential chatter to which any Senior Fellow might subject visitors or newcomers to Merlin: details of the College Charter; potted histories of the various *bâtiments*, statues, and other structures along their route; obscure facts relating to this or that College luminary and his discoveries, magickal and otherwise. Gray, to whom all of this was as familiar as his own name, scarcely listened, but 'Arthur' hung on Master Alcuin's every word, apparently following his characteristic mingling of English, Français, and Latin without difficulty, and again Gray was reminded of his own early student days. He had been just Sophie's age, then – a wide-eyed innocent, eager and shy together.

He trailed behind his companions, keeping his own eyes firmly above their heads, for if Arthur's face was an unsettling sight, Sophie in trousers was a thoroughly distracting one. Gray wondered that anyone could take her for a boy, even dressed as she was, and with that face on; despite her best efforts, she did not walk, or move, or stand, like anyone but her own dear self. It must be her magick that did the trick; was he, through close association, growing immune to its effects?

The Porter who kept the door of the Master's Lodge gave Gray and Sophie a narrow glance, but in the company of a Senior Fellow who came, as he said, on a matter of urgency for the Master's ears alone, they passed in without comment. The Master himself, it transpired, was taking tea alone in his study, and – a stroke of good fortune for which Gray silently thanked every god he could think of – would deign to see his visitors immediately.

Heart pounding, mouth dry, Gray followed Lord Halifax's superior manservant, Master Alcuin, and Sophie into the great man's study.

Selwyn, fifteenth Lord Halifax and Master of Merlin College, was a tall, imposing man of perhaps sixty years, with a mane of greying hair, a hawk's curved nose, and keen brown eyes. He looked to Sophie as though he should not suffer fools gladly. His study showed an odd mixture of tastes, or perhaps of histories: tall glazed cabinets covered most of the walls, filled with scrolls and codices, some obviously of great antiquity. Above these, secured by iron brackets all about the room, depended a collection of fearsome weaponry: several longswords and broadswords; a long pike; a grim, businesslike battle-axe. Sophie shuddered a little at this last; the Master of Merlin might be (as Gray had told her) a great and learned scholar, but if he chose to keep these things so close about him, she should not like to fall foul of the man's temper.

Temper, however, was not to be their difficulty.

Lord Halifax greeted Master Alcuin with a warm handclasp; he exchanged ceremonious bows with 'Dunstan' and 'Randal'; he frowned momentarily at Gray, as though wondering where he might have seen him before, and slowly dropped an eyelid at Sophie. Resuming his own seat, he gestured graciously for his guests to be seated also; they perched awkwardly on velveted sofas, Gray on one side and Master Alcuin and Sophie on the other.

Sophie had so much to do merely in remaining Arthur Randal that for some time she scarcely heard what was being said – until Gray's words pulled her back to reality: 'Not such proofs as might generally be recognised as such, my lord. I own they are more in the nature of deductions and inferences; the documents we have seen are copies, and name no names, but Master Alcuin agrees with me that the danger to you is genuine.'

It sounded absurd, and Gray must know it, but his tone remained confident, his gaze earnestly fixed on the powerful man before him. Sophie listened, impressed by his composure, as – still firmly in the character of Ned Dunstan, student in good standing of Marlowe College, whom no one had ever believed guilty in a violent death – he relayed the results of their various overhearings, the documents they had deciphered, and the testimony of a scry-mage (whose identity he skilfully evaded mentioning) as to the Professor's intent.

'It happens, my lord,' Gray continued, 'that a former student of Master Alcuin's is one of those on whose information our account relies. He has had the ill fortune to be suspected by Professor Callender, of knowing what he ought not; and as Master Alcuin will confirm, since receiving a letter on the subject from this man, sent from the Professor's country estate, he has been watched, and followed, both in College and in the town.'

'This is quite true, my lord.'

'And what of the student himself?' Lord Halifax enquired of Master Alcuin.

'I regret, my lord, that I may not name the man in question,' the latter replied. 'I have made a promise to that effect. But I may and do assure you that he is a man on whose integrity you may rely absolutely.'

Sophie fancied that Gray sat a little straighter.

Lord Halifax made no reply to this; instead he turned to Gray and said, 'The substance of your theory, then, is a conspiracy by Oxford Fellows and men at Court, whose goal is murder and possible regicide, and the presiding genius of this dread scheme is none other than Appius Callender.'

Sophie had feared that Lord Halifax must see their tale for the tissue of lies it was, but instead – worse – he threw back his head and laughed.

'Callender!' he said, still chuckling. 'This is good luck indeed! Of all men, I think I should best prefer that it be he who plots my downfall. An excellent joke, young Dunstan.'

'My lord, he has been ever your enemy,' Master Alcuin reminded his superior; his tone held a note of reproach.

'He has,' said Lord Halifax, sobering a little, 'and he has been ever a pompous, small-minded fool – he has not the wit, I think, to be anything more. It has always puzzled me, frankly, that he should ever have achieved either a doctor's robes or a Professorship. I do not doubt that he would very much enjoy plotting my death, and – who knows? – perhaps that of His Majesty as well. I should be very much astonished, however, if he should succeed in arranging either. You may depend, I think, on its being all a fanciful project of self-aggrandisement.'

The Master of Merlin sat back in his chair, folding together his long, sensitive fingers. 'Alcuin,' he said, smiling kindly, 'and you young men, I thank you for your concern for my welfare; I am touched indeed. I assure you, however, that I am quite safe, and beg you will not worry yourselves further on my account.'

It was unmistakably a dismissal. Sophie was half inclined towards one last, desperate outpouring of truth, in order to convince him, but what could she do but tell him what Gray had left out? And this would be a desperate stroke indeed; now he was amused, but if he should discover their deception, and, worse yet, the clandestine intrusion of a *woman* into Merlin's sacred groves . . .

Lord Halifax's manservant showed them out, and they retreated with all seemly haste to Master Alcuin's rooms. The latter again took up his informative patter, but his heart seemed no longer in it – nor could Sophie contrive to rekindle her fascination of only an hour before.

As she trailed the two men back through the oaken door, Master Alcuin stretched up to whisper something to Gray, who stooped down to hear him. 'Your *cariadferch* has done you a world of good, my boy,' he murmured, and Sophie, straining her ears, frowned at the unfamiliar word. 'You stand much straighter now than you used, and your stammer has quite gone.'

Quite unaccountably, Gray's ears went pink.

Gray slumped dejectedly into the long-legged wheelback chair he had been used to frequent as an undergraduate, which seemed to sigh a little and welcome him back into its embrace. 'I brought that humiliation on all of us myself, I suppose,' he said.

'Ought we to have told him the whole truth?' Sophie asked, hesitant. She had taken off her coat and rolled her shirtsleeves up to her elbows, and sat perched on the edge of an armchair with her chin in her hands. 'He must have been angry, I know, but perhaps he might have been . . . startled into considering the threat more seriously . . .'

Gray sighed and ran a hand through his hair. 'I was so *certain*,' he said, disgusted with himself. 'How could I have thought—?'

'That is quite enough, Marshall.' He had rarely heard Master Alcuin speak so sharply. 'Self-pity does no good to anyone. We must think what is best to do.'

'I must go back again, of course.' Gray had not meant to express his impatience so clearly. 'The question is—'

He stopped abruptly. What ailed him, that he should be prey to such stupidity? It was not only for the *Sapientia Delphi* that they had wanted Master Alcuin's bookshelves.

'Magister!' He caught feverishly at his tutor's sleeve. 'Have you still your collection of works on poisons?'

Sophie busied herself at the hearth and in Master Alcuin's spartan pantry, producing at length a pot of tea and a plate of bread-and-butter. She was not particularly hungry, but after an hour's frustrating attempts to help in the search for whatever the others might be looking for, it had seemed wiser to make some other use of herself. To find herself, in any collection of three people, the one most inclined to such domesticity, ought to have amused her; as it was, she was merely flustered and annoyed by her burnt fingers indifferent success, and regretted that she had not appreciated Mrs Wallis as she ought.

Carefully, balancing a heavy wooden tray laden with teapot and crockery and the heaping plate of bread-and-butter, she shouldered open the door of the study. The hinges creaked, but the sound drew no notice from the two men who sat on either side of the desk, leaning their elbows on strata of open codices and half-unravelled scrolls. Master Alcuin absently wound the end of his beard round one finger, first one way and then the other; Gray held a fistful of hair in his right hand, on which rested the weight of his head, and chewed the knuckle of his left forefinger in an abstracted manner. Sophie cleared her throat, to no effect.

'Master Alcuin. Gray,' she said loudly. 'I have made tea. Shall I pour some out for you?'

At hearing their names both of them jumped, and despite herself Sophie had to suppress a chuckle at the symmetry of their movements.

'I should very much like some tea, Miss Sophie,' Master Alcuin said after a moment, rising from his seat and smiling at her with anxious eyes. 'And I thank you. I daresay it would do us all good to rest from our labours for a little.'

'Yes,' said Gray, who was staring again. 'It is here somewhere, I know, but we can neither of us find it, and my eyes are quite . . .' He rubbed at them with one hand.

Sophie set out to pour the tea, only to remember that she had not been able to find any milk. As she began to apologise, their host waved a hand at her and said, 'Please, do not trouble yourself; I shall fetch the milk.' He murmured something under his breath and held out his right hand; there was a small sound from the direction of the pantry, and a moment later a small crockery milk-jug sailed through the door and floated neatly onto his outstretched palm. Sophie grinned, delighted. 'An unseen summoning! You must teach me to do that next,' she told Gray.

'Must you, Magister?' Gray rebuked his teacher, but there was the ghost of a smile in his eyes. He helped himself to a slice of bread-and-butter, appearing not to notice that the bread was an inch thick at one end, and almost translucent at the other.

Whilst they munched and sipped contentedly, Sophie, teacup in hand, drifted over to the desk and began idly turning pages. A small, ancient-looking codex had become almost entirely buried under its larger fellows, so that only a corner protruded from the mass; curious, she tugged at it gently. When at last it came free, she regarded its hand-tooled leather binding with a shock of recognition.

'I have seen this book before!' Sophie exclaimed, holding up a little leather-covered codex, crumbling at the edges. 'In the library at Callender Hall. Not *this* book, I mean, but another copy of the same one. I remember noticing it because—'

Gray swallowed a mouthful of bread-and-butter and deposited his half-empty cup precariously on the top of a bookcase. 'What is it?' he demanded, holding out his hand. 'Let me see.' Master Alcuin had put down his cup, too, and come to look over Sophie's shoulder. 'Fascinating,' he said. 'I believed this to be the only copy extant.'

Silently she handed over the book, and Gray looked at it in consternation, for he too had seen it before, atop a stack of codices on the Professor's desk in Breizh. '*Treatise* . . . *on the uses of* . . . what is that word? *both* . . . *and* . . . *deadly*? . . .' Defeated by his imperfect knowledge of the language, he returned the book to Sophie and enquired penitently, 'Could you translate, please?'

She smiled a little. 'Your Brezhoneg has improved,' she commented, and then turned her attention to the volume in her hand. '*Treatise on the uses of poisons, both noxious and deadly, with the methods of procuring and compounding them . . .*' she read. 'It is the only book in this language that I ever saw in the Professor's library that was not my mother's, and the only book of any sort devoted to poisons. And when last I looked for it – I had read only a little of it, you see, and meant to read the rest – it was not there. I thought it mislaid, but suppose the Professor had taken it, like the *Sapientia Delphi*?'

'He had,' said Gray. 'I saw it in his study, whilst I was—' He cast a guilty glance at Master Alcuin, and cleared his throat. 'During Lord Carteret's visit to Callender Hall.'

'Then . . . you think the "method" Lord Carteret speaks of is something in this book?' Sophie turned it over, then back again.

'Well,' said Gray, 'why else should he have such a book? I have never known him to take any interest in poisons, or seen any books on the subject in his rooms here, and by your own account he had none in Breizh either. And I think we may be sure that poisoning is what they plan. We know that they wish to ensure that no connexion is apparent between themselves and Lord Halifax's death, and what other sort of *method* could possibly take such a time to prepare, or—?'

Oh. *Oh.*

'Whatever Taylor and Woodville were after,' he said, 'on the night Gautier died, was something the Professor needed for . . . *this.* Something he could not otherwise acquire without arousing suspicion.'

'The name of this one means "heart's delight",' said Sophie, some three-quarters of an hour and twenty pages later; she underlined the words with a finger as she read. Absorbed in the work of translating, she was so close to Gray that his every breath brought him the faint, heady lavender-and-rosemary scent of her hair. Master Alcuin sat at her other side, taking rapid notes of Sophie's translations.

'A sort of horrible joke, I suppose,' she went on. 'The victim's heart, it says, "will appear to have stopped quite naturally"; a few drops only are needed, and it can be given in any draught of wine, ale, or mead.'

'If that is so,' said Master Alcuin, 'we have found the Golden Fleece of poisoners.'

'"To brew it requires—"' Sophie paused, frowning; after a moment her expression cleared, and she continued: '"To brew it requires three separate distillations, carried out over a period of several weeks or months . . ."'

As he listened, a series of hitherto baffling details slipped into place in Gray's mind, and he went cold with dread.

'. . . *too much groundwork left to lay* . . .'

'"Many of the ingredients are readily available,"' Sophie read, '"but three there are that may be more difficult to obtain: the fox-glove, which must be fresh and not dried or otherwise preserved; the distilled venom of . . ." Whatever can that be? Oh – "of the *Africk cobra*" – I should not like to think how one obtains *that*; and . . .' She paused again, evidently puzzled, and Gray's feeling of dread deepened so that he half expected his teeth to begin chattering. 'Look at this word,' she invited, 'and see if it looks like Cymric or Kernowek or . . .'

Gray looked, and thought, and clamped his lips shut against a rising wave of nausea.

'*A great pity your students failed you so badly, Professor . . . I know that you were counting on them to provide—*'

To provide what?

The answer presented itself to Gray's mind in the form of

Henry Taylor, clasping a carved teakwood box protectively against his chest.

'Yes,' he said bleakly. 'It could certainly have been that.'

Master Alcuin leant across to look at the place marked by Sophie's finger. He blanched and clasped his hands together. 'Do you truly believe this, Marshall?' His voice was low and urgent. 'Are you absolutely certain? To accuse a Senior Fellow of such barbarity—'

'We have accused him already of plotting murder, regicide, and treason, sir,' Gray reminded him.

'What barbarity do you mean?' Sophie demanded.

They looked at her, and then at each other; neither spoke. 'The man has been my father – well, stepfather – these sixteen years,' Sophie said caustically. 'I should like to believe I know the worst of him already. Tell me: what does that word mean?'

There was silence for some moments; and at last Gray said, very softly, 'It is Old Cymric. It means "beating heart".'

CHAPTER XVI

In Which Several Persons Are Unpleasantly Surprised

Sophie regarded the two pallid, green-tinged countenances before her, and her outrage at their secretiveness vanished in the face of this new horror. '"Beating heart",' she repeated, in an appalled whisper. 'Does this mean . . . must it be . . . ?' She could not quite bring herself to speak the word *human.*

The little leather-bound codex was still in her hand. Abruptly horrified by the very sight of it, she flung it across the desk and stood up, backing away and scrubbing her hands against her trousers like a child.

'Taylor had it,' Gray said, in the same low, despairing tone. 'The night the Professor sent us into the town. Taylor and Woodville were the only ones trusted to go into the place; the rest of us stood watch, outside the door and in the street below. I believe they had a great deal of coin with them, and so they must have done, if I am right, and there was murder done that night . . . When they came out again, Taylor was carrying something else' – here his long fingers mimed carrying something small and delicate – 'and he told us we must make haste. It was abuzz with magick . . . spelled, I suppose, to keep it . . . beating.' They all shuddered. 'Did Taylor and Woodville . . . ?' His throat worked; he wet his lips. 'They *must* have known – may the gods all curse them! If only I had asked –

demanded – but we were set upon in the street almost at once . . .'

Sophie had sat down again, feeling as ill as the others looked. Gray gave her a grim sort of half smile. 'I remember now that I heard one of them say we must be up to "nasty magicks". It was truer than I should ever have thought. Apollo, Pan, and Hecate!' he exclaimed suddenly, both fists striking the desk with a deafening crash. 'Taylor dared lay Gautier's death to my account. Yet he *knew* what we were after doing, all the time he knew . . . I wonder all the rest of us did not die that night, once we had served our purpose.'

Sophie stared at him, seeing but not quite crediting the gleam of tears in his eyes.

'We must go back again and warn him,' she said after a moment. 'Lord Halifax, I mean. But what if he still will not listen?'

Master Alcuin sighed. 'Then we shall at least have done our best,' he said grimly.

Gray drew one shirtsleeve across his eyes and sat back in his chair to look at both of them. 'I shall go alone, then,' he said. 'Sophie, Master Alcuin will see you safely back to the inn, and I shall join you—'

'No.' Sophie cut him off. 'We go together, or not at all.'

He began to protest but was again interrupted: 'She is quite right, Marshall,' said Master Alcuin. 'Whatever shielding-charm you carry may be ample protection against the general run of mankind, but Merlin College is full of powerfully talented mages. It is only Miss Sophie's concealing magick that protects you here. To leave these rooms without her would be slow suicide.'

Sophie stared; he gave her a half smile and an apologetic shrug. 'Seeing magick is a gift of mine,' he explained. 'And yours, young lady, is astonishingly strong. At another time, I hope you will permit me to—'

'*Tempus fugit*, Magister,' said Gray.

'Of course,' said Sophie. 'Time does fly, indeed, and we ought to get on. We ought to take all of this, I think,' she added, picking up the Brezhoneg book again with considerable reluctance and gathering up the ciphered documents and their transcriptions. 'It is not exactly proof, but . . .'

Silently Gray took the book and the papers from her and stowed them all in some hidden pocket, or pockets, of his coat.

'Magister,' he said, 'do you come or stay?'

In the moonlight, Sophie and Gray parted from Master Alcuin under the archway nearest his rooms, all of them hoping that their nearly silent, nearly invisible shadow would choose to follow him on his innocent errand to the Porter's Lodge, and not the two of them on their more delicate quest. He would go and return, he assured them, lingering only long enough to present a plausible appearance, and on returning would continue to search his books for anything that might counter the poison's effects.

More quickly even than before they crossed the College grounds, spurred by an inarticulable urgency.

They had been debating how best to approach the doorkeeper when they reached what ought to have been his domain and found his post deserted, the door completely unguarded. Sophie shivered and scratched her nose, which had suddenly begun to itch furiously. 'There's magick about,' she murmured, and Gray nodded; he was shivering, too, and rubbing the back of his neck with one hand.

The Master's Lodge was silent and dark – a darkness more profound than ought to have been possible on such a moonlit night. In the corridor, Sophie collided with Gray when he suddenly stopped; both of them pitched forward, and they tumbled together onto the floor.

They picked themselves up, knocking against one another in the gloom. Two voices murmured, one after the other, '*Adeste luces!*'; two small, soft globes of light spurted upwards, illuminating the cause of their difficulty: Lord Halifax's manservant, asleep in a high-backed chair, his legs outstretched across the corridor between them and the door by which they had entered. One of the lights vanished; Sophie looked up and her eyes met Gray's, wide with fright. 'Put out your light, for the gods' sake,' he hissed, and hastily she obeyed, plunging the corridor back into utter blackness.

The servant gave a gentle snore.

Gray clasped her hand and pulled her to her feet. Clinging together, they felt their way cautiously along the corridor. At length Sophie saw a gleam of unsteady light; as they stumbled towards it, it seemed to stretch and lengthen, until she recognised it as a line of firelight under a closed door.

It was perhaps foolish, she thought afterwards, to have opened the door, but open it Gray did, before either of them had given any thought to what might lie on the other side.

They were in the Master's study.

And there he sat, in the same large, velvety armchair by the fire which he had occupied that afternoon, with an empty plate and wine-glass on the little table at his elbow. For a moment Sophie thought that, like his man, he only slept; the hawk-like face was relaxed, the drooping lids closed over the penetrating brown eyes, and one hand hung limp over the arm of the chair. But it was all very still, too still, too silent; a growing unease propelled her across the too-warm room to Lord Halifax's side.

Gray was there before her, his longer legs covering the distance in a mere three strides; he touched the Master's arm, his shoulder, and held a hand briefly before his face. The slight motion disturbed the tableau of peaceful sleep, and the man's head lolled horribly sideways, his mouth falling open.

Sophie sprang back in horror just as Gray said, quite unnecessarily, 'He is dead.'

The cold iron fingers of panic closed about her heart. 'We must not stay here,' she whispered urgently. 'Come away, Gray, please. We can do nothing for him now.'

But he did not move; he seemed rooted to the spot, staring fixedly at what remained of the man whose life they had tried to save.

By turns cajoling and commanding, Sophie did her best to shift Gray from his paralysis. Her words seemed to wash over him, utterly without effect, and she grew increasingly anxious, dread chilling her from the inside out.

'*Think*, Gray,' she pleaded, tugging at his arm. 'Here we are, alone with a new-made corpse – and a book of poisons in your coat-pocket. How will it look—?'

He turned at last and looked down at her, torment written on his face. 'We might have saved him,' he whispered raggedly. 'I might have saved him. But he thought it all a great jest, and now . . .'

Frantic now, Sophie tightened her hold on his arm and leant back with all her weight, trying to drag him bodily towards the door. Desperation must have lent her strength, for she succeeded somehow in conveying herself and him across the room and nearly over the threshold.

But as her boot-heel struck the stone door-sill, there was a soft hiss, and a . . . *something* . . . descended on them both.

Sophie found to her dismay that she could scarcely move; she was weighed down by an overpowering lethargy, and all her limbs felt profoundly heavy and slow, as though she moved through deep water – or perhaps through treacle. Her nose itched more furiously than ever, but she could not seem to lift her hand to scratch it. The sensation of weight was not unpleasant, exactly; or it would not have been, had she not been so thoroughly terrified.

Turning her head, with considerable effort, to the right, she saw that Gray was similarly afflicted. He had closed his eyes and seemed to be murmuring something under his breath – whether spell or prayer or a string of curses, Sophie could scarcely guess.

'Well,' said a familiar voice behind them. Sophie's heart seemed to miss a beat, before a surge of anger set it pounding harder than ever. 'As well we thought to provide ourselves some insurance.'

Heavy footsteps approached, then stopped. In the next instant, with a sound like the tearing of silk, whatever spell had been holding them in thrall evaporated; there was a sharp intake of breath, and Sophie spun round, her left hand reaching for Gray's, to face the intruders.

'*You!*' gasped her father.

But he was not looking at her.

'I.' Gray surprised himself by speaking the monosyllable with perfect clarity. He let go of Sophie's hand and tried to push her behind him, to have his height and bulk between her and this new danger. She edged away, back and to the left, until he could not see her even from the corner of his eye. Willing her to conceal herself somewhere safe – and certain that she would not do so, whatever he said to her – he folded his arms and stared down at their would-be captors: Professor Callender and another red-robed Senior Fellow, as pale and gaunt as the Professor was ruddy and stout.

Almost before Gray spoke, however, the flash of outraged recognition on the Professor's face had given way to a puzzled frown; both he and his companion looked at Gray in apparent confusion. 'But it is not he – not Marshall after all,' the Professor muttered. 'Yet he looked so very like . . . Then who in Hades *is* this fellow?'

Puzzled for a moment himself, Gray nearly laughed aloud as recognition dawned. *Well played, Sophie!* He silently exulted.

But it quickly became clear that, in the circumstances, going unrecognised was of only limited use.

If Professor Callender was discomposed, his friend was not.

'Who are you?' he demanded of Gray. 'And what do you do here, at such an hour?'

Another link in the chain, thought Gray, recognising the basso voice. *Now, if only I knew who he is!*

'I might ask the same of you, Doctor . . .'

About to fall into the trap, the thin man stopped himself just in time. 'An undergraduate,' he snapped, 'dares question a Senior Fellow? Answer, boy! Who are you, and what do you here?'

'Dunstan,' said Gray, 'of Marlowe College. As for my business here, it is none of yours, sir.' Who would have supposed him capable of such exhilarating insolence?

The Professor had by now contrived to insinuate himself through the doorway and around Gray; from beside Lord Halifax's armchair, he produced a gasp of assumed surprise that would not have taken in a child: 'The Master! The Master has been taken ill!'

'He is *dead*,' said Gray bitterly, turning round, 'as you must know, sir, if you have looked at all.'

Perhaps Sophie's concentration had faltered for a moment; perhaps her magick could not disguise a voice so easily as a face. Whatever the event, the Professor's next words made it clear that he would no longer mistake his target. 'So it is Marshall, indeed; I might have known it. Is there nothing you will not poke your ugly nose into, boy?'

He raised one hand, drew a bolt of flame out of the air, and flung it at Gray.

Sophie had crept nearly all round the walls of the Master's study, frantically seeking any sort of egress; but the room's bow-window had no visible latch, and there was only that single door, with their adversaries between themselves and it. *We shall have to slink past them, somehow – or* make *them let us go . . .*

The fire-bolt aimed at Gray took her by surprise; she had had no notion that her father knew any battle magicks. Even if he knew only this one, it was one more than either Gray or herself.

Gray dodged out of the way, and the flame struck the door-jamb and set it smouldering. But another followed it, and another, and almost at once the Professor's friend joined the fray. Though managing to dodge many of the flames, hailstones, and small lightning-bolts that came at him, or to deflect them with some small shielding-spell of his own, Gray was visibly losing ground to his opponents.

Sophie crouched behind the sofa, clutching the damp handkerchief in her pocket like some talisman, and tried to shield him. She had only the vaguest idea how such protection might be accomplished – the library at Callender Hall being long on theory but short on practicalities – and little time to consider the problem; she did know how to conceal things, however, and this she tried with all her might to do. In the present case, however, it did not answer; though some missiles missed their target, more did not.

Something struck Gray's left shoulder, and he staggered; Sophie winced. *If only we had something to fling back at them . . . !*

Then, of a sudden, she remembered what she had seen on the walls above the bookcases – now but half visible in the increasing haze.

'Gray! Up there – on the walls!' she hissed, willing him to hear and understand – and the others to remain oblivious. Had he seen the armoury above their heads? Would he remember it?

The Professor and his accomplice indeed took no notice of her, but neither did Gray, preoccupied by the flurry of pebbles called down on his head by an ill-aimed lightning-bolt. He spoke a word that Sophie did not recognise, and the pebbles burst into dust, setting all three combatants coughing.

It is up to me, then. She took a deep breath and tried to remember everything she knew of seen and unseen summonings. *The spell is only an* aide-mémoire . . . *still, I should feel better if I knew a truly powerful one.*

A line of Gaius Aegidius wavered before her closed eyes. She opened them for a moment, grinning fiercely, then shut them tight, constructed a mental image of the long pike that she remembered seeing hung above the door, and stretched out both arms in what seemed the likeliest direction. '*Accedete*,' she whispered, reaching with all her magick and willing the weapon to her hands.

There was a creaking, splintering sound above Gray's head, and he glanced up to see one of the Master's antique weapons – a ten-foot pike, its iron tip rusted with age but still grimly pointed – pulling away the metal brackets that held it to the wall. As he and his antagonists paused in open-mouthed amazement, the heavy pole-arm flew across the smoke-clouded room and slammed into Sophie's outstretched hands.

She staggered but, letting the haft slide through her hands until its butt struck the floor, managed to stay upright. 'Gray!' she called hoarsely.

The Professor's gaze snapped round to her at the sound of her voice, but did not linger.

Gray crossed the room in two strides; she thrust the weapon towards him and he took it, hefting it as he might have held a pitchfork or a rake. It was heavy and unwieldy, and he had no real notion of its proper use. The two Senior Fellows, however – so close to triumph a moment ago – now looked very worried.

The Professor backed away. The gaunt man raised both hands; the Professor followed suit; their lips began to move, and a breeze gathered, sweeping about the room first gently, then with increasing force. The bookcases that lined the walls crashed open; glass shattered, and scrolls and codices and even loose shelves took flight, winging towards Gray and Sophie.

The first object to connect struck Gray full in the side of the head, and again he staggered, the tip of the pike dipping nearly to the floor. He heard an inarticulate howl, and fear clutched at him: *What have they done to Sophie?* When he regained his footing, he saw her well and whole, but her face was starkly white, her eyes huge and black, and tendrils of black hair writhed about her head like Medusa's snakes. Only once before had he seen her in such a fury.

This time, at any rate, I shall know what to expect.

The wind howled about them, flinging ancient and precious books in all directions, slamming them against furniture and walls till they began to break apart.

Hefting the pike, in trembling hands, so that its tip was level with the Professor's chest, Gray advanced across the room. The Professor left off hurling books and returned to hurling gouts of flame.

Gray saw rather than felt a flame sear the cuff of his coat; another ignited a flock of disarranged pages as they drifted past, then flared into ash. He swung his weapon round – it seemed to move achingly slowly – until the staff connected with the older man's outstretched left arm. There was a sickening crunch. The Professor shrieked in pain, lurched sideways, and then sat down in a heap on the floor.

His companion seemed at last to have remarked the existence of Sophie and was advancing on her cautiously, as though he feared she might bite him. She spoke a summoning-spell Gray was sure he had never taught her, and the poker from the fireplace behind her flew into her hand; Gray, averting his eyes from the fainting Professor, shouldered his own weapon and moved behind the other man. 'There are two of us,' he said quietly, 'before and behind, and only one of you. We know how you killed the Master, and what you mean to do next. Will you—?'

'I think not,' the older man snarled, wheeling about to fling another bolt of flame at Gray.

Gray sidestepped it, or nearly, and brought the pike up again. The wind abruptly died, and dozens of books fell to the floor, some of them smouldering and smoking; then, before he could react, Gray was trapped in a tight circle of flames higher than his head, half deafened by their crackle and roar. Through it he vaguely saw the thin man turning back to Sophie, his lips moving again to work the gods knew what dreadful spell.

Perhaps the flames are an illusion, Gray thought hopefully, though their heat was drying his eyes and baking his skin. He thrust the pike forward through the wall of fire; the staff burst into flame, burning his hands and setting his sleeves alight, and he was forced to drop it. The flames around him thickened and grew, till he could see almost nothing.

A howl of rage erupted from outside the fire-ring. While Gray tried frantically to discern what might have happened, that uncanny wind gathered again, now sweeping sparks and fragments of parchment about the room; all round him he heard the shiver and burst of shattering glass.

Then came a massive ripple of magick, and an almighty crash.

'Gray!' Sophie shouted. 'Gray, can you hear me?'

'Sophie!' Gray shrugged his coat up over his head, took a deep breath, shut his eyes, and dived blindly towards the sound of her voice. The heat was astonishing, but his passage through it mercifully brief; at the end of it Gray found Sophie, her face smeared with blood, standing amidst a very sea of broken glass.

'Come,' she said urgently, dragging him forward by the hand. Glass crunched under their boots. 'He will see us in a moment – I threw the poker at him, but it was only a glancing blow – *now*, Gray. Through the window!'

The oblong panes had shattered and the leads warped or even melted. Gray and Sophie clambered onto the wide sill and stood for a moment staring out into the darkness of the Master's garden. But it was only a moment, for behind them came a furious shout of 'Halt!'

Gray's coat wrapped about his forearm made a bludgeon to swing at the abused leads, and they parted like rotted wood.

He reached for Sophie's hand – turned to look for her – 'Sophie!'

'I shall not be a moment!' she called, breathless, from somewhere in the haze. A heart-stopping moment later she reappeared, jingling as she ran. In another moment the two of them were through the erstwhile window, out into the garden and running for their lives, with bellows of 'Proctors! The Proctors to me!' echoing in their ears.

Once over the low garden wall they paused under the shelter of a vast weeping beech tree, where Gray called the faintest light he could manage and they stood gasping for breath and staring at each other in its dim glow. Blood still streamed from Sophie's nose, dripping down to stain her collar and mingle with soot, ash, and plaster dust on the front of her ruined commoner's gown. She swiped one forearm across her face, seeming not to mark the smears on the sleeve of her coat.

'The Professor,' she said tremulously, 'is he . . . he is not *dead*?'

'No,' said Gray firmly. He coughed, his throat raw from the heat and smoke. 'Perhaps he fainted; I – I believe his arm is broken.'

'Thank all the gods,' said Sophie, who looked as miserably ill as Gray felt. 'He was warm, when I touched him – but he did not stir, and I thought—'

'*Touched* him? What possessed you?' said Gray. 'His companion was already calling for the Proctors—'

She put her hand into the pocket of her coat and brought out a ring of keys. 'I took these from his pocket,' she said. 'He always keeps them in the same one. I thought – we succeeded so ill in convincing Lord Halifax of the danger to his life, that I fear we shall have no luck at all in persuading His Majesty, without some proof of what they mean to do—'

Gray was torn between admiration of her presence of mind and retrospective terror – what if she had been caught in the act? 'That was very well thought of,' he managed to say. 'We must go quickly if we are to have any time to search.'

He let his small magelight die away. Clasping Sophie's hand, that she might more easily follow him in the dark, he peered out through the hanging boughs; seeing no one abroad, he pulled her after him back out into the night.

CHAPTER XVII

In Which Sophie and Gray Encounter Further Difficulties

'*What's the hour?*' Sophie whispered.

'Nearly midnight, I should think,' said Gray. 'Softly – I heard footsteps just now.'

Their progress was slow and erratic; the distance from the Master's Lodge to Professor Callender's rooms was not very great, but they were both so battered and fatigued that they could not go far without rest, and so dreaded pursuit that they flinched at every small night-time sound.

The footsteps came closer. Gray and Sophie crouched behind a statue of some Saxon king, so weathered that his face was a smooth oval, and waited for their owner to pass: a College Proctor with a magelight lantern – whether alerted by the Professor and his friend, or merely patrolling the grounds as usual, it scarcely mattered. Concealing magick was all very well, but solid stone, *ceteris paribus*, must be safer.

The Proctor paused a moment, perilously near, looking about him with narrowed eyes while Gray held his breath, desperately smothering a cough; then he shook his head and passed on.

The night was darker now; tattered clouds had blown in, by turns covering and revealing the moon. It had grown colder, too, and the air smelt of impending rain.

Gray shivered and suppressed a cough. His shirt and waistcoat were soaked through with perspiration, and in the chill air they clung unpleasantly to his skin. Sophie moved closer to him as they emerged from behind their stone protector; she too was shivering, and he hoped that she was only cold.

Her tangled, dirty hair smelt of soot and ashes; her clothes were singed and torn and bloodied, the purloined commoner's gown spotted with burnt-out holes and hanging limply from her shoulders. She coughed quietly, further muffling the sound by pressing her face into the crook of her elbow. Gray himself was in little better case – bedraggled and dirty, bone weary, his chest tight and aching, his throat raw. *If only one could lie down and sleep just a little . . .*

'Come along,' he whispered, taking Sophie's icy hand in his. 'This way.'

To gain entrance to the Professor's staircase they must traverse a grassy quad, some fifty paces across, with open archways to the left and right. In daylight, on legitimate business, a matter of moments; in their present circumstances, a tense, prolonged, perilous exposure, all the while waiting for a Proctor or a Senior Fellow to pass by or for someone not yet abed to spy them from an upstairs window. Still they might have passed unnoticed, had they not so lately survived a conflagration.

The wind freshened, driving ever thicker clouds across the face of the moon and plunging the College farther into obscurity; the air grew steadily colder, and each breath Gray drew caught in his smoke-roughened throat and threatened a new fit of coughing. Throat, lungs, and rib cage burned with the effort of keeping silence.

As they left the shelter of the wall, a gust of wind tore across the quad, scattering fallen leaves and rattling branches. Assaulted by the chill blast, Gray inhaled sharply; the cold air convulsed his lungs, and he bent almost double, racked with tearing coughs.

Sophie's arms went about his shoulders, and she whispered urgently in his ear, but what she said he could not distinguish.

Until, finally straightening and drawing a cautious breath, he heard the heavy, rapid footfalls approaching from the left side of the courtyard.

'*Now*, Gray!' Sophie hissed, tugging at his arm.

He caught her hand again, and they ran, but too late: 'You, there, boyo! Stop where yez are!' shouted the Proctor's bulldog rounding the turn into the quad. It did not occur to Gray to obey the order, but the man's next words, carried on the wind, stopped him in his tracks: 'Oi! Cleaver! Swithin! 'Tis yon long lad as Proctor Morris axed us to watch for! Look alive, men!'

More footfalls thundered towards the quad.

Sophie was staring at him, aghast, and he could well imagine what she must be thinking. He groped with his fingers for the shielding-charm tied about his wrist – had it been somehow damaged or disabled? – and found no charm there at all, only a circlet of burn-blisters where the silk cord had been seared away. Previously unremarked amidst his other hurts, they flowered into pain at his touch, and he set his teeth on a silent howl.

And there was Sophie still beside him, clutching at his hand, and three bulky Proctors arraying themselves across the quad to block their escape. 'Run, Sophie!' he urged, frantic with worry. 'They do not see you yet; you might still—'

She glared at him. 'No more do they see you,' she interrupted, sounding angry. 'Look.'

Gray did so – and was astonished to see the three men revolving on their heels, their faces screwed up in frank bewilderment. 'Where in 'Ades . . . ?' one of them began.

As if on cue, Gray's abused throat and lungs rebelled again, and this time, her body's endurance clearly at an end, Sophie joined in the choking cacophony. Though the noisy interlude was brief, when Gray looked up again he could see plainly enough that the Proctor's men were no longer fooled.

The closest was only thirty paces away; if Gray and Sophie tried to reach her father's rooms, they would be followed there and taken at once. On the other hand . . .

'There is another way out,' he hissed. He could breathe more easily now, he found. Still holding fast to Sophie's hand, he sprinted towards the entry to the Professor's staircase.

There was no time for Sophie to wonder where on earth Gray might be leading her, and when such a thought did try to obtrude itself, she quashed it sternly; here they were on his home ground. Now at least, with no one about to see them, she could abandon her increasingly erratic efforts at concealment. Still it was difficult not to protest when, after a mad serpentine dash up and down staircases, in and out of doors, she found herself face-to-face with a high stone wall, devoid of any evident foothold.

But Gray, somehow, was halfway up already; before Sophie could say anything at all he had shed his gown, scaled the wall, and flattened himself along the top, dangling the heavy black cloth down towards her as a sort of makeshift rope. Steeling herself, Sophie took hold of its lower edge with both hands and began to climb.

The wall was rougher-textured than she had first thought, and she found, in fact, plenty of footholds, but her blistered feet ached, her breath came short in her lungs, and when at length she reached the top she was gasping and dizzy with pain. Arms clasped about her knees, she crouched atop the wall – surprised to find it nearly two feet thick – and concentrated on slowing her rapid, ragged breathing.

At length Gray, now crouched beside her on all fours, put a hand on her shoulder and whispered, 'Drop the gowns inside the wall.

We shall be out of the College almost straight away, and they would only make us the more conspicuous.'

Shuddering, she scrambled out of her stolen garment, and they let them fall, vanishing into the darkness below.

Gray crept along the top of the wall on hands and knees, glancing back at her every few moments. 'Stop it,' she hissed at him. 'Look where you are going, for the gods' sake.'

He looked affronted, but did as he was bid. So profound was the chill, humid darkness by now that Sophie could see nothing before her but the soles of his boots, inching along the rough stone just ahead.

They had gone perhaps twenty paces along the wall, moving at a snail's pace, when Gray halted abruptly and sat up, swinging his long legs over the far side of the wall. 'This is where we jump,' he said calmly. Sophie's stomach clenched with naked terror, and she spoke sternly to herself: *You have survived far worse tonight already, you silly girl.*

Surely Gray would never lead her wrong.

Still, she nearly cried out when he dropped out of sight.

Gray landed, rather harder than he had expected, on the impromptu compost-heap that hugged the College wall just at this spot. He picked himself up, took a moment to catch his breath, and then, now they were outside the Proctors' jurisdiction, called just enough light to see by and sent it aloft to hover a little below the top of the wall, illuminating Sophie's dangling trousered legs, white-knuckled hands, and soot-streaked, terrified face.

'The jump is perfectly safe,' he called up to her. 'Do you see? I am quite all right – shall I catch you . . . ?'

She nodded, lips pressed together. Then she shut her eyes and pushed herself off the wall.

Gray caught her, stumbled a little, righted himself. She opened her eyes, her face only inches from his, and whispered, 'I thank you.'

Then he loosened his grip, and she slid to the ground and looked up at him expectantly. 'Where next?'

Gray was silent a moment, trying to see in his mind the quickest and safest return route. This was not quite so easy as he had anticipated; he had escaped the College this way many a time in his undergraduate days, but always with some less distant goal in view – an evening card-party in the town, or the wherewithal for some entertainment in College, to be purchased at a nearby public-house. No doubt many of his fellows had trod the path to Leda and the Swan, or to other houses closer and more unsavoury, but on this sort of expedition Gray had never been invited.

At last, however, he got his bearings, and they struck out to their right across the fields and woods.

They reached the South Road without incident, though once in it, passing such a number of lighted windows that they went always in fear of discovery. Some fifty paces along this road, Sophie caught Gray's arm and turned him back to look at her. 'Can you fly, do you think?' she said. 'Because, if you can, you ought to do it – I am so tired, I'm sure I could not hide us both if anyone should come, and aloft you might not be seen at all . . .'

'And if you should be unable to hide yourself, what then?' Gray hissed. 'Do you take me for a faithless oath-breaker, Your Highness?'

Her expression – the huge, shocked eyes, the trembling lips – called to his mind the only time he had made Jenny cry, the occasion when, in their childhood, he had been angry with her over some half-imagined slight and had said he should never speak to her again.

'I am sorry, Sophie,' he choked.

Her throat worked, and she drew one sooty, bloodied sleeve across her eyes. 'I meant nothing of the sort,' she said, with dignity, 'as you ought to know. I could not ask for a braver champion, Gray, or a kinder brother.'

These last words, which so recently would have warmed his

heart, Gray now absorbed in a spirit of profound melancholy.

'I thought,' she went on, 'that you could fly ahead a little way, and call a warning if you should see anyone coming—'

'Of course!' he exclaimed, and stooped down impulsively to kiss her upturned forehead. Buoyed by her trust, and ignoring the discomforting inner voice that wondered whether in his present state he could accomplish a shape-shift, let alone sustain it, he stripped off his coat and thrust it into her arms. 'There is not much left of it, I know, but Ned's clothes fit me a great deal better than my own, and I should not like to lose them . . .'

Her arms full of bundled-up clothing and dangling a pair of boots the size and shape of Breizhek fishing-boats, her ears pricked for Gray's warning call, Sophie paced cautiously along the half-familiar cobbled street. She braced herself up with the thought that before long they would be across the Cherwell and their chances of running against anyone at all, leave alone the Watch, vanishingly small.

'Oi!' called a voice behind her. ''Oo goes there?'

Sophie kept on, a little faster now; perhaps it might be addressing someone else. Next, however, she heard quickening footfalls, and the same voice, more urgent now: 'Stop, you! Halt for the Watch!'

With a sigh, she obeyed, turning about to face the men of the Watch.

There was only one, as it turned out; Gray had said the Watch patrolled always in pairs, and she wondered whether the other of this partnership was ill, or dealing with some genuine miscreant, or had simply decided to stop at home tonight. Her pursuer – slow-moving and solidly built, only a little taller than Sophie herself – approached at a sort of rolling gallop, holding aloft a magelight lantern.

'And 'oo might you be, then?' he enquired, thrusting the lantern into Sophie's face; she recoiled, squinting her eyes against the glare.

'Elinor Dunstan,' she said instinctively, then cursed herself for a fool, remembering – too late – Arthur Randal. But it was in any case not likely that she looked very much like Arthur Randal now.

The Watchman frowned at her and looked her up and down. 'Been in some trouble, 'ave we?' he said.

'None, I thank you.' Sophie spoke guardedly, not certain what the best answer might be – but as loudly as she dared, that Gray might hear her.

'Come now.' The grizzled face creased in a sort of leer. 'A little lass like you, alone on a dark night, dressed in yer brother's clothes . . . not as they don't suit yer, mind . . .'

Gray, where are you? Whatever do I say to this?

Sophie wished frantically that she were somewhere – anywhere – else, or that her interlocutor might lose interest in her. While the former desire, not surprisingly, went unfulfilled, she could see by the Watchman's changing expression that she had still sufficient magick left to give some force to the latter. His leering half grin gave way to a puzzled frown; he squinted at her, evidently wondering why he had found her so interesting a moment before. Slowly, Sophie backed away, still watching his face.

Thus it was that she saw his eyes widen and his jaw drop some moments before she identified the deep, angry hooting from behind her; then he dropped his lantern, which rolled across the cobbles spraying its light in all directions, and put up his arms to shield his face.

The owl had clearly no intention of hurting him, but it must be nearly as frightening, Sophie supposed, to be flown at by a large, angry bird of prey as to be genuinely attacked by one. In any event, a mere moment's hooting and flapping sufficed to thoroughly terrify her antagonist, who fled the scene, leaving his lantern behind him in the street.

'I thank you, Gray,' Sophie called softly to the grey shape circling above her head, stifling her laughter. 'I suppose we had best get on?'

The owl dipped one wing at her and glided away in the direction of the river. She followed as quickly as she could, pausing only to collect the Watchman's dropped lantern.

The exhilaration of flying – and of having rescued Sophie, however preposterously, from the attentions of the Watch – half succeeded in concealing from Gray that he was dangerously close to his limits. But he had not yet lost his senses altogether, and when the distant gleam of Sophie's lantern began to develop a prettily striated aura, and the rattle of the wind turning the leaves began to sing in his ears, it occurred to him that he would be of no use to anyone if he fell out of the sky and broke his neck.

Having seen Sophie safely over the Cherwell bridge, therefore, where the South Road petered out into rutted cart-tracks, he coasted rather drunkenly down to a tree beside the northbound track and alighted on a conveniently low branch a little way ahead of her. When she rounded the bend just past the bridge, he called, as loudly as he dared, until she stopped, draped something over the lantern, and stared into the trees, more or less in his direction. Then he dropped from his branch, shifting back into his own body as he fell, and landed on all fours behind dense strata of underbrush.

'Sophie!' he called softly. His human eyes strained to see her in the gloom.

'Gray? Where are you?' she called back, and he heard his own desperate weariness mirrored in her voice.

'Hiding,' he said. 'I shall come out, if you will toss me that bundle in your arms . . .'

There was no answer, but a moment later he had to dodge a large, heavy boot, then another, and in short order his entire toilette was draped among the brush and trees around him. 'I thank you,' he said, just loudly enough to be heard, and began looking for his shirt and trousers.

It was at this moment that it began to rain.

Dressing under these damp, thorny conditions, in profound darkness, was neither a rapid nor an agreeable process, but Gray managed it at last, and, scratched and dripping, emerged from the trees to join Sophie on the path.

Sophie, too, was damp and shivering and still very dirty, though the rain had washed the blood and soot from her face and plastered her hair in sodden tendrils against her head. 'How much farther, do you think?' she asked through chattering teeth.

'Far enough,' he admitted. 'Shall we get on?'

The rain eased; Sophie caught sight of a small structure to the left of the path. Close to, it proved to be a simple stone shrine to the Mother Goddess – old, but not abandoned – decorated with a bas-relief carving so weathered that the three figures were almost indistinguishable. Candle stubs, soggy remnants of flowers, and a scattering of grain bore witness to its recent, if not frequent, use.

Sophie knelt in the mud – she was now so thoroughly drenched that it could hardly matter – and addressed the shrine. 'Mother Goddess, bountiful and kind,' she began in ritual fashion, and then, hedging her bets, 'Juno, Diana, Ceres, Proserpina, I thank you for my life, this day, and for the life of this, my brother . . .'

But she found she could not go on.

With a damp squelching noise as his knees sank into the mud, Gray knelt beside her and began his own prayer: 'Mother Goddess, bountiful and kind, we pray you will see us safe out of our present troubles, and those that are to come.'

They had nothing to leave as an offering, no flowers or grain or coin, no incense to burn or wine to spill – nothing to yield up in exchange for the favours he asked. Nevertheless he bowed to the faceless images and spoke the ancient formula: '*Do ut des.*'

I give so that you may give in return.

As they struggled up out of the clinging mud, Sophie wondered anxiously what result such a bargain might yield.

False dawn had just begun to lighten the sky when they came into sight of their destination. By now they were beyond exhaustion, maintaining forward momentum only by leaning heavily one on the other; even thus supported, neither could go more than ten or twenty paces without rest. 'I hope we shall not be seen,' Gray sighed, 'for I am far too tired for explanations.'

Sophie did not reply.

Their ardent wish to re-enter the inn unseen – which ought not to have been impossible, being just such a house as might naturally leave its front door unbolted for the convenience of visitors in the night – was thwarted before ever they came near the door. A light burning in an upper window outlined a small, motionless form; when Gray and Sophie halted some fifteen paces from the house, the light shifted as this figure and its shadow, no longer motionless, loomed and leapt against window and walls, then vanished altogether – to erupt, sooner than seemed possible, from the very door by which they had meant to creep silently in.

'Elinor! Ned!' it shouted, in Joanna's voice. 'You are come back! Thank all the gods . . .'

'Joanna, hush!' Gray scolded her. He tried to see her face; there was light enough now, surely, yet everything he looked at seemed faded and blurred, dark around the edges.

'Take him indoors and feed him,' Sophie said, her voice a great way off. 'He is badly magick-shocked – and so am I, I expect . . .'

Then Joanna and the inn and the lighted window bent and swayed alarmingly, and the cobbles of the forecourt rushed upwards, and he heard no more.

CHAPTER XVIII

In Which Several Tales Are Told

Gray woke abruptly from an unpleasant dream filled with Gorgons and basilisks, in which he tried repeatedly to run to someone's rescue and repeatedly discovered himself to be turned to ice or stone, to find himself in his room at the inn. He could not have slept long, for the morning sun still streamed cheerfully in through the tiny window opposite the bed. Chill air streamed in with it, the landlord of the Swan having little concern for such fripperies as window-glass.

At first Gray thought he had woken (as sometimes happens) from one dream into another, for in the rickety chair wedged in next to the clothes-press slumbered a rumpled-looking, and strangely gownless, Master Alcuin. He was snoring very gently, the tip of his beard rising and falling with every breath.

'Magister?' Gray croaked, shading his eyes against the sun. 'What do you here?'

There was no answer but another delicate snore. Gray's throat still ached, his head was pounding, and, as he woke fully, he began to recognise that he was desperately thirsty – and desperate for something else as well.

Awkwardly he threw back the bedclothes and swung his legs over the side of the bed; he lurched to his feet, clutching the bedpost for support, and slowly bent down to retrieve the necessary from beneath the bed.

The room swam; he blinked, trying to clear his vision, but the moment his eyelids descended the swimming and spinning increased, so that his empty stomach heaved painfully and it was all he could do to stay on his feet. No sooner was the receptacle covered and replaced, than he was sinking again, until he found himself on hands and knees with his face against the floorboards. Laboriously he rose to his knees and attempted to scale the side of the bed.

But it was no use, and at last he subsided to the floor with a thump, both arms wrapped about his aching head.

There was a scuffling sound from behind him; he suspected rats, but could not bring himself to care very much. Then a familiar voice said, 'Marshall?'

Footsteps, a rustling noise, then the same voice sounding almost in Gray's ear: 'Marshall, my boy, whatever are you doing?'

Gray sat up – an undertaking requiring Herculean effort – and blinked in consternation at his former tutor. 'I am trying,' he said, the words clotting in his throat, 'to get back into bed – but – I do not seem to get on at all . . .'

Master Alcuin was a slightly built, sedentary man at least in the late sixties; Gray had a vague sense that such a person ought not to be asked to lift so much weight, but he was too grateful for the older man's assistance – and too much in need of it – to make any protest. At length he found himself tucked up into bed again, with Master Alcuin bending over him and fussing at him in a way that would have done credit to his mother.

'I am very disappointed in you, my boy,' he said, rather severely, and Gray, who had spent most of the return journey from Merlin in castigating himself for his failures, turned his head to the wall, fighting back tears. 'I am very sorry, Magister,' he choked. 'I wanted so much to save him, but—'

To his astonishment, he was lifted, and turned, and enveloped in a brief but crushing embrace. 'You misunderstand me,' Master Alcuin said, blue eyes kind under his snow-white eyebrows, as Gray sank back into the pillows. 'I have no fault to find with you for failing to exert the powers of a god. You did your best, and Lord Halifax chose to ignore your warning.'

He sat back in his chair and folded his arms. 'But that you should be so foolish as to attempt to *fly* home, after exhausting yourself in fighting off two more experienced mages – *that*, my boy, disappoints me greatly. I believed I had taught you better sense.'

Again Gray blinked at him. 'Then – *that* is what is the matter with me?' he said slowly. 'Magick shock?' A vague memory came to him, now, of Sophie saying—

Sophie!

He sat up abruptly, which made all of his various ills dramatically worse, and clutched at Master Alcuin's arm. 'Sophie,' he said urgently. 'Is she—?'

'Your young lady is quite well,' the older man said complacently. 'She appears to have been considerably less reckless than her companion. She has been up and about since yesterday evening, I am told.'

Gray stared, aghast – *yesterday evening*? – and his mentor chuckled. 'Ah, I see,' he said. Then he rose from his chair, snapped his fingers, and crossed to the door that led to the corridor. 'You must be very hungry,' he said, turning back. 'I shall sally forth in search of breakfast.'

Left alone, Gray struggled to think past his pounding headache. Everything about the present situation was perplexing and bizarre, but at least he knew now that Sophie was safe and well – though he would not entirely believe it, till he had seen her for himself.

I must ask Master Alcuin to stop calling her my young lady; I am sure she would not like it.

Food was brought, and devoured, along with two potfuls of strong tea, and afterwards, feeling much restored, Gray at last recalled that his first question had not been answered.

'Magister,' he said, 'you have not yet told me how you came here, or why.'

Master Alcuin sighed. 'Thereby hangs a tale, indeed,' he said. 'I think, however, I had rather tell it only once. By your leave, Marshall, I shall send for the rest of your party—'

He rose to go, but Gray stopped him. 'A little time, Magister, I beg,' he said. 'I fear I am hardly fit to be seen at present.'

It could hardly be denied that he looked quite dreadful, and smelt worse; if Master Alcuin was to be believed, he had slept a full day and night in this ruined shirt. His burnt hands and wrists stung fiercely, and rough, itchy stubble covered his cheeks and chin. He needed a hot bath, new clothes, and a healer; though these luxuries were not to be had at present, he could at any rate wash and shave and put on his ill-fitting old clothes, which were at least neither filthy nor singed. Mrs Wallis, presumably, could be prevailed on to repair the results of his adventures, provided that he did not look like a denizen of Newgate prison when next she saw him.

Half an hour later, looking as respectable as cold water, clean linen, and considerable elbow grease could make him, Gray sat on the edge of his hastily tidied bed, awaiting the arrival of Joanna, Mrs Wallis, and Sophie.

The door opened from within, and Gray (perched on the narrow bed along one wall) tottered to his feet to greet the ladies. He was pale and looked deeply tired, and his too-short shirtsleeves revealed the angry red of burnt skin on his wrists and hands; otherwise, however, he was much more himself than when Sophie had last seen him. He smiled at her, though his eyes remained grim and sad.

Mrs Wallis shut the door, and Sophie felt the now-familiar whisper of magick as Master Alcuin warded the tiny room. She wanted more than anything to fling herself into Gray's arms, but it would not be dignified and, besides, might very well knock him over.

Her sister, in any event, did it for her.

'Magister,' said Gray, having extricated himself from Joanna's too-enthusiastic embrace of his midsection, 'please allow me to introduce Miss Joanna Callender. Joanna, Master Everard Alcuin, usually of Merlin College.'

'Joanna,' Master Alcuin repeated, studying her and tugging thoughtfully at his beard. 'A most unusual name.'

'Joanna is a most unusual young lady,' Gray said dryly. Joanna sniffed – but she looked rather pleased.

'It is a name used among the Greek-speaking Judaei of the Mediterranean,' the don continued, 'derived from the Hebrew *Jokhanan*, meaning, roughly, "gift of God".'

'"Of god"? Which god?' Joanna enquired, frowning.

Master Alcuin chuckled. 'Most Judaei believe that there is only one,' he explained.

'How *peculiar*,' said Joanna. 'He must be terribly busy.'

'Interestingly, there are certain sects – some of those that call themselves "Christian" – whose belief is that their one god is a tripartite entity – in essence, not unlike our concept of—'

'Magister.' Gray's tone was a singular blend of impatience and affection. 'Another time, perhaps?'

'Of course, of course,' his teacher said. 'I ask your pardon.'

Joanna did not seem interested in pursuing the matter, but Sophie could not help remembering her mother's words on the occasion of Joanna's birth – *The gods withhold their gifts from me*, she had said – and wondering.

'Mrs Wallis,' Gray said, 'the Master of Merlin is dead, and we believe that the Professor and Lord Carteret intend to murder the King.'

* * *

Between them, haltingly and with many digressions, Gray and Sophie told their tale. Sophie's impressions of the battle (if such it could be called), and of their subsequent escape over the College walls, proved very different from Gray's own; it was startling to hear himself described as brave and quick-witted, when in fact he had been at all times clumsy, slow, and frightened out of his alleged wits.

'We should have had no chance at all, had Sophie not thought to provide me a weapon,' he argued at one point; turning to her, he said, 'When is it that you learnt to perform an unseen summoning? Only that afternoon you were asking me—'

'The spell is the one I learnt from Gaius Aegidius,' she said, 'as I expect you did yourself. And the incentive was very great. It was not so difficult as I expected.'

By way of demonstration, she summoned a codex from the stack beneath the dressing-table on which she was perched and leant across to put it in his hands.

Gray gaped at her – as he thought she must have intended.

'Remarkable,' Master Alcuin murmured. He took the book from Gray; as he listened, he rubbed the worn leather binding gently with his thumb.

Thus, for some time, the tale went on, until, interrupting Sophie's breathless recital of her rescue from the Watch, Mrs Wallis remarked, 'If we are to spend the next se'nnight in this excess of mutual admiration, perhaps it will be as well to lay in some provisions.'

When Sophie and Joanna glared at her, she assumed a bland expression and busied herself once again with the unidentifiable object she was knitting.

'For my part,' Gray said, looking down at the man beside him, 'I should like to hear *your* portion of the tale, Magister. You must also have had some manner of adventure, I think . . .'

'What young Marshall means,' his teacher rejoined, 'is that I am renowned for my attachment to my own rooms and my own books; he fears that some dire and dreadful calamity must have befallen me, to induce me to change my habits so suddenly.'

'It is . . . *unexpected*, you must allow,' said Gray.

'Well, as to that,' Master Alcuin said, 'it is very simple: I am no longer welcome at Merlin, and have therefore decided to throw in my lot with all of you.'

'But—' Gray began, and could not think how to go on. Everard Alcuin had been at Merlin College always, as far as anyone knew; it seemed quite impossible to imagine the place without him.

'You must tell us more than *that*, Professor,' Joanna scolded him – Joanna, Gray had often thought, would not fear to scold the gods themselves. 'It is quite unfair to begin so, and then not to finish your tale!'

'What Joanna means—' This was Sophie; but Master Alcuin raised a hand, gently compelling her to silence.

'Miss Joanna and I understand one another very well,' he said, with a little smile. 'And I trust you will all forgive an old man his odd ways. It seems,' he continued, abruptly sobering, 'it seems that the Master of our illustrious College has been foully murdered, and that I am one of the chief suspects in this dreadful crime. The other being, of course'– with a nod at Gray – 'my former student.'

If his aim had been to render them all speechless, he had succeeded admirably. For some moments, they could do nothing but stare, at one another and at him.

It was Sophie who broke the silence at last, in tones of mingled horror and disgust: 'Then this is what the Professor meant by "insurance".'

'On your own evidence, Miss Sophie,' Master Alcuin said, 'their original scheme must have been as we surmised – to test whether their poison could make death appear quite natural; I suspect that they altered their timing, however. The Master's manservant was seen delivering a message to Professor Callender's rooms. I believe that it was an invitation, and that Callender and his companion took advantage of the opportunity. Knowing you to be in Oxford, likely bent on exposing their plot, must have hastened them.'

As a boy, Gray had been on the receiving end of many a body blow; Master Alcuin's words struck him in much the same way, and he regretted his recent meal. 'We brought this upon him,' he said. 'If we had not—'

'No,' said Mrs Wallis firmly. 'Your visit may have hurried the hour of Lord Halifax's death, but it was Callender and his friend who chose him as their victim, and he himself who chose to ignore your warning. If indeed we must now prevent a further murder, Mr Marshall, as well as escaping arrest for the first, then we have certainly no time for self-pity and purposeless self-blame.'

Gray blinked and straightened his spine.

'I should guess,' Master Alcuin continued, 'that they arrived when they did intending to make quite sure that nothing in the circumstances could arouse suspicion. And, as they admitted quite openly before you the existence of a trap—'

'Arachne's Web,' said Gray, 'the easiest spell in the world to break.'

'For *you*, perhaps,' muttered Sophie. Joanna merely looked perplexed.

'I should imagine that it was intended to catch quite a different sort of prey,' the little don acknowledged. 'A curious Porter, for example, or the Master's own servant. They cannot have anticipated your presence, any more than we anticipated . . . In any event, when a man is dead, and his *sanctum sanctorum* thoroughly ravaged, the two facts are seldom unconnected, and someone must take the blame . . .'

'Did you see it, then, sir?' Sophie asked him.

'I did not,' he said, with a shudder, 'and glad I am, for to know it is dreadful enough. But all the College will have heard by now. The tale they tell – but it is so absurd, you know, that I know not how anyone can entertain it . . .'

The tale Master Alcuin related would have done credit to any market storyteller or tavern-minstrel.

'Professor Callender and his friend,' he began, 'a Fellow of King's College – he will be your mysterious *M*, I feel certain – paying a call on Lord Halifax at his express invitation, on arriving found his gate-keeper vanished; his servant was spelled asleep, and sounds of a dreadful struggle came from his private study. There my esteemed colleagues of course went, to investigate the disturbance; they found the Master dead – smothered – and his two assailants in the act of destroying his priceless library. On attempting to put an end to this outrage, they were themselves viciously assaulted, and the Professor left for dead when their attackers fled the premises.'

'But—' Sophie protested.

'One of the villains' – Master Alcuin nodded at Gray – 'was identified by the Professor, being well known to him, and proved to have been seen earlier in the day entering the Master's Lodge in the company of an accomplice' – here laying a hand over his heart – 'and later had been challenged by and subsequently escaped several Merlin Proctors – who, as you know, are considered incorruptible.

'Here the waters grow murky; for there is much confusion and dispute as to the identity of the other assailant. Some have mentioned a young man; at least one described a girl dressed in her brother's clothes, and others are equally adamant that there was no second fugitive. There is much wild talk of vanishing-spells and other complex magicks, but no one,' he concluded, in a tone of satisfaction, 'appears to have the least idea how any of it was managed.

'And still I am not come to the oddest aspect of this dreadful affair,' said Master Alcuin, 'or to the reason of my presence here. Though the Master's study was left in ruins, the contents of his desk survived unscathed, and among them was found a most unexpected document—'

'A letter foretelling his death, and naming his murderer?' Joanna broke in. 'Or the evidence of some secret society for the practice of forbidden magicks?'

Sophie hushed her irritably, but Master Alcuin looked thoughtful. 'Not exactly,' he said, 'although . . . No, the document in question purports to be a letter from the Master to the Senior Fellows of Merlin, to be opened in the event of his death, and is dated some two years since. Its contents, as I understand, are various, but among the miscellaneous directions and explanations is given Lord Halifax's choice in the matter of his succession—'

'But College Masters are appointed by the Crown!' Gray protested.

'Even so,' the older man said. 'But the King, of course, has but little interest in the affairs of any one College; in fact, therefore, the choice is made by the Senior Fellows, and confirmed by the Crown, unless there should emerge some serious objection to the candidate. The Senior Fellows, in turn, are often guided by the prior Master's opinion.'

With a rustling of petticoats, Mrs Wallis shifted in her seat. 'Can I be the only one who wishes to know the identity of this chosen successor?' she enquired. 'Although I rather think . . .'

'You are quite right, madam,' Master Alcuin said, nodding again. 'The man named is Appius Callender, Regius Professor of Magickal Theory.'

'It is a forgery, of course.' Gray's expression was unreadable, his hands clenched white-knuckled on his knees. 'And the letter, or that part of it at any rate, certainly does not date from so long ago. It is your – it is the Professor's doing, and the work itself – Woodville, of course, Alfric Woodville. The man was a forger in his cradle.'

'Woodville,' Master Alcuin repeated thoughtfully. 'One of Callender's protégés? Yes, yes, I see. I fancy I have seen one or two other such, following me about the town, as they supposed, in secret. In any event, though the appointment must of course be given royal assent, for the moment your erstwhile tutor, Marshall, is Master of Merlin, and you and I – as your accomplice, you know – equally in disgrace.' He looked up at Gray, who looked back at him; what could they be thinking? 'I must admit,' he went on, 'that when I once predicted our renewed collaboration, I had no notion of its taking place in such a context. But one must do one's best with whatever the gods provide!'

Then he looked round at the assembled company, so closely packed into Gray's tiny bedchamber that Sophie could almost hear each of the others breathe. 'I presume,' he said, quite briskly, 'that we go next to London?'

CHAPTER XIX

In Which Help Is Forthcoming from an Unexpected Quarter

'*You mean that* we must warn the King, of course,' said Sophie. 'But if Lord Halifax did not believe us, why should His Majesty do so?'

Joanna – who, Gray reminded himself, had witnessed none of the horrors of Lord Halifax's death – sat up eagerly and said, 'Because, Sophie, you—'

Then she broke off suddenly, her grey eyes widening in alarm, as Mrs Wallis and Sophie both turned to glare at her.

'Certainly we must warn the King,' said Mrs Wallis, 'but at present, as Mr Marshall has evidently worn out our welcome in Oxford, our most urgent task is to be elsewhere, and London surely offers our best and nearest opportunity of escape.'

'My sister Calanthe has a house in Town,' Master Alcuin said thoughtfully, 'or her husband has; in Half-moon-street, in Mayfair. I have not seen her in some time; perhaps she may welcome a visit, once she has heard our tale. Now,' he added, looking from Gray to Sophie and back again, 'since it seems likely that we may meet further . . . resistance, it would be as well for the two of you to become better versed in battle magicks. I shall begin your tuition after luncheon.'

Gray frowned and tugged at one ear, certain that he had misheard. 'I beg pardon, Magister, but did you say . . . ?'

His voice trailed off, and Sophie finished the sentence for him.

Master Alcuin nodded. 'I have failed to tell you of my misspent youth, I see,' he said.

Now Gray remembered his tutor's sympathy, even commiseration, on the day of that last, brutal letter from his father. Gray's father had always intended his second son for a military career, and the less Gray seemed inclined in this direction, the more insistent Edmond Marshall had become. Gray's three years at Merlin had been a trial to his father's patience, the culmination of which was a letter informing Gray that a mage-officer's commission had been purchased for him, and he was to hold himself ready to take it up immediately after concluding his course of study. Gray had devoted some hours to the composition of a courteous and respectful, but negative, reply, concluding, *I am grateful for the generosity of your offer, sir, but I regret that I cannot accept it.*

Edmond Marshall's reply was brief, bald, and coldly furious. Gray, upon receiving it, had read it through twice, then stood staring at it in a sort of trance; the words were plain enough, but he could not make himself accept their sense.

A drop of water had fallen on the paper and blotted the ink; the hateful words blurred. Gray had recognised, to his dismay, that he was weeping – a man of nearly nineteen, weeping like a child! Little wonder, perhaps, that his father should treat him so. But what was to become of him now? *I cannot submit. I know I ought, but I cannot do it.*

An enclosure from Jenny reported that she and Celia had used all their powers of persuasion, and Mama also, but to no avail: if Gray did not accept their father's terms, henceforth he would not know him.

Master Alcuin, observing his distress at their meeting that afternoon, had declined to interfere, but so kindly that the refusal carried no sting. 'I shall make certain that should you decide to remain here, it will be possible for you to do so,' he said. 'Your father may stop your pocket-money, but your scholarship remains, and no one will think it strange for so dedicated a student to remain in college between terms. But more than this it is out of my power to do.'

'I thank you,' Gray had said, grateful for even such a guarded show of support. 'I shall write to him myself this evening, and say that, much as I respect his wishes, I cannot bow to them.'

At this Master Alcuin had produced a brief, wry smile. 'I commend your decision, Marshall, and wish you well of it. Myself perhaps excepted, you are the last man in the world to make a good officer of the King.'

Had he been speaking not from mere speculation, as Gray had then believed, but from certain knowledge? He could scarcely imagine it, but it was also true that he knew little of Master Alcuin's past. And such a past would also explain, perhaps, his tutor's unexpected facility with ciphers. 'You were a mage-officer, Magister?' he hazarded.

'Even so,' the older man said. 'A very poor one, I own, for I had no more stomach for fighting and killing at twenty than I have now, but the magicks themselves were easily enough learnt – and easily enough taught, I should imagine, to two such gifted students.' He patted Gray's shoulder in a fatherly manner and gave Sophie a kind little smile.

Gray's room being far too small for five persons to eat their luncheon in, they repaired to what, at the Swan, passed for a private dining-room. Gray had an idea that the maid who brought their meal glanced at him suspiciously, but he dismissed it as mere lingering anxiety on his part. They discussed in low voices how best to reach London, how much it might cost, and what they ought to do, once there.

It was Joanna who gave the first alarm; her luncheon eaten, wearying perhaps of the endless discussion of ways and means, she had turned her chair so as to kneel upon it and peer through the shutters into the forecourt of the inn, which afforded always some matter for observation. 'Apollo, Pan, and Hecate!' she exclaimed, provoking a long-suffering sigh from her sister and a muffled snort of laughter from Master Alcuin. 'Come and look at this!'

They crowded about the window – Gray, who was nearest, arriving first to peer out over Joanna's head. When he saw what had drawn her attention, a dozen even less savoury curses rose to his lips, which he firmly stifled.

'The Watch,' he said instead, grimly. 'This bodes ill.'

The Watch it was indeed, and in force: four constables in their dark-blue cloaks, and a captain mounted on a large bay whose shoes struck sparks from the cobbles as he struggled to control it.

As Gray watched from above, the innkeeper emerged from the front door to converse with the Watch Captain, who had finally given up on his restive steed and descended to the cobbles. The officer spoke, gesticulated, spoke again; the innkeeper shrugged and shook his head. Then one of the Watchmen spoke to his superior, and the Captain began again.

Whatever he said this time had a quite different effect. The landlord began nodding slowly; to Gray's horror, he looked up, beginning to scan the inn's many shuttered windows, and then, worse yet, beckoned the Watchmen inside.

'The Watch may be interested in this house for many other reasons,' Master Alcuin pointed out, as Gray turned from the window. 'We ought not to assume the worst.'

Mrs Wallis nodded agreement, and even Sophie began to look less anxious.

'But if that is so—' Joanna began.

Whatever she had meant to say, however, was forestalled by a knock at the door.

* * *

Sophie froze, and the others about her stiffened into stillness at the same moment. The knocking came again, louder, more insistent; they looked at one another in consternation.

'*Quo vadis?*' Master Alcuin said at last. His voice might be rather formidable, if one could not see him.

The third knock conveyed a serious loss of patience. 'Open for the Watch!' cried someone without, rattling the doorknob.

Sophie wondered that they did not simply turn the handle and open the door themselves, till she recollected that, after the servant bringing their luncheon had departed, Master Alcuin had done something to the lock.

'Stand back!' another voice commanded, and after a moment something (or someone) large and heavy crashed against the door.

'Wait!' Master Alcuin cried. 'A moment, by your leave, and the door will be opened.' He turned to Gray and whispered, 'Hide yourself – shift, if you can, and get clear . . .' Then he advanced towards the door.

Sophie looked at Gray, who shook his head.

She felt less terrified than she might have expected, her mind on the question of whether she could conceal so many, and for how long. 'Come here,' she whispered to Gray, beckoning; he obeyed, and holding his hand tightly, Sophie crossed the small room to where Master Alcuin stood tinkering with the lock. She took hold of his arm with her free hand and smiled at him encouragingly. Then she shut her eyes, and took a deep, slow breath, and wished very hard that none of them might be noticed.

Master Alcuin finished with the lock, and the three of them backed cautiously away from the door. Hinges creaked. Sophie opened her eyes as the red-faced, ginger-haired innkeeper and three large Watchmen shouldered their way into the room. Her pulse hammered in her ears; Gray's long fingers clasped her hand painfully tight, and both he and his teacher stared at their would-be captors as if hypnotised.

But the intruders glanced towards them and then away, exactly as one of their confederates had done two nights since in the South Road.

Sophie prayed to every god and goddess she could think of, one after another, that they would simply give up and be gone, but the Watch Captain was not so easily put off. Addressing himself to Mrs Wallis – who sat, with Joanna, calmly eating grapes – he began, 'Madam, miss, I must ask your assistance. At the risk of alarming you, ma'am, we seek two very dangerous criminals, and have reason to believe they may have been seen here. Do you know, or have you seen, a man by the name of Graham Marshall – a very tall man, six feet and a half, or nearly – sandy-haired, with a crooked nose? Or one Everard Alcuin, a University don – in a black gown, you know, with a long white beard? They would have come here yesterday, or mayhap the previous night.'

Both Mrs Wallis and Joanna appeared to give these questions serious consideration. At last Joanna shook her head – for all the world as though she had liked nothing better than to assist the brave men of the Watch, but could not.

Mrs Wallis said, 'I fear we cannot help you, sir; my niece and I have seen no one of such a description. My nephew Edward, to be sure, is a very tall man, and sandy-haired, but he certainly is not called . . . what was it? Marshley? And I do not think he can be a dangerous criminal, as he has been here with us these several days . . .'

She is a glamourer, truly, Sophie thought. The innkeeper's two sons had carried Gray up to his bed not two days ago, insensible and all over mud, and must certainly have related this interesting venture to their father in the morning; yet the man said nothing, did not so much as look surprised to be told that this same Edward

Dunstan had been here all the time. Nor did the Captain of the Watch or either of his men seem at all suspicious, having heard a man speak to them from behind the closed door, to find only a woman and a girl within.

Still, if Mrs Wallis's magick at all resembled her own, its effects could not last for ever; though they might befuddle and trick their antagonists for a time, the only real solution to their predicament was, as it had ever been, to be away from here as soon as might be.

The Watch Captain surveyed the room once more and frowned thoughtfully in Sophie's general direction; she held her breath and concentrated even more furiously on remaining unnoticed.

He looked confused and shook his head. 'I am sorry to have worried you, ma'am,' he told Mrs Wallis, doffing his elaborately braided cap, and a moment later the four men were gone from the room, the door closed behind them.

No sooner had the sound of booted footsteps died away along the corridor than Joanna jumped up, almost overturning the table. 'You have done it, Sophie!' she whispered jubilantly. 'They were here, and so were all of you, and they looked *through* you, as though—'

'Mother Goddess!' Sophie breathed. She let go her hold on Master Alcuin's sleeve. 'I think,' she managed to say, wishing that the room would cease its whirling motion, 'I think that I should like to sit down.'

The miles of countryside sped by, and Gray fought his mind's tendency to wander.

'You tried, I collect, to adapt Thurimberg's weather-shield to the demands of combat,' said Master Alcuin, 'and found it did not answer?'

'Indeed it did not,' said Gray ruefully. 'Though I had more luck with a Slattery detonation. I think, however, it was wasted on mere pebbles; I reacted without thinking. Magister—' He leant forward and lowered his voice. 'I confess I was quite terrified.'

'Courage,' Master Alcuin intoned, 'consists not in lack of fear, but in mastering that fear so as to do what must be done.'

Gray had heard this aphorism before; now, as then, he did not find it particularly comforting.

He was, in truth, so weary, and the motion of the coach in which they sat – so well sprung, and six horses! He did not like to think what Mrs Wallis must have paid for its hire as far as London – was so soporific, that he found himself continually dozing off. To his left, Sophie was sound asleep, which was hardly surprising after her earlier exertions; to his right he saw only Joanna's back, and the back of her bonneted head; her face was pressed to the window in her eagerness to see all that they passed on the London road.

Finally Gray lost the battle, vaguely aware of his chin dropping to his chest just before he succumbed to sleep.

When he woke, it was to find his cheek resting on the top of Sophie's head, which was awkwardly pillowed against his shoulder; he had slumped down against the leather seat of the coach, polished smooth by many previous passengers, so that his shoulders were level with its back and his knees jammed against the opposite *banc*. Cautiously, so as not to waken Sophie, he straightened his stiffened, aching limbs and, blinking, looked about him at his fellow passengers.

Mrs Wallis was apparently asleep in her corner, her face invisible behind her bonnet-brim; Master Alcuin gazed out of the window opposite, one hand tugging gently at the end of his beard; Joanna seemed not to have stirred, still fascinated by the passing scene.

'Magister,' Gray said softly, reaching across to touch the older man's arm. 'Magister, where are we? What's the hour?'

Master Alcuin started, turned, and smiled at him. 'Of the hour,' he said, 'I have no notion, but we have done nearly a third of our journey, I should guess. You have been sleeping for some time.'

Gray began to apologise but quickly saw that there was no need.

'I wish my father had been more like you, Magister,' he murmured sleepily.

As his eyelids dropped again, he thought he heard Master Alcuin say, 'I have often wished the same myself, dear boy.'

They set down at an inn at High Wycombe to change horses and attend to various other requirements, and while there, Master Alcuin judged it high time to begin his pupils' tuition in earnest. Yawning, trailed by an uncharacteristically silent Joanna, they trooped out to a clearing in the little coppiced wood behind the inn and embarked on the oddest series of lessons Sophie had ever been set.

'The first and most important thing any user of battle magicks must learn,' Master Alcuin was saying now, 'is how to shield himself. Or, ah, herself,' he added. 'All the offensive spells in the world are of no use if one is felled by the first attack. You were very fortunate, but Dame Fortune is not always so kind. A shield must be strong, true, but as you discovered, Marshall, what is only strong is also vulnerable, in the end. Your truly effective shield, therefore, must also be *flexible*. Now, attend . . .'

Sophie was not at her best. She had slept nearly the whole journey thus far, and her mind felt much the better for it, but her body was stiff and bruised, and, try as she might, she could not shake off her fear of pursuit. This perhaps explained why she was so long in recognising that she had ceased to comprehend what she heard.

The first idea that suggested itself was that she was suffering from hallucinations. Only when Gray said, sounding puzzled, 'Magister, what tongue is that?' did it dawn on her at last that Master Alcuin had drifted into a language not known to her.

Master Alcuin's incomprehensible lecture abruptly ceased; he regarded his students with an expression of such honest bafflement that Sophie could not suppress a grin.

Then he frowned, and Sophie remembered herself. Fighting the instinct to hide behind Gray, or perhaps a tree-trunk, from the inevitable explosion, she lowered her gaze respectfully, peering sidewise at her teacher from the corner of one eye.

'Magister,' said Gray, 'you have not *forgot* it?'

His tone – not apprehensive, but warmly amused, a little disbelieving – made Sophie look up again in surprise.

'Certainly not,' said Master Alcuin; but he did not, in fact, tell them what language he had been speaking. Instead, he blinked primly, and tugged on the end of his beard, and said, 'Now, Miss Sophie! Tell me, where was I?'

Sophie gaped at him. Gray said, 'But . . .' and went no further.

Was Master Alcuin, Sophie wondered, perhaps very slightly mad?

At last, casting her mind back to the last thing she was perfectly certain of having understood, she said hesitantly, 'You were explaining, sir, what difficulties ensue when a shield is not sufficiently flexible.'

Master Alcuin's eyebrows flew up. 'By Jove!' he said. 'As far back as that? I had no idea.'

Then Gray began to laugh – a deep, musical chuckle that Sophie had never heard before, but which instantly felt familiar.

Master Alcuin's expression was, in fact, very comical, and when, on finding himself an object of his student's open mirth, he did not draw himself up and grow purple in the face with affronted dignity, but tilted his white head very slightly and gave a sheepish little smile, the taut line of Sophie's shoulders, the tension and strain of their near-capture in Oxford, flowed out of her in a peal of laughter.

'Speaking of languages,' Master Alcuin said, some time later, 'I hope you have studied your Cymric, Miss Sophie?'

Sophie shook her head.

'Well, you and I shall address that question at another time, for a lack of Cymric is a grave disadvantage to any serious scholar. Now, however,' he continued, '*retournons à nos moutons*, that we may live to fight another day. Marshall, demonstrate that last shielding-spell again, if you please . . .'

Gray did so, to some effect, and Sophie followed suit; they practised diligently until Mrs Wallis appeared to summon them back to their conveyance. And all the time Master Alcuin's words echoed in Sophie's mind: *to any serious scholar* . . .

'Number eleven, Half-moon-street,' Master Alcuin mused, staring up at the tall, narrow house before which they all stood, surrounded by their possessions and gradually dampening in the chill London drizzle. 'It is the same house, certainly; I remember the odd shape of the dormer-windows very distinctly . . .'

Mrs Wallis harrumphed, and Joanna wandered about, skirting the leavings of carriage-horses, to peer down into the areas of adjacent dwellings and up at their frost-nipped flower-boxes. Sophie sat on Gray's battered trunk, shivering and awash in homesickness.

The coach had brought them along the broad, noisy thoroughfare of Piccadilly, turned into Half-moon-street, and set them down in front of number eleven, at their request. They had waited below on the pavement while Master Alcuin made use of the ornate door-knocker, and at length the door had been opened by an elderly and excruciatingly correct manservant.

'I am sorry to tell you, sir,' he said to Master Alcuin, 'that you have come to the wrong house.'

'But indeed it is not the wrong house! I have visited my sister here often and often – that is – perhaps the house has recently changed hands?' Master Alcuin suggested hopefully.

'Certainly not, sir!' the servant replied. 'Not these ten years.'

'Perhaps we might speak to the present occupants . . . ?'

'I regret, sir' – he did not sound in the least regretful – 'Sir George and Lady Faraday are not at home.'

Mrs Wallis had at this point reassumed the persona of put-upon upper servant, while the others kept Master Alcuin below on the pavement, and exerted herself to be confidential and charming. Sophie could not hear all that was said, but at any rate the Faradays' man unbent so far as to bid Mrs Wallis a very civil farewell, and wish that she might succeed in finding the old gentleman's sister, before closing the door politely but firmly on them all.

The house, Mrs Wallis then informed them, had been the property of the lady's late husband; she had married again, and gone away, and thus had the house come into the possession of its current owners. What the lady's name might now be, and where they might find her, Mrs Wallis's new acquaintance could not or would not tell.

'And a pretty mess we are in now, sir!' she said to Master Alcuin. 'Ten years, indeed! This is quite the most hare-brained scheme ever embarked upon since—'

Then she shut her mouth abruptly, and turned away.

Gray approached Master Alcuin and laid a hand upon his shoulder. 'Magister,' he said, 'it was a good plan, but we must hatch another. Mrs Wallis will perhaps have some acquaintance who can help us, and in any case we cannot stand about for ever in the street. Ought I not to walk out to Piccadilly, and find a hackney-carriage?'

'Oh, yes, do,' said Joanna, appearing suddenly at Sophie's elbow. 'I shall come with you.'

An hour later a hackney-carriage deposited their damp and increasingly irritable party before a hotel of intimidating appearance, which Sophie feared they could very ill afford. A liveried man and a boy of Joanna's age descended the front steps and took their baggage in charge, and while Gray paid the driver, Mrs Wallis led the way up the steps.

The apartments in which they were soon installed were small but elegantly appointed, with Roman plumbing and every other comfort imaginable – save the woods and fields of Breizh, or the lawns of Oxford. Sophie, forgoing the promised dinner, spent a pleasant half-hour in a hot bath, after which she fell into bed, waking only briefly when, some hours later, Joanna tumbled in beside her and began to snore.

After breakfast the next morning Mrs Wallis took out paper and ink and sat for some time composing a mounting stack of letters.

'Who are you writing to, Aunt Ida?' asked Joanna.

'To the shades of former friends, it may be,' Mrs Wallis said, without looking up. 'It is many years since your mother and I were last in London, and, as you may recall, we departed in awkward circumstances. But if only one of these letters bears the fruit I hope, it will be enough.'

Joanna hovered at her elbow – attempting to read over her shoulder, as Sophie would have liked to do herself – until Mrs Wallis put down her pen and said, 'As you have nothing to do, *Harriet*, I am sure you will be glad to be of use. Go and fetch me a page-boy to take these to the post.'

Joanna fairly scampered away.

When the letters had been dispatched, and their luncheon brought, eaten, and cleared away, Master Alcuin warded the room against listeners and Mrs Wallis settled down again with her work-basket. Master Alcuin and Gray had spent the morning hunched identically over stacks of codices, and Sophie in determined study of the primer in Old Cymric which the former had produced for her from an overstuffed valise; she eyed it now with some disfavour. She could no longer say whether she were more daunted by the noise and bustle of the London street visible from the window of their sitting-room, or eager to escape out of doors.

'May we go out walking, Mrs Wallis?' Sophie asked.

'Oh, yes, please!' Joanna turned from the window. 'Gareth – the boy who took your letters, you know – says that there are public manor-parks to walk in, very near.'

'Perhaps tomorrow,' said Mrs Wallis.

'You need not come with us,' said Joanna, 'if you had rather not . . .'

'And if you lost your way? Or fell under the wheels of a hackney-carriage? I should be a poor chaperon indeed, to set the two of you loose in London before we have been here a day.'

'Perhaps Gray might go with us,' said Sophie diffidently.

Across the room, Gray looked up from his book.

'You know London well, do you, Mr Marshall?' Mrs Wallis enquired.

Gray admitted that he did not. 'But one who knows a good finding-spell or two can never lose his way altogether,' he said.

'And,' said Sophie, inspired, 'I should like to leave an offering to Mercury in thanks for our safe arrival; would that not be wise?'

Mrs Wallis appeared to consider all of this. 'Very well,' she said at last, and, with a meaningful look at Sophie, 'mind you do not draw attention to yourselves.'

The streets of Mayfair were far busier even than those of Oxford, and Sophie found the number of strangers overwhelming, but at length perceiving that they paid her small party little heed, she ceased to fear that everyone they passed might be a spy for the Professor. The crowds and the noise, however, soon enough made her long to turn back. Having left her small offering at the Temple of Mercury and Epona, whose roof-peak she had earlier glimpsed from the hotel window, she had no desire to further prolong the excursion, and she was grateful to see again at last the rooms that she had been so eager to quit not two hours since.

This first outing having passed so uneventfully, however, they had little difficulty in persuading Mrs Wallis to consent to its being repeated, and on the following afternoon they ventured farther afield.

On the third day of their sojourn in London, their now-daily walk took them into a vast park, on whose paths ladies strolled arm in arm and the occasional mounted gentleman walked or trotted by. Gray and Sophie kept a leisurely pace, letting Joanna dart ahead or linger behind as she chose, though never quite out of their sight or hearing.

The sun was well down towards the western horizon when they turned from the footpath into the Serpentine Road, returning in the direction of their hotel. Here was wheeled as well as foot and mounted traffic, and they kept a tighter rein on Joanna, mindful of Mrs Wallis's dire predictions about carriage-wheels.

Thus they both perforce paused with her, at the turning out of the park, to admire the elegant grey mares that were drawing towards them a little open carriage.

The driver slowed as he turned into the park, and thus gave Sophie a clear view of the carriage's occupant as it passed her. The cloaked and bonneted woman looked strangely familiar, but Sophie could not recall when or where she might have seen her before – until, unexpectedly, the woman turned in her seat and spoke, and Sophie saw her face.

'*Gray?*' The voice was incredulous, even frightened. 'Gray, is that you?'

Gray's face paled, flushed, and then split into a delighted, unbelieving grin. He sprinted towards the woman, who was already fumbling awkwardly with the carriage door.

'Jenny!' he cried, lifting her down and whirling her about. 'Jenny, whatever do you here?'

Lady Kergabet extricated herself from her brother's arms and stood on the pavement, staring.

'I have heard no word from you for so long.' She looked to Sophie as though she had seen a shade, or some other unearthly being. 'I thought – I feared that—'

'We are all quite well, Lady Kergabet, truly,' Sophie said.

'We are just now come from Oxford,' said Gray, 'and, Jenny, it has all gone terribly wrong . . .'

'Not here,' Sophie whispered, with a covert tug at his coat-sleeve, and to her relief he subsided.

'Where are you walking to?' Lady Kergabet enquired.

While Gray explained the direction of their hotel, Sophie studied Lady Kergabet. She seemed to have grown more plump since their last view of her, but it was not until she turned to speak to her driver, presenting her profile to Sophie, that the reason for this became apparent. Sophie was pondering what she ought to say – whether this were a suitable venue for congratulations – when Lady Kergabet began to speak again: 'Get in, all of you,' she said – though there seemed hardly room for two, let alone four – 'and I shall take you there, and then you may tell me all.'

When they had all packed themselves into the carriage like herring in a barrel, Lady Kergabet turned to Sophie. 'I must warn you, Miss Callender,' she said, low and grave, 'that you may be no safer from your father in my house. He has already been at Kergabet seeking you, before we came away, and I am not at all persuaded that he believed me when I said you had not been there.'

PART THREE

London

CHAPTER XX

In Which Sophie Is Thoroughly Astonished

'*This is quite* the most preposterous tale I have heard in all my life,' Sieur Germain de Kergabet declared, not two hours later. 'You ask me to believe that you' – he jerked his head at Gray – 'stand accused of a murder which you did not commit, *and* that you bested two master mages in some sort of magickal . . . *duel*, with the help of' – he glanced at his wife, and swallowed – 'of this young lady, and that . . .'

He spread his hands in a gesture of appeal. 'You cannot deny that it is all most implausible. Murders, poisons, and now plots against the Crown . . .'

'We have told you only truth,' Gray said, his voice tight. 'We did not come here to seek your help, but if you should be in a position to give it, I assure you that your efforts will not be misplaced.'

'I will vouch for the truth of what he says,' Master Alcuin offered.

'And I,' said Sophie.

'And so will I,' said Lady Kergabet, speaking for the first time since Gray and Sophie had begun their tale. All of them turned to look at her. 'Two months ago in Breizh,' she told her husband, who looked taken aback, 'when I scried Joanna's and Sophie's father, I saw that he meant harm to Gray; he was the importunate caller whom I told you of last month, seeking to retrieve Sophie, and I am quite willing to scry Gray or any of his friends, to prove to you that they are speaking truth.'

As she spoke Sophie remembered that they had something better even than this. 'Gray,' she murmured, 'the keys we took; have you them still?'

Gray looked briefly puzzled, and then delighted. He felt about in the pockets of his Ned Dunstan coat, from which Mrs Wallis had brushed the worst of the soot and grime; at last he extracted the jangling object and presented it to his sister.

'These,' he said, 'we thought to use to discover the conspirators' next step; we were forced to flee before we could search the Professor's rooms, but perhaps with your help, Jenny, we may yet learn what they plan . . .'

'Those keys are stolen property, I conclude?' said Sieur Germain mildly.

'They are, sir,' said Sophie. 'I stole them myself, and I assure you no man ever deserved it more.'

Sieur Germain raised his eyebrows at her, but said nothing.

Lady Kergabet took the keys, and Sophie watched, fascinated as ever, while she shut her eyes and murmured the still-unintelligible words of her scrying-spell. This time, when she raised her head, she was wide-eyed and pale. What manner of things had she seen or heard?

'I wish I had something of some use to tell you,' she said to Gray. 'He has killed a man who ought to have feared him, but did not; it is not he who wishes the death of King Henry, but they have given him what he asked, and he will keep up his end of the bargain. He has still every intention of seeking your death.' She turned to Sieur Germain and said, 'You shall do as you like in your own house, of course; but for myself, I shall help my brother, and our King.'

It was a brave speech – a brave stance, for a wife to defy her husband so openly; even a Breizhek husband, and even on such a point. Sophie hoped that Lady Kergabet – Jenny, as she had insisted they call her – would not regret it.

Sieur Germain appeared nonplussed, as well he might. Lord and lady faced one another in mutual defiance; Sophie held her breath.

Jenny's husband might have ordered her from the room and thrown the rest of them out into the street; he might have humiliated her before her friends by dismissing her words, or – as any stranger would certainly have done – accused Gray and Sophie of tampering with the keys in order to mislead her.

Instead he nodded sharply, raised her hand to his lips, and said, 'Of course, my dear; of course we must both help Graham and his friends.' He looked round at all of them. 'There will be time later to discuss what it is best to do. For the present – you must all be hungry and weary, after your journey, and we have as yet made you no proper welcome.' At his summons, a servant appeared as if from nowhere with decanter and glasses.

'We shall have refreshments set out in the morning-room,' Sieur Germain went on, when all had drunk in the rite of welcome, 'and, Jenny, perhaps you may like to show our guests their rooms? Miss Callender, Miss Joanna, I understand that you are countrywomen of mine . . . ?'

The recently purchased Carrington-street residence of the Kergabets was a typically tall, narrow Mayfair house whose second-floor bedrooms seemed to the country-bred Sophie to reach Olympian heights; it was elegantly but comfortably furnished, with much bright woodwork and many soft and yielding cushions. The chamber to which Jenny at length conducted her – having duly deposited Mrs Wallis and Joanna in their rooms and sent Gray on alone to the third floor – was bright and cosy, with wardrobe and dressing-table of some cheerful blonde wood, and a coverlet of bright kingfisher blue upon the bed. The shutters were open, and on the outer sill perched several small brown birds, their feathers fluffed out against October's chill.

'I hope you will rest comfortably,' Jenny said, smiling so kindly that Sophie had not the heart to tell her how unlikely this was. 'I am very happy to see you again, you know, though I should wish that the circumstances were different – I wish I were more certain that you will be safe here.'

Sophie – to whom Jenny presently seemed, despite all, a beacon of homely comforts – could think of nothing to say that might adequately convey her feelings.

What little remained of the day was spent mostly in eating (though Sophie, for her part, was too exhausted to feel very hungry) and talking over all that had occurred on either side, since Jenny's visit to Callender Hall. The Professor had been to Kergabet to seek them, but, it appeared, had first gone to Kemper, following their rumoured trail to the Sisters of Sirona. This unlooked-for piece of good fortune explained why, though travelling alone and openly, able to take a more direct route, he had not reached Oxford before them.

After dinner the ladies repaired to the drawing-room, and there, gleaming hospitably from the centre of the floor, was the most beautiful object Sophie had ever beheld.

Her weariness vanished; she only half heard Joanna's laughter at her eager approach to the pianoforte, the first she had seen since leaving Callender Hall. She had never before been so long without practising, and at first her fingers were stiff and uncooperative. She persevered, however, and soon long habit reasserted itself, and the instrument responded to her touch.

She found her way into a gloomy ballad which she had loved as a child, and had lost on the day when she made Mrs Wallis and the housemaids weep, and her parents had confronted her – Mama regretful, Father disapproving – and informed her that well-bred young ladies did not sing common ballads. She had understood from their decree only that, for no evident reason, they wished to take from her one of the few things she loved. But she had known better, by then, than to challenge the Professor, who, though kind enough to Sophie and her sisters when he was pleased with them, grew cross so very easily. Instead she had taken to disappearing from the house for hours at a time, roaming the gardens and, eventually, the park and tenant farms, in search of places where she would not be overheard. Even so, she had never dared to sing that particular ballad aloud; but she sang it now, for herself and for Joanna, feeling dimly that it symbolised an end of her stepfather's power over the children they had been.

And I'll watch all o'er his child while he's growing, she sang, ending the burden of the ballad's final verse, and looked up into an unnerving silence. Without her noticing, the men had come in to join the ladies; tea had been poured, fruit and cakes brought in and eaten; and now Mrs Wallis and Master Alcuin sat on one sofa, and Sieur Germain – with one arm quite openly curled about Jenny's shoulders – on another, and Gray in an armchair with Joanna curled catlike at his feet, all of them watching her. For a long moment no one spoke, and then Jenny seemed to rouse herself and said softly, 'I see that Gray was right, Sophie; yours is a rare talent indeed.'

Sophie's cheeks warmed, and she wished their rapt attention away. 'I am sorry,' she whispered to no one in particular. 'I – I am very tired . . . if I might retire, now . . .'

'Of course,' Jenny nodded. The three men stood, and there was a chorus of good-nights, and Sophie slipped out of the drawing-room and escaped up the stairs.

At first Gray thought he was hearing things – hearing again, perhaps, whatever odd manifestation had afflicted him in the temple at Kerandraon. Almost at once, however, he recognised that this sound was a physical voice, and a voice he knew. As before, he was helpless to resist it.

The song – not so much a song as a low, mournful keening – drew him out of his bed, out of the room, down the stairs, until he stood before Sophie's closed door. While his conscious mind shrieked at him to escape this compromising position with all possible speed, his left hand seemed to raise itself unbidden and gently rapped its knuckles against the polished wood.

The singing stopped abruptly, and with it vanished Gray's feeling of compulsion; and now, at last, wide awake and gobsmacked by his own stupidity, he understood.

He turned on his heel, prepared to flee, but before he could do so, the door opened, and he turned back to see Sophie's blotched and tear-stained face blinking up at him. Her hair hung in a thick plait over one shoulder, dark against her white nightdress.

Even in the half moonlight he could see the dark smudges under her eyes.

'Gray?' she whispered. 'Whatever are you doing here?'

'Your spell drew me,' he replied.

'What spell?'

'The one you sang.'

As Sophie only looked more bewildered, he went on: 'I see now how the magick works, and I promise to explain everything in the morning – I shall ask Master Alcuin to help me confirm – but I cannot stay here, Sophie, you must see that – if anyone heard, or saw—'

'No!' The desperation in that syllable belied her almost inaudible tone. To Gray's astonishment, she took hold of his dressing-gown and pulled him through the doorway, nearly cracking his skull against the lintel; then she released him, closed the door, and leant her weight against it. The moonlight showed her face more clearly now – the evidence of weeping, the lines of exhaustion that she hid so effectively by day. She looked desperate and defeated.

'I cannot sleep,' she confessed, as Gray moved out of range of the window. 'The nightmares have begun again, and worse than ever. I am frightened even to close my eyes. Mrs Wallis offers to spell me asleep, but . . .'

'Why do you not let her?' he whispered fiercely. 'You will do yourself harm, Sophie—'

'Will you do it? Please? I think . . . I think I should not mind it, if it were *your* spell.'

He stared at her in silence.

'Please,' she repeated, low. 'I cannot trust her, Gray. You cannot ask it of me – not after all of her lies to me, all these years . . .'

'Yet you follow her,' Gray said stupidly. 'All this way—'

'I follow *you*.'

The implications of this simple avowal made Gray dizzy with hope and despair. *But what does it matter what she thinks of me, if she drives herself mad with nightmares?* 'Go back to bed,' he said. 'I know a spell.'

He could almost feel Sophie's relief as she crept under the eiderdown, curling up like a child with her hand under her cheek. They had all grown used to her habit of nodding off at odd moments, and Sophie had always, after that first night on the road, refused to discuss the matter; but surely he – who loved her, and had sworn to serve her – ought to have seen how she suffered.

Crossing the room to kneel beside the bed, he laid one hand against her brow and, gathering up his magick, began to croon a spell for dreamless sleep. Slowly, Sophie's eyelids dropped; even after her deep, even breathing told him that the spell had done its work, he kept his station for some time, his gaze rapt upon her sleeping face.

At last, regretfully, he levered himself to his feet and looked about him, confronting the far greater problem of how to regain the safety of his own bed. For if any of Jenny's household were to find him here, barefoot and clad in nightshirt and borrowed dressing-gown, nightmares would be the least of Sophie's worries.

In the morning, Sophie was awakened by a knock at her door: one of the Kergabet housemaids, bearing morning tea. She felt disoriented and groggy, as though she had slept too long – though when the housemaid threw open the shutters, she saw that the sun had only just risen – and an odd impression nagged at her, of strange doings in the night. Still, she had slept more soundly here than in any bed since her own at Callender Hall, and, having been spared the usual nightmare procession of bloodied bodies and twisted limbs and dead, staring eyes, she felt it would be churlish to complain of how strange it was not to have dreamt at all.

Once washed and dressed, she leant her elbows briefly on the windowsill, looking out at the chill, bright October day. How peculiar to be surrounded by so many houses! But she felt oddly safe here, as though protected by the anonymity of this house, so like all the others.

She ran against Gray in the first-floor corridor that led to the breakfast room; he looked at her in a way she could not interpret and asked in a low voice whether she had slept well.

'Very well, I thank you,' she replied, puzzled, and was more puzzled at his smile.

The morning's post was brought in by a parlourmaid, who deposited a large stack of letters before Sieur Germain and handed on a salver a single thick epistle, sealed in violet wax, to his wife.

'This letter is from my mother in Kernow,' Jenny said, turning it over. She hesitated briefly, perhaps reluctant to exclude her guests by reading it at table, but in the end curiosity seemed to get the better of her; she broke the seal and read the letter through, whilst the conversation went on around her.

'My mother's news is *most* interesting,' she said at length, when the talk lagged for a moment.

'Indeed?' Her husband raised a sceptical eyebrow. 'How so?'

'She writes of her efforts to arrange a betrothal for her unfortunate second son.'

Down the table, Gray choked on his bread-and-butter.

After a moment he drained the remaining contents of his teacup and said to Jenny, 'And what result have these efforts yielded, then?'

'None, alas,' she replied, calmly. 'It seems that my father refuses to involve himself in the business – maintains, you know, that he has no such son – and she has "found it impossible, thus far, to persuade any respectable family to consider such a regrettable alliance."'

'*Regrettable!*' The word had left Sophie's lips before she could stop it; her teacup shattered, its contents overflowing the saucer and spreading a pale brown stain over Jenny's fine linen tablecloth. Every eye at the table came to rest on her.

'I do apologise, Lady Kergabet,' she muttered, too flustered and furious to concentrate on deflecting their attention. 'I . . . if Gray were *my* brother, I should be very angry to hear him slighted in such a way.'

'Jenny is quite accustomed to it, Sophie,' Gray said kindly, 'as am I. You need not fret over the blow to my vanity.'

She caught his bitter half smile in the instant before he schooled his expression to neutrality, and her heart seemed to miss a beat. For a moment she forgot the others at the table, plunged into a vivid memory of the past night's events, and she and Gray might have been alone in her moonlit chamber again.

Then his half smile grew into a crooked grin, and she looked down at her plate, her cheeks burning under Joanna's speculative gaze.

'She asks,' Jenny continued after a moment, as collectedly as though she had seen none of this, 'for my help, and my husband's, in convincing someone to allow his daughter to marry Gray.'

I, cried a voice in Sophie's mind whose existence she had not till now suspected. *I will marry him, with all my heart* . . . She kept her gaze fixed on her plate and pleated the edge of the tablecloth between her fingers.

'Marriage need not be such a *very* dreadful prospect,' Jenny was saying now, gently teasing.

'Jenny, must you?' Gray spoke quietly, but his voice held a warning note that Sophie had heard before, and Jenny must have recognised it also, for she quickly steered the discussion to other subjects. Sophie, preoccupied by her efforts not to make a scene, hardly knew what the others talked of.

'Sophie?' said Jenny's voice at her ear.

She looked up, startled, to find the table deserted; during her silent internal struggle, the others apparently had finished their meal and gone their separate ways. Jenny stood beside her chair, one hand on the curve of her belly and the other on Sophie's shoulder, smiling down with every appearance of compassion. 'My dear, you look quite overset,' she said. 'And I should like to talk with you a little. Might I persuade you to help me with my fancy-work . . . ?'

Numbly, Sophie nodded and rose to follow her out of the breakfast-room.

'You are angry with me,' Jenny said, when they had settled themselves in her airy, pleasant little sitting-room.

'Not with you,' Sophie protested. Though the baby's gown whose hem she was embellishing gave her an excuse to keep her eyes focused on her work, it offered no escape from probing questions.

'With my mother, then,' said Jenny. 'I understand your feelings perfectly.'

'I cannot see how,' Sophie said, her voice strange and choked in her own ears.

'You love and admire Gray,' said Jenny, 'and believe no one else values him as you do.' She appeared not to notice Sophie's discomfiture, but calmly continued, 'I have loved and admired my brother far longer than you can have done, Sophie, though perhaps not better.'

'I am sorry – I meant no disrespect—' She broke off, affronted by her hostess's expression of amusement.

'I do beg your pardon, Sophie,' Jenny said. 'I know that this must all be very trying. I had hoped, you see, that we might become better acquainted – that we might, perhaps, be friends . . .'

She spoke so kindly. She had put herself forward, had perhaps endangered her family, for their sake, when she might so easily have turned them away; not least, she was Gray's loyal and beloved sister. Sophie had a sudden, mad urge to kneel at Jenny's feet and confess everything – even acknowledge aloud, perhaps, this morning's new discovery. Jenny, she was sure, would not laugh at her. But had Sophie not done enough already to turn Gray's life on end?

Instead, therefore, she forced herself to smile calmly, to set her stitches neatly as she said, with perfect though greatly abridged truth, 'I should like that very much.'

They spoke, as they worked, of inconsequential things, and Sophie was surprised to find herself enjoying the conversation; it was a relief from poisons and treason and shielding-spells to turn her hands to fancy-work, and her thoughts to considering the relative merits of green velvet and blue lustring.

She and Jenny were laughing happily over the latter's tales of kitchen prankery when, to Sophie's astonishment, the door burst noisily open and Gray, breathless and frantic-eyed, ducked under the lintel. 'Jenny!' he exclaimed. 'Have you seen—?'

Then his gaze lit on Sophie, and his whole bearing relaxed – then stiffened again in something very like accusation. 'Why do you hide in here?' he demanded. 'Joanna has been quite frantic, and Mrs Wallis—'

'I am not *hiding*,' Sophie retorted, holding up her embroidery. 'I am helping Jenny.'

Gray frowned at her, and, blushing, she dropped her eyes.

'I asked Sophie's help, Gray,' Jenny said. 'She has had far too much of excitement and distress of late, and she needs quiet and peace, and a little female company. If you persist in worrying her,' she went on, more severely, 'I shall be forced to ask that you amuse yourself elsewhere.'

There was a brief, tense silence. Then Gray said, very quietly, 'I shall be in the library, Sophie, with Master Alcuin. What we have been discussing concerns you very directly. When you have finished your work, perhaps you would join us there.'

'Of course,' Sophie whispered; her hands trembled as she set stitch upon stitch. She did not look up, however, until she had heard the door close, and then she found Jenny studying her with such a lively interest as made her drop her gaze to her work again, gritting her teeth in an effort to restrain her tears.

CHAPTER XXI

In Which Are Discussed Magick, Plots, and Counterplots

Gray returned to Sieur Germain's library in a morose temper. Quite why he felt so disappointed in Sophie and Jenny, he could not exactly make out; he had no good reason to take umbrage with either . . .

'Marshall?' Master Alcuin looked up from his energetic note-taking at the sound of the closing door. 'You have not found her?'

'I have found her, indeed,' Gray replied; 'she is with my sister, *embroidering baby-clothes* and talking of . . . of fripperies, as though we had nothing of more importance to do.'

The older man shook his head. 'Miss Sophie does her best, Marshall,' he said. 'As do you. You must not expect too much of her; she has not had the advantages of a systematic education, and she has far more magickal talent than most, nearly all undisciplined and unexplored. And, besides all this, she is very young, and has been accustomed to a much more . . . retired style of living than—'

Gray slumped dejectedly into a seat across the table. 'It is not that, at all,' he admitted. 'If it were that she is unwilling, or did not learn quickly enough . . .'

'Well, then,' Master Alcuin prompted, 'what is it that disturbs you so? This is not like you, Marshall.'

Gray was spared the trial of attempting to explain, however, for at that moment the door opened, almost silently, and Sophie – looking as colourless and insignificant as in her father's dining-room – stepped into the library. Though she did not greet him or even look at him, he felt, now that she was near, like a wandering sailor at last sighting his lodestar.

'Here I am,' she said softly, taking a seat at the end of the table and addressing herself to Master Alcuin. 'Magister, Gray tells me that there is something you wished to discuss with me?'

'Indeed,' their teacher replied. 'A discovery of great import to your magick – though it is his more than my own. Did you not tell me, Marshall,' turning to Gray, 'that the answer came to you in the night?'

At once Sophie blushed and looked down at her hands, and Gray wished heartily that he had not said even this much to any other person. 'I ought not to have alluded to the circumstances,' he said, leaning towards Sophie and pitching his voice for her ears alone, 'but I should not wish to . . . to steer you awry . . . on such a matter.'

She raised her face to his, eyes wide. 'What matter?' she asked. 'Gray, whatever do you mean?'

'Your spell,' Gray said; 'or, rather, your *spells*. Your *magia musicae*. I – we – I understand, now, what it is you do.'

Sophie remembered, now, that last night he had promised to explain something.

'You found it yourself,' he continued, 'in the marginalia of Gaius Britannicus's commentary on Orpheus; but I did not understand, then, what it meant.'

'*The singer may work various magicks, even as the Sirens of Homer*,' Sophie quoted, remembering. 'It does mean something, then?'

'It means exactly what it says,' Master Alcuin replied. 'The Sirens are – were – the first recorded to possess this particular magick. It is very rare indeed, but the histories document various other exercises of such a power, though in such a haphazard way that its course is difficult to follow.'

'What power?' Sophie was bewildered. 'The Sirens' song lured men to their deaths, the histories say . . .' She paused, and in her mind things shifted subtly, fragments slotting into place. She looked up in horror. 'That?' she demanded. '*That* is my talent?'

Gray's expression told her she had guessed aright.

'*Magia musicae* is not inherently malevolent,' Master Alcuin said gently, holding her gaze. 'Its effects depend on will, on intent. The same is true of any magickal working, as I am sure you understand.'

'What Master Alcuin means,' Gray added – Sophie turned to him, hopeful – 'is that though you certainly *could* do such a thing, anyone admitted to the privilege of knowing you, must understand that you never *should*.'

'Exactly, exactly,' the older man agreed, and patted Sophie's hand. 'The vital words are *various magicks*; you may leave the Sirens out entirely, if you wish.'

'Yes,' said Sophie after a moment. 'Yes, I think I should prefer it so.'

'It is all in Orpheus,' Gray explained. 'Gaius Britannicus did not quite comprehend it; perhaps he translates the Greek too literally. I am not sure how well I understand it myself. But here – in Claudius Varo's translation – we have this . . .' One long finger trailed along the line of cramped Latin print as he read, '*That which we name "the magick of music" has generally several discrete parts: the power of drawing persons for diverse purposes, or of holding captive; a species of foretelling, in general sadly unreliable; the means to evoke a sanguine or melancholy mood in the hearer; the power of soothing a savage or enraged beast* . . . There is quite a bit more in this vein; and at last we have this: *It is generally agreed, that the human voice is the most powerful channel of this magick, and that only the most powerful possessors of such a talent may exercise it in other wise* – with an instrument alone, I suppose he means. Then, eventually, he tells us that a person possessing such a talent may exercise all of its aspects or, more usually, a few only.' Laying the codex gently down upon the table, he looked up at Sophie. 'What do you think? Have we found our answer?'

'I . . .' Sophie could not think what to say. *Your spell drew me*, Gray had said, and she supposed that he must have the right of it, for certainly she could offer no better explanation. 'Does Orpheus,' she began again, 'condescend to explain the particulars of the workings he mentions?'

Gray looked down at the book again. 'If he does so,' he said dryly, 'it is not in a manner I should consider practically useful. My own opinion . . .'

There was a brief silence before, almost simultaneously, both Sophie and Master Alcuin prompted, 'Your opinion?'

'I believe that this magick must work in the same way as your . . . more evident talent,' said Gray. 'But – tell me—' His eyes held Sophie's, and she found herself, absurdly, admiring their depth of colour: gold and brown and green mixed all together. 'What were you thinking of, when . . . ?'

'Of you, of course,' she replied, without pausing for thought.

'And those other times?'

'Other times?'

'In the small drawing-room at Callender Hall,' Gray elaborated, and now she recalled his – at the time, mystifying – remarks on the subject of displaced magick shock: *There was magick in that room. I felt it – it called me there.*

'I cannot now recall,' she said, 'or not precisely; but I was thinking, I suppose, how much I should miss your company when the Professor took you away again.'

She smiled, a little tremulously, and was inexpressibly comforted by his answering smile.

'And on that first night in the library?'

Sophie blinked. 'Then, too?' she asked. 'I . . . I was wishing for someone to help me make sense of Gaius Aegidius.'

She remembered thinking, at the time, what an odd coincidence it was that Gray should have appeared in the doorway of the library just then.

'It does seem that we have made some considerable progress.' Master Alcuin's pensive remark startled Sophie from her thoughts. Both she and Gray turned to give him their full attention.

'Of the workings mentioned by Orpheus,' he began, 'we can be sure only of the drawing-spell; what else you may be able to achieve, we shall have to determine by experiment – at some other time, when we have leisure for such researches. But, Marshall, this discovery of yours raises more questions than it answers. Tavener's *Historie*, you see' – before him lay another, newer codex, which he patted affectionately as he spoke – 'names the royal house of Tudor as connected to *magia musicae*, and as for Miss Sophie's other, equally unusual magickal talent . . .' He paused.

Sophie found that her hands had curled into fists, and carefully unfolded them.

'I am an old man,' Master Alcuin went on, 'old enough to have seen a great deal of what the two of you may consider "history", and heard tell of considerably more, accounts both reliable and . . . rather less so. It occurs to me that some years ago – perhaps as many years, Miss Sophie, as you have lived – the kingdom was full of tales of another young woman who seemed able to disappear at will. A woman who fled one night with her infant daughter, and never was seen again . . .'

We must tell him. He has guessed it all already . . . Sophie fought the urge to look to Gray for confirmation of her decision; this was her own secret, her own tale, and the telling of it must be hers to undertake.

'You are quite right, Magister,' she said at last, raising her head to meet his kindly, penetrating eyes. 'That woman was my mother; she has been in the realm of Proserpina these past nine years, and – and the infant daughter with whom she fled, you see before you now.'

Master Alcuin's blue eyes widened; then, to Sophie's dismay, he began to rise from his chair.

'I should not advise kneeling, Magister,' said Gray. 'You will find that Sophie does not much care for it.'

By the time they had done explaining matters to Master Alcuin, Sophie had come to another decision. 'Gray,' she said firmly, 'we must also tell your sister and brother-in-law. It is not fair to ask for their trust, and then to abuse it by withholding the truth.'

He looked at her – doubtfully, it seemed – and fetched a sigh. 'You are right, of course,' he said at last.

Sophie stood – triggering a cacophony of scraping and clattering as her companions hastened to follow suit – and squared her shoulders, saying, 'We had best get it over, then. Unless . . .' She looked from Gray to Master Alcuin, biting her lip. 'Ought I to go alone? If—'

'Of course not,' Gray said. He patted Sophie's shoulder in a vague, kindly way and, opening the library door, waved her through before him. Master Alcuin followed her out, remarking, 'Perhaps we should do better to suspend our study of battle magicks until tomorrow, when we are all feeling more composed.'

Sophie stopped in her tracks and turned to gape at him. 'Surely . . . surely we cannot learn battle magicks indoors, in a London house!'

'Indeed,' Gray said, 'that seems most inadvisable.'

Master Alcuin looked pleased with himself. 'But your sister,

Marshall, thinks it *most advisable* that you both learn to defend yourselves, and has offered us the use of a cellar room for the purpose. I spoke to her on the subject this morning,' he added, 'before breakfast; we have arranged it all between us.'

'One of Master Alcuin's few defects,' Gray remarked dryly, 'is a propensity to be up and about when wiser folk are still abed. It is a fault he shares with my sister, alas.'

They found the other ladies in the drawing-room, Jenny pottering about at the pianoforte while Mrs Wallis darned stockings, and dispatched Joanna to fetch Sieur Germain. Mrs Wallis put down her work and rose to demand of Sophie, sotto voce, what she was about; before any explanation or justification could be attempted, however, Joanna returned with Sieur Germain in tow, and Mrs Wallis took her expression of alarm back to her seat.

There was no knowing what tale Joanna had spun for their host. He was out of breath and looked anxious; when Master Alcuin murmured a warding-spell, his expression of anxiety deepened, and Jenny, too, began to look alarmed.

'Sophie, dear, whatever is the matter?' the latter enquired. 'You look very grim.'

Sophie attempted a reassuring smile; even she was conscious of its not succeeding very well.

'We have not been entirely forthright,' Sophie began. She ought properly to look at her audience, but though she might have made herself meet Jenny's eyes, to look at Sieur Germain was quite impossible.

'That is . . . we have told you nothing but truth; but we have not – *I* have not – told all the truth. But I have decided—'

'Think before you speak, Miss Sophia,' said Mrs Wallis, with a meaning look.

'I have thought, thank you.' Sophie's fingers gripped the edges of the piano-bench on which she sat, as though she could somehow draw courage from the polished wood. 'My mind is quite made up.'

'There are other considerations, child! Think – is this wise?'

'Perhaps not, but—'

'Enough!' Sieur Germain thundered, making them all jump. 'Miss Callender has something to say to us,' he went on, more moderately, 'and anyone who does not wish to hear it may leave the room.'

With a wary glance at him, Mrs Wallis subsided.

'I am very sorry, Sieur Germain, Lady Kergabet, for having deceived you, when you have been so kind and generous to us,' Sophie went on. 'I hardly know where to begin . . .'

'Begin at the beginning, Miss Callender,' Sieur Germain suggested patiently.

Sophie laughed – a choked, horrible sound. 'The beginning would be long in the telling,' she said, her gaze on the elegant pattern of the carpet at her feet, 'but the end is that I am *not* Miss Callender, at all. I am – I am—'

But she found she could not go on.

The fraught silence of the drawing-room was stirred by a rustle of skirts, the sigh of upholstery released from someone's weight, soft footfalls on the thick carpet. An arm gently encircled Sophie's shoulders; on her other side, a large, warm hand clasped hers.

'She is the lost Princess Royal,' said Jenny, to Sophie's astonishment. 'She whom we have heard so much talked of, since coming up to Town – the daughter of the vanished Queen Laora, whom His Majesty seeks so eagerly of late . . .'

'You *knew*?' Sophie whispered.

'I have still your father's key-ring – your stepfather's, that is.' Jenny raised her voice a little to be heard over the exclamations of her husband and brother. The two men fell silent, and her next words were spoken in the gentler tones Sophie knew: 'When one scries an object more than once, things inscrutable may grow clearer, and the strongest emotions leave the most tangible impressions. When your stepfather came to Kergabet, he told us that he was seeking his daughter. But when last he used one of the keys on that key-ring in the door of his library in Breizh, he was locking it against his stepdaughter, and the shade of her mother, the—' Jenny's voice faltered, and she continued apologetically, 'the Breton harlot.'

Sophie flinched and stole a glance at Mrs Wallis; she was stony-faced but – perhaps resigned to her indiscretion now that it was proved redundant – looked less splenetic than before.

Sieur Germain opened his mouth, clearly about to take his wife to task for keeping this secret from him. Jenny silenced him with a look.

'And Gray?' Sophie asked anxiously, catching at her hand. 'Does my stepfather seek him? Does he suspect where we have gone?'

'I cannot tell,' said Jenny. 'I am sorry not to be of more use.' Head on one side, she regarded Sophie with a crooked smile very like her brother's. 'I ought to have seen long ago that you were not what you seemed,' she said. 'You do honour to my house, Your Royal Highness, and you are most heartily welcome.'

Sophie clasped her hands in the folds of her skirt, to hide their trembling. 'The honour is mine,' she whispered.

The servants had poured the wine and handed the dishes, and Sieur Germain had dismissed them until the next remove, which seemed to signal a council of war. 'I have been thinking,' he began, 'what is best to do—'

'We cannot do anything,' said Gray (unleashing on his brother-in-law, in the form of ill-mannered impatience, the frustrations and anxieties that preyed upon his mind), 'without more information—'

Jenny frowned at him, and he subsided. After a moment it occurred to him that this conversation would be much better carried out without benefit of listeners, and he drew up his magick and began to mutter a warding-spell.

'I have been thinking what we had best do,' Sieur Germain repeated calmly, 'if we are to have any hope of foiling a plot of whose form we have as yet no clear idea. Let us canvass what we do know. A conspiracy exists, which involves, at the least, four men: Viscount Carteret; Appius Callender of Oxford; Callender's comrade-in-arms, who may or may not be identical with the mysterious *M*; and *W*, whose identity we do not know, but whom we may assume to be close to His Majesty, or at any rate to the Court. We know also that at least one man has already fallen victim to this plot, and we can be fairly certain that his death was in the nature of a rehearsal for the true purpose of the conspiracy. What else?'

'We believe,' said Gray, 'that Lord Halifax was killed by means of a particularly arcane poison, which is intended to mimic the appearance of a natural death, and which requires considerable time and at least one ingredient that could not have been obtained except illicitly; from which I think we may conclude that, for some reason, the conspirators' plan depends on creating that appearance of natural death. We believe that their purpose is treason and regicide, and we can, I think, be fairly certain that their plans, whatever they are, require the reappearance of the Princess Royal.'

His throat was dry; after a swallow of wine he continued. 'What we do *not* know is how they intend to administer the poison, or when, or where; we do not know what they hope to gain from their crimes, nor' – he could not keep the frustration from his voice – 'nor do we know what they want Sophie *for*.'

'I should imagine,' said Sophie, in a voice so tightly controlled that it seemed to cut across Gray's skin like a blade, 'that they still expect me to be their princess, and marry some elderly Iberian prince; or, if not that, then to marry someone else to whom my position and powers may be useful.'

The idea of marriage so obviously repulsed her that Gray was almost ashamed to meet her gaze.

'Even had we not the evidence of Carteret's diary and his references to "the girl",' said Sieur Germain, 'everyone in London – and half the kingdom, very likely – has heard the rumours of the King's irrational obsession with his lost child. A year ago the talk at Court was all of His Majesty's desire to make common cause with the King of Alba against the claims of Eire, and his proposal to grant the Duke of Breizh and the barons in Cymru the same power as those of Maine and Normandie to levy taxes and militia, as Breizh's border is equally threatened from the south – he was known to have had several acrimonious disagreements with Lord Carteret's faction of the Council on those very points – but now—'

'Oh!' Gray said, as the possibilities unfolded before him. Often and often, he had been baffled by the meaning of a passage until, by some minute shift of the context in which it appeared, a tutor or fellow student had cast just the right light upon it to change everything. His brother-in-law had just done the same. 'They have been encouraging him,' he went on, his gaze unfocused on the shining curve of the wine glass in his hand. 'He was making plans which Lord Carteret and his friends did not like, and they have hit upon this means of distracting and discrediting him. If all the world believes that he has lost his senses, if he seems to have no thought but of his lost child, then who could fault his closest advisor for taking the reins in his stead? Of course any political move His Majesty makes will seem crackbrained to those who believe him to be acting under the influence of such an obsession, and Lord Carteret can then do as he likes.'

'But if that were so,' said Sophie, 'why should they wish him dead?'

Gray looked up and saw her frowning in puzzlement. 'How old is the Crown Prince?' he asked Sieur Germain.

'Rising fifteen,' said the latter.

'The sooner he takes the throne, then,' said Mrs Wallis, 'the more time his regent will have to consolidate his influence over the new King, and what better regent for young Edward than his father's faithful advisor, who so ably kept the kingdom afloat when we might all have run aground on the rocks of Henry's obsession?'

'Oh,' Sophie whispered. 'Yes, I see.'

'And if Lord Carteret *does* mean to marry Sophie off for some advantage of his,' said Joanna, 'he will have an easier time of it as regent to King Edward than as advisor to King Henry.'

'I do not see how it could be any easier,' said Sophie bitterly, 'considering how our present predicament came about.'

There was a silence, then, which ran on too long to be entirely comfortable – except, apparently, for Joanna, whose enjoyment of her *ragoût de veau* continued unabated.

'His Majesty is presently at Caernarfon,' said Sieur Germain at last, 'and does not return until shortly before Samhain; and we know that Callender and *M* are at Oxford, and Lord Carteret here in Town. *W* we may suppose to have gone to Caernarfon with the royal family, as Lord Carteret clearly meant to order him thither—' He broke off with a soft *Oh!* and a pained expression.

'My lord?' Jenny's voice was low, but such was the tense, expectant silence around the table that all eyes turned to her. 'Are you well?'

'Quite well, my dear,' said her husband, but he scrubbed the knuckles of his right hand against his brow as though his head pained him. 'I have had an idea which I do not much like. My dear, do you remember the man whom you danced with at Lady D'Aubigny's ball, just before you and I were introduced?'

Jenny's expression said quite clearly that she did not.

'A fair-haired man,' Sieur Germain prompted, 'not tall, and not much younger than myself. You told me, I recall, that he thought very highly of himself.'

'Ah!' said Jenny, her eyes lighting in wry recognition. 'Yes, I do remember him. The Earl of Wrexham, yes?'

'Yes,' said Sieur Germain. 'Brother to Queen Edwina, and presently in Caernarfon with his sister and her husband and sons.'

There was a long, thoughtful silence.

'If Lord Wrexham is the *W* of Lord Carteret's diary,' said Gray, 'or even if he is not – so long as *W* is at Caernarfon with the King, it is of no use to send a warning to the King there; it would only be intercepted and destroyed.'

'And in any case,' Sieur Germain said, 'we cannot approach His Majesty – or anyone at Court, for that matter – and simply tell him that his closest advisor and his brother-in-law are plotting an attempt on his life; we should only be laughed at.'

Gray winced at this unintended allusion to the late events at Merlin; Sophie had now stopped eating altogether and was staring down at the veal, carrots, and parsnips congealing on her plate.

'And as there are five mages among us,' said Master Alcuin, 'it will be taken as read that any evidence we might offer for scrying has been tampered with by one or other of us.'

'But if *W* travelled into Cymru with the royal family, or soon thereafter,' said Gray, thinking aloud, 'then he was already there before Lord Halifax's death, and has had no opportunity to lay hands on the poison. Caernarfon, if I do not mistake, is His Majesty's place of retreat from the duties of the throne?'

Sieur Germain nodded.

'Then,' said Jenny, catching at Gray's line of argument as she always had, 'if we cannot reach him there, equally he is beyond the reach of . . . others. Whatever their plan may be, they cannot put it into execution until His Majesty returns to London.'

'But that is only half true,' Gray said, speaking the thought as it came to him. 'His Majesty may be inaccessible at Caernarfon, but *Sophie is here*.'

He could not, he reminded himself sternly, pack Sophie into a hired carriage and flee to Alba or Eire; no one else here present had witnessed the conspirators' conversation in the Professor's rooms, the finding of the ciphered documents, the brawl in the Master's Lodge. Besides, in so doing he might well only be drawing her into further danger. But just at this moment there was nothing he wanted more.

'That is so,' said Sieur Germain, 'but all of us are here with her, Graham. Miss Sophie,' he said, turning to her, 'you may be assured that we shall not let you come to harm.'

Then turning again, he met Gray's eyes with a firm, determined nod.

Gray considered his brother-in-law.

His parents had not invited him to his sister's wedding; alerted by a letter from Jenny and Celia, however, he had prevailed upon Crowther to lend him the price of the journey to Kernow by the mail-coach, and thus contrived to appear at his father's house in time to see Jenny Marshall become Lady Kergabet, and to join in the procession that accompanied the new bride to her husband's temporary lodgings in Truru.

He had been reassured, on making his new brother's acquaintance, to find that Sieur Germain seemed genuinely enamoured of Jenny, and to hear him speak as admiringly of her talent and her wit as of her beauty. He would have been much the happier, however, for any evidence that Jenny was likewise fond of her bridegroom.

'And are you happy, Jenny?' he had asked her anxiously, when they contrived a few moments alone. 'I should not mind about Father, and your going so far away, if I could think of your being happy there . . .'

'He is a good man, Gray,' said Jenny. Her fond, sad smile had given him the sudden vertiginous sense that their ages had been reversed. 'And he has been very kind to me – and to Mama, which you know is not always very easy. I beg you will not be unhappy on my account; I shall be quite as well contented in my new home as I could possibly be elsewhere. And' – she caught Gray's arm – 'and you will write to me very often, will you not? And come and visit me, whenever we may go up to Town?'

Gray had given her as reassuring a smile as he could manage, and stooped to embrace her. 'I shall certainly do so; you shall hear of all my doings, till you are quite weary of me. Though I do not know if your husband is quite as eager as yourself to give me house-room . . .'

At this, he remembered, Jenny had stood a little straighter and said firmly, 'I shall persuade him.'

Gray rather wondered, now, whether Sieur Germain had in fact required so very much persuading; the first shock being over, he seemed as game for an adventure as Joanna.

CHAPTER XXII

In Which Sieur Germain Makes Himself Very Useful

In the days that followed, Sophie became drearily familiar with the four walls of the Carrington-street cellar, and was so much occupied by day, and so thoroughly exhausted by night, that she had little opportunity for anxiety and a merciful, if partial, release from seeing those she loved die bloodily in her dreams. She and Gray, under Master Alcuin's tutelage, practised summonings and shielding-spells, spells to fling small objects at putative foes and to move large ones (more sedately) at need, spells to confuse, spells to call blinding light. In the absence of other opponents, they soon began sparring against one another, for the straw-and-canvas targets on which they had begun, as their teacher pointed out, could not return fire, and he was continually urging less caution.

'You have much to learn of elemental magick,' Master Alcuin said, thoughtful. 'For earth-magick I see no application suited for our purposes, but the control of water, air, and fire may prove invaluable – and the last particularly. To begin with we shall try a few useful fire-spells . . .'

Sophie tried to conceal her shudder.

They settled themselves against one wall to listen whilst Master Alcuin expounded the uses of fire in battle. At last Sophie, seizing the opportunity offered by a brief pause in the spate of theories and *exempli*, raised her voice a little to say, 'Magister, if it is all the same to you, I think I had rather forgo the practical side of this lesson.'

Master Alcuin paused and looked at her consideringly.

'Fire is like magick,' said Gray softly, for Sophie's ears alone. 'Controlled, an invaluable tool; uncontrolled, a catastrophe. I pray you need never *use* this knowledge, but you are wiser and safer for having it.'

Sophie could not deny the truth of this, but a memory loomed of Lord Halifax's study, and Gray staggering through a wall of flames.

Her fingers clenching against the flagstones, she looked up again at Master Alcuin. 'But I *cannot* – please, do not ask me—'

'Of course you can, Sophie,' said Gray. 'Did you not master unseen summoning in a single afternoon? Perhaps you do not recognise how unheard-of . . . I was your age, or thereabouts, when I learnt that spell; it cost me a week's effort, as I remember.'

'It – that is quite different,' said Sophie, distracted by this turn of the discussion. 'I had no idea of – and I was abed nearly two days, afterwards . . .'

Her voice trailed into silence as she stared, puzzled, at Master Alcuin; he was chuckling, shaking his white head. 'How long, Marshall, Miss Sophie, how long would you guess that it took me to master that working?'

Sophie looked at Gray, who looked back at her with equal puzzlement. 'Perhaps . . . three days?' he said.

'A week?' Sophie hazarded.

Smiling, Master Alcuin shook his head.

'A month,' he said, 'less perhaps a day.' He looked earnestly from one of his apprentices to the other. 'Do you begin to see, now, what power the two of you might one day command?'

'What do you see, Jenny?' Joanna asked eagerly.

Sieur Germain was away from home, visiting some mutual

acquaintance of himself and Lord Carteret, and Master Alcuin resting upstairs; the rest of the family were gathered in the morning-room.

Jenny shook her head as she laid the Professor's key-ring upon her worktable. 'These have been too long parted from their owner, I think,' she said, 'or I have exhausted them; there seems nothing new to be gleaned today that was not there before. Your stepfather is very angry with you, Sophie,' she added. 'It makes anything else difficult to see.'

Sophie lifted her chin. 'He has always been angry with me, more or less,' she said, 'when it suited him to take notice of me at all. I should be the more surprised if he were not.'

'*I* am not afraid of Father,' said Joanna.

'Then you would do well to be afraid of his friends,' said Gray, rather sharply.

Mrs Wallis, hitherto silent over her work, looked up at this. 'Wise advice, Mr Marshall,' she said.

'I wish,' said Sophie, in a voice of suppressed passion, 'I wish there were something we might *do*. I am half mad with waiting. And it is all very well to learn to defend ourselves, but surely . . . surely if things go so far, we shall have lost already.'

Jenny rose from her seat and went to the window, where she stood looking down into the street.

Sophie turned to Gray and went on, 'I read once of a king who wore rings and jewels spelled to resist poisons, but perhaps it was only a tale, for I cannot at all remember where I read it.'

'It was Henry the Great; he of the many wives,' said Gray at once. It was that Henry, it occurred to him, who in a sense had begun the story of Sophie's exile, when by divorcing his first Queen, Catherine of Aragon, he had given such gross offence to what were then the several courts of Iberia. 'There is a brief account in Tavener's *Historie*, and I believe one of Master Alcuin's books – the poisons, you know – describes how the magick was managed by his Court mages. Only—'

'Yes, I see.' Sophie looked discouraged. 'We should have to borrow some piece of jewellery from His Majesty, or send him one and make him wear it, and how should we ever manage *that*?'

They subsided for a time into a disconsolate silence.

'We are marching towards our battlefield in the dark,' said Gray at last, 'on the strength of last month's intelligence.'

Gray had been used to consider himself a prudent and sensible man, but sequestration in Carrington-street had begun to wear away his prudence and good sense. 'Sophie,' he said, dropping his voice and leaning towards her, 'what do you say to a little reconnaissance?'

Sophie looked up eagerly.

'Mr Marshall!' Mrs Wallis had evidently much keener ears than Gray had supposed. 'Have you forgotten already what befell your last reconnaissance mission?'

Gray sighed, and sighed again as Sophie's eager interest visibly deflated. 'No, ma'am,' he said.

Gray and Sophie grew more skilled both at attacking each other and, to everyone's relief, at shielding themselves from attack. Sophie assured Gray that she was no longer troubled by nightmares, even as signs of sleeplessness grew plain upon her face. He began to feel shut in, and he longed to go flying – just once – but a large woodland owl in the middle of London would no doubt draw a quite unwelcome degree of notice, and so he remained resolutely earthbound.

Mrs Wallis absented herself from the house most mornings and declined (whilst tending grimly to their various injuries, in the interval before dinner) to go into any detail as to where she had been. Jenny meanwhile entertained a steady stream of morning visitors, although, pleading fatigue and indisposition, she contrived to decline all proffered invitations to dinners and evening parties, apparently without giving offence.

'I cannot accept all of them,' she explained to Gray, 'or we should be never at home; and I cannot accept one without offending all the others, which I dare not do at present.'

These visitors were full of gossip, and many of them – or their husbands – were regularly at Court. Though few had anything really interesting to say, the King's search for the lost Princess Royal was a popular topic, which meant, so Jenny said, that she was at least as likely as her husband to learn something of interest to Sophie. Thus far this approach could not be said to have borne any very valuable fruit, however, unless it were useful to know that the Queen was rumoured to have sought a famous healer's advice on what she might do to conceive a girl – surely the first British queen to do so at least since the time of the Romans.

Once or twice Gray detected in his sister's glance the familiar sympathy that made him yearn to pour out his heart to her. Whenever a proper moment offered itself for doing so, however, there arose some interruption to prevent his beginning; and so he spoke of everything but what most occupied his mind.

They had been in London an interminable se'nnight when, the company being all at dinner, Sieur Germain watched the last servant out of the dining-room after bringing in the second remove and, turning to Gray, said in a low voice, 'May I trouble you once more to secure us against eavesdroppers?'

Startled and intrigued, Gray paused with fork halfway between plate and lips to begin a warding-spell, and when he had nodded to Sieur Germain, indicating that he might safely speak, the latter said, 'I have news.'

A taut silence fell.

'I believe I have discovered a fifth member of the conspiracy,' he said grimly. 'I have been to see an acquaintance of mine, a neighbour of ours in Breizh, who was at Court all the summer, and just now returned from a fortnight at Bath. He agrees with others I have spoken to, that His Majesty's desire to locate the lost Princess has led him to keep some very inadvisable company – priests and priestesses of the cult of Arawn, dedicates of Hecate and of Taranis, and all manner of foretellers, and even a man reputed to be a necromancer.'

Gray shuddered. Sophie, across the table at Jenny's right hand, looked positively ill. What would be the effect of this new intelligence on her goodwill towards the father she had never met?

'But he told me also,' Sieur Germain continued, 'that the King is almost constantly attended, even one might say *shadowed*, by one of the Royal Healers, a Lord Spencer, who whispers in his ear and is said to brew him sleeping draughts and tonics.'

'And is he gone to Caernarfon, too?' Sophie asked him urgently. 'This Lord Spencer?'

'No,' said Sieur Germain, 'or, at any rate, he has certainly been seen in Town since His Majesty's departure.'

In the face of Sophie's evident relief, Gray revised his opinion of her feelings towards her father.

'Joanna and I have not been idle, either,' said Jenny unexpectedly. 'This morning we – Joanna being of course a young cousin of my husband's – entertained Viscountess Lisle and her mother.' When no one gave any sign of recognition, she elaborated, 'Lady Lisle, as you may know, is a close friend of Her Majesty's, and her mama – Lady Brézé, you know – is very fond of telling people so.'

'It is an extremely tiresome habit,' Joanna muttered, helping herself to more veal collops.

Jenny's serious expression did not waver, but her eyes glinted at Gray. 'Tiresome it may be, but in this case it has been useful, as it encouraged Lady Brézé to inform me that the King and Queen intend returning to Town only on the day before Samhain.'

Sophie looked up sharply from the roasted parsnips which she had been pushing about her plate. 'Can we rely on her information?' she asked.

'I believe so,' said Jenny cautiously. 'Though her mother is so very ambitious on her behalf, Lady Lisle has known the Queen since they were girls together in Shropshire, and I believe would stand just as much Her Majesty's friend if she were yet only Lady Edwina Ashley. Her understanding is not particularly good, I fear, but there is no malice in her.'

'You will be pleased to learn, then,' said Sieur Germain, producing from the pocket of his coat, with some satisfaction, a thick engraved card edged in the royal purple, 'that we have received an invitation to Their Majesties' Samhain ball.'

CHAPTER XXIII

In Which Lady Kergabet Receives an Unexpected Caller

Sieur Germain's announcement fell among his listeners like Thor's own war-hammer, and produced a stillness very like the moment after a thunderbolt.

It was Joanna who first broke the silence: 'A *ball*? A *royal* ball? How marvellous! Think what the girls at school will say . . .' Then she seemed to remember that it was mid-October, and she very far from returning to school, and subsided.

Everyone else began talking at once.

'A brilliant stroke!' Master Alcuin exclaimed.

'But, my dear,' said Jenny, 'I am by no means fit to be seen—'

Sieur Germain looked at once disappointed and relieved. 'You are much mistaken, my dear, if you think so! But of course you need not come with us if you dislike it.'

'Is it wise to expose ourselves so publicly?' said Mrs Wallis. 'Though it may be that we shall be safer in a crowd, and the Samhain ball is certainly the best place to seek one.'

'What is more to the point, madam,' said Sieur Germain, 'as we are none of us personally known to the King and Queen' – Sophie could not help glancing at Mrs Wallis, but she continued perfectly inscrutable – 'the circumstances of a ball, and the traditions of Samhain, offer us the best opportunity we are like to have to convey a warning.'

'I must ask once again,' Gray said, 'what reason we have to suppose that His Majesty will give any credence to such a warning. And I cannot like a scheme which throws Sophie into the path of persons who certainly wish her ill.'

'To say nothing of their attempts on Gray's life,' said Sophie, who had awoken that morning panicked and tangled in her coverlet, from a nightmare vision of Gray slowly burning alive in Lord Halifax's study.

'I am sure there could be no such attempts on any of our lives in such a public venue,' said Gray, looking across at her with what he presumably supposed was a reassuring smile. 'And they cannot poison all of us along with the King; nothing could be more suspicious. But you remind me that in Oxford, at any rate, Master Alcuin and I stand accused of murder, and from Oxford to London is but sixty miles.' He grimaced and tugged at his ear. 'Still, we must try to warn him; what else can we do?'

'Mrs Wallis,' said Joanna suddenly, 'you are personally known to the King. Or at any rate you were. He could scarcely be expected to recognise Sophie, after all this time, but if you—'

'You quite mistake the nature of my acquaintance with His Majesty,' said Mrs Wallis dryly. 'He is not altogether a fool; he must know that Laora could not have made her escape so thoroughly without my . . . connivance.'

At the same moment Gray, eyes fiercely alight, said, 'If you imagine that I – that we should allow Sophie to be handed to him on a platter, to be married off to some Iberian princeling—'

'Indeed not, Mr Marshall,' said Mrs Wallis, looking at him in what might almost have been approval. 'But, Sophia, your mother believed . . .' She stopped, and was for some moments silent, gazing at nothing and no one.

At last she turned again to Gray and said, 'Mr Marshall, may I trouble you to lift your wards?'

Gray's eyebrows rose almost into his sandy curls, but he snapped his fingers obediently. Sophie shivered as the magick of the ward evaporated.

Mrs Wallis rose from the table and quietly left the room.

In her absence, the remains of the second remove were cleared away, and the next brought in – though only Joanna seemed likely to do it any justice.

When Mrs Wallis returned to the table, she held in her left hand what looked very much like a letter: faded ink on yellowing paper, the two halves of a broken seal in pale wax. She nodded to Gray, who closed his eyes and muttered his warding-spell again.

'Perhaps I erred in so long withholding this letter from you, as it concerns you so nearly,' she said, when the spell was done. Sophie had rarely heard her speak so hesitantly. 'But it is . . . I have never wished you to remember your mother as she must have been when she wrote it.'

She held out the paper to Sophie, who grasped it in fingers that shook. The letter was dated to the year following Joanna's birth.

My dear one, it began.

I have written this letter and hidden it, that you may discover it if anything should befall me. I have kept from you, my more-than-sister, more secrets than even you suspect; if all goes well, then they will out, or I shall take them to my grave; and, if ill . . . But I shall not dwell on such matters.

You will know already, that in the character of my husband I was most unhappily deceived. For myself, this no longer signifies – I have made my choices, despite all your warnings, and must bear their consequences; but I weep to think of my girls left in his power. Amelia is his own child, and his favourite; I think he will not use her ill. Joanna too – poor unwanted babe! – you cannot take from him;

but Sophia is none of his, and her I leave to your faithful guardianship.

Do what you must – you will know best – to keep her safe, in his house or elsewhere, as events decide. I have made him agree that I may teach her the use of her talents, when she is of an age to employ them; but if I know him, he will not honour his word – he has the prejudices of his race, for all his Breizhek birth – and there is none else to teach her, if I be not by. He little suspects how powerful she will one day grow, nor would I have him know it, for he would only seek to make use of her, as he has tried to make use of me. If she is not taught, Maëlle, she will be a danger to all about her; I beg that, so far as is in your power – which I know may not be far – you will put her in the way of learning. I judge her a clever child; it will perhaps be enough merely to give her the freedom of the library. I beg you will not let her be parted from you . . .

There followed a passage so much blurred and spotted that Sophie could not decipher it. She turned the paper over and read,

I spoke of secrets. The most of these concern Sophia herself, and though what I write may seem preposterous, I beg you will not dismiss it. Sophia, you see, is favoured of the gods, and has some great destiny before her. I have dreamt true dreams, and prophetic ones: her father's life, and the fate of the kingdom, will one day depend on her. I well know how absurd it sounds. You will say I know not foretelling from fancy; but I speak truth, for all that.

If she returns too late to her father, the consequences will be dire – but if too soon, then all these dreadful years will be for naught. The gods grant that she – that we – that you, *my dear – will know the moment when it comes.*

By the time Sophie reached the end of the letter – or, more exactly, the point at which it stopped, without at all seeming to conclude – the words had begun to blur before her eyes, and the paper shook with the trembling of her hands.

'This . . .' Sophie gestured with the letter. 'You believe that she knew . . . something? That this is not mere madness or self-delusion?'

Mrs Wallis sighed. 'I have never known what to believe. But as we have all seen for ourselves, she was not deluded with respect to the matter of your talent.'

Sophie looked down again at the letter, which seemed to draw her gaze like a lodestone.

'Sophie,' said Joanna, sounding oddly unsure of herself, 'what . . . what does the letter say?'

Briefly Sophie considered handing it over to Joanna, who, after all, was Mama's daughter too. But to show her those words – *poor unwanted babe!* – no, it was not to be thought of. Sophie had, the gods knew, made no very great success of protecting her small sister from the vicissitudes of life, but this much at least she could do.

'That Mama believed me fated to save my father's life one day,' she said instead, low. The weight of Lord Halifax's death rode on her shoulders, a burden felt now heavily, now lightly, but never long absent.

'And it may be that she knew whereof she spoke,' said Gray, in a simmering tone, 'but it does not follow that you need bear that burden alone.'

As Sophie looked across the table at him, one side of his mouth quirked up in a grim half smile.

Sophie went early to bed and lay for some time under the kingfisher-blue coverlet with Master Alcuin's primer in Old Cymric open against her drawn-up knees. With the best will in the world, however, she could not force her eyes to take in, or her mind to make sense of it; at last, admitting defeat, she left her bed to replace the battered codex on the dressing-table and stood before the window, gazing down at the street.

What could Mama have been thinking, to write such a letter? Had Sophie not known its author, she should certainly have judged it the product of some sort of delusion; but Mama, though so often melancholy, had never seemed other than perfectly sensible. *Yet there were so many other things I did not see . . .*

The truth was that she no longer felt sure of anything.

Worse, the Kergabets' elegant little house – which had once seemed a refuge – was in fact just as much a prison as Callender Hall had been. Her gaolers were kinder, certainly; she had Gray and Joanna always with her, which was as unlike being thrown upon the company of Amelia as a purring cat is unlike a hedgehog; but she was penned here just the same. London itself Sophie found altogether dreadful, noisome and clattering and airless, and the thought of remaining here for any length of time more dreadful yet.

And still there was something worse in store. For either they would fail to save His Majesty – her father, as she supposed she must learn to consider him – and would all be in the conspirators' power, and worse, known to have acted to thwart them. In such a case, a quick death would be their best hope.

Or, if they should succeed – what then?

Sophie continued as determined as ever to avoid taking up the mantle of Princess Edith Augusta, and she trusted her friends not to reveal her identity without her consent; but with at least three other persons now in the secret, it was all too probable that the choice would not be hers at all. And Mama's letter . . .

I am very sleepy, she had said, and returned that epistle to Mrs Wallis to do with as she liked – purely in order to escape the discussion that followed her reading of it, for never had sleep seemed farther off. Could it be true that Sophie herself must somehow intervene to save her father? If so, must she reveal herself in order to do so? Having done so, was there any possibility of retreat, of escape?

And the ordeal had only been exacerbated by Joanna's evident persuasion that if only the threat of elderly Iberian princes could be removed, Sophie must of course embrace the idea of becoming the Princess Royal – as though no other objection could be made to a life consisting of public scrutiny and private isolation. As though Sophie had not had enough of being locked up.

Sighing, the tears to which she refused to yield by day coursing silently down her cheeks, Sophie turned from the window and crept back to bed, praying to Morpheus for peaceful dreams.

Her prayers were not answered; even the sleeping-spell Gray had taught her, though she fell swiftly enough into sleep, brought her no peace.

In the morning, feeling as little rested as though she had not slept at all, she drank her morning tea and dragged herself down to the breakfast-table, where she sat silent, hovering at the verge of tears, while the others ate and debated. They looked at her – anxious, puzzled, sympathetic; she willed their attention away, and, obligingly, they turned it elsewhere. All but Gray, who continued to cast a worried glance at her every few moments; they were not placed near enough to one another for any private conversation to be possible.

After breakfast, she joined Master Alcuin and Gray as usual, and they started for the cellar, but even before they had reached the top of the staircase Sophie was having second thoughts, and at last she said, 'Magister, if you will excuse me . . . I have not slept very well . . .'

He stopped, and his blue eyes studied her keenly under the snow-white brows. 'I think,' he said after a moment, 'that we should all be the better for a rest from our labours. Both of you have made commendable progress, and have earned a holiday.'

Avoiding Gray's eyes, Sophie gave Master Alcuin a grateful smile.

So it was that all of them were with Jenny, Joanna, and Mrs Wallis in the morning-room, and not safely out of sight belowstairs, an hour before noon.

Gray and Master Alcuin were discussing antidotes, a miscellany of books stacked between them on the chessboard, and Sophie apparently trying to keep awake long enough to finish stitching together a baby's nightdress, when Joanna turned from her station at the window, her round face gone as pale as the pages of the codex open in Gray's hand.

'Gods and priestesses! He has found us,' she whispered.

Sophie's head jerked upright; Gray dropped the book, which fell splayed face down across the carpet, and sprang up from his chair; Mrs Wallis put down her mending and looked up at Joanna, alert but unalarmed. The others seemed not to take her meaning immediately, but all were gathered round her station at the window in time to see the stout, elegantly dressed figure stop before the Kergabets' door and raise the brass knocker. Two taller, slighter figures loitered on the pavement opposite, whom Gray recognised with unpleasant conviction as Taylor and Woodville.

'Apollo, Pan, and Hecate!' said Gray. 'Horns of Herne!' said Master Alcuin. Sophie, clutching at Gray's arm with trembling fingers, whispered, 'We are undone.'

After a longer delay than he seemed to expect – for he paced about impatiently, even knocking a second time – the door was opened and the visitor admitted to the hall. Then Jenny turned from the window and said briskly, 'Nonsense! I have only to ask Treveur to say that we are not at home, and he will have to go away.'

Mrs Wallis nodded, evidently satisfied. For a moment, indeed, it seemed that this simple and elegant solution might suffice, but the servant who opened the morning-room door a few moments later was not the formidable Treveur but the young housemaid, Daisy, who had been in the household only a month. She curtseyed swiftly and not very neatly to her mistress, darting frightened eyes at the various occupants of the room, and announced in a terrified whisper, ''Tis a Professor C-c-callender, the M-m-master of Merlin C-c-college . . . I asked 'im to wait b'low, m'lady, but 'e would not . . .'

Jenny, moving more quickly than Sophie had thought possible, propelled Daisy back out into the corridor, whispering in her ear, and shut the door. Whirling to face the room again, she began hurrying her guests away from the window and across the room, where, disguised by potted shrubs and an ornately carved wooden screen, a connecting door led into the breakfast-room. They tumbled through the doorway – first Joanna and Mrs Wallis, then Master Alcuin; then Gray, a stack of incriminating books swept haphazardly up in his arms; and at last only Sophie, whose feet seemed as staggered and dazed as her mind, tripping over each other and hampering her efforts to flee, remained in the morning-room with Jenny.

Just as Joanna was reaching for Sophie's hand to pull her through after the rest, the other door opened again, and poor Daisy, stammering more than ever, repeated her announcement.

Jenny, her flushed cheeks the only indication that anything was amiss, sailed back across the room to greet her importunate caller. Behind the carved screen Sophie stared, frozen, ignoring Joanna's outstretched hand and Gray's increasingly frantic whispers. Just in time she spied the book Gray had dropped, and summoned it to her hand. When her fingers closed about the worn leather binding, she found them clutching at it like some sort of talisman.

The Professor was now actually in the room, and he was, she found, not so terrifying here as he had been in the abstract. Though her first thought had been to flee, she had now a strong desire to see how her erstwhile paterfamilias conducted himself, and to hear what he would say. Batting the reaching hands away, therefore, she pulled the breakfast-room door to as quietly as she could, before ducking down behind the rose-tree.

After all, if she could not conceal herself from one overconfident and unimaginative man, whom she had been used to regard as supremely stupid, what hope was there that she and her friends could somehow foil the more formidable part of his confederacy?

'Professor Callender,' said Jenny calmly, 'this is a most unexpected honour, indeed; I had not thought to meet you again so soon. Will you not sit down?'

The Professor was evidently not in a temper for polite conversation. 'You have something of mine, Lady Kergabet,' he said.

'I beg your pardon, sir.' Jenny's distant courtesy conveyed both puzzlement and disapprobation. 'I do not take your meaning.'

'My daughter Sophia,' said the Professor, between set teeth. 'I beg you will not play games, Lady Kergabet. I have every reason to believe that she is here.'

'I am afraid, sir, that you are quite mistaken.'

'You continue to deny, then, that you conspired with your unscrupulous brother to lure my daughter away from her home and her friends?' the Professor demanded. 'To persuade her into a foolish elopement, with the object of—'

But Sophie, fuming at his adjectives, was not to discover what he imagined Gray's object to have been, for Jenny had had enough. 'Certainly I deny it,' she said frostily. 'I am heartily sorry that you should have lost your daughter; such a fate is to be pitied. If, however, you have come here only to frighten my housemaid and to impugn my brother's honour and my own, then I shall thank you to take your leave, sir.'

It was impossible to imagine a clearer dismissal, but Appius

Callender was not so easily put off. Peering stealthily through the gap between two carved oak-leaves, Sophie saw, to her dismay, that he had begun striding about the room, thrusting his umbrella-tip under and behind the furniture and dragging aside the window-curtains, as though he imagined them all to be concealed there. Jenny exclaimed indignantly, but to no avail.

Sophie herself was safe enough, presumably. The Professor had scarcely seemed to see or hear her when she lived under his own roof, except on that last, dreadful day, but she trembled for the others, who might still be just beyond the door at her back. At any moment it might occur to him to employ a finding-spell – she wondered that he had not done so already – and even if it did not, they were hardly well enough concealed to escape a determined seeker. Creeping on hands and knees, therefore, she inched backwards until her boot-toes touched the door-sill, then sat up and leant her back against the door, reaching one hand up to grasp the handle. While the Professor had his back to her, peering under Jenny's worktable, she turned the handle sharply and fell backward into the breakfast-room, where she fetched up squarely against her sister, knocking her, and Gray's stack of codices, to the floor.

'He is searching the room!' she whispered urgently, as Gray and Master Alcuin helped her and Joanna to their feet. 'He will try a finding next – you cannot stay here – he will see the door in a moment—'

Gray already had hold of her left hand, and Joanna of her right; Master Alcuin was gathering up the scattered books; and before she could continue, all five of them were along the corridor and creeping down the service stairs.

At length they found themselves in the kitchen, where they were greeted with considerable displeasure by the large and redoubtable Mrs Treveur; her consternation vanished, however, to be replaced by a wide smile, when she caught sight of the youngest member of their party. 'Dim'zell Zhoanne!' she cried. '*Mont a ra mat ganeoc'h?*'

'*Mantret on*, Itron Treveur.' Joanna returned a breathless apology for their intrusion. No sooner had she begun to explain their situation than Mrs Treveur broke in with a torrent of reassurances.

'It is quite all right now,' Joanna told Master Alcuin, who was all too plainly defeated by the tide of rapid Brezhoneg, 'for Daisy ran straight away to fetch Treveur and Harry – the footman, you know – and they are gone upstairs to throw him out.'

A moment later they were joined by all three of the aforementioned and by Jenny herself, in a state of formidable wrath.

'He suspects,' she told her guests, as they followed her upstairs. 'He is certain that Gray and Sophie, at least, are concealed somewhere on the premises; he was certain that I had you both hidden at Kergabet, when he came there in pursuit of you, and with far less reason—'

'Alas,' said Sieur Germain, who had joined them in the morning-room – and in some haste, for he still wore his gloves and carried his hat, and his great-coat was beaded with water. 'Alas, Dimezell Sophie, I fear that he has excellent reason to seek you so fervently now.'

'You have learnt something new at Court, then?' Gray demanded eagerly.

'I am very sorry,' Sieur Germain began, with an apologetic look at Sophie. 'My efforts to investigate, I fear, have alerted some member of the conspiracy to your being in Town—'

'Or perhaps,' said Joanna, 'it is only Mrs Wallis's morning calls, and her letters to half of London.'

'Whatsoever I have done, Miss Joanna, has been always in your sister's interest,' the latter declared. 'There is more at stake here than you appear to understand.'

'My dear,' said Jenny, 'we know already that Sophie's stepfather suspects her presence here; what I cannot understand – nor Sophie – is *why*, after so many weeks' apparent indifference to her whereabouts, he should suddenly be prepared to risk making a spectacle of himself . . .'

Sieur Germain looked grim. 'He has need of her,' he said.

Gray glanced at Sophie, who sat forward in her chair with her face in her hands.

'Lord Carteret and Lord Merton – he, I believe, is both your second Oxford assailant and the *M* of Lord Carteret's diary – have lately been spending a great deal of time with the Iberian ambassador,' Sieur Germain continued after a moment. 'Carteret has, according to some at Court, ambitions of completing the great alliance contemplated by His Majesty more than a decade ago; the knowledge that the lost Princess is within his grasp perhaps suggested to him a swifter and less costly means of cementing it than whatever he had previously in view. The Iberian royal family have not forgot that once a princess was promised them in marriage and not delivered. The prince who was to have been Dimezell Sophie's husband has been wed long since to a daughter of Bordeaux, but the present Emperor has no son and has recently lost his second wife. The more the ambassador learns of the powerful magick that is said to run in the late Queen Laora's family, the more he enters into His Majesty's lively interest in finding her daughter. His Majesty has proved more difficult to persuade of the merits of the scheme, but Lord Carteret, it seems, presents at least the appearance of perfect confidence in his eventual agreement.'

Sophie raised her head. Her dark eyes were enormous; only the fading marks left by the pressure of her fingers lent any other colour to her face.

'Then,' she said – she it was, though the voice in which she spoke was so unlike her own that all of them turned to gape at her – 'should they find me now, I am condemned now as surely as I have ever been.'

She rose, moving slowly as if dazed, and went silently out of the room, waving a hand vaguely above her head as she passed through the doorway.

Jenny stood up and made to follow her, but was stopped on the threshold by Master Alcuin's warding-spell. He snapped his fingers to release the wards; as Jenny hurried after Sophie, and Joanna after Jenny, he and Gray looked at one another in utter amazement.

'She walked through my wards,' Master Alcuin breathed, awed. '*Straight through*, as though they were not there at all.'

There was an odd, choking sound, from somewhere behind them, which Gray could not at first identify. He turned to look and could not quite believe his eyes: Mrs Wallis was laughing. It was a laugh with no joy in it, and very little mirth.

'She is so very like her mother,' she said. 'May the gods help the Iberians.'

CHAPTER XXIV

In Which Jenny and Joanna Solve a Difficult Problem

Dinner that evening was a subdued and melancholy meal, which no one seemed eager to prolong.

In the drawing-room, Sophie, intending to occupy her hands with fancy-work in hopes of calming the turmoil of her thoughts, found herself and her baby's bonnet inextricably cornered by Master Alcuin and Joanna, apparently in collusion. All through dinner she had felt some undercurrent – gazes averted, quiet conversations cut awkwardly short – whose meaning, set against the events of the morning, she trembled to consider.

'Jenny and I have found the answer, Sophie,' Joanna began, characteristically both cryptic and blunt.

'The answer . . . ?'

'No matter what you may have been told, Miss Sophie, you cannot be *made* to marry anyone, if you refuse,' Master Alcuin told her gently. 'But it is certainly within the rights of the paterfamilias – and certainly of the royal paterfamilias, whether father or brother to yourself – who must consider the good of the kingdom above all else – to make your life a misery until you do agree. And princes and princesses, in general, cannot expect to marry for love.'

Sophie stitched doggedly, and would not raise her eyes. *Next he will begin to speak of my duty to the kingdom.*

But instead he said, 'A prior legal marriage, however, and particularly a marriage *confarreatio*, must materially weaken their cause . . .'

Here Master Alcuin paused delicately, and Joanna leapt into the fray. 'Jenny says the Iberians are very much concerned with virginity, you see. They require an ordeal, as part of the wedding-rite—'

Sophie's needle pricked her finger, and she yelped in pain.

'What,' she demanded, looking up at last, 'what on *earth* are you suggesting?'

'Really, Sophie,' said Joanna, with some impatience, 'you must see that we are thinking of your marrying Gray.'

This time Sophie ran the needle deep into her thumb.

'And supposing,' she said, folding the injured digit into her fist, 'supposing *me* willing to take such a step, why should you imagine that *he* will agree to it?'

Master Alcuin looked puzzled; Joanna threw up her hands and exclaimed, 'You must be altogether blind, if you cannot see that he has been violently in love with you since – since—'

'"Violently in love", indeed,' Sophie scoffed. 'I cannot think where you find such expressions, Joanna.'

'It is perfectly true,' retorted her sister. 'Have you not seen how he looks at you? And besides – Gray has said himself that your magick is more powerful than his, and his, as you must have heard Master Alcuin say fifty times, is very great indeed; do you expect to find many other men who . . . ? He is not very handsome, certainly, and rather an odd sort of man altogether, but as you are rather odd yourself—'

'And *that* is your reasoning – that he *must* love me, and I him, because *you* consider both of us "odd"? Joanna, *really*.'

'That is not what I meant, at all!' said Joanna.

'I hope that you will not dismiss this idea out of hand, Miss Sophie,' said Master Alcuin.

Sophie again took up her *broderie anglaise*, sighing over the minuscule spots of blood she had left on the fine white muslin. Resolutely ignoring both sister and teacher, she bent her head and plied her needle as calmly as she could manage, but beneath that calm exterior roiled feelings more agitated, more violently alternating between fear of the future and a certain ludicrous hope, than Joanna could possibly have conceived.

Gray stood at the window of the breakfast-room, gazing fixedly out at the ubiquitous autumn fog that blanketed Mayfair. Their breakfast eaten, the rest of the household had gone about the business of the day – all but himself and Jenny, who had waylaid him as he made to leave the room.

'Tell me,' she said, stepping up beside him, 'supposing that we succeed in foiling this plot of Lord Carteret's, what will become of you? And what of Joanna and Sophie?'

Gray frowned. 'I hardly know,' he said. 'We have not had much leisure, you know, to consider such things.' He tried out in his mind the words *I shall go home*, and found them wanting. What manner of home could Merlin be to him, or his father's house either, if Sophie were not there? 'I shall go up to Oxford, I suppose, and petition the College to regain my place there, and Sophie . . .'

What might be Sophie's fate, indeed, if nothing was done to stop it? If a betrothal agreement was signed and sealed by King Henry, could even incontrovertible proof of Lord Carteret's perfidy invalidate it?

'I – I shall miss her,' he went on, doggedly, 'both of them, that is – and you also, of course—'

'But you could do very well without me, I think,' said Jenny, 'and without Joanna, if Sophie were not in question.'

The room was silent, but for the cheerful crackling of the fire, while Gray considered how to refute this too-apt observation. Then he looked down at Jenny, whose wide hazel eyes were fixed on his face with deep compassion, and at last gave up the battle. 'I love her,' he confessed, simply.

'That is very fortunate,' she said, 'for she is thoroughly besotted with you.'

'I understand, of course,' Gray continued, 'that she cannot possibly—*What* did you say?'

His mouth hung open, and he knew he must look a fool, but Jenny only smiled fondly up at him and said, 'Do you think yourself so very difficult to love?'

While Gray struggled to adjust his mind to the idea of Sophie besotted, Jenny pressed her advantage: 'And you must see, of course, that a prior marriage – a marriage by contract, properly witnessed and consummated – will be her surest protection against—'

'You cannot be serious, Jenny.' She must be mistaken, surely; she had not seen Sophie's sweet, reproachful face as she said, *I could not ask for a kinder brother . . .*

'I am quite in earnest, I assure you; is not this just what you have wished yourself? I should not dream of jesting on such a subject.'

'But – but if—' Gray stammered. 'If indeed Sophie has any regard for me, it must be only the effect of gratitude, for I am sure I am the first man who ever was kind to her.'

'Breaking my china when Mama dared to disparage you,' said Jenny mildly, 'does not seem very like mere gratitude.'

'But, Jenny – even supposing her to return my feelings, this – it is like one of Joanna's minstrel-tales . . .'

'And why not?' His sister folded her arms. 'You have rescued the imprisoned princess, have you not? You have gone on a quest and fought a battle; you seek to save the kingdom from—'

'And in a tale, no doubt,' Gray interrupted, rather savagely, 'I should prove in the end to be a wealthy knight, or a prince, and only disguised as a disgraced and impoverished student. In life, alas, it is not quite so easy a thing for a princess to accept an offer of marriage from a man of no fortune, homeless, fatherless, friendless—'

'You dare call yourself *friendless*, Graham Marshall?' Jenny demanded. 'Here, in my husband's house, where you have had help and refuge, and all that is in our power to give you? You account our friendship as nothing, and your tutor's too? I should never have thought such a thing of you.'

It was all true, every syllable; Gray could offer nothing in reply but the basest self-justifications.

'I am sorry, Jenny,' he said instead. 'Truly sorry. I meant – I did not mean—'

'I know very well what you meant,' said Jenny, relenting. 'We are both out of temper; I ought not to have spoken so.'

'You said nothing to me that I did not deserve,' said Gray ruefully.

'Gray, hear me.' Jenny sat on the sofa and motioned him to join her, then reached up to take his face in her hands for a moment – gently, as a mother might with a beloved but inattentive child. 'Sophie loves you, and you love her; I can think of no other woman who would suit you so well, and she . . . there cannot be many men, Gray, who would esteem her as you do.'

'But who could help loving her?' he cried, indignant on Sophie's behalf. 'All courage and generosity as she is, with such intelligence – and so beautiful—'

'There has been some material change in your opinion on that point, I conclude?' Jenny cast a sidelong glance at him. 'For only two months ago, you know, you described her to me as "very clever and accomplished, and altogether agreeable, though by no means pretty . . ."'

Gray opened his mouth to deny this accusation, but as quickly closed it again.

'Perhaps the Professor's interdiction clouded my mind,' he said, 'for she is certainly the most beautiful woman of my acquaintance.'

'I saw it, you know, in August. You had not yet understood your own feelings, but, being so much in each other's company, I felt sure that you would come to an understanding before summer's end, and when you came here—'

Gray tried to frame some objection to this but could not.

'I had intended to let things take their natural course,' said Jenny, folding her hands together in her lap, 'for a man in love will seldom take a sister's interference kindly, but circumstances do not allow . . . You both are as good as orphaned; there is nothing at present to be settled on either of you. But – have you not thought? – neither can there be any objection from anyone to your marrying, for apart from His Majesty, here in this house are all the friends and relations that either of you can claim, and you may be sure that all of us wish you joy. A wedding will be awkward to arrange – we can hardly begin it in her father's house, and you have none of your own to bring her to – but . . .'

Having canvassed all these difficulties, she looked earnestly at him and concluded, 'Not one pair of lovers in a thousand, Gray, has such a chance, and besides the danger to Sophie, I shall think you very stupid indeed if you do not take it.'

Gray blinked at her.

'I never was so fortunate – or so unfortunate – as to be in love,' Jenny continued, low, 'but if I had, I hope I should not have thrown away such an opportunity of happiness for such a reason.'

She had turned her face away.

'Jenny, dear,' Gray said, 'are you so very unhappy?'

'I am quite as happy as I deserve,' she said, and, before he could ask what she meant, added briskly, 'Now, go and find your Sophie – and send Joanna in to me, for she has been listening at the door quite long enough.'

* * *

Gray's hand was on the door-handle, turning it, when he heard the scuffle in the corridor – and a moment later, Sophie's outraged voice: 'Joanna Claudia Callender! Mother Goddess, have you no manners at *all*?'

He opened the door; there before him was the author of these words, looking startled and dismayed. 'Joanna,' he said absently, looking into Sophie's dark eyes, 'go in and speak to Jenny.'

He vaguely heard Joanna's affronted *hmmph!* and the click of the latch as the door closed behind her.

'Gray?' Sophie whispered, stepping forward to touch his arm. 'Gray, whatever is the matter? You look . . .'

'Hush,' said Gray. 'Not here.' He thought a moment. 'The drawing-room! There will be no one there now.' Taking Sophie's hand, he pulled her after him towards the drawing-room door.

She stopped him on the threshold, tugging her hand away from his and turning him to face her. 'Gray, what on *earth*—?'

He smiled down at her in mute apology. 'I should like to speak to you,' he explained, 'without an audience.'

Sophie ducked silently under his outstretched arm and into the room, where, like a turtle dove returning to its nest, she took up her by now accustomed seat at the pianoforte. Half closing her eyes, she began to play a soft, slow melody in the Aeolian mode.

Gray quietly shut the door.

'Sophie,' he said, sitting down beside her on the piano-bench. Their arms touched; his pulse thundered in his ears. Though Jenny's assertions had quite convinced him at the time, he now began to doubt again whether she had seen aright.

'Joanna tells me,' Sophie said, to his surprise, 'that she and your sister have had a – a mad idea.' She did not look at him; her fingers played over and over the same four chords. 'She thinks – but it is too absurd – she thinks that you . . .' Her voice grew thick and choked, and she fell silent.

Gray was strangely comforted to find her as flustered and uncertain as he. 'Joanna,' he said softly, 'is much more often right than you allow.'

Sophie's fingers stilled but did not leave the keys; the unresolved cadence hung fading in the air, a question unanswered. 'Do you mean . . . you cannot mean . . . ?'

'But I do,' said Gray.

At last she turned to look at him, and he seized the opportunity to take her hands in his – hardly able to discern whose trembled more. Her eyes were deep and dark as a moonless night. 'I think – I begin to believe that it – that their mad notion is not mad at all.'

But it was no use; he could scarce string three words together while sitting so close beside her, and was in danger of conveying quite the wrong impression. Loosing her hands, he sprang to his feet and began to pace the room, his mind seeking some means of rescuing this scene from absurdity.

Reaching the window, he turned about and nearly ran against Sophie, who had risen from her seat and, to all appearances, followed him across the room. As he drew breath to apologise, hoping that he had not hurt her, she looked up at him – a challenge in the set of her lips, and all the hurts of her girlhood in her eyes.

'Sophie,' he began again, 'This is not . . . it was not *all* our sisters' idea, and I should not wish you to think . . . I have been wishing, these many weeks – but I did not think that . . .' Nothing could be more ludicrously awkward than this frantic search for words. But she began to take his meaning now; the smile glimmering in her eyes was encouragement enough. 'I have nothing to offer you, Sophie – nothing but my own poor self, which is pledged to your service already – but, Sophie – *cariad*, dearest love – Sophie, will you . . . ?'

The question was never finished, however, for, by way of an answer, Sophie stood on tiptoe and tugged on the lapels of Gray's coat, drawing his head down to hers until, for an eternal, intoxicating moment, their lips met.

Magick shivered the still air around them – whether hers, or his, or both together, Gray neither knew nor cared.

She loves me! his mind repeated exultantly.

Sophie felt Gray's arms close tight about her, and her feet left the floor to dangle in mid-air; losing her grip on his coat-collar, she wound her arms about his neck. Her ears hummed; through the frantic hammering of her own pulse she felt the pounding of his heart, as strong and urgent as though their bodies were not separated by layers of linen and muslin and wool.

They were both of them awkward and uncertain, to be sure; had she harboured any illusions that Gray might be more experienced in this arena than herself, they would have all been done away. For all that, she could no longer doubt what he felt for her, and she might have laughed aloud – had she had breath enough – to think how far her earlier fancies had fallen short of reality.

Gray raised his head, his brows drawing together in a puzzled frown, and set her gently on her feet. Head on one side, he stood for a moment looking down at her; his face was flushed pink, his chest rising and falling as rapidly as Sophie's own, and she had a sudden urge to giggle. 'Listen,' he whispered.

The strange, discordant humming which Sophie had believed to be some fancy of hers, she now understood was quite real. Looking about them, she and Gray fixed their gaze at the same moment on the source of the sound: Jenny's gleaming cherry-wood pianoforte, whose strings, Sophie saw as they stepped closer, vibrated wildly, as though every key had been depressed at once.

'I am very sorry,' she said, 'but I have not the least notion how to make it stop.'

'Oh, my Sophie,' he cried, subsiding onto the piano-bench and pulling her into his arms. 'I should not love you half so well, *cariad*, if you were like other people.'

He bent his head and kissed her, eagerly, and she as eagerly replied. The discordant hum grew louder and louder, but neither of them heard it any longer, until at last – never meant to withstand such usage – the pianoforte's strings began to snap.

CHAPTER XXV

In Which Mrs Wallis Is Surprised

At the first jarring *twang!* from behind them, Gray and Sophie sprang apart, recoiling from one another as from an open flame. From opposite sides of the long, narrow room they stared at each other, Sophie's dismay mirrored in Gray's suddenly ashen face.

Another string snapped, and another, and Sophie cried out, distressed by the sight and sound, for already the instrument was a beloved friend. Abruptly the humming of the remaining strings began to die away, and only moments later the drawing-room was silent – but for their rapid, panicked breathing.

'What . . . ?' Gray began, looking from Sophie to the pianoforte and back again.

Then Sophie's teeth began to chatter, and at once he was at her side, folding his arms about her and murmuring words of reassurance. For a moment she relaxed gratefully into his embrace, remembering every fright, every scrape and misadventure, from which he had extricated her in the months of their acquaintance, and comfortably certain that he would do so again. Then the precise nature of the present difficulty burst upon her once again, and she stiffened in alarm.

'Sophie.' His voice was gentle, full of concern. She looked up into his face, tears standing in her eyes, and caught her breath at his expression. 'Please, *cariad*, tell me – what is the matter?'

'*That.*' Trembling, she gestured with one arm at the damaged pianoforte. 'How can I – how can we—?' The numberless other times when her magick had shattered or smashed or mangled things, and, much worse, had injured *people* – most frequently, Gray himself – paraded themselves before her mind's eye, echoing and strengthening the nightmare images that, despite half a lifetime's familiarity, had never lost their power to terrify. The tears would no longer be restrained, and she buried her face in her hands as she sobbed, 'I am good for nothing but destroying things! Even what I love, I—'

'No,' Gray said fiercely, tightening his arms about her shoulders. 'Sophie, you must not think so. The pianoforte is . . . *attuned* to you – as am I, it seems,' he added in a lower voice, with a shadow of laughter in it. 'You have not destroyed it; only . . . only overwhelmed it. Some connexion must have amplified the resonance of your magick – yours and mine, rather – in the aether, and—'

There was a timid knock at the door; Sophie made to disentangle herself, but Gray seemed to have no idea of letting her go.

'Gray? Sophie?' came Jenny's voice from the corridor. Sophie flinched, wishing that she could disappear altogether. 'May I come in?'

'Yes, of course,' Gray called, relaxing his grip very slightly.

The door opened slowly; Jenny looked about her, and seemed to relax when she caught sight of her brother with his arms about Sophie.

'The two of you have reached some sort of understanding, then?' she said, smiling.

'We—' Gray began, but Sophie – unable to bear being greeted so warmly, after what she had done – rushed to forestall him. 'I have ruined your beautiful instrument, Jenny,' she cried, at last extricating herself, 'and I am most dreadfully sorry. I beg you will let me pay for—'

'Whatever do you mean?' Jenny stepped closer to the pianoforte and began to examine it. Sophie, watching, saw the precise moment at which she recognised the damage, and braced herself for a storm of angry accusations, but, though Jenny looked deeply shocked, none came. 'I . . . I shall write today to have the strings replaced,' she said instead, then, steadying, 'It will not sound quite itself in the meantime, to be sure, but I should not call it *ruined*.'

She turned back to Sophie and Gray, her smile perhaps a little uneasy. 'This explains the odd sounds I have been hearing, I suppose,' she said. 'I rather feared—But, Sophie, tell me: I hope that . . . you will not think me presumptuous, I hope, if I ask whether I may call you "sister". . . ?'

Sophie blinked. 'I . . .' Turning, she looked up at Gray; with a tentative half smile that set her pulse racing again, he took her hands in his and whispered, 'What say you, Sophie?'

'Do you mean' – she no longer cared whether Jenny might hear – 'that you still – after – *that*—?'

Gray looked perplexed. 'Yes,' he replied. 'Of course, yes.'

'There is my answer, then,' said Sophie. Joanna had been quite right, after all; surely no other man would repeat his offer of marriage, having witnessed such a display. 'Of course, yes.'

Gray's look of confusion gave way to an expression of unalloyed delight. He bent to kiss her upturned forehead, and through all her doubts and trepidation, she felt certain of having chosen aright.

'Then I wish you joy!' said Jenny, so unexpectedly that Sophie jumped in surprise and knocked her head against Gray's chin. 'And perhaps you will both come with me, and put an end to everyone else's suspense.'

'Gods and priestesses,' Sophie muttered – for she had had a dreadful thought: 'I shall have to tell Mrs Wallis, and ask for her consent.'

* * *

When it came to the point, Sophie was not quite brave enough for a private audience with Mrs Wallis. They resolved, therefore, to make the petition for their families' consent a general one, hoping that whatever objections Mrs Wallis might raise would be sufficiently answered by the enthusiastic approval which Jenny predicted from everyone else.

Sophie could not imagine how they would begin, but she had, despite so many years' experience, reckoned without her younger sister.

'Well?' As Jenny ushered them into the morning-room, Joanna put down her work and jumped up from her chair. 'Are we to have a wedding, then?'

In spite of everything, Sophie began to laugh. 'Joanna, *really*,' she said, for at least the thousandth time. 'What a question!'

But this seemed to be answer enough, for at once she was nearly bowled over by her sister's congratulatory embrace. 'Did I not tell you?' Joanna whispered smugly into her ear.

Over Joanna's shoulder, Sophie saw broad smiles on the faces of the assembled company – all but Mrs Wallis, who was nowhere to be seen.

'Jenny?' she said, hesitant. 'Where has Mrs Wallis gone?'

Frowning, Jenny cast a questioning look at her husband. 'I believe,' Sieur Germain began, 'that Mrs Treveur—'

But before he could elaborate, footsteps were heard in the corridor, and Mrs Wallis's crisp voice saying jovially, 'Miss Sophia! Mr Marshall! You have at last decided to rejoin the mortal world, I see?'

This made Sophie blush – and Gray, too – as perhaps nothing else could have done.

Mrs Wallis sailed past them into the morning-room and seated herself composedly on a sofa; the not-quite-acknowledged lovers regarded one another in silent consternation. There must be some accepted protocol for such circumstances, and, given a more usual sort of courtship, one or other of them must have taken the trouble to discover what it was. As things were, however . . .

'Sophie and I have something to say to all of you,' Gray began at last, boldly taking her hand. 'I have made her an offer of marriage, and – and she has accepted it, and, as the five of you are all the friends and relations we have, we . . . we ask all of you to give us your consent.'

As though Master Alcuin and Sieur Germain had been wanting only this precise turn of phrase to match Joanna's exuberance, Sophie suddenly found herself and her betrothed – for so she must now consider him – enveloped in a flurry of cheek-kissing, back-slapping male felicitation. Jenny and Joanna stood back, exchanging self-satisfied looks, and Mrs Wallis—

'Mrs Wallis,' said Sophie, addressing her self-proclaimed guardian rather recklessly than politely, 'have not *you* anything to say?'

To her astonishment – there seemed no end of astonishments today – Mrs Wallis laughed aloud. 'Indeed I have not,' she said. 'I should not myself have chosen quite this means of carrying out your mother's wishes, but above all she wished you safe and happy, and the latter you undoubtedly appear. And, besides, I am quite speechless with surprise.'

'You cannot be serious, Mrs Wallis!' Joanna exclaimed.

'Quite serious, Miss Joanna, I assure you,' said Mrs Wallis solemnly – though her dancing eyes declared her quite otherwise. 'I had not thought that any two persons so apparently blind to one another's wishes could manage to reach any sort of understanding in so short a time . . .'

'Well, you may thank *me* for that,' cried Joanna, 'and Jenny, too, of course – I am sure they would never have spoken two words to each other about it, if we had not *made* them.'

'Mind it does not go to your head,' was Mrs Wallis's only reply.

Though such a kind of humour was not very much to Sophie's

taste, it did at least suggest that her fears of opposition from this quarter had been misplaced, for which she was duly thankful.

'There is much to be done,' Mrs Wallis resumed, putting aside her unaccustomed mirth. 'We must agree on terms, and engage a priest – not too highly placed, I think – to draw up the contract and oversee the promises; and, of course, as to witnesses—'

'That does not sound like any wedding I ever heard of,' Joanna objected.

Mrs Wallis gave her a disapproving look. 'That, my child, is because you have been accustomed to consort with Breizhek servant girls and farmers' daughters,' she said. 'Such affairs are conducted rather differently among persons of gentle birth . . .'

But Sophie could not attend to her disquisition on the legal differences between handfasting and marriage by contract, and the advantages of the latter for women, in the event of divorce; she found herself wishing, with more honesty than propriety, that she and Gray had not left the drawing-room quite so soon.

'They cannot have so very much to discuss,' said Gray, with a rueful smile, 'if they are settling the amounts of our respective fortunes.' Then leaning down to her, he lowered his voice to ask, 'Are you happy, Sophie?'

Sophie stood on tiptoe to kiss his cheek. 'I am frightened out of my wits,' she admitted, 'but I cannot bring myself to mind it very much just now.'

Sieur Germain and Mrs Wallis retreated to the former's private study to continue their discussion of contract arrangements; Jenny and Joanna, looking like cats in a dairy, descended to the kitchen to pester Mrs Treveur for wedding delicacies. Gray was considering how he and Sophie might best escape everyone's notice for an hour or two when Master Alcuin approached them, smiling broadly, to remind them of the lessons they had been neglecting.

The rest of the day passed very much as usual – if a day spent belowstairs, drawing water from the air to fling hailstones at one another, and (despite Sophie's objections) learning to expand a tiny utilitarian flame into a large and menacing one, could any way be called usual. When the whole household met again before dinner, Gray and Sophie were both too tired to pay much heed to the general conversation; they sat together on a sofa in the drawing-room, companionably silent, and finding themselves placed next to one another at table, they clasped hands beneath the tablecloth and spoke, in low voices, of everything and nothing. Gray felt so extraordinarily fortunate that he could have laughed aloud.

At last his attention was called perforce another way, by Sieur Germain's asking him a direct question.

'I beg pardon, sir?' said Gray, drawing a chorus of tolerant amusement.

'We are deciding your wedding-date,' said his brother-in-law. 'Have you any objection to being married on the day after tomorrow?'

Gray, astonished, looked at Sophie, whose shoulders lifted minutely.

'We cannot act too soon, I think,' said Mrs Wallis, 'for he may well return to investigate more thoroughly.' There was no need to ask whom she meant.

'I have written to the Temple of Tamesis,' Sieur Germain continued cheerfully, 'and tomorrow we shall see what can be done.'

'I almost wish that Father *would* come,' said Joanna, spearing a piece of mutton with her fork. The rest stared at her, dumbfounded. 'Not until afterwards, of course,' she added hastily, 'but I should so like to see his face, when he finds that it is true after all, and he can do nothing about it . . .'

'*I* should like never to see his face again,' said Sophie.

* * *

The priest of Tamesis, presiding goddess of the River Thames, was punctual to his hour, though he seemed ill pleased by the circumstances of his summoning. Having perused the sheet of paper on which were set down the proposed terms of the marriage contract, he looked up at Sieur Germain, frowning.

'This is a most peculiar document,' he said, disapproval in every syllable. 'I find it difficult to believe that any two persons of gentle birth should agree to be married on such terms – or that their families should permit it.'

Sieur Germain shrugged his shoulders. 'These are peculiar times,' he said blandly, 'and we find ourselves in peculiar circumstances.'

'Neither of us has the least objection to the terms,' said Sophie, too anxious to be cautious about speaking out of turn.

'Certainly not.' Gray reached for Sophie's hand and pressed it reassuringly.

The priest fixed his eyes on them, and his frown deepened. 'And do I understand you all to be living together in the same household?' he enquired. 'This also is most irregular.'

'The circumstances, as I have said, are somewhat unusual,' Sieur Germain repeated patiently. 'Miss Callender's home is in Breizh, and Mr Marshall's at Oxford; as both at present happen to be resident in my home, it seemed far more sensible . . .'

'The bridegroom is your kinsman, is he?' Sieur Germain nodded in reply, and the priest continued, 'And who speaks for the bride's family?'

'I do,' said Mrs Wallis, chin jutted. 'She is orphaned; I am cousin to her late mother, who left her to my guardianship.'

Again the priest looked deeply sceptical, and for an anxious moment Sophie expected him to announce his intention of refusing their request. After a moment, however, he shook his head and sighed. 'These hasty love-matches are of all marriages the least likely to endure,' he remarked, 'but equally there is no reasoning with their authors.'

Pocketing the paper, he nodded to Sieur Germain. 'I shall return tomorrow, an hour before sunset,' he said. 'Mind you have your witnesses assembled; I do not like to be kept waiting.'

'I thank you, sir,' Sieur Germain replied with a bow.

The priest nodded again, curtly, and took himself off.

'Impertinent puppy!' said Mrs Wallis, as soon as he had gone.

'Never mind, ma'am,' Sieur Germain soothed her. 'He will do as well as any other, and we need suffer his impertinence only once more.'

Sophie had sprung to her feet and was pacing round and round the sofa. 'And if he does not come back?' she demanded of no one in particular.

Gray rose from the sofa to plant himself in her path. 'He will come back,' he said, laying a hand on each of her shoulders.

'Of course he will,' said Sieur Germain, dryly, 'because otherwise the Temple of Tamesis would forgo the very generous marriage-tithe we shall pay him; and they have need of it, to shore up their riverward wall.'

Sophie bowed her head against Gray's chest. At once he folded her into his arms, and she drew comfort from the steady rhythm of his heart. *After tomorrow*, she told herself bracingly, *after tomorrow no one can part us if we do not wish it.*

'Sophie.' Jenny's voice interrupted her reverie, and she raised her head in some confusion to locate its source. 'Sophie, a moment?'

Gray let her go, bestowing on her briefly the particular smile that spread a warm flush over her cheeks, and, turning away, she followed Jenny out of the room.

'I have a difficult request to make of you,' said Jenny, when they were closeted in her sitting-room. 'But first I think I ought to speak to you about—'

'I beg you will not,' Sophie interrupted hastily. 'I was brought up by a healer, you know; I am not in the least need of *that* sort of lecture, I assure you.'

Jenny declared herself well pleased, but still she insisted on quizzing Sophie on a long list of herbs, with their precise uses. Having thus satisfied herself that her new sister should not find herself in unexpected need of baby's bonnets, she seemed about to speak, but at Sophie's enquiring look fell silent, suddenly intent on the hands clasped in her lap.

'You will think me a most contrary creature,' she said at last, colouring a little. 'It is not that I have any wish to interfere in your . . . but, you see, you have both of you so *much* magick, and it appears that, in certain circumstances . . .'

'Jenny,' Sophie began, now rather flustered herself, 'has this . . . has what you wished to say anything to do with your pianoforte?'

'It shames me to speak of such matters, when you are a welcomed guest in my home,' said Jenny, with a wan chuckle, 'but, you see, if the house should be blown to bits around our ears, or . . . or all the windows melt—'

'Of course,' said Sophie, 'someone might be hurt.' It had surprised her that Jenny, of all people, should be discomposed by a discussion of marital relations, but that she should fear to breach the laws of hospitality was easily understood. 'I believe I may safely promise you that we shall be extremely careful. I thought perhaps an interdiction – or a very strong ward – Gray and I have been reading a great deal about warding-spells . . .'

'I thank you.' Jenny smiled gratefully. 'And I hope I have not given offence.'

Sophie smiled in return, to conceal her dismay. 'None, I assure you,' she said. 'But I wonder . . . might I ask a question of you?'

'Of course you may.'

'It is . . .' She hesitated. 'It is a very personal one. Of course you need not answer, if you had rather not . . .'

Jenny looked at her expectantly, and her courage failed her. 'It is nothing,' she said instead, lamely.

'You are not having second thoughts?'

Sophie laughed, perhaps a trifle raggedly, but said nothing. What was there to be said?

Leaving her chair, Jenny sat beside Sophie and took her hands. 'Sophie, you need not take this step if it makes you unhappy. We will find some other way to—'

'I am not unhappy, Jenny, truly,' said Sophie, anxious to make herself understood – to herself as much as to Jenny. 'If I must marry someone, I can think of no other who – but—' She paused, feeling wretched. 'I had not thought to marry so young . . . nor in such haste.'

To her surprise, Jenny gave her hands an understanding squeeze. 'Of course not,' she said. 'Your life has been turned quite upside down, and I cannot wonder that you feel harried. But, Sophie, listen. My brother is . . . he is an unusual man. He will certainly not expect you to sit at home and embroider baby-clothes, if you do not wish it. If you had rather study ancient languages, or go out riding every day – he will be very happy for you to do so, I know.'

Sophie could not help but smile at Jenny's way of putting things. 'You do not seem so very unhappy to be embroidering baby-clothes,' she ventured.

'No, indeed.' Jenny returned the smile. 'But, you see, I have everything I want, more or less.' Releasing Sophie's hands, she gestured vaguely about her. 'I have never expected to go about having adventures, you know, or to be a great mage or a great scholar. Had I indeed expected it, I should have been greatly disappointed, I think,' she added with a laugh, 'small as my talent is for any of those pursuits. But yours is quite a different case, is it not?'

'Because I am a *princess*, you mean.' Spitting out the hated word with bitter emphasis, Sophie rose abruptly from her seat and began to pace about the small room.

'Not at all,' said Jenny mildly, 'though that must have some bearing, certainly. I only meant, however, that you are very much cleverer than I, and very much more talented. And then, to be so much in love as you appear to be . . .'

At this reminder – however little intended – of her most recent magickal disaster, Sophie's cheeks burned, and she cast a guilty glance in the direction of the drawing-room. She hardly knew how to express what it was that frightened her so: that they would all be soon involving themselves in mortal peril, and she could not bear to think what the end of it might be, if all their preparations should prove insufficient. *If I cannot protect him – or if he will not let me.*

But all this would be equally the case, whether she married him or no.

'Jenny,' she said, finally coming to the point, 'do you – please forgive my asking – do you love your husband?'

Jenny's smile grew a little rueful. 'He loves me very much,' she said. 'Not, perhaps, as my brother loves you – but very much, in his own way. And I am very fond of him. He is a good and an honourable man, and he has been very kind to me.'

'And to all your odd acquaintance,' Sophie added. She had not at first been much disposed to like Sieur Germain de Kergabet, but for her – as perhaps for Jenny? – he had improved upon closer acquaintance.

'Indeed,' Jenny laughed, 'though that, I fear, is rather a recent development. From his behaviour to all of you here, one would not guess that only this summer he was annoyed that I should insist on corresponding with a brother whom my father had very reasonably thrown off.'

'But he trusts you,' Sophie persisted, rather shocked. 'He was reluctant to take us at our word, but yours convinced him at once.'

'Yes, he trusts me.' No trace of mirth now remained in Jenny's voice. 'I could not have agreed to marry him else. I learnt early –

at my mother's knee, one might say – a lesson I hope you shall be spared: we should both be miserable, could we not trust one another.'

'Jenny, do you think – do you think I do right, to marry for love? You do not think I shirk my duty to my father, or to the kingdom?'

Jenny was silent for a time, her face very still. 'I can only tell you,' she said at last, 'what I have already told Gray: that not one pair of lovers in a thousand is given such a chance as this, and I should think you a fool to disdain such good fortune.

'No: I shall tell you one thing more. It was given to me once, long ago, to have my prayers very clearly answered for the good of one I loved, and I have long prayed for my brother's happiness in marriage, as I am sure he once prayed for mine. I do not presume so far as to call you the Great Mother's answer to my prayers; yet I cannot think how they might be better answered.'

Sophie flushed, and knew not where to look.

'I shall pray, also,' she said after a moment. 'I shall beg the Lady Juno's blessing on my wedding day – that is most proper, is it not?'

'Most proper, indeed,' said Jenny, smiling.

CHAPTER XXVI

In Which We Witness the Making of Promises

Breakfast on the morning of the wedding was a hurried affair, every member of the household having some pressing task. Sieur Germain had gone out very early, despite a settled rain; the moment they had eaten, Jenny and Joanna whisked Sophie away to try on her wedding-dress, while Mrs Wallis disappeared to join Mrs Treveur in the kitchen.

Gray alone wandered the house in search of some occupation. Too restless and distracted to read, and disinclined for conversation, he yearned to escape the house. Instead he paced and fretted, until at last he was waylaid by his brother-in-law in the corridor outside the drawing-room.

'I have discharged your commission,' Sieur Germain said cheerfully, handing him a small paper packet, slightly damp and sealed with the mark of a renowned family of goldsmiths, 'and I believe that Jenny has something to show you, also . . .'

'Has she?' he said. 'Where shall I find her?'

'She is in the morning-room, I believe.'

'I thank you,' said Gray. He started down the corridor in the proper direction, only to turn back, the little packet clasped in one hand, to cry, 'And I thank you, a thousand times, for – for—'

'Another time,' Sieur Germain replied, waving away his thanks.

'The gods grant you many more years in which to discharge all debts of gratitude.'

'The gods grant,' echoed Gray.

Jenny received him in the morning-room – where she sat with Joanna amidst what must surely be a full cartload of hothouse flowers, whether destined for marriage-offerings or simply to decorate the house for the occasion, it was difficult to guess – with an expression of affectionate impatience.

'I had forgot, after all these years,' she said, 'how difficult it is to gain your attention when you have something on your mind.'

Joanna produced a most uncharacteristic giggle; Gray frowned at her, but to no effect.

'I did have your things here,' Jenny continued, greatly increasing his bewilderment. 'I wished to show them to you myself. But as there was not room enough for everything, once the flowers arrived, I have asked Treveur to put them in your bedroom—'

'*My* things? What things?'

'Graham Valerius Marshall, you did not think I should permit you to be married in those appalling clothes?' his sister demanded.

He glanced down at the outgrown trousers, the threadbare waistcoat, the coat that – despite the best efforts of Mrs Wallis and several Kergabet servants – still bore traces of its misadventures at Merlin.

'I . . . I had not thought at all,' he admitted.

'Well, go and look.' Jenny shook her head in good-natured despair. 'My lord will send his man up later to do something about your hair.'

In his bedroom he found neatly laid out a suit of clothes, recognisably much finer than any he had ever owned – and as to size (of which he was a rather better judge) more accurately cut than he would have thought possible. Not for the first time he wondered, with a groan, how he should ever succeed in repaying his brother-in-law for the tremendous outlay of coin which he must be making; to repay his even greater outlay of effort and goodwill was, of course, quite impossible.

Sophie woke to a hesitant knocking at her bedroom door and rose from her bed, against whose coverlet she had collapsed, exhausted from experimenting with warding-spells, some unknown while before, to open it. She had expected Jenny or Joanna – perhaps Mrs Wallis, or Jenny's maid – come to harry her into new clothes or carry out their threats to dress her hair 'just like the Queen's'. Instead the knocker was Gray, wearing the diffident expression that she so seldom saw of late, from which she deduced that his errand concerned matters of the heart, rather than of the intellect.

'Sophie,' he began, 'might I – have you a moment to—?'

'Come in,' she said, rubbing one eye, and, when he hesitated, 'Gray, we shall be married in a few hours' time; surely there can be no impropriety . . . but do not close the door, if you had rather not.'

Rather to her surprise, he ducked under the lintel and pulled the door to.

'I have . . . I should have liked to give you a proper betrothal-gift,' he said, stepping close to her and taking her hand. At his touch she smiled, warmed to her toes. 'This . . . it is not exactly mine to give – I have had to ask my brother-in-law to find it for me, and to pay for it – but the thought, at least—'

'There is no need to give me anything,' Sophie told him, indulging herself by stretching up to tuck a stray lock of hair behind his ear. '*You* ought to know that, if anyone does.'

Gray returned the smile; he put up a hand as though to touch her cheek but halted it in mid gesture. 'Still,' he said, 'one ought to do things properly, and, besides . . .' He let go of her hand and reached into a coat-pocket, from which he extracted some small, glinting thing. Then reaching again for her hand, he turned it palm up, and gently folded her fingers round the object.

Opening her hand, Sophie looked down at a slender gold ring.

'Oh,' she said softly, rendered quite as inarticulate as Gray had ever been. She turned the ring around in her fingers, admiring the delicately chased laurel-leaves that decorated its outer surface, and marvelled that he should have contrived to choose for her so exactly what she might have chosen for herself. Then, looking up at him, hoping that he would read in her face what she could not quite manage to say, she slipped it onto her finger – against the vein which, so said healers' lore, leads most directly to the heart.

About to attempt some expression of thanks, she was forestalled by another, more importunate knock at the door. This time it was Jenny indeed, with Joanna and a brace of maids.

'Baths,' the mistress of the house announced succinctly, and, pointing an imperious finger at her brother, 'Upstairs with you.'

Though the traditional festive visit to the public baths was out of the question, the Roman-plumbed facilities *chez* Kergabet were quite luxurious enough for Sophie's taste. On this occasion a fire crackled merrily on the marble hearth of the second-floor bathroom, and the large bath was already filled with steaming water.

Properly steamed and scrubbed, Sophie drank Mrs Wallis's vile-tasting tincture of wild carrot seeds and was ceremoniously attired in her makeshift wedding-clothes. Jenny performed the motherly office of tying the broad sash in an elaborate knot, and her maid, Henriette, took firm charge of Sophie's hair.

By the time she was summoned to appear downstairs, Sophie felt she would go quite mad from the suspense.

The drawing-room was lit by half a dozen candelabra and filled with the scents of flowers blooming out of season – roses and lilies, hyacinth and eglantine. The priest had set up his altar, lit his incense, pronounced his opening invocation; he summoned the bride, and Jenny led Sophie forward. Sophie answered his questions in a sort of haze, declaring (not altogether truthfully) that she was indeed Sophia Lavinia Callender, of an age to marry and contracted to no other man, and had come here of her own will to be married to Gray; her family's consent was sought, and Mrs Wallis gave it. She heard Gray called likewise, and likewise declare himself, and Sieur Germain give consent on behalf of his family. Bride and bridegroom bowed to the altar. The priest – who looked rather cross, for no reason that Sophie could discern – led them in making their offerings to those deities concerned with marriage.

Amidst all this strangeness, only Gray himself – though resplendent in new clothes, his hair freshly trimmed and so neatly arranged that it might have belonged to some other person – seemed at all familiar, and Sophie gazed at him steadily, casting only occasional glances at the priest and the invocations and offerings on which she ought to have been concentrating her mind.

'Graham Marshall, Sophia Callender,' the priest said sternly, 'having given your consent to this marriage, signify it now by joining your hands.'

They did so, and he wrapped the leathern marriage-cord round and round their clasped right hands, intoning as he did so the ancient formula: *Bond of love, mild as silk; bond of trust, strong as iron; bind these two for all their lives. May the gods grant it.*

'May the gods grant it,' echoed the assembled company: Jenny and Sieur Germain, Joanna, Mrs Wallis and Master Alcuin, and nearly all the Kergabet servants.

Rain lashed the drawing-room windows; from time to time a bolt of lightning darted a brief unearthly light on the candlelit chamber, casting each face, each gesture, each object into stark relief, and was swiftly followed by a roll of thunder.

The priest broke one spelt-cake in two, handing one half to Gray and the other to Sophie, and offered others to Juno and Hymenaeus,

Brigid and the Great Mother, on his little charcoal brazier. Sophie's mouth was so dry that she could scarcely swallow her portion. She choked it down, however; a marriage sealed by this means, a marriage *confarreatio*, was of all bonds the most difficult to break.

The priest read the terms of the marriage contract once more, that bride and bridegroom might give their formal agreement. Having done so, they were freed from the marriage-tie, which the priest handed to Gray. Without, the thunder had grown less frequent but more ominous; rain washed down the windowpanes in sheets.

'Attend,' the priest said, rather sternly, and for a moment Sophie looked him full in the eyes. When she turned back to Gray, he was holding out one hand, palm up, and smiling down at her; instinctively she returned a glad smile of her own. '*Ubi tu Gaius, ego Gaia*,' the priest prompted: *Where and when you are Gaius, I am Gaia – where you are, what you are, I shall be also.*

'*Ubi tu Gaius, ego Gaia*,' Sophie repeated, gazing up into Gray's wide hazel eyes and laying her hand atop his upturned palm. *Great Mother*, she prayed, *Juno and Venus, from your great bounty, bless my wedding-day . . .*

'*Ubi tu Gaia, ego Gaius*,' Gray replied.

The last syllable fell into a sudden and profound silence.

'How funny!' said Joanna – sotto voce, but perfectly audible in the abruptly soundless room. 'The rain has stopped.'

Jenny shushed her, and the rite proceeded through the few blessings and entreaties that remained; it must be only his own fancy, Gray decided, that the priest had begun to look distinctly frightened.

He and Sophie made their first offering as man and wife, and a final bow to the altar, and the company adjourned to the dining-parlour, where they were greeted by a wedding-feast which, though on a smaller scale, appeared to Gray at least the equal of Jenny's own. The priest of

Tamesis, though earnestly pressed by Sieur Germain to stay to dinner, as earnestly declined, and had taken himself, his tithe-purse, and his paraphernalia away into the reinvigorated thunderstorm before the first morsel of food was eaten in the adjoining room.

'The priest would not stay?' Gray heard Jenny say to her husband, in a low and worried tone. 'I do not like that omen.'

Sieur Germain only laughed, however, and said, 'I see no omen in it, my dear. This weather makes him want his own warm bed, no doubt. We shall do better without such a dyspeptic guest, in any case.' Catching Gray and Sophie about the shoulders, he added, 'Now, into the dining-room with you!'

For this occasion Gray and Sophie had perforce to sit together at the head of the table, and, had either been at all inclined to eat, they must still have gone hungry, so frequently were they congratulated, wished joy, long life, and good health (and, by a slightly tipsy Mrs Treveur, many children), and called upon to speak. Gray hardly knew what he said when thus applied to; if he had been distracted by thoughts of Sophie earlier in the day, when she was elsewhere, here in her presence he found it quite impossible to think of anything, or anyone, else.

The hour was nearing midnight when, in lieu of the usual festive torchlight procession of the bride to her new home, the household took up candles and escorted Sophie up one staircase after another, to Gray's bedroom on the third floor. Sieur Germain – Mrs Wallis not being of a size to perform this office – lifted Sophie over the threshold; and, with much good-natured teasing, the door was closed upon them.

CHAPTER XXVII

In Which Master Alcuin Draws an Interesting Conclusion

They stood for a long moment staring at one another, hearing no sound but the tattoo of raindrops on the window-glass and their own ragged breathing.

'We had better ward the room, I suppose,' said Sophie at last, blushing, and Gray, with some relief, nodded.

'It will be enough?' she said. 'You are quite sure?'

He was less completely confident than he had led Sophie to believe, but the theory was sound enough. 'Two days since,' he said, 'when Master Alcuin warded the dining-room – did you feel the wards at all, when you walked through them?'

Sophie's eyes widened. 'I thought,' she began, 'I thought I had brushed away a cobweb. I felt the merest touch – like gossamer – and – I wanted so *very* much to be out of that room, and away from everyone . . .'

'Exactly,' said Gray. 'No one else in this house could have passed those wards. *My* wards alone would not likely suffice to contain your magick, but a joint effort, using a particularly effective spell—'

Sophie drew a deep breath and nodded.

It took some little time, in the circumstances, to achieve the proper state of concentration on the spell that Gray had carefully transcribed and they had both committed to memory; by Sophie's silence he deduced that she was in the same difficulty. '*Tego, saepio, custodio*,' he began at last, and heard her voice echoing his own: '*Saepio, cingo, amplector . . .*'

At the final phrase – *Ego obsecroque impero* – a double whisper of magick passed through him; the hairs on his neck and arms rose shiveringly for just a moment, and he opened his eyes to see Sophie scratching her nose, her dark, intent gaze focused on his face. He attempted a smile and made to take her hand, but she turned away, moving towards the dressing-table where, somehow, her *toiletteries* had appeared, tidily disposed beside his own. 'My head aches dreadfully,' she said, sitting down before the mirror. 'Every hairpin in this house is in my hair, I think.'

She bent her head and began pulling out the pins. 'Let me help you,' Gray ventured, and crossed the room to stand behind her chair.

Her hair, freed gradually from its constraints, was as wonderfully soft as ever he had imagined it, but there seemed no end to the flowers and ribbons and pins. As he worked them free – gently, cautiously, for this was territory as unexplored as any that might come after – he could not resist occasionally stroking his fingers through the silky strands. He looked up, startled, when a soft chestnut-coloured tendril wound itself momentarily about his hand, but Sophie's head was still bent just enough to render her expression unreadable.

From time to time their fingers met, and he thrilled to every momentary touch. It was of all things the most absurd that such a slight thing should so affect him *now*, but so it was; by the time the last pin chimed softly on the polished surface of the dressing-table he was breathing rather fast.

Sophie raised her head; his eyes met hers in the looking-glass, and he saw that her face was as flushed, her eyes as nervously bright as his own. She stood abruptly, turning away from her reflection. 'It ought not to be so very difficult to begin,' she said.

* * *

'You could sing to me, you know,' Gray murmured, 'and I should be utterly in your power.' He stood perhaps four paces' distance from her, one hand white-knuckled on the nearest carven bedpost.

'But that,' replied Sophie (who had read one or two books far more unsuitable than her stepfather had any idea of), 'would be most unfair.'

She took another step towards him.

'Indeed – and' – a moment's pause; then, striding forward and pulling her into his arms – 'and quite unnecessary, besides.'

She was never afterwards sure exactly what happened next; only that, somehow, Gray's coat and waistcoat, collar and neck-cloth, were quite elsewhere, and the bodice of her gown sliding off her shoulders, at the moment when their fingers collided around her elaborately knotted sash.

They laughed uncertainly; Sophie let go the knot, and Gray's long fingers fumbled with it. 'Let me,' she said after a moment, but Jenny had tied it so thoroughly, and pulled each separate twist so tight, that they could neither of them make any headway.

'When fair means fail,' Gray said at last, 'we cheat.' And, closing his hand about the recalcitrant knot, he whispered three words.

Then he looked down at his hand, and blinked. 'Oh,' he said.

Sophie, following his gaze, saw at once the source of his consternation: rather than simply untying the knot, his spell had unravelled the sash itself into a mass of silken threads. 'What was it you said to me, a few days since?' she said, restraining her laughter as best she could. '"I should not love you half so well, *cariad*, if you were like other people . . ."'

Gray stared at her for a long moment, a smile tugging at the corners of his mouth, then looked again at the ruined fabric in his fist. At last he spread his fingers and let the gossamer threads fall to the floor. 'Come to bed,' he said – half command, half entreaty – and opened his arms once more.

And, smiling, Sophie went.

She woke with the twittering of sparrows at false dawn, half under the tangled bedclothes, half firmly wrapped in the arms of her husband, who slumbered deeply, his warm breath tickling the back of her neck. She had been dreaming, she remembered: a pleasant dream of wandering in a forest in spring. She shivered, then frowned; the room was far colder than it ought to be, surely. Had the fire gone out altogether?

With some difficulty she wriggled out of Gray's embrace and, eventually, out of bed. By now thoroughly chilled, she retrieved and shrugged on the first garment to catch her eye: Gray's discarded shirt, whose hem fell past her knees. Wrapping the rumpled fabric twice round her body, she approached the hearth and found that, indeed, last night's cheery blaze was now a heap of cold ashes; they had not thought to bank the fire. More puzzlingly, the hearthstones bore signs that the flames had blazed up spectacularly before burning themselves out.

Only yesterday Sophie had dreaded what she might behold on waking, her mind's eye conjuring splintered wood, shattered glass, cracked hearthstones – things fractured, charred, fragmented, crushed by the power she had never sought and now could not control. Though as yet she had seen nothing so very dreadful here, she could not be sanguine; the odd half light of this hour just before dawn might hide a multitude of horrors.

Trembling a little – and not only from the cold – she raised a hand and called a timid, fragile globe of light.

She was very near the window, and so it was the window-curtains that she noticed first of all: had not the heavy damask borne a quite different pattern yesternight? But she had been thinking of quite other things; perhaps she might be mistaken. Determined to know the worst, she strengthened her light a little and, moving to the centre of the room, revolved slowly on her heels, examining every visible object intently. From time to time, as she moved, an unfamiliar twinge recalled to her mind fragments of the night just past. They had neither of them truly known what to expect, but – Sophie smiled a small, secret smile – such things, it seemed, had a way of working themselves out.

She had been able to forget, for a time, how much she was afraid, but now she could not help remembering.

They had not destroyed anything, in the strict sense of the term; this gave her some comfort. But that the wards on this room had been necessary, she could no longer doubt. She had only to hope that they had also been sufficient.

The beautifully carved rosewood bed had sprouted little leafy shoots, all along the headboard and up and down the tall posts; the small rosewood bookcase seemed similarly afflicted. Not only the window-curtains but the costly hearthrug, the damask coverlet twisted about Gray's long legs, the drawn-back bed-curtains – all had somehow been reworked into new and phantastickal motifs. The little flowers carelessly discarded upon the dressing-table had apparently taken root there and nodded their unseasonable heads before the looking-glass like tiny ladies of fashion.

The looking-glass itself, paradoxically, remained quite unmarred, and cast Sophie's reflection back at her just as though she – as though *everything* – were not profoundly, irrevocably changed.

Gray stirred in his sleep and mumbled something, and Sophie – who had crept into bed again and, shutting her eyes against the bizarre phenomena around her, allowed his slow, even breathing to lull her back into sleep – sat up abruptly to see full daylight, a cold, bright, wintry sun, throwing bright shutter-stripes on the walls and floor. *At least*, she thought absently, *it has stopped raining at last.*

'Gray,' she said softly, laying a hand on his bare shoulder. 'Gray, wake up.'

His face showed a momentary confusion; then he opened his eyes, and blinked at Sophie, and smiled a wide, delighted smile.

'The sun is long up,' she said. 'I am sure we ought to be downstairs; everyone will be thinking—'

But Gray was laughing at her – the low, musical sound she heard so seldom, and loved so much – and pulling her down into his arms, among the rumpled pillows. 'That we are new-married and lying late abed,' he said. 'What else should they be thinking, pray?'

'Gray.' Was it possible that he did not see what she had seen? 'Gray, look about you.'

Raising his eyebrows, he sat up and surveyed the oddly new-furnished room. One long arm reached up to pluck a leaf from the nearest bedpost. 'Is this . . . ?' he enquired, peering at it.

Sophie nodded.

'Well,' said Gray. He looked at her, and back down at the tiny yellow-green leaf. 'This is not quite what we had expected.'

When at length – long after the morning meal had ended – the new-made *conubii* made their appearance downstairs, they were greeted by what Gray supposed to be the usual sort of friendly raillery, but though there was quite enough of this to make both of them blush, he could see very well that no one's heart was in it.

'Something has happened,' he said, looking from Jenny to her husband to Master Alcuin. 'Or something new has come to light – what is it?'

It was Joanna who spoke, while the others seemed to be considering how to begin. 'He has come back again,' she said. 'My father. With another man – Master Alcuin observed them from the window as they departed and believes it was one of Father's students – and two constables of the Watch.'

'During *breakfast*!' added Jenny. 'I suppose he meant to catch us in a lie by arriving at an hour when no civilised person would think of calling.'

'They were at length prevailed upon to depart,' said Sieur Germain, with a grimace, 'but although the good men of the Watch appeared persuaded of our innocence in the matter of Professor Callender's missing daughter, I fear the Professor himself was not.'

Sophie's grip on Gray's hand had tightened painfully, and his hand clasped hers with scarcely less ferocity. Joanna said, 'I shall go and fetch you a fresh pot of tea.'

'It is very fortunate that you warded your room so completely,' said Master Alcuin. 'I am not certain which of our visitors worked the rather potent finding I observed – perhaps it too was a joint effort, by Callender and his young friend – but certainly it must otherwise have located you, Marshall, worked at such close range.'

'Located *me*?' said Gray, startled. 'Are you quite sure?'

'Oh, certainly,' Master Alcuin replied.

'I left the others here in the breakfast-parlour to intercept Callender and his party below, in the hall,' Sieur Germain explained. 'It was necessary, of course, that Master Alcuin not be questioned by the men of the Watch. I can assure you that when not impugning your honour and that of your sister and myself, and threatening retribution for my intransigence, Callender spoke particularly of a finding-spell directed at you.'

'But why . . . ?' Gray had wondered that the Professor, on his previous visit, should have wasted time seeking Sophie under sofas and behind occasional tables, when he might have found her so much more quickly and easily by magickal means. Now a thought struck him. 'Perhaps,' he said to Sophie, 'he cannot picture you accurately enough to work a finding.'

Sophie, Jenny, and Sieur Germain protested the absurdity of this idea, but Mrs Wallis and Master Alcuin looked thoughtful.

'Indeed, Miss Sophie,' said the latter, 'it seems entirely possible that your magick could have such an effect.'

'Or perhaps his companion worked the spell,' Gray continued, 'and had no means of knowing what you look like. In any event, however, we are none of us safe so long as he still suspects our presence here. A finding may be less reliable at greater distance, but—'

'Perhaps . . . if we set a ward on the whole house?' said Sophie. 'Or a shielding-spell? Might such a spell be constructed particularly to evade findings?'

Master Alcuin's thoughtful frown deepened, and he began toying with the end of his beard. 'Such a construction ought certainly to be possible—'

'He is still there,' said Joanna, erupting suddenly into the breakfast-parlour.

Sieur Germain rose from his chair, glowering, and strode out of the room, calling for Treveur.

'I thought him gone away,' Joanna continued, 'before Gray and Sophie came down, but he is still there, or he is come back. He is alone now, at least.'

'And will see us the moment we pass by any window facing the street, I suppose,' said Sophie, 'or venture a single step out of doors.'

'Then you must not let him see you,' said Jenny firmly. 'Perhaps he will give up and go away.'

Below, the front door opened and closed with some violence.

'An excellent plan, Lady Kergabet,' Mrs Wallis said dryly, 'save that it may cause us some difficulty in accepting Their Majesties' invitation to the Samhain ball.'

Gray, who had been thinking exactly this, raised his eyebrows. 'Have you any alternative to propose, madam?'

'Of course I have,' said Mrs Wallis, smug. 'You did not think I had been visiting about Town all this time, to no purpose?'

Their attention caught, they all of them waited in silence for her to explain herself, until at last Joanna burst out, 'Well, then? Tell us what it is!'

Mrs Wallis smiled – a slow, inward-looking smile. 'All in good time, Miss Joanna.'

'But you must tell us *something*, Mrs Wallis,' said Sophie.

'Indeed,' said Master Alcuin, 'how can we form a strategy, in the absence of full intelligence as to our own defensive capabilities?'

'And if my efforts should prove unsuccessful – what then?' Mrs Wallis retorted. 'You may rest assured, all of you, that I shall tell you all that is necessary, at the proper time.'

Sophie, anxious not to violate the Kergabets' hospitality by expressing her opinion of this behaviour, excused herself, sans breakfast, as quickly as politeness allowed. She took refuge in the library, whither she was followed by an anxious Gray.

'There is nothing the matter with me,' she assured him, with some impatience. 'I am only feeling *extremely* annoyed with Mrs Wallis, and trying not to show it.'

'You felt, then,' said Gray, perching on the edge of the table and smiling crookedly down at his wife, 'as though you must get away, or else shake her secrets out of her.'

Sophie was smothering a very unmatronly fit of giggles when the library door opened and Master Alcuin stalked into the room.

'Your guardian,' he said to Sophie, fairly quivering with irritation, 'can be most infuriatingly secretive.'

'Can we not ask Jenny—?' Sophie began, but Gray shook his head.

'I have asked her,' he said gloomily. 'She first took me to task for suggesting that she spy on a guest in her house – after being treated so shabbily as a guest of the Professor, she wondered that I dared ask such a thing, and how should I have felt had she used her talent on you, Sophie, or on the Magister, in such a way? And when I persisted, she admitted at last that she had tried it already, in secret, and could see nothing at all.'

'Well.' Master Alcuin shook his head ruefully. Then, with a more cheerful look, he rubbed his palms together in the manner of one settling down to work. 'Our host appears to have rid us of our besetting Fellow, at any rate for the time being, by dispatching young Harry in pursuit of the Watch.

'And now – I have no wish to pry, you understand, but – tell me – the warding-spell you worked upon your room: apart from deflecting our unpleasant visitors, it was successful? Or – unnecessary, perhaps, after all?'

Instinctively Sophie glanced at Gray, wondering whether she ought to let him answer this question. Then giving herself a mental shake, she looked into their teacher's keen, kindly eyes and replied, 'Not unnecessary, Magister. But successful, yes – or, at any rate, I have not seen any damage elsewhere in the house—'

'It was not *damage*,' Gray protested.

'*Not damage*?' she repeated, incredulous. 'What do you call it, then?'

He frowned in thought, settling back in his chair and folding his long arms across his chest. 'Metamorphosis,' he said. 'Transformative magick. Or perhaps . . .'

'Transformative magick?' Master Alcuin asked. By now Sophie had half forgotten that a third person was present, and she started a little at the interruption. 'Transformative of . . . what, exactly?'

Between them they detailed, as best they could, their observations, and when they had done, Master Alcuin looked from one to the other, twisting the end of his beard about one finger.

'There must be some precedent,' he said at last, 'but I cannot recall encountering it in my reading. I shall have to look farther . . . would that I had all my books to hand!' A pause, and a rueful smile: 'You will both be too fatigued, then, I suppose, to experiment with warding the house against finding-spells.'

It was only now that Sophie recognised what was perhaps the

oddest aspect of this thoroughly odd affair: that, far from being exhausted by that tremendous expenditure of magick, she felt rested, refreshed – almost buoyant. She closed her eyes and slowed her breathing, slipping down into the centre of herself; sure enough, the blue-white flame-flower of her magick burned as brightly and sang as high and clear as ever. Perhaps, in fact . . .

Through her confusion and discomfiture she heard Gray's voice, slow and incredulous, speaking her own thoughts: 'No. No, indeed – it is impossible, but – I believe I have *more* magick now than I had yesterday.'

She looked at him, and then at Master Alcuin – who had once told them that he had a talent for seeing others' magick. He scrutinised each of them in turn, head on one side, eyes narrowed; his face paled a little, and he opened his eyes wide and shook his head like a hound after rain. 'It is true,' he said, sounding awed. 'Quite impossible, but perfectly true. Both of you – more than before . . .' Now he was scrabbling among the scholarly detritus that littered the table, at last unearthing a pen and a scrap of writing-paper. 'For *this* I am sure there is no precedent. Fascinating! It is the sort of thing spoken of in oracular prophecies, the stuff of legends . . .'

Sophie's mouth was dry. 'Magister,' she said softly. But he was writing frantically, and seemed not to hear. Gray reached across the table to lay his hand over hers. 'What does this mean?' she whispered.

'I cannot think,' he said, in the same tone, 'but we shall not let it part us, whatever it may mean.'

This thought gave Sophie courage, and she smiled.

CHAPTER XXVIII

In Which Joanna Is Disappointed Again

'*If you have* nothing to do, Gray, cannot you at least keep *still*?' said Jenny, closing her book with quite unnecessary violence. 'You will drive us all mad with your pacing and prowling, and wear my carpets to shreds.'

Gray – who had indeed been pacing the length of the drawing-room for more than an hour – turned on his heel to glare at her. 'I might say the same of you,' he said. 'You have quarrelled with your seat five times this evening, by my count, and fetched down three different books—'

They might have continued thus, had not Master Alcuin growled from across the room, 'Children! May we not have a moment's peace?'

These days of waiting for the eve of Samhain had begun to seem a foretaste of Tartarus. They had done what they could. They had their means of entry to the Royal Palace: the invitation to the Samhain ball for Sieur Germain and Lady Kergabet, Lady Kergabet's uncle and aunt, and two young cousins of Sieur Germain's. They had planned, as well as was possible, the moves of the game they should have to play once there – had composed a letter to King Henry and commissioned Sieur Germain's helpful informant to deliver it as early as possible after the royal family's return from Caernarfon; had marshalled what real evidence they had, and discussed *ad infinitum* how best to make that evidence persuasive. It was maddening to possess, in the form of the Professor's ring of keys, what might have been damning evidence in the hands of a skilled scry-mage, were it not for the inevitable suspicion of magickal tampering.

Then – only a few days before His Majesty's expected return to London – Gray had received a letter from Oxford, enclosed in one directed to Jenny which read, simply, *Please send on after reading.*

He had half forgot the letter to which this one was a reply – a hastily scrawled note to Henry Crowther, dispatched from a posting-inn somewhere between Aleth and Rostrenen, asking for news of Crowther himself, and of Evans-Hughes and Gautier – and it had evidently languished in the Porter's Lodge at Merlin until very lately, awaiting his return from his parents' home in Yorkshire.

My dear Marshall, it ran,

Have just received yours of Midsummer, and hope that your sister will forward this on to you, wherever you are, for I have been at some pains to find out her direction. First things first: as you must know by now, it is true about poor Gautier. Whatever anyone says, Marshall, you are not to blame: Taylor was occupied, and Evans-Hughes was knocked flat, but I was neither, and you may take my word on it. I am perfectly well now, and Evans-Hughes also; I pray the same may be true of you. It is true then, I collect, that you went to Finisterre with Callender? When you disappeared, Evans-Hughes told me that Callender had made off with you (and other things of which the less said, the better), but then C returned without you, and the next any of us heard was that you and old Alcuin had broken into the Master's Lodge and run Lord Halifax through with that great, rusty old spear that used to hang upon the wall of his study – you remember it, I am sure – which of course no one could believe. At any rate, I felt I must warn you and your sister that C has managed to get himself elected Master, and has been going up to Town more often than anyone can at all account for; and I cannot help thinking that he must also have discovered Lady K's direction. And he has made known that he intends to be in London on Samhain-night, which as you may imagine has caused some consternation: the Master of Merlin, to absent himself from the College's Samhain rites? I think therefore that he must have some particular business afoot; and as he has not boasted of its importance to all and sundry—

'Listen to this,' Gray said, breaking into the murmur of breakfast-table conversation, and read the letter out. 'Does this not look as though they mean to make their attempt on Samhain-night itself?'

This conclusion was not universally embraced – Sieur Germain, in particular, arguing that while a public festival might be the ideal setting for cutpurses and pickpockets, surely a poisoning was more easily conducted in privacy – but the danger was acknowledged to be sufficient that they must plan for this contingency as well.

The remainder of that morning was therefore spent in composing what proved to be a distressingly long list of the means by which a poison might be administered to the most recognisable man in the kingdom, in full view of thousands of his guests, and in devising strategies by which they might keep both His Majesty and the members of the conspiracy under their collective surveillance. If the poison in question was the one they believed it to be – that which Master Alcuin's book named *Levenez an kalon*, 'heart's delight' – then its flavour and odour were such as to be remarked in a bland dish but readily enough concealed in any sufficiently strong wine or 'well-flavoured meat', which might have helped to narrow the field at an ordinary family dinner but was of no use at all in the present case. That the conspirators could not afford the suspicions that must arise from any further deaths in the course of the ball, and that their supply of a poison so difficult to manufacture must be limited, suggested that there could be no question of adulterating whole tureens of soup or decanters of wine; the poison must be introduced more directly. If, therefore, His Majesty could not be persuaded by their warnings, they must try to catch the conspirators in the act, and to prevent its consequences. More they could not do, until Samhain-night itself.

By now the occupants of the house had begun in earnest to grate on one another's nerves. Sophie and Joanna bickered; Sieur Germain was by turns morose and garrulous, and Master Alcuin began to display a lack of patience that Gray, had he not been himself in a state of tension bordering on distraction, would have found quite shocking. Mrs Wallis continued both infuriatingly vague and uncharacteristically fretful.

For Gray, the vexatious daylight hours were made bearable by the long, blissful nights, which seemed almost to belong to another existence. If nothing else, he told himself, he and Sophie should at least have had these few nights together – *alone* together, with their wards shutting out all the rest of the world.

That the wards had in fact been intended to shut *in* something else, however, was difficult to forget. Though that first morning's strange metamorphoses had reversed themselves by nightfall and were every day less persistent, the accompanying phenomenon seemed concomitantly stronger; to wake each morning abuzz with magick not only replenished but, to all appearances, increased was not only a source of puzzlement and worry but made the coming day's enforced captivity all the more exasperating.

At breakfast the next day – the last before Samhain-night – Mrs Wallis received a letter which caused her to smile in a satisfied manner and, having enveloped herself in a voluminous cloak and strung about her throat an oddly familiar necklace, to absent herself from the house for several hours. When she returned, the rest of the family were summoned to the drawing-room, where – now wearing an assortment of peculiar jewellery – she at last acquainted them with her plan.

'Your mother,' she began, nodding at Sophie and Joanna in turn, 'was for some time in the habit of granting favours to persons who had urgent need of dissimulation or disguise. She was sometimes not particularly . . . discriminating in her choices . . .' Here Mrs Wallis's mouth twisted in the way Sophie had known all her life, but her eyes grew soft and distant. 'In any case,' she went on after a moment, 'there remain in London some few beneficiaries of Queen Laora's assistance whom I have been able to locate, and who proved willing, eventually, to return to me the tokens they had received from her hands.'

Ignoring Sophie's exclamation of surprise at this cavalier treatment of the secrets her guardian had always been at such pains to conceal, Mrs Wallis bent her head and lifted a thin gold chain up and over her coils of dark hair. Raising her face again, she presented the chain – and its small teardrop of polished obsidian – to Master Alcuin, who sat nearest. 'Look at it,' she invited, 'and tell them what magick you see.'

'It is another of my mother's charms against unwelcome attention,' said Joanna impatiently. 'Are there – how many are there?'

Mrs Wallis did not reply.

Examining more narrowly the various ornaments that Mrs Wallis had not been wearing at breakfast, Sophie spied a slender silver ring set with a tiny globe of onyx; two bracelets – one, like that Gray had lost in Oxford, an obsidian bauble on a silken cord, and the other a heavy silver chain set with three midnight-black ovals; an elegant little copper hairpin topped by a trio of jet beads;

and, last of all, a shawl-pin of elaborate design, in which a gleaming black teardrop made one petal of a parti-coloured flower.

'Laora always favoured black stones for this purpose,' Mrs Wallis said. 'Sometimes jet or onyx, but obsidian was her favourite; she could feel their memory of the fires of Vulcan, she said.' Then she shook her head as though she had said something foolish.

While Sophie had been remarking on the varied motifs of these objects, and Jenny and Sieur Germain exclaiming in surprise and wonder, Joanna, it appeared, had been counting them. 'There are six,' she crowed, 'and six of us, besides Sophie. There is no reason in the world why I should not come with you—'

'*No*, Joanna.' Never before, perhaps, had the rest of them been so well united.

'Concealment is not everything,' Gray explained.

'There will be mages present with sufficient talent to see through such charms,' added Master Alcuin, 'and it may be that Miss Sophie will need to husband her own magick for other purposes . . .'

'We must have other means of defending ourselves,' said Sophie, adding, with a nod at Sieur Germain, 'magickal or otherwise, and we have no very clear idea of what we may have to do . . . Joanna, if you should be hurt . . .'

Sophie thought she could perceive a softening in her sister's eyes, and such kind of arguments might at length have reconciled her, had not Mrs Wallis then said, 'It is quite out of the question, Joanna. Your mother would never have consented to my involving you in such danger, at your age.'

'I am only four years younger than Sophie,' Joanna retorted, blinking furiously, 'and quite as clever – it is not right that I should be made to sit at home, doing nothing—'

Quite plainly she could remain here no longer without material loss of dignity; Sophie was therefore not at all surprised when, abruptly, she sprang up from her chair and ran out of the room.

Shooting a last glare at Mrs Wallis, Sophie followed her – along the corridor, up the stairs and, at last, through the door of her bedroom, which Joanna tried, but failed, to slam in her sister's face.

'It is not *fair*,' she sobbed. Hot tears soaked into the front of Sophie's gown. 'I am always left out of everything, and – and—'

'Not *everything*,' said Sophie, stroking Joanna's hair. 'But—'

'And how *dare* she say that I am too young? As though I were a *child*, or—'

'Jo, dear,' said Sophie, 'we all know that you are wise beyond your years, but it is quite true that there would be no one else of your age, apart from the Princes perhaps – it would only be one more means of drawing attention to ourselves, which you know we must not do. And as Mrs Wallis says, Mama—'

'Mrs Wallis may care whether I live or die,' said Joanna bitterly, 'but Mama never did. You need not pretend it to spare *my* feelings.'

This came so near the truth that it would be futile to dispute it; instead Sophie kissed her sister and said, '*I* should care, very much.'

At last Joanna raised her head, and, startled, Sophie saw in her face the mirror image of her own deepest fears. 'I have no one but you, Sophie,' she whispered, 'and you are always getting into dreadful trouble. If – if you were to go off to the ball, tomorrow evening, and never come back again . . .'

Sophie hugged her fiercely. 'Of course I shall come back,' she said. This was a side of her sister she had seen only a few times in their lives – and that none other, she suspected, had ever been permitted to see at all. 'But, Jo, I should feel so very much less anxious if I knew that you were safe at home . . .'

Joanna sniffed loudly, dragging one wrist across her eyes. Her expression was blank, unreadable.

'Jo, you will stay here?' Sophie repeated. 'You will stay out of danger? Promise me, Joanna, please . . .'

At first the only reply was a long, considering look, and Sophie, remembering half a hundred episodes of ingenious disobedience, could not think what to do next, but finally Joanna folded her hands in her lap and said, with great composure, 'I promise that I shall stay out of danger.'

Sophie was too much relieved to think of pressing her farther.

The morning of the last day of October dawned cold, crisp, and oppressively bright. Gray woke with Sophie still soundly asleep in his arms, which caused him to smile and thank the gods for his good fortune; then he remembered what day it was, and smile and thanks evaporated together.

Breakfast was tense and nearly silent. Jenny – who had been first to come down to breakfast as always – was pale and heavy-eyed, and abandoned her brioche after only two bites. When Sophie and then Gray asked whether she was quite well, she produced a brave but ultimately unsuccessful attempt at a smile and said, 'I am only a little tired.' Mrs Wallis, however, on arriving in the breakfast-room, gave her a single shrewd glance and declared that she was to spend the day resting, and was on no account to stir out of doors, most especially not to the King's Samhain ball or any other.

That afternoon, as soon as he had finished dressing, Gray was shooed out of what had until recently been his bedroom, so that Henriette, Jenny's maid, might work her magick upon Sophie. At loose ends for more than an hour, he wandered about the first floor, peering into the drawing-room, the library, and Sieur Germain's study; noticing everywhere an unaccustomed disorder, he concluded vaguely that the housemaids must have been pressed into service to help the ladies dress. At length he determined to try his luck with Joanna, who had spent most of the day behind closed doors, in sulky silence. His enquiries after her welfare being met with stony silence, he descended the stairs again and sat down at the foot of the staircase, gloves in hand, to await the arrival of his wife.

Down she came at last, moving slowly and carefully. Jenny's dressmaker had enveloped her in deep green velvet, bodice and hem crusted with gilt embroidery; gilt threads and strings of seed pearls glimmered in the phantastickal construction of her hair. She looked so unlike herself that for a long moment Gray could only stand and stare.

'I wish you would not look like that,' she said at last, in her own beloved voice. 'You frighten me.'

He closed his mouth and blinked. 'You look very beautiful,' he managed.

So she did – but it was a hard, unyielding beauty that she wore, glittering and cold – the fearsome, inhuman beauty of Helen, of Circe, of Venus or Diana. Gray felt he would be very glad, when all this was over, to have his own warm, mercurial Sophie back again.

Mrs Wallis came down a few moments later, equally splendid and strange in her festival attire of midnight blue, and before long the entire party were assembled. Mrs Wallis examined the disposition of her charms – the ring on Sophie's finger, the bracelets concealed beneath Master Alcuin's and Gray's shirt-cuffs and the long slender neck-chain looped about Sieur Germain's throat and tucked out of sight. The garish brooch, she had pinned at her own waist; the hairpin, Gray supposed, must still be on Jenny's dressing-table. Treveur and Bertha brought cloaks and wraps, and as the ball-goers were donning these Jenny herself came slowly down the stairs, still pale and wrapped in a dove-grey dressing-gown, bearing in her arms the last essential element of their apparel: five stiff, elaborate velvet masques, painted in gilt and silver, trimmed with glittering beadwork and ribbons and feathers.

'Joanna helped me to make them,' she said, as she distributed each to its intended wearer. It scarcely needed saying: Gray's was as ill suited to him as could possibly be imagined, so much beaded and embroidered that its black velvet ground was scarcely visible, and edged in peacock-feather eyes sewn in place beneath some sort of thin, silvery cord.

'Must we look so . . . so *gaudy*?' he protested weakly, holding it at arm's length.

'We must,' said Mrs Wallis. 'My cousin's charms will carry us only so far, and a charm, as you know, Mr Marshall, may easily be lost. It would be foolish to draw attention from the merely curious by failing to look our parts.'

Sophie held her own masque briefly before her face, and for a moment disappeared entirely into the character of Sieur Germain's pretty young cousin.

'The carriage, my lord,' said Treveur, holding out the last, voluminous cloak for his master.

Jenny stood on tiptoe to kiss Gray's cheek and murmur a blessing; she embraced Sophie, clasped hands with Master Alcuin and Mrs Wallis, and at last, looking troubled, stepped forward into her husband's arms. 'You will be careful?' Gray heard her whisper, as Sieur Germain kissed her brow.

Finally she stood back and looked them over, her pale face carefully expressionless. 'May Fortune smile on you,' she said softly, 'and all the gods protect you.'

They descended the stairs; Harry arrived, inexplicably breathless, to open the front door and let down the carriage steps; Gray and Sieur Germain handed Sophie and Mrs Wallis into the carriage; and in no time the Kergabet coach had joined the throng of similarly festive traffic along the road to the Palace.

Sophie's hand found Gray's, and he clasped it tightly. *There can be no turning back now.*

CHAPTER XXIX

In Which a Princess Goes to a Ball

The carriage shuddered to a halt, and the footman sprang down to open the door and unfold the steps. The travellers descended into the great forecourt of the Palace, hung everywhere with sheaves of grain, horns filled with fruit, strings of tiny magelight lanterns. Concealing their faces behind their phantastickal masques and their urgent purpose beneath an air of festivity, they ascended the wide, white marble staircase.

Sieur Germain reached into a pocket of his coat, where Sophie had earlier seen him conceal their warning missive to the King:

> *Your Majesty is in mortal danger. Do not trust Lord Carteret, Lord Wrexham, or Lord Spencer, for they mean you and your children harm. If you will consent to speak with me, send word by the bearer of this letter. If you will not, then at least, for your own sake and the kingdom's, I beg you will take great care with your meat and drink.*
>
> *– A loyal subject and friend*

'Wait here,' Sieur Germain commanded. 'I shall return as quickly as I may.'

Then he was caught up in the swirling, laughing, flirting crowd, and carried away beyond their seeing.

The rest of the party stood hard by the west wall of the vast Octagon Room – of which Gray had so often heard from those of his fellows more in tune than he with London society – near a large bas-relief of Perseus slaying Medusa. In the main, the noisy throng paid them little heed. Every so often a curious eye came their way, and as quickly turned again; from time to time, too, some young man cast an appreciative glance at Sophie and tried to catch her eye. But her attention was all on the marvels around her – and who would fault her, Gray asked himself bleakly, if she should prefer *all this* to a life of genteel poverty with her hastily chosen spouse?

Then an ostrich-feathered dandy, whose neck-cloth dripped with costly lace, gave her a gallant, smiling bow as he passed; she put a hand to her mouth and turned her face away, hiding laughter. Gray recollected with a smile what manner of woman he had wed, and was reassured.

The longer they stood waiting, however, the more restless he became. There were a great many guests already arrived, to be sure, and all of them masqued, but how could it take such a time to locate an acquaintance with whom one had arranged a rendezvous and put a letter into his hand? Was their presence discovered so soon, and Sieur Germain made prisoner, or worse? Were they, in fact, altogether too late?

A hand on Gray's arm startled him from his increasingly melancholic reflections; Sieur Germain was at his elbow, gesturing discreetly for the others to lend him their ears. 'The King and Queen are expected within the hour,' he said, his voice scarcely above a whisper. He spoke in Brezhoneg; Gray murmured a translation, in Old Cymric, to Master Alcuin in even lower tones. 'My friend is gone to speak with His Majesty now, bearing our letter, and he will find me out again – even if he has no reply to bring – to say how his errand has sped.'

'So now we wait,' said Sophie.

* * *

Their only task, for the moment, was to observe without attracting observation, and much was there to be seen. Magelight lamps and lanterns of every conceivable shape and size hung all about the walls and on cords criss-crossing the high ceilings, illuminating painted scenes from Virgil and Homer, Ovid and Apuleius. Displays of flowers, of fruits, of tree-nuts and grains and wine, competed for space with the numerous statues of gods and goddesses, long-dead monarchs and famous mages, that filled every corner and alcove. From high-hung galleries near and far drifted snatches of music – strings and flutes, horns and clarionets; as the party made their slow circuit of the vast reception rooms, Sophie caught now this tune, now that, till her head began to ache with the effort of following three or four melodies at once.

And more splendid yet was the spectacle presented by Their Majesties' invited guests.

Sophie's own gown, and Mrs Wallis's, which she had thought such a mad extravagance, seemed moderation itself beside the attire of the women around them: gowns of satin and velvet, so heavily embellished with satin roses, jet beads, gilt embroidery, silk lace, that it was difficult to imagine how their wearers remained upright; jewels marvellously wrought, draped about throats and wrists, across décolletés and bodices, as though each lady wore her whole fortune on her person; masques and headdresses heavy with feathers, pendant jewels, strings of pearls.

The male contingent, Sophie saw as she scanned the glittering throng for any sign of the three conspirators she knew by sight – her stepfather, Viscount Carteret, and the second man they had confronted in the Master's Lodge at Merlin, the presumed Lord Merton – was scarcely less gloriously adorned. Its evening full-dress was grander than anything in her experience, its masques – in character ranging from the elegant to the flamboyant to the macabre – testifying to the anxious labour of many a milliner and many a lady. Of her own party, only Sieur Germain came near to equalling the ostentation of the rest. Master Alcuin could scarcely help looking what he was, an elderly man profoundly indifferent to matters sartorial, and Gray's fine new wedding-clothes were built on more simple lines, far better suited to himself than to present company. That preposterous peacock-feather masque – surely Joanna's doing – could not quite disguise his incredulity at the scene before him.

This, then, Sophie marvelled, *is what Mama and Mrs Wallis left behind them, all those years ago.*

What a relief it must have been!

An age seemed to pass before, at last, a man of about Gray's own age, dark-haired and solidly built, approached Sieur Germain. 'I have not sped,' he said.

Sieur Germain drew him aside, into the shadow of the nearest piece of statuary, and the others, without discussion, discreetly moved to screen them farther from view. Gray, standing nearest, thus heard clearly what was surely meant to be a private confession of failure.

'I was able to gain His Majesty's dressing-room,' the young man began, still in the language of Breizh. 'And I gave the letter into his own hand, before there was time for anyone to ask my business. But I had chosen my moment ill, for he was not alone; with him, besides his body servants, were the Queen's brother, and the healer Lord Spencer . . .'

Gray felt the colour draining from his face, and at last found reason to be grateful for Joanna's peacock feathers. *We are too late. Once more we are too late.*

'And then?' Sieur Germain demanded.

'I made my bows and went away,' the messenger admitted. 'I lingered some time in the corridor, to see whether one of His Majesty's servants might be sent with a message for me, but to stay longer must have aroused suspicion. I know not, therefore, whether the King has read your letter or no, nor can I know who else may have done so.'

Sieur Germain's curses were none the less vehement for being delivered in an undertone that few could hear. 'Were you recognised?' he asked at last. Gray, scanning the room in the direction from which the stranger had come, held his breath in anticipation of the answer.

'I cannot be certain,' said the young man. 'I believe that I was not, but my lord Wrexham, I know, is a far more subtle schemer than you or I. I am very sorry, my lord . . .'

'It is of no matter,' Sieur Germain assured him, rallying. 'Your errand was not our only stratagem. You have already been of very material help to us, and—'

'Cousin,' Gray hissed, reaching behind him to attempt a quelling gesture, for at that moment he had seen, amidst the milling, light-hearted festive crowd, two men – masqued, but moving with a purpose and determination which set them quite apart from all the rest – making their way towards the Kergabet party. He doubted that any of the others had seen them; the one advantage to being taller than anyone else in nearly any room was that of seeing one's adversaries approaching from a great way off.

After one last, covert glance at these pursuers, Gray spun round and bent to address Sieur Germain and his companion more directly. 'You have been followed,' he told the latter, and to his brother-in-law he said, 'Shall we ask . . . our cousin to hide him, or had he better get quite away?'

Though conducted in the lowest possible tones, their conversation had by now attracted the notice of the rest of the party, who equally needed no telling that their first attempt at saving King Henry's life had not gone as intended. They arrayed themselves now in a tighter arc, shoulder to shoulder, so that Gray heard the others' breathing as loudly as his own.

Gray glanced across the circle at Sophie, who met his gaze with a brief, anxious lifting of her shoulders. Looking over her head into the crowd, he saw the two men he had remarked earlier, drawing ever nearer – not speedily nor directly, but inexorably. 'Whatever we do,' he murmured, 'must be done with all possible dispatch.'

'Take this,' said Sophie quietly; there was a small, disapproving sound from Mrs Wallis, and Gray saw that Sophie had removed her mother's charmed ring and was holding it out towards Sieur Germain's ill-fortuned messenger. 'What . . . ?' he began, but stopped, staring goggle-eyed at the delicate object in his hand.

'You may go or remain, in equal safety,' Sieur Germain said, laying a broad hand on the younger man's shoulder. 'The lady has given you a charm to conceal you from unwelcome eyes.'

'I shall return it to you as soon as may be, m'lady.' The stranger bowed deeply to Sophie, who looked perplexed. Then, with another backward glance, he took a hasty, quiet leave of them all and melted away into the throng. His pursuers came near; looked, but saw nothing to interest them; and passed away again.

The Kergabets, real and counterfeit, looked at one another. 'Next, then,' said Sophie, 'we seek out our . . . friends.'

This task required that they disperse themselves, for each of them knew some of their quarries by sight, yet none knew all, and they dared not yet risk the use of a finding-spell. It was now, as they hastily redistributed the six conspirators among five watchers, that they felt the absence of Jenny – though Gray could not deny that it was a relief to him, to know both Jenny and Joanna safe at home. This, after a hurried prayer that the Mother Goddess and Ceres of the harvests – whose festival, in part, this was – might speed their search, they had begun to do, when, at some signal that Gray could not at first discern, the whole teeming, chattering crowd fell into an expectant silence, and every gaze turned upwards, to the head of the great staircase that made one side of the Octagon Room.

Trumpets sounded. 'His Majesty, Henry, King of Britain,' a voice (surely projected by magickal means) intoned.

The twelfth Henry stepped out onto the landing and saluted his guests; a cheer erupted from the assembly, though Gray thought it was not so unanimous as might have been expected.

'Her Royal Highness, Queen Edwina.'

The plump little queen, her blonde hair coiled atop her head in a shining coronet, emerged to join her husband. The crowd's approval now was unequivocal; shouts of '*Vive la reine!*' echoed in Gray's ears.

The three young princes were announced, to the same hearty acclaim: Edward, Roland, Henry. From behind his peacock feathers, Gray studied the Crown Prince – a sturdy towheaded boy just a year older than Joanna, and not very much taller – and tried to imagine him taking Sophie's part against Lord Carteret and the Iberian ambassador. It was as well that Sophie and he had taken the decision out of others' hands.

The royal family having been announced, it occurred to Sophie that no one else had been. 'No names, and no faces, and no welcome-oaths,' she murmured, incredulous. 'It is an assassin's dream.'

'Indeed.' Master Alcuin appeared to have heard her self-directed remark. 'It has long been the custom for Samhain, but you will find that when a monarch believes himself less than universally beloved, he will always discover some reason that the custom ought not to apply *this* year . . .'

Sophie sank her voice still further to reply, 'Would that His Majesty had been more perceptive.'

Then Gray, whose arm she held in what she hoped was a maiden-cousinly manner, moved another way, pulling her with him. Master Alcuin too moved slowly off, nodding affably at everyone he passed, till he was lost to her sight.

The royal hosts having at last made their appearance, the festivities could now begin in earnest. Very soon the great doors opened, with ponderous slowness, and the King and Queen led their guests into the Palace ballroom. They took their places at the top of the room; hundreds of other couples arranged themselves below, and a great consort of musicians – half a hundred at the least, thought Sophie, awed – struck into the evening's first *contredanse.*

Sophie and Gray took up a station suited to observe their fellow guests and, standing a little apart, turned once more to the search for those conspirators whom they might reasonably hope to recognise – the Professor, of course, as well as Lord Carteret and Lord Merton.

Sophie cast many a wistful glance at the long lines of dancers. She had never before attended so much as a neighbourhood ball in Breizh; Amelia and Joanna, having both learnt at school, had taught her dances enough, but except when some evening party of Amelia's ended in an impromptu dance, she had never seen them properly performed – and even then she had been always pressed into service to supply the music.

You are not here to dance with handsome young men, you silly girl, she admonished herself, scanning the dances, and the surrounding mêlée, for any sign of their quarry. But perhaps she did not do it so well as she had meant – perhaps she allowed her body too much sympathy with the rhythm of the music, or her face too much admiration for the dancers' graceful movements – for after some moments Gray's hand fell softly on her shoulder, and she lifted her face to hear him say, '*Petite cousine*, you will perhaps do me the honour of dancing the first two dances with me?'

Sophie regarded her husband in some consternation. 'But . . .'

Stooping down to murmur in her ear, he answered her objection before she could articulate it: 'We should be just as well placed to observe from within the dance as from outside it; should we not?'

'That is true,' she said.

'And you are most eager to dance,' he went on, more loudly, holding out his hand, 'are you not, little cousin? We do not often see such grand assemblies at home . . .'

Smiling, Sophie took the offered hand. 'I thank you, *ma c'henderv*,' she said – though it cost her some effort, when he looked at her as he was doing now, to continue the pretence that they were no more to one another than cousins, attending the ball with a family party.

Then they were joining the end of the nearest dance, and all her energy went into observing its steps, until at length she was mistress enough of them to return her attention to the hunt.

Gray quickly decided that he had made rather a dreadful error in judgement.

Though Sophie appeared to have no difficulty in learning – remembering? – the steps of the dance they had joined, moving through the figures more effortlessly and gracefully even than the fine ladies around her, he himself, possessing not much more experience and rather less natural grace, was not in such good stead. He had as yet made no misstep sufficient to impede the progress of the dance, but if he had ever danced these figures before, it was too long ago to remember, and following them left him no attention to spare for more vital matters.

Yet just as he was cursing himself for a fool and considering on what pretext he could extricate himself and Sophie from this predicament, his gaze happened to fall on her face, and through the glittering velvet masque her dark eyes glowed at him in silent thanks. Their hands met across the gap between them; they turned about, separated, bowed; and when Gray returned to his place, his eyes still on Sophie, it occurred to him that he had done all this entirely without thinking. *Perhaps this was not such a terrible mistake at all*, he thought, raising his eyes to look about him.

It was not surprising, perhaps, that none of the men he sought should be found among the dancers. Still, others enough – observers, hangers-on, the occasional gentleman casting a jealous eye on some dancing lady – were there to be scrutinised for any resemblance or connexion to the three he sought, to make him feel this time not entirely wasted. And, after all, the King could not be poisoned while actually dancing.

The first dance was finished, and he and Sophie had gone halfway down the second, when a couple standing up in the next dance over – that led by the King and Queen – caught Gray's eye.

Both seemed younger, and rather smaller, than the rest of the assembly. Though the golden-haired boy had now donned a masque – adorned beyond anything Gray had yet seen – still he was recognisable as one of the Princes; it could not be young Henry, certainly, but whether Edward or Roland was more difficult to guess. It was not he but his partner who had triggered that little shock of recognition, but again Gray could not quite think where he might have seen her before.

Then – bowing to the lady at Sophie's left, then the one at her right – he saw the mysterious young lady execute a haphazard sort of curtsey with which he was most assuredly familiar. He stared hard at her as he and Sophie turned about once again, observing her manner of walking, the colour of her hair, the expression of that small part of her face which he could see, and the more he looked, the more dreadfully certain he became.

'Look at that young lady,' he murmured, when next the figures of the dance permitted a word in Sophie's ear, 'the one who dances with the Prince. I am very much afraid—'

But there was no need to finish the thought, for Sophie had contrived to look, without appearing to do so, and now turned back to clutch at his hand with desperate urgency. He had not mistaken, then: it was Joanna indeed.

'She *promised* me!' Sophie hissed between clenched teeth. 'The little fool!'

'We shall find her,' said Gray, 'and send her home straight away, before there can be any danger. Be easy, *cariad* . . .'

But how they were to accomplish this feat, without resorting to a too-revealing magick, he had no idea whatsoever.

CHAPTER XXX

In Which an Error Is Turned to Advantage

For Sophie, the quarter-hour that remained passed with agonising slowness. Only her knowledge that exposure meant the direst of consequences restrained her from bursting through the ranks of dancers and dragging her sister bodily away, and she was kept from some equally ill-advised magickal outburst only by Gray's steadying presence – for which Joanna too, she thought grimly, would soon have cause to be thankful.

She watched Joanna and her grandly dressed partner all up and down their dance, while Gray watched the King and Queen; yet when the music ceased and the dancers began to drift away, and Sophie made to follow them, Joanna was nowhere to be seen. Desperate, Sophie looked up at Gray, whose height must give him a better view, but he was looking down at her at the same moment, frowning and shaking his head.

They moved nevertheless in the same direction as the generality of the dancers, hastening lest they be caught up in the formation of the next set, and trying to look every way at once. Joanna had prudently acquired, for this outrageous escapade, a gown of green velvet in the precise shade favoured by the Duchess of Norfolk, and thus worn by nearly half the ladies present. Where she had found it, and how (and with whose connivance) cut it down to fit her,

Sophie did not like to guess, but as a disguise, it could hardly have been better chosen. If indeed Joanna remained in the ballroom, she had contrived to conceal herself as effectively as even Sophie could have done.

Though Sophie's furious anger with her sister was hardly a useful emotion in the circumstances, she kept it stoked and burning, for not far beneath it lay the naked, gibbering terror to which she must on no account give way – whose very existence it would be fatal to acknowledge.

And so absorbed were she and Gray in their efforts to catch some glimpse of Joanna, so forgetful of their original purpose, that all the rest of His Majesty's guests might have been mere painted scenery.

Then, quite by chance, they were separated for a moment by the haphazard stumbling of some young nobleman, partaking too freely of the King's hospitality, and Sophie half fell against a man who stood just to her left. The feeling was like leaning against a cattle-fence; but still, her mind all on Joanna, she did not at once recognise what – whom – she had found.

'Your pardon, mademoiselle,' the man said, gently steadying her, and that deep voice, together with the scarecrow-like frame, announced in no uncertain terms that here at last was one object of their search. Sophie stifled a yelp of alarm and reached out blindly for Gray, drawing breath again only when his hand clasped hers.

A glance beyond Lord Merton, now favouring her with a gallant if creaky bow, revealed the well-fed, richly accoutred form of the Professor. Here, then – *Oh, gods and priestesses!* – were two well-educated mages who had, on their last meeting, been more than a match for her concealing magick – and for her mother's. Though Sophie had learnt a great deal in the intervening weeks, the shielding-charm Gray now wore was surely no different from that which had failed to deceive the Professor on that other occasion. They had meant to spot their quarry and observe from a safe distance, remaining themselves unobserved, but now . . .

How could *she be so foolish?* Sophie's anger at Joanna flared again. *And how could* I?

But even with the thought, she was tightening her grip on Gray's arm and concentrating on shielding him as well as herself from their adversaries' notice. And almost instantly, to her immense relief, Lord Merton's mouth, visible below his ornate masque, twisted in the puzzled frown with which she had lately grown so familiar, and he turned away from her and resumed his conversation with her stepfather. The latter glanced briefly at Sophie as she turned away, with frank suggestion in his eyes.

She swallowed her revulsion. Might she turn this mischance to good account? By some flirtation tempt the Professor and Lord Merton away, perhaps, and lock them up somewhere until tomorrow morning? Then there would be only three conspirators to watch, and if one of the Oxford men was carrying the poison—

Then there passed a woman clad in green velvet, and Sophie forgot for the moment all thought of subterfuge. 'Joanna,' she said. 'We *must* look for Joanna—'

She felt rather than heard Gray's sharp intake of breath as he propelled them into the dubious shelter of a potted rose-tree, which topped him by less than a hand's breadth. 'Remember what we have come here to do,' he admonished her, sotto voce. 'We cannot—'

'She is a foolish, thoughtless child,' Sophie retorted, dropping his arm, 'but she is *my sister* – the only one I am ever like to have – and I have no intention of abandoning—'

Gray took her by the shoulders, almost roughly, and seemed about to shake her – or worse; instead, after a moment, he loosed his grip again and drew her into his arms. 'You are not alone in loving your sister,' he murmured, gentle again. 'But think: she will be in as much danger if – if our opponents succeed, as she could possibly be in witnessing our attempt to stop them . . .'

Sophie was forced to concede the truth of this. 'But what if they – what if *he*—'

Looking earnestly up into Gray's eyes, she could scarcely fail to see the shadow of dread that passed across them, but he answered her with every indication of confidence. 'They have no reason to seek her – even to consider that she might be present here. And if *we* cannot find her, for all our searching, it is not very likely that she will be found by anyone else.'

Cogent though his analysis undoubtedly was, Sophie might yet have protested – had she not chanced, in glancing to her right just at that moment, to see the Professor and his friend moving away.

'Mother Goddess, bountiful and kind, keep my foolish sister safe,' she muttered under her breath, as they meandered through the crowd, a careful ten paces behind their quarry.

And still her attention was drawn by every flash of green velvet that she chanced to see out of the corner of her eye.

'He has got something in his pocket,' Gray muttered, as if to himself. With a guilty start Sophie followed his gaze to her stepfather; indeed, the Professor was continually darting one hand into the pocket of his waistcoat, then removing it again, as he spoke and laughed with his companions. It was a quick, nervous gesture, instinctive rather than deliberate; to one who did not perfectly know his ways, it might seem merely the fussy, fastidious habit of a fussy, fastidious man.

'Yes, I see,' she murmured in reply. 'Is it, can it be – is he to be the one, then, do you suppose?' Oh, if only she or Gray could summon the poison away from him, and so end this painful game at once!

Obeying her frequent injunction to Joanna, however, by thinking before she spoke, she quickly saw that it was quite impossible. How could they summon an object they had never seen, having no idea what it might look like? And if the Professor did not see or recognise them, he would certainly notice the absence of this object of which he was so solicitous. Almost she could feel his hand closing about her wrist. He would raise a hue and cry, claim assault, even, perhaps, denounce his assailants as the murderers of Lord Halifax; Lord Wrexham or Lord Spencer, seeing the resulting commotion, would claim knowledge of a plot against the Crown and to have found the authors of it; Sophie and Gray would be detained, arrested, searched, and found to be in possession of an obscure and deadly poison – whose recipe must eventually be discovered in a book belonging to Master Alcuin and presently kept in Jenny's house . . .

And, in any event, the thing in the Professor's pocket might be something else entirely, and they should have given the game away to no purpose.

With a sigh, she resumed her watchful waiting.

It was not very easy to follow the Professor through that vast assembly without appearing to do so, but follow him they must, for he was not content to remain conveniently in one place; with Lord Merton hovering shadow-like at his elbow, he buzzed from one conversation to the next like a portly, rubicund housefly spreading flattery and officious goodwill – eagerly playing his new role as Master of the kingdom's oldest College. Gray could not help thinking that Lord Halifax would have done all of it with more dignity. Though, for the matter of that, Lord Halifax would never have left Merlin College to its own devices on Samhain-night to begin with.

Preoccupied by the effort of keeping their quarry in sight without attracting suspicion in turn, Gray did not for some time ask himself where the rest of their allies might be, or whether they had found the men they sought – though his eye could not help seeking one small, green-clad figure, even as, within, he roundly cursed his young sister-in-law and plotted the angry lecture which he would read her, once caught.

At his side, Sophie drew in a startled breath. He looked down at her in some alarm, then followed her gaze to the form of Lord Merton – who had turned away from the Professor and seemed about to move off in another direction entirely.

'Will you go after him?' Gray said. 'Or will I?'

'They will see you!' Sophie's furious whisper startled him; had this not always been their plan? 'Whichever we choose, he will see you, and—No. Besides, it is the Professor who—'

Of the two, the Professor certainly seemed the most likely to be carrying the poison, yet they could not let one of his collaborators slip away unpursued. But if Sophie had been shielding him all this time, they could not know how far they could trust Queen Laora's charms. What profit all their careful surveillance, if Gray should be revealed to his quarry the moment they were parted?

Then, of a sudden, the answer came to him. 'I shall be quite all right,' he said. 'Do you not recall how you befuddled them, in the Master's study at Merlin, from clear across the room? If you could do it then, think how much better you shall do it now . . .'

Sophie stood for a moment clutching his arm and pressing her lips together, while Gray gritted his teeth, fighting the urge to importune her farther. At last her eyes brightened, and she nodded sharply and loosed her hold. *Be careful*, said her lips below the masque; he glanced away for a moment, so as not to lose sight of the Professor, and when he looked again it was to see her disappearing into the throng on Lord Merton's heels. 'May all the gods protect you, *cariad*,' he whispered prayerfully.

Knowing that, so thinly stretched as her concentration now was, any small lapse might be fatal, Sophie forced herself to look straight ahead, at the retreating back of her target – to shut out not only her own urge to pursue Joanna but the distracting, attracting sights and sounds that bubbled and seethed all about her; she must restrain herself at all costs from attending to the music, which would occupy her mind to an extent she could very ill afford. Not only her own concealment but Gray's, too, depended now on this singleness of purpose: Mrs Wallis might place all the faith she liked in Mama's concealing charms, and where the rest of the conspiracy was concerned might be justified in so doing, but mages were a different matter.

With one sister so much in her mind, it was very disconcerting to see the other pass directly between her and the object of her surveillance.

Sophie stopped dead, though only for a moment. *Was* it her sister, indeed? The full red lips were Amelia's, the fair curling hair and the rather supercilious carriage, but the woman before her was masqued, of course, and (like Sophie herself) attired with a magnificence quite foreign to the erstwhile denizens of Callender Hall. The voice, however, settled the matter instantly.

'My dear Mr Woodville,' she heard Amelia say, with a simpering laugh, to her companion, 'you are too kind . . .'

And he returned a fatuously adoring smile, patting the gloved hand that rested on his arm.

Woodville. Sophie frowned with the effort to remember as they moved beyond her view. One of the Professor's students, but which? *And whatever can the Professor have been thinking of, to bring Amelia with him on such an errand? He must be very sure of its success . . .* But the discovery that she had lost sight of Lord Merton drove these lesser considerations from her mind.

To her immense relief, she spotted him again almost at once; he had stopped to speak with someone, just out of her view. After a moment he moved on, only to stop again, and again, so that she was obliged to pause likewise, and return the nods and smiles of strangers, lest she draw uncomfortably near.

At length, however, Lord Merton – though not ceasing to

meander, apparently at random, through the increasingly loquacious crowd – began to pause more rarely, and to linger less, until at last he passed out of the public rooms altogether. Having so ruthlessly narrowed her focus, Sophie could not help seeing how much more purposeful he now looked, how alert were the occasional glances he threw over either shoulder, but the import of these signs quite escaped her, until – seeing her quarry come to a halt before a large, imposing oaken door, and rap upon it a complicated rhythmic pattern – she paused to look about her, and saw nothing and no one between cat and mouse but a silent, empty corridor.

Lord Merton cocked his head. Slowly his face turned towards Sophie, and for a moment she stood frozen, terrified, as though she could possibly have come this far unnoticed and yet be discovered now. He looked directly at her; she did her best to vanish into her surroundings; and after a moment he shrugged his bony shoulders and with a rueful chuckle turned away.

Then the door swung inwards, opened by some unseen hand, and he stepped forward. Quickly, before she could think better of it, Sophie stole up behind him and followed him in.

A fire crackled below a ponderous carven mantelpiece – merrily, one might have said – and was the room's only source of light. It illuminated, besides the scarecrow in scholar's clothing that was Lord Merton, a man of middling height and middling girth, altogether undistinguished but for the shock of golden curls, gleaming in the fitful light, that showed above his green velvet masque. Having motioned the newcomer to a chair, this man paced to and fro before the hearth, passing sometimes so near to Sophie that she could see the tiny beads of perspiration that bedewed those artfully disarranged curls. In his hand he clutched something – a slip of writing-paper, she saw at last.

'Calm yourself, Wrexham, I beg,' Lord Merton said, leaning

negligently back in his seat. He pulled off his masque to fan his face, a slow, hypnotic motion. 'What can have happened to put you in such a state?'

'You shall know soon enough,' the other snapped – yes, it was the Queen's brother, of course.

Sophie started when the complicated knock came again. Lord Wrexham crossed the small room and opened the door to admit Viscount Carteret and another masqued, elegantly dressed stranger, and after them, narrowly avoiding the backswing of the great oaken door, Sieur Germain de Kergabet, who secreted himself in the shadows on either side of the door.

'Why have you summoned us now?' demanded Lord Carteret. 'Have we not duties to perform?'

Lord Merton half turned towards the door, and Sophie's heart leapt into her throat. Hastily she extended her concealing magick to embrace Sieur Germain, as well as Gray and herself; she now felt stretched very thin indeed, but there was nothing else to be done.

'Shall I set the wards?' the don said. 'Or do we wait?' He spoke delicately, as though the question meant much more than appeared.

The others, too, had now removed their masques, so that Sophie could clearly see Lord Wrexham and the handsome young stranger – surely the healer, Lord Spencer – exchange a hard, cold look. 'Set them now,' said the former, and, with another shrug, Lord Merton did so. His spell was long and elaborate, yet Sophie scarcely felt the whisper of his warding-magick.

'My friends, we are betrayed,' announced Lord Wrexham. He held up the letter in his hand and read out the indictment of himself, Lord Spencer, and Lord Carteret, so recently composed in Carrington-street. 'It is Callender's doing,' he continued, his face livid in the dancing firelight.

Lord Carteret reached for the letter. 'This is not his hand,' he said.

'It will be the work of that student of his, then, to put us off the scent,' Lord Wrexham returned, impatient; in her mind's ear Sophie heard Gray's voice: *Woodville, of course. The man was a forger in his cradle.* 'Callender has lost his stomach for the affair, I suppose, or he has discovered—'

'Nonsense!' said Lord Merton. 'He is a fool, certainly, and hard-pressed to see beyond his own interest, but what would it profit him now, to turn on you? He cannot expect his word to be taken over Carteret's, or yours.'

Lord Wrexham still looked unconvinced, but the others were nodding. Sophie fidgeted. 'You judge rightly, I think.' Lord Carteret's high nasal voice was startling after Lord Merton's basso. 'Has the old man seen it?'

'He has.' Lord Spencer folded his arms across his lace-frothed breast.

'The old man would read it, of course,' said Lord Wrexham, 'and did, before anyone could prevent him – and seemed half inclined to believe it, too, but naturally I—' At a raised eyebrow from Lord Spencer, he amended, 'naturally *we* made haste to persuade *His Majesty* that his enemies are not so close to home.'

Lord Merton's gaunt cheeks creased in an approving chuckle. 'Naturally,' he repeated.

The younger men smiled.

'A child might have done it,' said Lord Spencer. 'We told him that a truly loyal friend would not fear to put his name to his warning, and reminded him that the men named have ever been his devoted servants, one of them his own brother.'

'The messenger awaited a reply,' Lord Wrexham added, 'but he had not the patience to wait us out; you may be sure that no meeting has been arranged by that means.'

'Well enough,' said Lord Carteret. 'Merton – we may depend on Callender to play his part as agreed?'

'Certainly, my lord,' said the latter, rather stiffly.

'And you have no reason to believe he suspects our plans . . . ?'

'Certainly not!' Now Lord Merton's tone was positively scandalised. 'I have been entirely discreet, I assure you.'

'See that you remain so,' Lord Carteret went on, sternly, 'until we have persuaded him to yield up the Princess. After that, of course . . .' And the wave of his hand as he spoke left Sophie in no doubt as to her stepfather's eventual fate. *If only he knew*, she thought, pressing her hands together to still their trembling, *he would thank all the gods that he has not yet found me* . . .

Just then a bell began to tell the hour: *one, two, three* . . . At the final chime the four men exchanged looks of consternation. 'It begins,' Lord Wrexham intoned dramatically. He made for the door, avoiding a collision with Sieur Germain only because the latter stepped smartly out of his path, and wrenched it open; but he was stopped on the threshold by Lord Merton's wards, as were the others who followed him.

After a long moment Lord Merton smiled a thin, humourless smile and snapped his fingers negligently to release the wards. The other three tumbled over one another out the door.

Sophie lingered, torn. Clearly, whatever the conspirators had planned for tonight was about to begin, but ought she to leave Lord Merton to his own devices, however peripheral he appeared?

The hour was growing later, and Gray had followed the Professor, he felt sure, over every inch of the Palace ballroom. He had not again sighted Joanna, though he had several times been half convinced of glimpsing her out of the corner of his eye, nor had he seen any of the rest of his own party. He had at first stayed well back, wary of being recognised, but, emboldened by his quarry's apparent ignorance of his presence, had drawn gradually closer, till the temptation to knock the Professor on the head and turn out his pockets, or attempt to summon their contents, was very strong indeed.

But the first was too crude and would attract too much attention, charms or no, and the second was very unlikely to succeed; the first thing every mage learns about finding and summoning is that one can do neither without an accurate image of the thing sought.

As he was contemplating this problem, he heard an unexpectedly familiar voice. 'Professor Callender, sir,' it said, in tones of obsequious respect, 'a word in your ear?' And Gray raised incredulous eyes to find himself, in very truth, almost face-to-face with Alfric Woodville.

CHAPTER XXXI

In Which Several Stratagems Fail, and Others Succeed

Sophie had been lurking along the corridor, still concealed, for mere moments when Lord Merton emerged and made his way past her, returning in the direction of the great ballroom. She followed some half-dozen paces behind as he rejoined the chattering throng that drifted and surged, by turns, towards the great double doors leading out into the courtyard.

Shadowing her quarry as closely as she dared, she found herself at length on the north side of the large inner courtyard, facing the great altar – and the King – through a screen of people some three or four rows deep. The rites of Samhain were just beginning; around her there persisted a faint hum, the muted voices of those unready to suspend the pleasures of conversation, yet not daring to disturb too far the solemn dignity of the occasion.

Her attention was so much divided – her eyes between Lord Merton and the King; her thoughts between half a dozen objects; her magick tenuously extended, now, to all her allies, wherever they might be – that Sophie felt she might fly apart. Never had any sacred rite claimed less of her concentration. She knew it, and felt all the disrespect of a wandering mind at such a time; but her task, too, was a kind of sacred duty, and had its own urgency. Perhaps not every life is sacred to the gods – but surely, that of Britain's King . . .

The murmurs were gradually fading, so that Sophie could now hear more clearly the voice of that king – not only the paterfamilias of the kingdom but her own. It was a pleasant voice, lighter and higher than Gray's or Master Alcuin's but possessing the same warm timbre, the same easy command of the several languages in which it spoke the prayers. From Sophie's current vantage point – gazing up at the dignitaries ranged around the altar steps – King Henry looked a small man, fine-boned and none too stoutly made. His face in the torchlight was earnest, his attention all on the act of worship entrusted to him on this night. For the first time she felt a rush of affectionate concern for him – so trusting, so much burdened with duty and care, and surrounded by men who wished him ill.

For surrounded he was. To his left and right stood Queen Edwina and the princes, but just beyond them – at the short ends of the oblong altar – were stationed Lord Wrexham and Lord Spencer, and at the opposite end, together with a sharp-faced, supercilious man of middle years, Appius Callender – Master of Merlin – stood behind Lord Carteret.

If these four were here to be seen, then somewhere close by must be their shadows. It was not to be supposed that Mrs Wallis and Master Alcuin would be easily visible, in all this press of humanity, but surely Gray must be, here as elsewhere, at least half a head taller than anyone about him.

Sure enough, when next she took her eyes from Lord Merton to glance eastward, in the direction of her stepfather, she was rewarded with the briefest glimpse of her heart's desire: a flash of sandy hair, a gleam of peacock feathers, a neck angled in the stoop-shouldered attitude of one attempting to hide in plain sight.

'*Sacramus Cereris aristifer, Jovis celestis, Matris tergemina, Patris magnum, dei magnique dei parvuli, bordeum primum . . .*' His Majesty lifted a gleaming sheaf of barley. He held it aloft for a long moment, while around him echoed *sacramus, sacramus.* Then, slowly, deliberately, he bent to deposit the offering on the altar, already heaped high with the fruits of earth and tree, shrub and vine. King Henry bowed to the altar; his subjects, sincerely or cynically as conscience decreed, followed his example.

And now, rustling and whispering through the crowd from the eastern gate of the courtyard, came the next, and nearly the last, offering. Gray craned his neck to see the fat golden sheaf of wheat, the *triticum primum*, its heavy heads nodding with each passage from arm to arm. Voice after voice murmured blessings and private petitions, *May the gods grant it.* Hands reached out to touch the offering, and those farther away seemed yet to bend towards it as it passed them; he fancied he could feel their prayers and pleas hanging in the air, heavy as incense.

The great persons of the kingdom – Saxon and Breizhek, Kernowek and Cymric, Briton and Normand – were not, perhaps, so different from their tenant farmers who would, at this hour or near it, be making their own bargains with the gods for the year ahead.

'*Sacramus Cereris aristifer, Jovis celestis . . .*'

The rite of offering was repeated. Gray looked and listened, spoke and bowed, with the rest. The near-encounter with Woodville had been a shock; though no flicker of recognition had shown in the other man's eyes, his very presence was an unexpected complication. Had the Professor expected opposition and brought reinforcements? If the worst should come, would they face one more mage-warrior than they had expected?

But at any rate, there could be no question of poisoning at present; the offerings now piling on the altar were destined for the gods, not for men.

The wheat-sheaf was laid atop the altar, its weight causing the heap to shift dangerously before it settled again. By the stir in the throng around the western gate Gray recognised the moment when the *vinum primum*, the first-pressed wine in its heavy golden chalice, began its journey towards the altar dais. Its path differed, apparently, from those of prior offerings, circling the edge of the courtyard before beginning a slow spiral in towards the central altar.

More than any other period of this endless evening, the libation's journey seemed interminable. Gray clenched and unclenched his hands; he crept as close as he dared to the altar steps, eyes on the Professor. At last he saw the chalice approach – an ancient, elaborate thing, glowing with the bright warmth of that most precious of metals.

The cup travelled round the lower steps of the dais, at length reaching the top on the far side of the altar, where stood a row of dignitaries – foreign ambassadors, by their dress – whom Gray could not identify. Beginning at the north-east corner, it passed slowly from hand to hand until it reached the north-west, and the hand of the Master of Merlin.

Gray did his best to keep half an eye on the King, but thousands of eyes were trained on His Majesty, and his true task was to watch Professor Callender. He watched, only half understanding what he was seeing, as the Professor's left hand accepted the sacred chalice and his right dipped into his coat-pocket. Then comprehension arrived in a horrifying flash – *He is going to poison the* libamen*!* – and Gray desperately gathered his magick for a summoning-spell.

When the hand reappeared, however, a sort of fog blurred it and its contents. Gray scarcely needed the familiar shiver of hairs rising under his collar to recognise a clumsily rendered spell of misdirection. Odd, this – the Professor was not a rank amateur, to work such a small magick so poorly.

Clumsy or not, however, the spell served its purpose, for Gray could not see the poison clearly enough to summon it away.

While the Professor muttered his blessings over the cup, his hands shielded from behind by his own body, and from before by Lord Carteret's, Gray worked his way closer, dodging around well-heeled spectators who muttered accusations at one another in his wake. But he had not been quick enough; Professor Callender was already passing the chalice to Lord Carteret.

Well, thought Gray, chagrined beyond any thought of concealment, *at any rate I can summon* that.

To his astonishment, however, he found that he could not.

By now the *vinum primum* had passed from Lord Carteret's hands to Prince Roland's, and thence, quickly, to the Crown Prince. In a few moments the King would receive it, and, if Gray's conclusion was correct, then all might be lost.

As he stared ferociously at the glowing chalice, collecting his wits for a second attempt, a hand touched Gray's arm; looking down, he found Master Alcuin close beside him. '*Conjuncte,*' he murmured – *together.* 'Before the King can drink.' Gray nodded sharply. But even their joined efforts could not shift the chalice from the Prince's hands.

Master Alcuin looked again, narrowly, at the object of their concern, and muttered, 'Of course . . . it is warded against magickal interference.'

'We must stop *him*, then,' Gray replied, sotto voce; the older man inclined his head. How much simpler and safer their task would have been, could they only have borrowed some piece of the King's jewellery and found a means to spell it against the poison!

Bowing ceremoniously, Prince Edward offered the cup to his father, who accepted it with an answering bow. As he made to lift the *libamen* above his head, Master Alcuin and Gray directed at him a spell intended to freeze an attacker in his tracks.

But this too, it seemed, their enemies had anticipated; their combined magicks met some palpable barrier, and His Majesty continued his invocation undeterred.

Sing to him, Sophie, Gray silently pleaded, as though there were some possibility that she might hear. Had she seen what her stepfather was doing, or guessed it? Did she understand what might be at stake?

Then the rolling Latin cadences faltered, and – yes, *there* – from somewhere far to Gray's left, in the fraught, puzzled silence, a clear, sweet voice was singing.

The voice grew stronger. Lowering the chalice, the King stared out into the throng, his brow furrowing. For one exulting moment Gray thought the danger past. Then Lord Carteret leant across the corner of the altar, apparently remonstrating with his monarch, and from the ends of the dais a fair-haired man and a dark one edged over to join the conference.

All about them, people began to whisper, and the whispers grew as Gray wove through the crowd, towards the sound of Sophie's voice.

'Your Majesty.' Lord Carteret's voice was low and urgent. 'Remember your duty – to the gods – to your kingdom – to your people . . .'

The King made no answer – or none that Gray could hear.

'The King of Britain,' said the fair-haired man, 'surely will not be persuaded by a *siren song* to dishonour Britain's gods . . .'

'Remember Ulysses at the mast, Your Majesty . . .'

The low, cajoling voices went on and on – working some persuasion, magickal or otherwise, which Sophie could hold at bay but not defeat. The tide of whispers ebbed and flowed, but Gray could hear nothing clearly but her voice. It seemed to him that all the world revolved around the two fixed points of Sophie and her father – revolved at an excruciating crawl, as though caught in some immense Arachne's Web.

Some instinct warned him in the nick of time that a more immediate danger threatened. He ducked sharply, just avoiding the spurt of flame that passed harmlessly over his head to scorch the opposite wall; on one side of him a woman screamed, on the other a man cried, 'Jove's blood! What foolery is this, on such a night?' Turning, he muttered a hasty shielding-spell to fling a wall of magick between himself and his assailant. Somewhere just behind him, Sophie sang on – an Erse melody in the Mixolydian: *It will not be long, love, till our wedding day* . . .

Around him, vaguely, Gray heard more people shouting, shrieking. He struggled against a tide of panicked flight as his fellow guests took to their heels. At last, across an empty expanse of cobbled courtyard littered with festive debris, he spied the source of the threat.

Sophie's voice faltered.

'Sing!' he hissed, risking a backwards glance. 'I can hold off the others, but *you* must stop him from drinking; the poison is in the wine, I am sure of it. Look, they are whispering at him still.' As he spoke he held out one hand; when Sophie clasped it, he drew her forward and pulled her tight against his side. Though her eyes were wide, her face ashen, the words of her oddly chosen spell-song again rang clear and true. Reassured, he let her go.

But the effort of fighting her father's sense of duty had taken its toll of her other magick. 'You had better have stayed at home, boy,' Lord Merton taunted, with a mocking smile of recognition, as he raised his hands for a renewed assault.

Gray poured magick steadily into the shielding-spell wrapped about himself and Sophie, and held resolutely still as a rain of fire-spurts, increasingly large and numerous, fizzled into nothingness about them. His opponent's confounded expression gave him more satisfaction than he cared to admit, but it would not do to be overconfident. For now they were safe enough – but no mage could hold a shielding-spell for ever.

'To me!' cried Lord Merton, staring wildly about him. 'Foul treachery! They mean harm to the King!' Flames streaked towards

Sophie and Gray, only to rebound harmlessly. Their author roared in frustration.

And why, indeed, Gray wondered, should Lord Merton be fighting all alone?

He spied his brother-in-law, just east of the altar, in the act of subduing some elegantly dressed stranger; Master Alcuin had come to magickal blows, not, to Gray's surprise, with the Professor, but with Woodville. Of Mrs Wallis he could see no sign; she might, he supposed, be on the far side of the altar – or, indeed, have sensibly taken shelter from this storm, no place for a healer's magick.

But for the group round the altar, frozen between panic and devotion to duty – the spellbound King and his earnest lecturers; the plump little Queen sobbing; the foreign dignitaries crouched on the steps with their arms about their heads – none now remained in the courtyard but attackers and attacked. Those of the invited guests who had not vanished altogether were ranged along the outer rim of the courtyard, hugging the walls or cowering behind pillars or the half-denuded trees. The men of the King's Guard standing to attention on either side of the gates had come forth, pikes at the ready, to defend their monarch – but against whom, or what? Though Sophie had let go her own concealing magick, all but she were still shielded by her mother's charms, which few guardsmen would be equipped to defeat. Rather than level their fearsome weaponry against one unarmed girl, they stood and looked bewildered, while Lord Merton, the Professor, and Sieur Germain's prisoner bellowed orders at them, which they could not understand how to obey.

Though the courtyard was nearly empty, the noise seemed to have tripled, the confusion multiplied; fire-spells left the air thin and shimmering with heat. But Sophie's song-spell still held King Henry from drinking the fatal draught.

* * *

Suddenly a stocky little figure scaled one corner of the dais, to balance precariously atop the altar beside the heap of offerings. The Queen scrabbled frantically at her son's ankles, but he shook her off. 'What is this madness?' Prince Roland demanded. 'Who are you? What is it that you want?'

Everyone ignored him – or nearly everyone.

At the sound of her half-brother's furious voice, wavering uncertainly between baritone and treble, tears stung Sophie's eyes. Blinking furiously, she pulled off her masque, the better to scrub them away, but her own voice caught in her throat, and her song died into choked silence.

She stared up at him – Joanna's age, or nearly, bewildered by the flames and noise but prodded into reckless bravery by fear for those he loved – and felt that to be this boy's near kin might be something.

'Sophie!' Alerted by Gray's urgent summons, she saw, to her horror, that the whisperers had prevailed; King Henry was lifting the chalice again, preparing to finish the rite she had interrupted.

'No! Your Majesty, please, you must not!' she cried, half sobbing with frustration and dismay. From all directions familiar voices echoed her words, but the invocation went on – though even from this distance she could see the trembling of her father's hands.

'Sophie, *you must stop him*!' Gray's voice was ragged. He had put off his masque and shed his coat; his shirt was damp, and his face ran with perspiration.

Sophie searched her mind frantically for some fragment of melody, and – for the first time in her memory – could think of none. Her heart seemed too large for her breast; its desperate pounding threatened to burst her ribs; the prayer was almost at an end, and then—

I am safe from Lord Carteret and the Iberian Emperor now, even if they discover who I am. But my father is not. Surely this is the moment Mama's letter spoke of, the moment I must recognise when it comes.

King Henry bowed low to the altar; straightened; began to raise the cup to his lips. Gray tried to shout one last warning, but the words would not come.

But from behind him there came another voice – familiar yet utterly strange: 'Henry!'

The King raised his head.

'Henry, as you love me, *do not drink*!'

The King's eyes widened. His face drained of all colour; the chalice slipped from his fingers and rang against the stone steps at his feet.

Lord Merton – Woodville – allies and enemies wheeled to stare at him. The fair-haired man alone did not seem drawn to the spectacle; even before the sound of chalice's impact died away, he was reaching into the breast of his coat – metal gleamed briefly in the torchlight – Gray heard Sophie cry out in alarm.

The long poniard was whisked from the stranger's hand just as Gray was beginning to summon it; it rose high into the air, then fell, hilt down, to strike its owner smartly on the crown of his head. He staggered, and Master Alcuin, appearing behind him seemingly from nowhere, dropped him where he stood with a neat, sharp blow to the back of the skull.

The Queen cried, 'Edric!' and fell to her knees beside the fair-haired man; the King, however, seemed not to have noticed the momentary disturbance.

Gray turned on one heel, following Henry's gaze, and drew a deep, shuddering breath. Though he had seen only once, and not in life, the face Sophie wore, he knew it at once for the young Queen Laora – the Midnight Queen herself.

All around them the air buzzed with gasps, whispers, the rustle of heavy skirts, as His Majesty's guests surged forward, forgetting their terror in the wonder of this revelation.

Then – after a moment that seemed to last an age – King Henry's voice, heavy with some strong emotion: 'Laora . . .'

And Queen Laora vanished, giving place to a slender young woman of middling height, dark-eyed and chestnut-haired, who clasped her slim sun-browned hands and said, 'Your Majesty, I ask your pardon, for indeed I am not she . . .'

But all those present could guess, now, who this stranger must be, and – save perhaps for her father – found the return of the lost Princess at least as scandalously exciting as that brief, misleading glimpse of the long-dead Queen.

'Your Majesty.' Sieur Germain turned his prisoner over to the nearest guardsman and approached the dais with a respectful bow. 'The Princess and her friends, myself among them, ask pardon also for this . . . disruption. That cup, from which you would have drunk, contained a poison—' Indignant protests from the conspirators, and gasps of horror from the crowd.

Gray shivered; so near the river, the night air was growing chill and damp. He bent to retrieve his coat, and shrugged it on over yet another ruined shirt and waistcoat.

'The same, we believe,' Sieur Germain continued, 'that felled Lord Halifax, late Master of Merlin College. Our warning to you was perhaps not . . . In short, I beg Your Majesty will forgive us our transgressions against the laws of hospitality, for they were motivated only by our earnest fear for Your Majesty's life.'

It was a pretty speech, but its object seemed to have caught little of its meaning. 'The Princess . . . ?' he said, staring.

'The Princess,' called someone whom Gray could not see, 'has saved King Henry's life.'

First a few voices, then many, from all about the courtyard;

first ragged and uncertain, but quickly gaining authority: '*Vive la princesse! Vive la princesse!*'

Then a man's voice rose above the ovation: 'Sons and daughters of Breizh! Have foreigners not ruled our country long enough? Must we wait forty years more for the old Duc to make up his mind? Or shall we unite behind a new champion? Here is our Breizhek Queen – *here*, friends, is our true monarch! You see her lineage; you have seen her power – and her mercy. Will you follow her?'

The cheering faltered for a moment; then a new chant was taken up by fewer, but more vehement, voices: '*Vive ar rouanez* – Long live the Breizhek Queen!'

From those whose allegiance still lay all this side of the Manche, rose opposing shouts of 'Long live the King!' – 'Britain undivided!' – '*À bas la bâtarde!*' For if the Midnight Queen was a kind of heroine in Breizh, here in England Laora was only 'that Breton harlot', the faithless traitoress who had met her death while fleeing with some illicit lover.

At first Sophie seemed struck dumb with sheer surprise. 'Stop!' she cried at last, her hands clenching into fists. 'Stop it, all of you!'

Disconcertingly, she seemed to have gained several inches in height.

'I am Queen Laora's daughter, indeed,' she went on – the crowd having gone abruptly silent – 'and a daughter of Breizh, but there the tale ends. If you have been led to believe otherwise, I am heartily sorry.'

Then, with a determination in which only Gray, perhaps, could have recognised bewilderment and alarm, she approached the dumb-founded King, her eyes downcast, and knelt to him in all her Samhain finery. Her voice low and earnest, but reaching somehow to every corner of the courtyard, she repeated the very words which Gray himself had once been so foolish as to speak to her: 'Your devoted servant, Your Majesty.'

Of what happened next, Gray would later remember only that, alerted by the commotion, those of the royal guardsmen on duty – or off it – elsewhere in the Palace, now arrived in rather bewildered force, to swell the noise and confusion of the gathering, and that Lord Carteret, abruptly trimming his sails to this new breeze, gestured expansively at Sophie as though to say, *You see? I promised you your Princess, and here she is . . .*

In the presence of so many formidable men-at-arms, Lord Merton prudently took his cue from Lord Carteret by choosing to melt away into the crowd. But young Woodville – actuated perhaps by the now apoplectic Professor, or perhaps by his own enthusiasm – launched an ill-aimed volley of hailstones at Gray and Master Alcuin, who stood between him and Sophie. Gray threw up another hasty shielding-spell and cried a warning to Sophie, who, springing to her feet, did the same.

The only one of Woodville's missiles to connect at all struck the Crown Prince a glancing blow to the temple; he glared at its source, and with a look of contempt drew from the damp air a brief, drenching shower of rain.

The resulting wave of nervous laughter sent the dripping Woodville into a fury. Hailstones and fire-bolts erupted from the air, directed wildly and none too carefully at the Princes, at Sophie, at Master Alcuin, and at Gray – and thus threatening everyone in the general vicinity of the altar dais.

Titters gave way to a new access of shrieking and panicked flight. Now however, the men of the King's Guard came into their own; officers bellowed terse orders, and in short order the milling crowd had been tamed and the unfortunate Woodville was sprawled face downward on the cobblestones, with a guardsman's boot firmly planted in the small of his back.

And so, for a moment, all seemed to be well.

Then someone cried, 'A healer, quickly!' and all eyes turned thither on the instant.

Several gentlemen and ladies clutched heads bruised by hailstones or nursed limbs from which the clothing had been singed away; some stood, others sat or knelt on the cobbles, looking dazed. In their midst, however, a single, half-familiar figure lay supine, her arms outspread, her heavy midnight-blue skirts awkwardly twisted about her lower limbs.

Gray saw it and cried out in dismay, but his exclamation, like everyone else's, was lost in Sophie's high, horrified shrieking.

CHAPTER XXXII

In Which Sophie Makes a Confession

Sophie stared at the still, supine body of Mrs Wallis and, for the first time in nearly a decade, remembered.

She remembered a day in early spring, a timid beginning after a long and bitter winter. The girls had teased Mama all the morning to walk out with them, and at last she agreed, though warning them that they must go slowly. She had grown round again, and Sophie was old enough now to understand what this meant, but this time, for some reason, she seemed more cheerful.

The day being mild, they decided at length to strike out from the park into the lanes and byways of the manor. Here Sophie was the leader, knowing as she did almost every corner of the estate, and every tenant, but so happy were they to be free of the house that before long they had wandered beyond even Sophie's knowledge.

They stopped to rest beside an old well in someone's disused orchard; the trees were uncared for, full of deadwood, and the ground beneath them awash in the remains of last autumn's windfalls. It was a lovely spot, in its own way; wild birds and small beasts had come to feast on the bounty of tree and field. But here, too, they met with less congenial company: a brace of adventurers, deserting officers by their dress, who had tried their hand at poaching and were building up a fire to roast their catch.

They had killed a hare, and with an obsequious civility that concealed something quite other, invited Mama and the girls to help them cook and eat it; Mama's polite refusal made one of them angry, but the other only tried harder to persuade her.

'Girls!' Mama called to them, just before the taller man approached her, cupping a hand under her chin to lift her beautiful face to his. 'All of you, run away home! I shall follow you in a little while. Go, now!'

Amelia, not waiting to be told again, turned and fled; Joanna hesitated, but at Sophie's urging retreated a little way.

Sophie herself could not seem to move, could not stop herself from watching. The men were grinning, leering, hateful and hopeful at once; Mama twitched away, but they had her cornered against a tree-trunk. She could not speak, it seemed, could scarcely move.

Sophie was both terrified and furious. Whatever the men intended, Mama did not like it; she looked at them as Sophie had often seen her look at Father, a look like a caged fox. Sophie did not stop to think but reached for the pebbles she had been collecting and began hurling them, with more vehemence than care, at the nearest of the attackers. At first her missiles, not surprisingly, scarcely even drew his notice. At the same time, however, a wind sprang up, swift and biting despite the day's mildness, and growing increasingly savage, and now the pebbles began, inexplicably, to burst on impact, while the stones of the old well set up a curious, angry humming and at last begin to splinter and crack.

The tall man took notice now, and turned to glare at her.

'Sophia!' Mama cried. 'Sophia, stop it at once, and run away home!'

But Sophie stood frozen, unwilling – unable – to obey. The tall man still held Mama around the shoulders, grinning, and Mama's face still wore that caged-fox look; how could Sophie even contemplate running away? Yet what good did she do by remaining?

The wind had died down a little, and Sophie hurled another stone while no one was looking. Then the smaller man turned, strode towards her, and slapped her face, once – twice – again – she staggered – and once more the wind howled dementedly about them all, fetching down dead twigs from the trees overhead.

Mama's lips moved, and she made a sort of twisting motion with one hand, and Sophie, all unwilling, found herself turning on one heel and setting off towards home. Behind her Mama's voice rose, shouting words she did not recognise or understand. In her panicked fear Sophie managed to surmount whatever force compelled her homeward; the wind gathered strength and speed, and overhead boughs creaked and snapped as she ran towards Mama, just in time to see the two men slide to the ground, as if they had suddenly fallen asleep.

Mama was safe – thank all the gods! – and Sophie pelted towards her, weeping with relief and the aftermath of terror, to fling herself into those outstretched arms.

But before her eyes a deadfall branch, loosened by the sudden breeze that had now died as abruptly as it sprang up, leant away from the trunk of an apple tree – split – plunged – and Mama lay still between her fallen assailants, her arms outflung, and a spreading pool of bright red seeped out into the muddy ground.

Sophie remembered Mrs Wallis arriving at a dead run, falling to her knees beside Mama, weeping, imploring, importuning the gods of healing to save Mama's life; remembered the shade of a smile on Mama's ashen face as she whispered something that Sophie could not hear. Remembered Mrs Wallis saying, in a voice that shook, 'I swear it, Laora. By the love I have for you I swear it.'

Then she had found Sophie and Joanna clinging together – Sophie sobbing, shaking, with blood smeared over her face and trickling sluggishly from her nose, Joanna dry-eyed, ashen-faced, and silent – and knelt to gather them into her arms.

'Your Mama has gone to live in the Elysian Fields,' she told them, her voice breaking, 'but I shall always look after both of you – all of you . . .'

Sophie had tried to speak but succeeded only in wailing. At last she managed to get out the single word 'Mama,' and then all the rest came tumbling out higgledy-piggledy, and Mrs Wallis's round, kind face went very still, and she held Sophie tighter.

'We are beyond the interdict,' she muttered to herself. 'Laora, Laora, you were right to fear for her. How could you be so foolish, love, how could you?'

Sophie remembered those words, quite without meaning to her at the time, and felt that her heart would break.

Mama was gone, Mrs Wallis had said so, but the men who had tried to hurt her were only sleeping, and when they awoke a little time later, Mrs Wallis made them forget.

Mrs Wallis was calm and kind and dependable. She shepherded Sophie and Joanna back to the house, back to the familiar comforts of the nursery, where Amelia was waiting tearfully, and tucked them all up into their beds, with the nursery-maid to watch over them.

Amelia and Sophie had awoken the next morning while Joanna was yet asleep, and run downstairs calling for Mama. Mrs Wallis called the whole household together in the kitchen and explained that Mrs Callender had found a very difficult experimental spell in an old book in the library which she had wished to study, and had tried to work it alone; that the spell had proved even more difficult and dangerous than she had expected; that they must all take good care of the little girls now that Mrs Callender was no longer here to do so. She had written to the Professor, she said, to acquaint him with the sad tidings.

Sophie and Amelia wept, and remembered the tale, and Sophie's waking mind forgot the true one.

A shattering roar erupted from the circumference of the courtyard as every torch blossomed upwards, every magelight lantern flared into a blinding little sun. For a heartbeat the ravaged courtyard showed bright as day; then, just as suddenly, all was plunged into darkness.

Gray had ducked, for a moment, instinctively. Now he called as much light as he could muster and stood straight, battling a sudden, furious, swirling wind. All about him, heedless of their costly finery, people were flattening themselves against the reassuring solidity of the cobblestones.

The source of this elemental chaos stood quite still, oblivious, howling her grief and rage at the night sky. Her nose was bleeding heavily, crimson tracks against her waxen skin – too vast, too wild a release of magickal energy taking its toll of her body, again . . .

'Sophie!' Gray shouted as he struggled towards her, trying in vain to make himself heard over the cries of panic, the keening of the wind in the denuded trees. 'Sophie, *stop*!'

When at last he reached her, he saw at once that further speech would be of no use. Mrs Wallis would have slapped her face, or shaken her, to bring her to her senses; but Mrs Wallis . . .

In any case, Gray had never in his life struck a woman, and he had certainly no notion of beginning with Sophie.

Instead he drew her rigid, trembling body against his and held her tight. Briefly she fought his encircling arms; then – so abruptly that his ears rang in the unexpected silence – the wind and Sophie's howling ceased together, and she sobbed in his arms like a child.

'Sophie, *cariad*.' Again she seemed not to hear him. She shivered, and clung tighter as he bent to slide one arm under her knees.

Magelights pulsed into existence, small and larger, all over the courtyard, and people staggered to their feet. Guardsmen had surrounded the King and his family, weapons out; stewards with fire-pots emerged from the direction of the ballroom and rushed hither and thither, reigniting the snuffed-out torches; men, and a few women, in the garb of healers followed at a run. All these doings Gray saw but dimly as he passed by, his attention all on Sophie.

Through a gateway whose guards had left their post, they found the light and relative warmth of an interior corridor; round the next turning Gray discovered two gilt chairs and a velvet-covered sofa, on which, with a sigh of relief, he deposited Sophie. Her shivering had grown worse, though at least the flow of blood from her nose was slowing; he shed his coat once more and wrapped it about her shoulders, then sat beside her and drew her into his arms again.

Words began to emerge through the racking sobs, the chattering teeth. 'Mama! Mama!' Gray heard, incredulous; then, more inexplicably still, '*Mantret on,* Mama, *mantret on* . . .'

I am sorry.

And what in Hades had Sophie to be sorry for?

'Sophie.' That voice – familiar, beloved – at last began to break into Sophie's confused and desperate misery, forcing her to recognise the arms that held her, and behind the iron tang of blood, the scent of the body that supported hers. For just a moment she was herself again – was no longer a terrified child – was confident and comforted; until the weight of what she had seen, what it had made her remember, descended again to crush all hope. To think that her most terrifying nightmares, these nine years, had been simple truth!

Gray let go of her shoulders and slid gentle fingers beneath her chin. Irrationally dreading lest he should read in her face the secret of her guilt, she twisted out of his grasp, regained her feet, and made to flee, nearly losing her balance; when he stood and came towards her, she pushed him away, eyes averted, both palms flat against his bloodied breast.

He staggered back, one step, two; then, steadying himself, he stepped forward again and caught her by the shoulders. Confused and frightened, she exerted herself not to be seen – but to no avail.

'Whatever dreadful thing you believe yourself to have done, *cariad*, will be no less dreadful, being hidden.' He spoke so mildly, so reasonably, that once more she took heart, and then she saw again, in her mind's eye, the plunging branch, the spreading blood . . .

'No,' she said, denying – what, she hardly knew. 'No, no . . .'

'*Sophie!*' A new voice, frightened, urgent; the sound of rapid footsteps against stone, away down the unfamiliar corridor in which they stood. Gray's hands dropped away from her face; she felt rather than saw him straighten into tense alertness, gazing over her head to locate the speaker. Turning to follow his gaze, Sophie had a vague impression of dark hair, a white face, a rumpled green gown—

'*Joanna?*' she whispered, incredulous, as the apparition flung itself upon her.

Joanna it was, miraculously unscathed, and in the same breath berating her sister and thanking all the gods that she yet lived. Half strangled by the younger girl's frantic embrace, Sophie closed her eyes and returned it in grateful silence.

Joanna released her at last and, looking from her face to Gray's, seemed to take in their wretched state. 'What has happened out in the courtyard?' she demanded. 'You are all over blood! They have not . . . they have not *won*? There was so much shouting and running about – but then I heard Sophie singing – and then more shouting – and the most *dreadful* noise . . .'

Sophie blinked. 'I – I hardly know—'

'Sophie,' said Gray urgently, turning her to face him and clasping her shoulders with both hands. 'You will be well, now?'

How am I to answer that question? She nodded, feeling dazed, and clung tighter to Joanna's hands.

'Joanna, look after your sister,' Gray commanded. 'Both of you, stay here. I shall be back directly.'

And without another word to Sophie, he strode off in the direction of the courtyard.

'He has gone without his coat,' said Joanna, hefting the mass of deep brown velvet. 'You had best put it on; you are shivering.'

'Jo.' Sophie sat quite still as her sister draped the coat again about her shoulders. 'Jo, I have remembered something dreadful . . .'

Quite what he had expected to see on re-entering the courtyard, Gray hardly knew. There had been time enough, at any rate, for the interrupted rite to come nearly to its end, for the first sight to meet his eyes was that of the King – flanked by three smaller figures that must be his sons, and two larger ones whom Gray could not identify – preparing to add the crowning tribute to the haphazardly reassembled heap on the altar.

For a moment Gray could only think how odd it was that His Majesty should choose to finish his prayers before addressing the other, more urgent demands upon his notice. But though the traitors had spoken with malign intent, in urging that he let nothing prevent him from fulfilling his obligations, they had also spoken truth: it would be a poor sovereign indeed who placed his innocent subjects in jeopardy by slighting the gods.

The final invocation drew to a close; the broken cake of wheat, oats, and barley was piled atop the rest. After a brief, silent consultation, one figure detached itself from the group round the altar, to return bearing a torch borrowed from a passing steward.

Gray squinted through the smoke, at once fascinated and perplexed, as the King hefted the crackling torch and cried aloud the Latin words that meant, *Grant that I may lead my people another year in prosperity and peace*, and set the heap of offerings alight.

'May the gods grant it.' Gray spoke the response by instinct, only then remarking other voices murmuring the same hopeful words. The courtyard, so apparently empty, in fact hummed with quiet industry. Healers moved with steady purpose among the injured and those suffering from exhaustion and nervous strain; stewards and footmen gathered the debris of revel and calamity, slowly restoring that ravaged place to its accustomed sobriety. Guardsmen manned the gates to gardens and ballroom; even the gateway through which Gray had emerged was, he now discovered, flanked by two large and formidable men-at-arms.

He wondered for some moments that they should have failed to challenge him, before at last recollecting the charm he yet wore.

Though the stewards did their best, they had no means to dispel the haze that filled the air, and which the light of the rekindled torches and the smoke of the burnt-offerings were every moment increasing; worse, at the eastern end of the courtyard, where a gate gave onto the Palace gardens, a late-autumn mist crept in from off the river. Already the altar and its attendants had all but vanished from Gray's sight; around the circumference of the courtyard, guardsmen were now indistinguishable from statues. There was, to his relief, no sign of Professor Callender or any of his confederates, but to find those he sought began to seem a daunting task indeed.

'Your pardon,' he mumbled, half stumbling over a man in healer's robes who knelt beside a weeping noblewoman. The healer raised his head, surveyed Gray incuriously, and, without a word, returned to his task.

Gray wandered among the groups of deflated revellers, every one a stranger to him, until he began to despair. He was nearly halfway across the courtyard, as best he could judge, when his ears caught at a fragment of familiar speech and, turning abruptly, he beheld at last one of the objects of his search.

Not dead – no longer even insensible – Mrs Wallis sat composedly upon a stone bench, conversing with the healer whose fingers probed the impressive bruise on her temple. 'Mr Marshall!' she greeted him, smiling.

Having assured himself repeatedly that he would certainly find her safe and well, Gray was unprepared for the magnitude of his relief – the more so because it was only on Sophie's account, and Joanna's, that he had sought her to begin with. For his own part, he was so angry that he cared not whether she lived or died, but to have brought them such ill tidings . . . No, it did not bear thinking of.

'And what,' Mrs Wallis enquired, 'have you done with Mrs Marshall?'

Gray blinked. 'Oh!' he said, after a moment. 'She is . . .' He pointed vaguely, unable to get his bearings in the thickening haze. Then, indignantly, 'She is terribly frightened. You must come to her at once, and show her that you are not dead—'

'Marshall! – is that you? *Quid agis*, Marshall?'

Gray turned towards the voice, narrowing his eyes to no avail, and at the same time taking a firm hold of Mrs Wallis's elbow. This precautionary gesture, even as he made it, struck him as slightly foolish – but with Mrs Wallis one never knew. 'Magister?' he called. '*Satin bene istic tibi?* I am here, and I have found Mrs Wallis, but—'

Master Alcuin loomed quite suddenly out of the smoke and mist and reached up to clap Gray on the shoulder. 'I am exceedingly glad to have found you,' he said. 'I made sure you had moved this way, but in this gods-accursèd mist . . .' Then looking about him, he demanded, 'And Miss Sophie? She is safe? Where have you left her?'

'Just inside the south gate, and I shall take you to her. But I beg you will hurry, for' – with a wave of his hand at Mrs Wallis – 'I have news that ought not to be delayed. And, while we go, you must tell me – where are the Professor and his friends? They have not—'

'They are made prisoners; His Majesty ordered their arrest,' said Master Alcuin. 'I fear, however, that we shall be next. A moment only, and I shall tell you all—' And turning, he called out, 'Kergabet! This way, if you please – I have found them!'

There was a sound of hastening footsteps, and Sieur Germain appeared behind Master Alcuin, relief writ plain on both their faces.

'Ah!' Sieur Germain's nod of satisfaction took in Mrs Wallis as well as Gray. 'Well met, madame. Now, let us make haste—'

Then his face went stiff and wary, his gaze focused on something beyond them. Gray turned to look – still holding fast to Mrs Wallis's arm – and beheld a guard captain and a quartet of guards.

One of the guardsmen peered at them and said, 'I do recognise those two, sir: the tall one, and the little old man. I cannot vouch for the others.'

'Very well.' The guard captain surveyed them wearily. 'They are all in it together, I daresay. You, you, and you' – nodding at Gray, Sieur Germain, and Master Alcuin in turn – 'I arrest you in the name of His Majesty the King.'

Almost before he had finished speaking, each of them had a guardsman looming at his shoulder.

'I must protest, Captain,' said Sieur Germain. 'What offence have we committed?'

'Disturbing the peace,' said the guard captain, wooden-faced. '"Arrest them all, and let this appalling mess be sorted out in the morning," His Majesty said. I hope, gentlemen, I may rely upon you to consider your own dignity?'

'That other lot carried on most dreadful,' Gray's hulking young guardsman confided, sotto voce. 'M'lady was in a great taking, for—'

'Reynolds!' At his captain's stern look, Reynolds shut his mouth with a snap.

'Now then,' said the captain, and his little troop was in the act of forming up its prisoners to be marched away, when out of the mist a firm, commanding voice said, 'Captain Prichard, a moment, if you please.'

A moment later there emerged, flanked by another pair of guardsmen, none other than the King himself.

'My daughter,' he said, addressing the prisoners. 'You will take me to her – at once, if you please. By all the gods, if she has come to any harm—'

'The wind . . . *you* made the wind blow?' said Joanna, wide-eyed, when Sophie had finished her tale. 'I had thought . . . But I hardly know what I thought. Foolish things. The Mother Goddess, protecting Mama, or—'

Astounded by this reaction to her miserable confession, Sophie caught her sister by the shoulders: 'Do you tell me that you have *known*, all these years, how Mama died, and said never a word about it?'

Joanna shrugged and looked away. 'I did not know it was to be such a secret,' she said. 'Of course Father and Mrs Wallis told a different tale, but I did not think you could believe them, any more than I did; and you dreamt of it so often, you know, that I thought—'

'But – how did you—?'

'When we were children in the nursery,' said Joanna, with all the dignity of her rising fourteen years, 'you talked in your sleep.'

As she spoke she rummaged in the pockets of Gray's coat, and extracted therefrom a further handkerchief and, inexplicably, a tiny bottle of scent; opening the latter, she sniffed appraisingly, then emptied it into the handkerchief and began gently to sponge the blood from Sophie's face and hands.

'I had the same dreams, you see,' she said, as though Sophie had wanted telling. 'But you – you thought it only a nightmare?'

'There were so many,' said Sophie – pleading, helpless to explain. 'That was perhaps the worst, but they were all of them so dreadful – full of killing and death, and all manner of horrors . . . How was I to know it for truth, Jo?'

Joanna looked thoughtful.

'I see now why the gods sent such dreams to plague me,' Sophie went on. 'Once already I had used my magick to – to do great harm, and—'

'You must not say such foolish things,' Joanna said sternly. 'You were a child of eight – no one had taught you the least thing about your magick – you had no reason even to *suspect* – truly, Sophie' – this in a more conciliating tone, as she subsided next to Sophie on the settle – 'no one could fault *you* for what happened. You were only trying . . . the worst that can be said, is that you were foolish enough – *brave* enough – to throw stones when you might have run to fetch help; and any help you found must have come much too late.'

Sensible words, of perhaps considerable truth, but Sophie, exhausted and distraught, was not in a humour to give them much credence. 'Still, you cannot deny it, Jo,' she said. 'It was my doing, whether meant or not . . . Mama was well able to protect herself, and she must have known what might happen – the only end of my foolish bravery, as you call it, was to – was to—'

But she could not say the words aloud.

'Sophie.' With a gentleness of which few would have suspected her, Joanna drew her weeping sister into her arms. 'Tomorrow, when you are rested and well again,' she murmured, smoothing Sophie's tumbled hair as she might have stroked her pony's mane, 'you will see it all quite differently. Gray will explain it to you, and Mrs Wallis, and it will all be quite all right . . .'

But this only made Sophie cry harder. She ought, she knew, to tell her sister what had happened – to explain what had prompted her horrifying recollection – but Mrs Wallis had loved Joanna as Mama had not, and she found it was quite out of her power to break such news as this. *Gray will tell her. Gray will know what is best to say . . .*

* * *

'Sophie?' Gray called. 'Joanna?'

Rounding a corner just ahead of the remainder of the party, he beheld his wife, wrapped again in his discarded coat, shivering and sobbing in her sister's arms. A moment later the guardsman Reynolds trod on his heel, and he was forced to make way for the others.

Sophie raised her head, displaying for half a heartbeat a face cleansed of blood but swollen and blotched with much weeping; before Gray had had time to blink, the ravages of her distress had disappeared, and her expression showed only her present alarm. Joanna had started to her feet and, apparently heedless of the reproaches due to her profound disobedience, ran to embrace first Master Alcuin, then Mrs Wallis and even Sieur Germain. Only when she found herself face-to-face with King Henry, and surrounded by half a dozen solid guardsmen, did her self-assurance fail her, and then with a hasty, slapdash curtsey and a murmured 'Your Majesty,' she retreated again behind Mrs Wallis. Gray doubted very much that the King had noticed her at all, so hungrily was his gaze fixed on Sophie.

But she, throughout the whole of her sister's exuberant performance, only stood and gaped at her erstwhile guardian.

'Mrs Wallis,' she said at last, with a sort of hiccough, stretching out a trembling hand. 'I thought – I had thought that—'

'You are a foolish child, Sophia,' Mrs Wallis returned, with such uncomplicated affection in her tone as made Gray blink in surprise. She stepped forward to kiss and embrace Sophie. If she had expected some return for this display of feeling, however, her disappointment must have been great, for Sophie continued still and silent.

But not so her father.

By her proximity to Sophie, Mrs Wallis now commanded the King's notice, as previously she had not; as he studied her profile, frowning, he appeared to grow ever more astonished.

'It is you, indeed,' he said at last, astonishing the rest in turn. 'Lady Maëlle – is't not? You have a great deal to answer for.'

Her back stiffened; then, slowly, deliberately, Mrs Wallis loosed her hold of Sophie and turned to face the man whose daughter she might fairly have been accused of abducting. 'Your Majesty.' A deep, graceful curtsey, rather at odds with her frosty tone.

But his attention had already left her, as it must, to fasten once more on his daughter. 'I can scarce believe my eyes,' he murmured, as though to himself. Gray felt half ashamed to witness such private anguish, but he would not have left Sophie to face her father alone, even had it been in his power to choose.

'You have the look of your mother,' whispered the King, and came forward – one step – two; he stood before her with outstretched arms, while she gazed up at him like one spellbound. 'And her magick also; that face, that voice . . . On Samhain-night, it's said the dead may walk among the living . . . But I am so glad you are come back to me, my little Edith Augusta!'

This at last seemed to break the spell. 'You are mistaken, Your Majesty,' said the Princess Royal, drawing herself up. 'My name is Sophie Marshall.'

CHAPTER XXXIII

In Which Old Scores Are Settled

Sophie Marshall. She had never so styled herself before, or not aloud, and the sound of it, the look on Gray's pale, sooty face when she glanced his way, went some distance towards restoring her equilibrium. *Perhaps Joanna spoke truly*, she thought; *perhaps it was not all my fault; perhaps I may be forgiven.* Despite the hollow terror of the memory, the cold knot of guilt and misery under her heart began, just perceptibly, to loosen.

'Sophie,' Gray began, and then fell silent. She held out a hand; he smiled and reached towards her, clasping her fingers with his. When he would have drawn closer, however, she shook her head; this battle she must fight for herself.

But it seemed she was to have a moment's reprieve, for the King, his advance halted by her brief show of defiance, now turned, frowning, to enquire of Gray who he might be.

'Graham Marshall, Your Majesty.' Only Sophie herself, she thought, could have detected the tremor in his voice. 'Late of Merlin College. I am brother-in-law to my lord of Kergabet, and I am Sophie's husband.'

His Majesty's visible consternation provoked Mrs Wallis to speech. 'You cannot have believed, my lord,' she said, 'that Sophia's friends, however great our fear for Your Majesty's life, should betray her once more into the very danger which her mother sacrificed so much to avert?'

'I beg your pardon, Lady Maëlle; I have not the pleasure of understanding you,' he replied, so stiff and regal now that it was difficult to credit his pleading of a moment since.

Mrs Wallis had plainly some retort in mind, but Sophie, wishing only to have this moment over, saw her chance and seized it.

'Your Majesty,' she said, 'I am heartily sorry to have played you such a trick as to show you my mother's face, but I assure you there was no alternative. You shall hear all the tale another time, no doubt, but what I should wish you to know at once, is . . .'

The words caught in her throat, and she swallowed – weary, ravenous, chilled bone-deep, but determined that, at all events, she should make her position clear.

'What I must say,' she went on at last, her voice no longer sounding like her own, 'is that I have not come back to "claim my place", or to beg your hospitality, or to – to discompose your family in any way. Had I been able, I should have gone away again at once, and no one the wiser—'

But she was brought up short by her father's inarticulate cry of distress.

'Edith – *Sophie!*' the King began again, his jaw working. 'I – you cannot mean—No, indeed, you shall not go away again, before we have so much as spoken—'

And he took another step forward, his hands raised as though to take her by the shoulders.

Sophie recoiled.

'Your Majesty may perhaps forget,' Sieur Germain interjected, chillingly civil, 'the debt which he owes to the Princess this night . . .'

'Or perhaps,' Mrs Wallis continued, as though to her companions, 'His Majesty is merely carried by the exuberance of his gratitude into too violent an expression of hospitality.'

Halted once more, the King stared in silence from one of them to the other. Sophie turned in their direction, opening her mouth to voice some rebuke, but fatigue made her eyes darken and her knees give way beneath her before a word had passed her lips. She reached out blindly for some means of support; strong hands steadied her on her feet.

When she came to herself again, Mrs Wallis and Gray were supporting her between them, and she heard Joanna in full spate: '. . . and I do think it too bad of you, Your Majesty, to keep poor Sophie standing here in such a pitiful state – and Gray, too, and the others – when, if you had only heeded our letter—'

'Dim'zell Joanna,' Sieur Germain warned, and Joanna shut her mouth at once, though looking rather bellicose than chastened.

'Your Majesty,' murmured the guard captain who stood at the King's elbow. 'May we proceed?'

'A moment, Captain. The Princess and her attendants shall be our guests,' said the King, 'until such time as this affair is settled. Where is—? No; no, that would be most unsuitable. You, Girard' – turning to one of the guardsmen – 'fetch me one of the Queen's ladies, to escort our guests to suitable quarters.'

Girard trotted away down the corridor and returned only moments later with a bewildered-looking young woman in tow. She curtseyed deeply to the King, and goggled at Sophie.

'Madame de Courcy,' said His Majesty. 'You will find suitable accommodations for these ladies, if you please.'

'Your Majesty.' Another curtsey, and to Mrs Wallis, 'If it please you, ma'am . . . ?'

She set off back the way she had come. Joanna trotted after her, almost without a backwards glance; Sophie tried to cling to her husband, but Mrs Wallis pulled her firmly along.

'Rest well, *cariad*,' said Gray, low, as he let go of her hand. 'I shall see you in the morning, no doubt.'

She cast a last desperate look over her shoulder at him; he gave her an encouraging smile.

Then the King said in a flat voice, 'You may proceed, Captain Prichard.' The captain gave a low-voiced order, and the guardsmen took Gray and the others by the shoulders and began to march them away.

'Gray!' Sophie tried to shout, but what emerged was a sort of whispered croak; then they were out of sight, and it was too late.

'Come, child,' said Mrs Wallis kindly, and Sophie stumbled after her.

There was but one chamber in the Royal Palace both held under interdiction of all magick and large enough to accommodate so many; into this apartment, already occupied by the conspirators, Gray and his friends were conducted by their captors. The spell settled like a weight of misery on Gray's shoulders, worse by far than the Professor's interdiction on Callender Hall, and he knew from their waxen faces and dispirited expressions that the other mages present felt it likewise.

Curiously, however, the Professor himself seemed unaffected – or perhaps his towering rage still masked the symptoms of illness.

'You!' He levelled a furious glare at Gray. 'Is there no ridding the world of you, accursèd boy?'

Gray returned his gaze levelly but said nothing, being preoccupied with swallowing back a wave of nausea. Woodville, though his face was green in the intervals between bruises, managed a sneer. The Professor took a step towards Gray but halted, still glowering, when one of the guardsmen posted at the door cleared his throat meaningly.

Sieur Germain pointedly turned his back on the Professor and his allies and peered up into Gray's face, and down into Master Alcuin's, with furrowed brow. 'You look very ill, both of you,' he said. 'Will you not sit down?'

He took them each by an elbow and propelled them to an unoccupied settle.

'It is only the interdiction,' Master Alcuin explained, mopping his forehead with a handkerchief.

Gray closed his eyes, found this did not answer, and opened them again, staring up at the blessedly featureless ceiling. 'Magister,' he said, attempting to divert his thoughts from his rebellious stomach, 'that guardsman – how came it that he recognised us? Has he a strong magickal talent, to see through our charms?'

His teacher gave a wan chuckle. 'You have not puzzled it out? Recall, Marshall, the charms protect against *unwelcome* notice. It was that guardsman who subdued your friend Woodville, when you and I and Miss Sophie were under attack, and his attention to us at that moment, therefore, was very welcome indeed . . .'

Of course. Gray nodded – blinked – swallowed hard.

Sieur Germain, perched on a chair opposite, looked from Gray to Master Alcuin in growing alarm. 'You, there,' he called to the guardsmen at the door; when one of them left his post to investigate, he said, 'My brother is very ill; you must see that he cannot stay the night here. I would speak to your Captain Prichard . . .'

Gray did not hear the guardsman's reply; he closed his eyes, and drifted, and knew no more.

Sophie shifted in her seat, covertly lifting her gaze to the frescoed ceiling of the King's great audience chamber. She was hungry, thirsty, and desperately tired, having slept long but unquietly, disturbed by Joanna's nightmares as well as her own. She dreaded the ordeal still to come and, though she believed the truth must prevail, was continually recalling examples from history in which the reverse had occurred. And having resolved, before succumbing to magick-shocked exhaustion, that she must tell Gray everything she had remembered, as soon as they should be permitted some private speech, she was impatient to have it over. His troubled glances at her, from where he sat between his brother and Master Alcuin against the right-hand wall of the long, narrow room, suggested that he guessed at her distress – though surely he could have no notion of the truth.

From time to time – covertly, and with some trepidation – Sophie shifted her gaze to the opposite wall, where, beneath a fresco depicting the twelve labours of Hercules, their opponents were gathered. Viscount Carteret stood in close conference with Lord Merton; Lord Wrexham and Lord Spencer slumped in gilt-and-velvet chairs, one at either end of the row along the wall, while Woodville slowly paced, and the Professor muttered to himself, with furrowed brow, occasionally casting a venomous glance at his accusers.

Gray and Master Alcuin, Lord Merton and Woodville, all alike looked worn and pale and ill. 'They will have been confined under a powerful interdiction,' Mrs Wallis said quietly, when Sophie exlaimed at their wretched appearance. 'The stronger one's magick, the worse are the effects. Do not be alarmed, however; it will not last.'

'Mother Goddess!' Joanna declared, 'I am so hungry, I believe I could eat a whole roast ox. Whatever can be taking such a *time*?'

'Hush, child,' said Mrs Wallis. 'The King is returning.'

At last, thought Sophie. He had left the audience chamber an hour since, to consult with the guard captain, Prichard, and Master Lord de Vaucourt, chief of His Majesty's mages; the two sets of prisoners, together with their guards and the small party of ladies, had in the interim had ample leisure for discussion, explanation, and recrimination, as circumstances suited, and to speculate as to what results this conference would produce. Sophie had attempted twice to speak to Gray, but his guards, though she saw sympathy in their faces, had on each occasion escorted her firmly back to her own seat.

Sieur Germain had presented their evidence, such as it was, of Viscount Carteret's planned coup d'état, calling on Master Alcuin to explain the nature and effects of the poison used, and on Gray and Sophie to confirm its prior use on Lord Halifax. To Sophie's ear, he made the whole phantastickal tale sound – if not perfectly reasonable – less incredible than she could have managed herself, and while he spoke she was in great hopes of the King's seeing everything as he ought. Lord Merton's turn came next, however, and from then on she had been in dread of the outcome. The Professor's tale of Gray's assault on Lord Halifax was rehearsed again, and a motive for it adduced, by the assertion that 'young Marshall' had been finally sent down in punishment for his misdeeds – including the suspicious death of a fellow student – and had returned to exact his revenge. Upon discovering that his stepdaughter might in fact be the lost Princess, Lord Merton explained, the Professor had naturally wished to see her restored to the bosom of her family and had sought Lord Carteret's advice on how best to do so. That Lord Merton and Woodville had done their best to injure Sophie, Gray, and Master Alcuin – and succeeded in injuring Mrs Wallis – they could scarcely deny, but neither could Sieur Germain disprove Lord Merton's indignant protest that it had all been done in defence of His Majesty and not with any will to harm him.

'A conspiracy?' Lord Carteret, rising from his seat to answer his accuser, breathed indignation at the very suggestion. 'But why should *we* be supposed to be in collusion? And what reason can Your Majesty possibly have to value the word of these . . . *interlopers*, above that of your most trusted advisors? And *Bretons*, Your Majesty! Has my lord so soon forgot the attempted *insurrection*, which was so obviously the object of their presence here . . . ?'

It had soon become clear that of the two versions of events presented for his consideration, Henry was strongly disposed to favour his chief counsellor's. Still, if one party could not prove their case beyond doubt, no more could the other.

The King now resumed his seat, flanked by Captain Prichard and Lord de Vaucourt, in whom Sophie now recognised the sharp-nosed man who had stood with the King at the altar on Samhain-night.

'My lord of Vaucourt reports that a poison has been detected in the dregs of the chalice, and on the stones before the altar, such as Master Everard Alcuin has described,' the King announced to the room in general. Sophie breathed a sigh of relief. 'This circumstance is much in favour of the explanation offered by my lord of Kergabet.'

Protests arose from the Professor's side of the chamber, which the King quelled with a look.

'However,' he went on, 'there is no evidence to suggest whose hand placed the poison therein – whether some person here present, or some other person unknown. Neither can we be certain whether Professor Callender's knowledge of' – the King's voice faltered for the first time – 'of his stepdaughter's identity is of recent date, as he claims, or of long standing, as alleged by Lord Kergabet. There is also the matter of the death of Lord Halifax, Master of Merlin College; and, as Lord Carteret has reminded us, of the apparent attempt to sow dissent among our subjects.'

No one spoke.

'That the truth of all these questions may be known, and this matter settled expeditiously, therefore, we have determined to beg the assistance of the gods. From the Temple of Apollo, Watcher of the Heavens,' said the King, 'we have summoned those priests, renowned as truth-seers, who judge where the King's Magistrates declare themselves defeated. These holy men, I trust'– looking sternly from Sieur Germain to Lord Carteret – 'you will neither of you consider liable to corruption by the other?'

Sieur Germain joined so readily with this drastic proposal that Sophie felt sure he must have had the same in mind all along; she saw, too, how neatly their opponents – believing their influence with His Majesty so steadfast, as must in the end win him to their side – had been trapped. An impartial truth-seer would have no choice but to declare against them, and well they knew it, but so too would a refusal to submit confirm their guilt.

The ordeal was nearly over, then, and could surely have only one end. For the happy fortune by which those she loved had won through in safety, or soon would, Sophie gave thanks to every god, great and small, whose name she could recollect. Still she felt she would go mad with waiting; when at length the great oaken doors swung open, she leapt to her feet as eagerly as any prisoner sighting freedom from his chains.

Three tall white-robed priests of Apollo there were – two crowned with flowing white locks, and the third perhaps in the middle thirties, whose strikingly good looks were spoilt by an arrogance of expression, which quite undid the effect.

Sophie had sprung up at their entrance and now stood quivering with tension; at her side, Joanna shifted from foot to foot, scarce able to contain her impatience. Gray's skin prickled. He glanced across to where the conspirators had gathered in an anxious bunch; he fancied a storm-cloud of despair forming overhead and was seized with fear lest they – lest Woodville, in particular – should make some last, desperate attempt. It would be calamitously foolish, before so many witnesses, but, if they had nothing to gain from defiance, neither had they much to lose.

Just as this thought occurred to him, the gooseflesh-prickling of his skin intensified, and he saw Sophie rub furiously at the bridge of her nose. He reached for his magick, ready to work a shielding-spell – and felt only a sickening jolt as it failed to answer his call.

I know this feeling. Knew it but too well, and too lately. Alarmed, he looked down the room at Sophie, whose face had gone tallow-white, and across at their enemies. Only Lord Merton and Woodville appeared to have noticed anything amiss, but their identical expressions of outrage confirmed Gray's hypothesis that someone had lately worked an interdiction on this chamber. Catching Sophie's eye again, in a silent effort at reassurance, he turned to look at Master Alcuin.

The little don smiled up at him, and winked.

The priests addressed to their King a bow just deep enough to avoid offence, and, straightening, the first of them looked down his long nose at all present and began, 'Your Majesty has, I hope, some good and pressing reason for summoning us here?'

'We have sought your Lordships' assistance,' the King replied, 'in a matter of vital import – for us, and for all our kingdom.' His tone was frosty. The priests of Apollo showed signs of curiosity, and His Majesty was beginning to explain the facts of the case, when the doors again burst open to admit a breathless and dishevelled woman and three half-grown boys.

'Henry!' the woman cried. One of the boys stopped to gape a moment at Sophie and Joanna before joining in his brothers' futile attempts to restrain their mother.

Queen Edwina was a little woman, plump and pink-cheeked and scarcely taller than Joanna; in her striped muslin gown and knitted shawl, she looked like nothing so much as a flustered country gentlewoman. But the passionate terror in her face and voice permitted neither amusement nor contempt. 'My lord – *Henry*,' she went on, 'you surely cannot suspect Edric of any intent to harm you? There is some mistake, there must be! Please, my lord, this is madness!'

The King continuing resolutely silent, she appealed to Lord Wrexham: 'Edric, please, you must explain! Tell Henry, tell him that you did not mean any harm! Tell him there is some mistake—'

But her brother silenced her with a savage exclamation, and, defeated, she stood staring from one of them to the other, before at last suffering her eldest son to put an arm about her shoulders and help her to a seat. As they passed him, Gray heard her murmuring, 'But Edric would not, Ned. You must know that he would not. It is all some terrible mistake . . .'

Lord Wrexham was still and white with fury.

'Your Lordships will pardon this unseemly disruption,' the King continued. Gray wondered at his monarch's collected manner until, chancing to see the man's clenched white-knuckled hands, he began to grasp the effort of will that lay behind it. 'The Queen, I assure you, is as eager as I to see truth told and justice done . . .'

But his tale proceeded to the accompaniment of a low, disconsolate weeping.

'Then,' the priest declared at last, 'let us proceed. You' – levelling an imperious forefinger at Master Alcuin – 'will first lift your interdiction on this chamber, if you please.'

Here Woodville so much forgot himself as to use language that even Joanna blushed to hear, and Master Alcuin queried mildly, 'Is this wise?'

The priest folded his arms and glared Woodville into silence; then, turning to Master Alcuin, he replied, 'Until Apollo Coelispex has revealed to us the truth of this affair, we may take no position as to the innocence or guilt of either party. Civility is no sure token of good intent; nor do the chosen of Apollo Coelispex require the assistance of mere scholar-mages.' He paused, then repeated, 'You will lift the interdiction, if you please.'

Master Alcuin raised his eyebrows and shook his head, but he began to murmur in what eventually became discernible as archaic Cymric. When after some moments Gray felt the upwelling of magick that meant the spell was at an end, he reached immediately for the strongest shielding-spell he could think of, lest any danger threaten, but at once the three priests set up a strange chant – half spell, half prayer – that effectively forestalled him.

With the first repetition, intoned in unison, Gray found himself gently divested of the power of speech, and, glancing at his companions, saw them all likewise affected. The chant was begun again on parallel fifths, this time producing a sort of *stillness*: neither the heavy, lethargic pull of Arachne's Web nor the stiff insensibility of a freezing-spell but simply a lack of motion, disconcerting but not unpleasant. Had His Majesty known of *this* magick, Gray wondered, when he sent for help to the Temple of Apollo? But of course he must; was it not close kin to that magick which he had himself bequeathed his daughter?

Gray had rather expected that they would all be directed to supply some personal article to be scried. The methods of Apollo Coelispex, however, proved considerably more direct.

The priests separated to move among their prisoners – only the King himself remaining free of their spell. The youngest approached Sophie, who stood nearest, and, laying one hand on her shoulder and the fingertips of the other against her brow, spoke to her in a low murmur. Gray could not see her face, nor, even at such close quarters, clearly distinguish what the priest said to her, or what she said in reply. But he could see her back and shoulders stiffen and then, slowly, relax, before she again lapsed into that curious bespelled stillness; he derived from this the comforting conviction that, at any rate, she had suffered no permanent harm from the ordeal of speaking truth to divine power.

The same emissary of the oracle-god next questioned Master Alcuin before approaching Gray himself; meanwhile Gray had also had ample opportunity to observe, though at an uncomfortably oblique angle, the rather different effect of the experience on Lord Carteret and Lord Merton. The priests who spoke to them wore the same impassive look, spoke in the same low murmur, but whereas Sophie had appeared to be replying willingly – or at any rate voluntarily – to her interrogator, both Lord Carteret and Lord Merton seemed under some compulsion, which they were at pains to resist.

Then the tall priest repeated his ritual gesture, and Gray was suddenly freed from his enforced silence. He could not help at once inquiring of his captor, 'What is the name of your song-spell?'

'We do not deal in *spells*.' The priest accorded the syllable all the contempt with which another man might speak the word *night-soil*. 'This is the power of Apollo Coelispex, which his chosen exercise by his favour.' And seeming to recollect that Gray and not he was under interrogation, he demanded a full accounting of the events of Oxford and of the royal ball.

This Gray was happy to supply. The chosen of Apollo listened in earnest silence; when the tale was done, he looked hard at Gray and demanded, 'What part did you play in last evening's display of disloyalty, which Lord Carteret has characterised as an attempted rebellion?'

Gray, startled, said, 'None whatsoever!'

The priest gave a brief, terse nod, declared himself satisfied, and, by a murmured phrase and some gesture that Gray could never afterwards remember, silenced his latest victim once more before moving on to the next.

At last the priests, having questioned all those present, returned to the top of the room. Here they conferred, briefly and in apparent silence, after which the eldest of them turned to face the King. 'Apollo, Watcher of the Heavens, has deigned to render us his verdict,' he intoned, in the most formal and florid Latin Gray had ever encountered outside the pages of Gaius Aegidius, 'and it is now in our power to reveal to Your Majesty the truth of this unfortunate affair.'

They had reasoned correctly, it appeared, on the subject of Lord Carteret's motivations. The notion of an alliance with the Iberian

Emperor had been his own more than King Henry's, and he had taken Laora's departure with the infant Princess to heart for strategic reasons that, in the intervening years, had grown gradually more personal.

'Lord Carteret had many plans for the furthering of such an alliance,' the priest explained, 'any of which, in his view, must have been jeopardised by any such devolution of powers as His Majesty has lately been contemplating, in the provinces of Cymru and Breizh. Iberia is a valuable ally, but empires do not become such by respecting the borders of their neighbours' possessions. What might the Emperor offer the Duke of Breizh, in return for turning the military forces newly under his control in another direction?'

The outraged exclamations of the Breizhek contingent were silenced with a look.

'To discredit His Majesty required no very great effort on Carteret's part. The kingdom had embraced Queen Edwina and rejoiced in the arrival of each of her sons, hale and hearty and, best of all, male. The succession was not in doubt. No good could come of wishing the Princess back again; surely, if she were not dead, she must have reappeared by now. To seek her was throwing good coin after bad; what manner of king spends his time seeking a dead girl-child to the neglect of his living sons? The more Carteret secretly encouraged His Majesty's search – while meanwhile the Queen and her brother openly protested it – the more the kingdom began to doubt.'

Gray felt vaguely that he ought to derive some intellectual satisfaction from this confirmation of so much of his own prior reasoning, but could not.

'Carteret had long planned to arrange His Majesty's death, and take advantage of the general doubts as to his competence to install himself as regent to Prince Edward, but he wished very much to avoid the disruption of an assassination, even one which he could safely blame on some unconnected party. He had already consulted a healer, Lord Spencer, who could tell him only that poisons exist to mimic a natural death. But a mage of Merlin College, having the run of the most comprehensive magickal library in the kingdom, surely could discover what those poisons are and how to create one. Lord Merton knew of this interest on Carteret's part and befriended Appius Callender as a means to gain access to that library; only later did he discover, because Callender is foolish and boastful, that he had another card to play.

'Callender's apparently absurd claim to be harbouring the lost Princess Royal,' the priest continued, 'presented an opportunity too perfect to ignore. Having confirmed that the girl existed, and could at least pass for the Princess – he did not greatly care for the truth of her claim, you understand, for at worst he could credibly argue that her parents' magicks were latent in her and might be expected to resurface in a later generation – Carteret recognised that by furnishing the promised bride at last, he could avoid months of tedious negotiations and attempts to arrive at an equally acceptable quid pro quo. Moreover, he would be giving up something on which, by this time, no one appeared to place much value; best of all, he would have his revenge upon Queen Laora by foiling her scheme as she had once foiled his. In fact, of course, Callender's claim was perfectly true.

'The poison itself presented some difficulties. Chief among these were its long maturation period – in excess of two months – and the requirement that the blood used in its manufacture be added directly from a beating human heart. Carteret had no wish to take responsibility for this aspect of his plan; eventually it fell to Callender, who delegated it to two students whom he trusted, one of whom you see before you.' With a long finger, the priest indicated Woodville. 'These men recruited others, among them this man.' The finger swung towards Gray. 'There were three others, one of whom perished in the course of the expedition; only Henry Taylor and Alfric Woodville, however, knew the nature of their errand. To their credit, the heart with which they returned, eventually, to Merlin College belonged to a man already condemned to death for killing his wife and son.'

Gray was not as much comforted by this as he might have expected, though at least it did obviate the lurking nightmare-image of Woodville and Taylor with their hands in the bloodied chest of a dead child.

The priest reported Gray's frantic flight to the College, Gautier's death as witnessed by Woodville – as Crowther had suggested to Gray, an unlucky accident that no one present could have prevented – and the Professor's decision to protect his own reputation by laying the blame for the entire debacle on Gray.

'Carteret is a cautious man; Callender, in his way, is cautious also. While Carteret insisted on meeting the putative Princess to judge her fitness for his purposes, and on testing the efficacy of Callender's poison, Callender – though drawn to Carteret's plan for its own sake, as an indication of his importance in the world, and for the opportunity it offered of exchanging his troublesome stepdaughter for what seemed a guarantee of future advantage – demanded a reward of his own: he wished to be Master of Merlin College, and Lord Halifax stood in his way.

'The test of the poison – which is to say, the murder of Lord Halifax – was to take place after the beginning of the Samhain term, when the College would be busy and the Fellows disinclined to brangle over the election of a new Master. Callender commissioned Mr Woodville, who has what is apparently a well-justified reputation as a forger, to create a letter purportedly from Lord Halifax, suggesting Callender as his successor.

'Unfortunately, several events took place during the College's Long Vacation which led to alterations in both of these plans.

The first was Mr Marshall's inconvenient failure to perish in an "accident" which Callender had arranged for him to suffer in the Temple of Neptune at Kerandraon; instead, the accident befell Miss Joanna Callender, whose life Mr Marshall subsequently saved. The second was his theft of two letters written by Lord Carteret and a portion of his personal diary, copies of which were later deciphered by Mr Marshall, Mrs Marshall, and Master Everard Alcuin, also of Merlin College. The third was that Mrs Marshall – Miss Callender, as she then was, and of course originally the Princess Edith Augusta – discovered herself to possess considerable magickal talent, and the fourth was that, as a result of these circumstances, Madame Maëlle de Morbihan' – here the priest nodded at Mrs Wallis – 'determined that Callender Hall was no longer a safe refuge for the Princess Royal, and therefore aided and abetted Mr Marshall and Miss Callender in fleeing to England.'

The priest paused and looked about him as if to judge the effect of his words on his various listeners.

As Master Alcuin had surmised, the Professor and Lord Merton had killed Lord Halifax – the poison had been in his wine – several days earlier than planned because they feared he might after all take Gray's warning to heart. The Professor had been in bad odour with his co-conspirators as a result of Sophie's disappearance, and the noisy catastrophe of Lord Halifax's death persuaded them that he had become a liability to their cause, but he remained their best chance of locating Sophie.

At length the priest's narrative arrived at the feast of Samhain. 'The death of Lord Halifax,' he said, 'had proved to Carteret's satisfaction that the poison – which is of Greek origin, incidentally, though found in a Breton book – could produce the appearance of a natural death. This was essential to his scheme, for he meant not only to murder King Henry but to discredit him utterly.

Also essential was another property of the poison: if given in the suggested dose, it will kill its victim approximately one half-hour after it is ingested. In this case, the dose was to be administered in the chalice holding the *vinum primum*, which would pass through thousands of hands on its way to the altar but from which no one else would dare to drink.

'The King would drink from the cup, then pour the libation; then he would continue the rite, to the final offering – the cake made from the first wheat, barley, and oats harvested from the royal lands – and ask the gods to show their acceptance of his prayers on behalf of his kingdom, by answering in the affirmative his closing plea: *Grant that I may lead my people another year in prosperity and peace.* From the *libamen* to the close of the rite takes, in ordinary circumstances, approximately one half-hour; Lord Carteret's plan, then – understood and condoned by all of his co-conspirators – was for His Majesty's heart to stop within moments of his plea for the gods' favour.'

The priest, so far utterly impassive, now turned to look at Lord Carteret. Gray could no longer see the priest's face, but he could see Lord Carteret's, which was pale and slightly green. 'The gods' will is not yours to bend to your own, nor is it yours to mock,' the priest said. Then he turned once more to the King and inclined his head. 'Your Majesty.'

The royal family and the King's mage excepted, it was impossible that anyone present should be surprised by Apollo's verdict; but for these six, though even they must have had their suspicions, the shock was all too real. The Princes stared; Queen Edwina wailed, 'Edric! Oh, Edric!' and fell sobbing into Prince Edward's arms. Sophie longed to offer some comfort, some word of understanding – but surely she was the last person in the kingdom whose attentions the Queen might welcome. Released from the priests' spell, she and Gray and Joanna had instinctively crowded together, and in Joanna's tightly folded arms, in the tense pressure of Gray's hand on her shoulder, Sophie felt their sympathy with her unexpressed dismay.

The King swayed on his feet for just a moment, passing his hand over his eyes as though to expunge a nightmare vision. But immediately squaring his shoulders and straightening his back, he gravely thanked the priests, adding, 'We shall not forget the service rendered here by the chosen of Apollo Coelispex.'

The eldest priest smiled thinly. 'See that Your Majesty does not.'

The verdict had been rendered. The Kergabet party were exonerated of any suspicion; Lord Carteret and his companions, their plans and intentions laid bare, were declared guilty of high treason and, prisoned still in silence, would now be taken from this place to attend their fate. Unable to protest the verdict aloud, they maintained a posture of dignity in defeat – all but the Professor, who paced up and down, gesticulating, and his protégé, who continued to sulk.

It might be, Sophie reflected soberly, that she would never again see any of them alive.

The holy men bowed in valediction, with no more genuine deference than before, but their disdain seemed no longer to trouble His Majesty. 'Captain Prichard,' he said, 'you will summon the rest of your men and escort these prisoners to the Tower; Vaucourt, you will go with them and put in place the necessary magickal precautions . . .'

Lord de Vaucourt, who must have been intimately acquainted with most of the conspirators, was pale and tight-lipped, but he did not presume to question the King's orders. There was silence for some moments, but for the Queen's despairing sobs.

Sophie could bear the sound no longer; shaking off Gray's restraining hand, she half ran the few steps that now separated her from her stepmother. The Crown Prince frowned at her; Prince Roland smiled – but his welcome, she saw, was for Joanna, only half a pace behind her.

'Your Royal Highness,' said Sophie, 'I am most dreadfully sorry . . .'

Edwina raised her blotched, reddened face from her son's shoulder; her expression was transformed, from bewilderment to bitter hatred. 'This madness is *your* doing,' she choked. 'Yours and your gods-accursèd mother's. Why must you come here? Why could not you leave us in peace? Why—?'

'*Mother!*' Prince Edward's voice quivered with indignation. 'Her High—The Pr—She has saved Father's life – all our lives perhaps – and she and her friends are Father's *guests* . . .' The Queen staggered away, into the arms of her younger sons, and the Crown Prince turned to Sophie a face pink with embarrassment. 'I do apologise, most sincerely, for my mother's behaviour,' he said. 'I beg you will not take offence. She does not know what she is saying.'

'Of course she does,' said Joanna, impatient. 'And—'

'And I should not think of taking offence.' Sophie trod meaningly on her sister's toes. 'She has had a most dreadful shock. I should feel just the same in her place. And so should you, Joanna,' she added, sotto voce.

Joanna rolled her eyes.

'Ned!' This from Prince Roland, who darted back from some distance to chivvy his brother into action. 'Ned, do come along. Harry and I have persuaded her that she can do no more good here, but we shall want you to sing her to sleep.'

Edward seeming about to embark on an elaborate farewell, Roland tugged him away by the arm; a moment later they were gone, in the wake of little Prince Henry and the Queen.

'You had much better have held your tongue,' said Joanna.

Sophie sighed and shook her head. 'I cannot blame her,' she

said. 'But I could not stand there like a stone when she was in such distress.'

They turned back again to see the King conferring in quiet earnest with Sieur Germain and Master Alcuin, apparently quite oblivious to the scene just past.

His Majesty had, of course, to do his duty. But Sophie felt that she must have liked her father a great deal better, had he instead thought first of comforting his wife.

CHAPTER XXXIV

In Which Sophie Makes Up Her Mind

Captain Prichard returned with a round dozen guardsmen, men of impeccable discipline whose eyes widened only slightly when they understood the nature of their errand. From the prisoners' expressions – her stepfather's particularly – Sophie guessed that their escort would have good reason to be thankful for their enforced silence.

With the prisoners' departure, His Majesty's tension and determination seemed abruptly to desert him – and with them, all awareness of his being observed. He sank into the ornate chair – meant to evoke the Royal Throne, Sophie supposed – at the top of the audience chamber, like a wilting autumn daisy, and dropped his head into his hands, and wept.

His guests, no longer prisoners except of custom, looked at one another in alarm, and knew not what they ought to do.

'Edwina,' Sophie heard her father say, on a sort of quiet sob.

'She is—' she began to reply, only to recollect that she had not the least idea.

'Roland and Ned and Harry have taken her away and put her to bed,' said Joanna, with perfect self-possession. Sophie bit back a shocked exclamation and heard a strangled laugh from one of the men; the King seemed oblivious, however.

'They are twins, you know, she and her brother,' he said, addressing Joanna. His eyes, damp and pink-rimmed, were very blue; for the rest, he might have aged thirty years since Sophie last beheld his face. 'All manner of torments await him in Hades, I hope, to reward him for involving her in this business! I thought him a man of better sense.'

He urged them to consider themselves his guests, but – to Sophie's relief – stopped short of an outright command, saying only, 'You will undertake not to leave London for the present,' before at last taking himself away.

For some moments Sophie and her friends blinked at one another in silence. At last Sieur Germain ventured, 'What say you all? For myself, of course, I had much rather return to Carrington-street, but . . .'

The others, Sophie found, were all looking at her. 'His Majesty was kind enough to the three of us,' she admitted, 'but I should like to go—' She had been about to say, *to go home.* 'Jenny will be frantic,' she said instead, for indeed Jenny had had nothing for nearly two days but written messages of reassurance and strict instructions not to stir from home.

'We are agreed, then,' Sieur Germain smiled, and the whole room let out its breath in relief.

They now separated to make their preparations for departure. A steward appeared as if from nowhere to conduct the ladies to their borrowed apartments, and another whom Sieur Germain dispatched to give orders that his carriage be readied for their journey, and who politely informed him that four members of His Majesty's household guard were to accompany them.

Sophie would not again be parted from her husband, however; ignoring Mrs Wallis's raised eyebrows and Joanna's knowing grin, she dragged him after her into the bedchamber, communicating with Joanna's, which had briefly been hers. Hardly had the door closed behind them when, turning, she was lifted from her feet, caught up in so tight an embrace that she could scarce draw breath. 'Oh, Sophie,' Gray whispered, his breath warm against her neck. 'My Sophie . . .'

Quite unable to speak, she contrived to make a sort of strangled squeak in reply, at which, with a startled apology, he set her on her feet again and let her go.

At once she put her arms about him and leant her head against his chest, merely for the familiar pleasure of feeling his heart beat under her ear.

'Do you know,' Gray said, 'have you any notion, *cariad*, how near we came to disaster?'

'I was dreadfully afraid,' she admitted. 'But every word they spoke was falsehood, and we were in the right. His Majesty must have seen reason in the end . . .'

'And if he had not chosen to seek the truth?' Gray reminded her gently. 'If he had taken the word of his trusted advisors and dismissed our own, as he might so easily have done?'

Sophie shivered, and turned away to begin gathering up her few belongings. The sight of her heavy cloak – how had that come here? – in the bright, cold sunshine of a winter's afternoon made her feel doubly foolish in her Samhain evening finery, sponged and pressed with great care, while she slept, by some no doubt bewildered laundry-maid.

She and Gray were alone now for almost the first time since her disastrous outburst. His words echoed in her mind: *Whatever dreadful thing you believe yourself to have done, will be no less dreadful, being hidden* . . . She had resolved already to take the first opportunity of telling him the truth. She *must* tell him, and at once; it was the height of foolishness, after all their misadventures together, to suppose that there could be any danger in doing so.

The difficulty was that she could think of no way to begin.

'Sophie.' His hand on her shoulder startled her so that she dropped the cloak on the floor. A murmured *adeste* brought the tangle of heavy fabric up into Gray's hands; then, laying the cloak over a chair, he drew Sophie against his side and looked earnestly down into her face: '*Cariad*, will you not tell me your trouble?'

Sophie turned her face away. 'I have remembered,' she said softly, 'how my mother died . . .'

They had been in Carrington-street less than three days, under the affectionate care of Jenny and her household, who in their own ways echoed the flurries of doting attention, and the storms of tearful recrimination, alternately bestowed by their mistress; and all the family were gathered in the breakfast-parlour when they were interrupted – with the utmost civility – by one of the guardsmen whom King Henry had insisted upon seconding to the Kergabets' house while Sophie was resident there.

The chief of his commission was to deliver a letter from His Majesty to Sieur Germain, acquainting him with the details of the traitors' fate. This Sieur Germain instantly unsealed and read through, whilst the others watched him in an expectant silence broken only by the clink of Joanna's knife and fork against her plate. Treveur had brought up a second letter for Mrs Wallis – *Cousin Maëlle*, Sophie reminded herself for the hundredth time, to little effect – and a third which, circling the dining-table, he silently deposited beside Sophie's place. She looked at the neatly written direction, *To Mrs G. Marshall*, and slipped the letter off the table and into her lap, in hopes that it might go unremarked.

At last Sieur Germain laid by the sheaf of heavy paper and looked down the table at Jenny, wearing an expression of disquiet.

'Whatever is the matter?' Joanna demanded, putting down her fork. Sieur Germain appeared not to hear her.

Sophie glanced across the table at Gray, whose face expressed profound confusion, and back at Jenny, who looked alarmed. 'My dear,' said the latter, 'please, tell us – what does His Majesty write?' Her face paled a little more. 'He – he has not . . . had a change of heart?'

Sieur Germain blinked. 'Not in the way you mean, my love,' he replied after a moment, and took up the pages again. 'Listen . . .'

The King's letter used the formal Latin of a royal communication. The circumlocutory language, the long periods, were so difficult to follow by ear, and the narrative meandered so in setting out its argument, that Sophie did not at once understand the letter's import; once grasped, however, its message was unmistakeable.

The charge was high treason, and the penalty death by beheading, for these traitors so highly placed as to escape the indignity of the noose. Or so they had expected, from their knowledge of the law.

Indeed, William, Viscount Carteret, Lord President of the Privy Council – author and architect of the conspiracy – was to be executed in seven days' time. But for the rest – as also Henry Taylor of Merlin College, Oxford – the sentence of death was commuted to that of imprisonment in the Tower of London.

His Majesty had been moved to this display of clemency, his letter explained, by the relative youth of some of the conspirators, the prior faithful service of others, and, most particularly, by their role as instruments of the gods' benevolence in restoring the lost Princess to her family.

Sophie looked down at her plate.

Sieur Germain and all his family, the letter continued, were desired to wait upon His Majesty on the fifteenth day of November, when a great public feast-day would be held to give thanks to the kingdom's many patron deities for the gift of His Majesty's life and the defeat of the traitors.

'He has gone mad,' Mrs Wallis said at last, wonderingly. 'Truly he has gone mad, and believes himself inviolable. Cannot he see that he has enemies enough?'

'He is King of Britain, by favour of the kingdom's own gods,' Sophie objected. 'It is his right—'

'He is mad, or a fool,' said Joanna flatly. 'The Queen has begged him to spare her brother's life, I suppose, and Amelia has cried a few pretty tears, for the sake of my father—'

'Perhaps, Joanna,' Gray interjected mildly, 'His Majesty wishes to show his subjects that he is no vengeful tyrant, and perhaps he is sensible of the risk of making martyrs of your father and those others whom he believes to have acted at Lord Carteret's behest.'

Sophie nodded; whatever the consequences might be, she could not be sorry that both Amelia and the Queen should find their sufferings diminished.

'That may well be,' Sieur Germain said, 'and such an impulse does him credit, but it is susceptible of other interpretations, Graham, that we may all one day have cause to regret. As for His Majesty's other decision . . .'

Glancing along the table, Sophie judged the rest equally at sea. 'Which decision?' she enquired.

Sieur Germain looked at her, and then at the letter in his hand. 'His Majesty finds himself bereft of his closest and most trusted advisors,' he said slowly. 'He professes himself in need of wise, sober, and impartial counsel, and . . .' A long pause, in which once more he looked down the table at Jenny, as though to read in her face the answer to some unasked question. 'He wishes *me* to offer him such, in the capacity of Lord President of the Privy Council.'

Sophie stared.

Master Alcuin was the first to recover. 'It is a sensible course,' he said, tugging thoughtfully at the end of his beard. 'A man of good birth – but not too high – and of good intellect, who has proved his loyalty so incontrovertibly, and in so practical a fashion . . .'

Harry and Bertha came in to clear the plates and, finding all but Joanna's still nearly full, went quietly away again.

'The Normand faction will be furious.' Mrs Wallis sounded (thought Sophie) unnecessarily smug. 'And all those stolid Saozneg nobles too. Has he considered that, do you suppose?'

'You speak as though I meant to accept the appointment, Lady Maëlle,' said Sieur Germain, with the shade of a smile.

'Do you not?' Joanna asked. To all appearances, she had forgot already her denigration of His Majesty's intellect.

'I am as little qualified for such a post as any man could be,' he replied, and, when the others protested, he reminded them (though with a little return of his usual aplomb) how little he had lived in Town, how seldom involved himself in politics or appeared at Court.

'On the contrary,' said Master Alcuin, letting go of his beard and leaning forward. 'It is for all these reasons, I think, that – Old Breton as you are – His Majesty does not fear to trust you now.'

'You think as I do, then.' Sieur Germain was nodding slowly, his expression thoughtful. Had he been intending all along to accept the post? 'It will mean living much more in Town, and less at Kergabet,' he went on – speaking to Jenny, now, as though no person else were present. 'We should be forced to live a great deal less quietly than we have done, and you, my dear, should be under constant siege, by ladies whose husbands seek preferment at Court . . .'

'But we should be in a position to do a great deal of good,' said Jenny, decisively, 'and it has been some time, I think, since last His Majesty had the counsel of any who wished him well.'

His Majesty's second letter was read in the morning-room after breakfast, when Master Alcuin and Sieur Germain had retired to the library to write letters of their own.

'Well, Sophia,' Mrs Wallis announced, 'did not I call your father mad this morning? I am sure you will doubt it no longer, when I have told you what he writes.'

Gray looked up from his book, and Sophie from the game of chess into which Joanna had dragooned her, when she would have joined him on the sofa; her cousin shook her head in apparent disbelief, and Jenny said, 'Lady Maëlle, you would perhaps be wiser to speak less plainly . . .'

Joanna frowned. 'I do wish,' she said, capturing Sophie's priestess with quite unnecessary force, 'that people would *say* what is in their letters, and not make such a great mystery of it.'

Mrs Wallis, instead of reproving her, began to laugh. 'Well, then, Joanna,' she said, 'here it is: your father being no longer suitable for the post of guardian, you and your sister Amelia are made wards of the Crown, so as you remain unmarried – which is to say, that His Majesty has taken upon himself the responsibility of the most disobedient young woman in all his kingdom, and the most empty-headed.'

Joanna stared.

'He goes on to enquire whether I have any suggestion to make on behalf of either of you, as to where you might like best to live for the present—'

'But that is all settled!' Joanna looked from Mrs Wallis to Jenny, with some alarm. 'That is – I have no notion what Amelia may like – but *I* am to stay with Jenny.'

Sophie looked at Gray and bit back a laugh; was this not exactly what they had settled as ideal, during one of those long evenings spent debating and deciding the futures of all their acquaintance?

'Of course, Joanna, you are most welcome,' Jenny was saying, with a merry smile, 'but you may find our life here fuller of tiresome morning callers and offering much less of intrigue and excitement than has been true of late . . .'

Joanna grinned. 'You will need my help, then, to amuse you. And if I cannot live with Sophie—'

She stopped, putting her hand to her lips, and at once all eyes were on Sophie. But it was the work of a moment to turn all this curiosity away – this time entirely without magick. 'Cousin Maëlle,' she said, quietly, carefully, 'have you thought where *you* will make your home?'

'For the moment,' Mrs Wallis replied, not in the least discountenanced, 'I shall stay here, where I am most needed; Joanna may be a most amusing companion, but her training in midwifery, I regret to say, has been sadly neglected.'

Jenny was trying unsuccessfully to hide a grin behind her hand.

'As far as my future is concerned,' Mrs Wallis continued imperturbably, 'I have had a dozen invitations, at the least, since arriving in Town; you need not concern yourself for *my* welfare, I think.'

Sophie thought of the unread letter secreted in her work-basket. Whether it contained some similar invitation, or quite the reverse, there was no knowing, and she could not settle in her mind which possibility she most dreaded. *I used to pity Joanna so, because Mama would not love her; and now I should give anything to be in her place . . .*

Well. Anything but Gray.

'How dare he? How *dare* he!'

Woken abruptly in the half light before dawn, Gray saw Sophie fling a sheaf of papers from her with such force that the row of twittering sparrows on the Carrington-street windowsill took flight in alarm. 'How dare who, and what?' he demanded ungrammatically, rubbing his eyes, as the pages settled to the floor. 'What is the matter, *cariad*?'

She turned to him with the ashen face and black, blazing eyes of violent wrath. 'He—How can he think—? To suggest that I might choose – that *anything* might induce me to—' She held out one hand, and the scattered pages reassembled themselves between her fingers and thumb; then, furious, she thrust them at Gray.

Startled, he rubbed his eyes again with his free hand. Had he indeed seen her execute a wordless summoning? Some instinct of self-preservation led him to set the question aside for a more propitious moment, and instead peruse what proved to be a letter to Sophie from her father, written two days since.

'He may perhaps misunderstand the nature of our attachment,' he ventured, having read the missive through.

There was nothing in its intent, he felt sure, but affection for Sophie and a wish to improve her circumstances; the method, however, plainly would not answer.

Did not Sophie wish to know her brothers? His Majesty enquired. They were eager to be acquainted with her. Did she not wish to be launched into the best society by the Queen?

Gray snorted.

Should she not like to have at her disposal the extensive library of the Royal Palace, its renowned gardens and generously furnished music-rooms? To study with the finest masters of music, drawing, riding, and dancing?

Hmm.

Lastly, His Majesty's dearest Sophia was assured that no effort or expense should be spared in releasing her with all possible speed from the marriage into which she had been forced by Lady Maëlle's fears for her and Lord Carteret's machinations, and that no future alliance should be entered into without her express prior approval.

Ah. Now I see. But enough of the old Gray Marshall remained to feel astonished and grateful that such a woman as Sophie should be outraged at the thought of giving him up.

'Should you not like to see the Palace library?' he said, seeking a less inflammatory approach to the subject. 'And the harp your mother played, and the gardens where she must have walked—?'

'Have you forgotten how my mother came to leave that harp, and those gardens, and that library? Perhaps *he* has – but *I* have not, nor will such an offer as *this* ever induce me to consider myself his debtor. I have saved his life; I have sworn my allegiance, when – apparently – I might have led a rebellion; let him be satisfied, and leave us in peace.'

'But, *cariad*,' Gray objected, 'he makes no mention of any debt on *your* part; quite the contrary. He wishes only to know you better, I think, though I must concede that he has not chosen the best means to effect a reconciliation . . .'

Sophie folded her arms, shivering; the worst of her anger had evidently burnt itself out. Gray reached out a hand to her, and she crept into bed again.

'It is not only that,' she admitted, once settled in the curve of his arm, her head against his shoulder. 'I cannot help thinking, you know, what insult I should be offering to Queen Edwina, and how much she must dislike me; can he not see how unpleasant it must be for all of us – and for her most of all?'

She paused for breath, and Gray was about to suggest that the Queen might one day come to appreciate her merits, when she went on: 'But the worst of it . . . it is no wonder, I suppose – I was a babe in arms when last he saw me – but to offer me a home, as though I were still a child – to suggest that I am anxious to be released from our marriage—'

'I am sure your father meant no insult, *cariad*. He has drawn a wrong conclusion, but not an unreasonable one, in the circumstances.'

'Perhaps so, but the insult is none the less for being unintended. He might have *asked* me why I married you – might he not? Assuming, that is, that he believes me capable of knowing my own mind.'

There could be no arguing with this.

'How am I to accept his assurances that I shall be allowed to choose my own husband, when he cannot see that I have done so already? I am to take him at his word, after – after *everything*?'

'Sophie.' Gray shifted a little, so as to look down into her face. 'Sophie, your father loves you; a blind man could see that he loves you, and loved your mother, and that he bitterly regrets the choice he once made. I am sure, indeed, he felt there *was* no choice. You know very well that the monarch must sometimes do what the man abhors.'

'And what of it?' A challenge – though she was not unaffected by this view of the question. 'It is all very well for him to be sorry, but his regret can do no good to anyone – can it? If it cannot make him consider his wife's feelings or her dignity, or respect his sons – if it cannot show him that I am a woman grown and not the child he once sold away—'

Sophie's words were swallowed in a choking sob, and she scrubbed at her eyes with white-knuckled fists. At last she drew a ragged breath and sat up, wrapping her arms about her drawn-up knees.

Gray laid one hand on the curve of her back. 'You need not go and live in the Royal Palace, if you do not wish it,' he said. 'Your father knows better now, surely, than to attempt to command you. But . . .' He paused, considering, and after a moment went on: 'You spoke once, long ago, of wishing for a brother; should you not like to be better acquainted with the three you have? And a father who loves you, and wishes to know you better – this is not a gift to be lightly thrown away . . .'

Sophie turned and put her hand against his cheek, and for some time sat silent and still.

'You are right, of course,' she said at last, with a sigh. 'He means well.'

'Of course he does,' said Gray, encouragingly. 'And I am sure, when you have properly explained the situation—'

There was a discreet knock at the door: young Daisy, leaving morning tea on a tray outside their door.

Both of them released their wards; Gray threw back the bedcovers and crossed the room to retrieve the tray.

'I am sure,' he repeated, setting the tea-things down on the dressing-table, 'he will be perfectly satisfied that you made the choice yourself, and are happy in it.'

Sophie's expression brightened as she considered this, which encouraged him to add, 'You have only to tell him the whole story from the beginning – how you fell madly in love with me from our first meeting, and nothing would do for you but to marry me at once—' He broke off, laughing, when Sophie flung a cushion at his head, an expression of wifely ire rather spoilt, however, by her subsequently bouncing up out of bed and kissing him.

'We must take thought, however,' he said; 'before we have quite exhausted the hospitality of my sister and brother, I must endeavour to find some gainful employment, so we may have something to live on, and somewhere to live.'

'But – Gray—' Sophie looked stricken. 'Will you not go back to Oxford, to finish your studies? After defying your own father, at such a cost, you will not let – *this*—'

'Merlin cannot be my home now, Sophie,' he replied, as gently as he could. 'Even were my petition accepted and my place assured – which is by no means certain – I should be no more willing to live in College without you, than you to play the dutiful royal daughter without me. A married Fellow is one thing; a married student is quite another. But our friends will see to it that we are not without books, you know, and I hope we shall neither of us give up our studies . . .'

Sophie was silent a long moment, gazing into the banked fire.

Then she slipped out of bed again to stand before him. '*Ubi tu Gaius, ego Gaia*,' she said, looking up into his eyes.

Above this echo of their marriage-vows, Gray's ears rang for just a moment with the high, clear singing of many voices. He smiled down at Sophie. She returned the smile, so that all her face blossomed into exquisite beauty; then she bent her head and began to pour out the tea.

CHAPTER XXXV

Thereafter

In London, the twelfth day of November dawned grey and damp. The sentence of death had been carried out on Viscount Carteret, who had once had the ear of King Henry; the feast of thanksgiving was yet to come; and Sophie and Gray were bidden to a private audience with their King. Sophie's many letters to him ought surely to have made her position clear; it was difficult to guess, therefore, what had prompted this insistence on a meeting. But here they sat, waiting to be summoned into His Majesty's presence.

Gray was lost in thought, pondering the half-mad idea that had begun to possess his idle moments. Sophie, he knew, dreaded some renewal of her father's pleas to her, to 'return to the bosom of her family'; she knew that her refusal to play the fêted, cosseted Princess puzzled and confounded her father. Nor was either of them comforted by Sophie's growing conviction that the King valued her chiefly for her resemblance to her mother.

A steward emerged into the corridor where they waited. 'Mr Marshall?' he said. 'His Majesty would speak privately with you.'

Gray gave Sophie's hand a reassuring squeeze and rose to follow the steward and make his leg before the King.

'Mr Marshall,' the King began, 'I have been considering your future.'

Gray blinked.

'First, however, we must consider my daughter's.'

He sat back in his chair and studied Gray, who returned his gaze as calmly as he could manage. There was something in the King's tone which, though he could not have said precisely why, he did not much like.

'Mr Marshall, let us be frank with one another,' said His Majesty. 'I have no wish to give offence, nor am I in danger of forgetting the very great service which you and your friends have rendered to your kingdom, both in exposing and frustrating a most malicious plot and in rescuing the Princess Royal from the hands of the traitors. I shall not insult you by suggesting that your motives in entering into this marriage were of an ambitious or mercenary nature—'

'I thank you for that courtesy, Your Majesty.'

'I would point out, however,' the King continued, smoothly ignoring this interruption, and Gray's rather less than courteous tone, 'that to an impartial observer, the circumstances suggest that Lady Maëlle chose you as her . . . instrument in this matter rather because you happened to be at hand, than because the match suited either my daughter or yourself, and that, the marriage having accomplished the purpose for which Lady Maëlle designed it, there can be no necessity for its perpetuation.'

'Sir—'

'You and my daughter are both very young, Mr Marshall, with all your lives before you; it seems hard that you should be tethered to one another by a choice made in such haste, and made by others—'

'Your Majesty.'

The King closed his mouth and raised his eyebrows.

'With respect, sir, I fear you are labouring under a grave misapprehension,' said Gray, choosing his words with care. 'I did not offer marriage to Sophie at Lady Maëlle's instigation – though

I do not deny that I hoped to defeat Lord Carteret's plans for her, such as we understood them to be. I wished to marry your daughter, sir, because I love her.'

This the King evidently had not expected; his eyebrows rose further, and he made no reply.

'And though I cannot speak for Sophie in this matter,' Gray went on, doggedly, 'she has certainly given me to understand that she accepted me for the same reason.'

His Majesty appeared to consider this idea.

'You are a talented mage, I am told, Mr Marshall,' he said at length. 'It would not be beyond your powers to persuade a young woman, innocent of the world, to believe herself in love?'

'Beyond my powers? I cannot say,' said Gray, clenching both hands to steady his voice. Any man might be overcareful of his daughter's welfare; an accusation of this kind was another thing entirely. 'I should as soon exercise persuasion of that kind upon any woman as use my talent to kill a man for his purse. Sir.'

'Pray do not take offence, Mr Marshall!' the King exclaimed. 'I do not accuse you of malicious intent. It had occurred to me, however, that a man – or any other person closely concerned in the matter – might resort to such means of persuasion in service of some unexceptionable goal. To reconcile a woman of delicate sensibilities to a marriage of necessity, for example.'

'Sir, with respect—'

The heavy doors crashed open, and between them stood Sophie, pale with alarm. 'Gray!' she cried, flinging herself towards him at a run.

He advanced to meet her and folded her tightly into his arms. 'Sophie—'

'What has he been saying to you?' she demanded, pushing him a little away from her so as to look up, searchingly, into his face.

'I believe your father wishes to know what – since it cannot have been my fortune, my prospects, or my looks – could have induced you to marry me.'

'But – but I have told him again and again – I have written so many letters, explaining—'

'Your protestations, however,' said Gray gently, controlling his anger for her sake, 'might have been made under the influence of some spell that made you believe you felt what you did not.'

Sophie stared up at him in bewilderment. He saw the moment when understanding dawned in the darkening of her eyes, and he felt it in the rigid tension of her shoulders under his hands.

She shook off his grip and turned, slowly, to face her father. 'This accusation is infamous, Your Majesty,' she said, in a voice that trembled. 'You insult my husband, and so insult me. I think we can have nothing more to say to one another.'

'Sophie—'

'*No*, Gray. We shall not stay here to be insulted and abused.' She caught his arm and tried to propel him through the door.

'A moment, Sophie. Sir,' said Gray quietly, standing fast despite her, and turning back to the King – who had risen from his seat and stood looking at Sophie in an agony of indecision. 'You have one last opportunity, I think, to begin to undo the damage you have done. Were I you, I should not waste it.'

The King cast him a glance in which opposing impulses were strangely mingled – hope and fear, gratitude and resentment. Then both turned their eyes to Sophie, who had halted on the threshold, staring at the floor.

'Sophia,' said the King, in a choked voice. 'The name your mother gave you. You are so very like her, my dear.' He swallowed, then drew breath. 'I would not repeat my errors. Sophia, do you indeed love this man?'

Sophie turned to look at Gray, and her furious eyes softened. 'I do,' she said firmly.

'And it is your determination to continue in this marriage, even if it should condemn you to penury? Yes, Mr Marshall,' he added, his gaze still on Sophie, 'you see I know all about you.'

'It is,' said Sophie.

'I am not altogether destitute, Your Majesty,' said Gray stiffly. 'I have—'

'I should not care if you were,' Sophie interrupted, catching his hands in hers, and holding his gaze.

'To say true, *cariad*, I had rather be your husband and a pauper than the richest man in the kingdom.'

'That is all very finely spoken,' said the King dryly. Gray gave a guilty start and tore his attention away from Sophie's luminous brown eyes. 'I should find you singing a different tune, I fancy, after a year's trial. However: you have both been punished enough through your involvement in this business; I think we shall not undertake the trial, for the present.'

They stood, hands clasped, and regarded him in puzzlement. What could this mean?

'Mr Marshall, your erstwhile tutor's property being forfeit for his treason, as you know, I have it in mind to grant you his Breton estate, in recognition of your service to your kingdom. It is not the very finest in the kingdom, to be sure,' he added, 'nor even in the country, but its possession certainly must serve to hedge you against, as you put it, destitution.'

It was a bewitching vision: to live amidst the beauties of that country, Sophie's country, almost within sight of the sea – to have that library for their own, and the pleasure of improving it – and surely such lands and wealth must win even Edmond Marshall's respect. But—

'But what of Miss Callender, and Jo – and Miss Joanna?'

'You know very well that they cannot be permitted to inherit, given their father's crime,' the King said. 'That does not mean, of course, that your house may not welcome what friends you choose, to live in it with you, or even in your stead.'

'I – I thank you, Your Majesty. Very much.'

'We both thank you, Your Majesty,' Sophie added in a small voice, 'for my sisters' sake.'

Gray understood her: how could she desire to be mistress of that house, where she had so long been a prisoner? 'I think, however,' he said, 'that we had rather not make our home there for the present. If – if I may make free, Your Majesty, to propose an alternative?'

The King sighed. 'By all means, name your price, Mr Marshall,' he said dryly.

Gray imagined the newly named Chief Privy Counsellor casting up his eyes.

'Recent events, as you know, have interrupted my studies,' he began, 'and Sophie has seen almost nothing of the world beyond the Pr—beyond our small corner of Breizh. Nor has she had opportunities to study as she ought. I should very much like to have my former place at Merlin College restored to me; but . . .' He hesitated a moment, very much aware of Sophie's hand in his; she had not authorised, not directly, the request he was about to make on her behalf, but if he did not press their joint victory now, would Fortune grant him another chance to do so?

'But Sophie must have a place also,' he said at last, and, ignoring her quick indrawn breath, hurried on: 'She has earned it, a thousand times over – besides her talent, she has all the makings of a thorough scholar – and though the Senior Fellows would refuse her at her own request, or mine, surely they cannot refuse an admission by royal fiat. I understand, Your Majesty, that it is not—'

But the King was waving a hand to quiet him. 'Of course, of course you are right,' he said. Gray could not conceal his astonishment. 'Your mother would have wished it,' His Majesty added, to Sophie. 'She was a scholar herself, you know, and dreamt of being another Lady Morgan one day, the sponsor of a college for clever young ladies. Perhaps you shall be her heiress in this as well. But, Sophia – Sophie – you will come and see your old father now and again, will you not?'

Sophie was pressed close against Gray's side; he could feel her pulse racing.

'I . . .' she began. She looked up at Gray, her face mirroring his own disbelief. Could it be? Such a gift to them both – to make a place for them – for both of them, together – where they most longed to be?

At last, squaring her shoulders, Sophie turned back to address the King. 'Yes,' she said, more firmly. 'Yes, Father, I shall.'

ACKNOWLEDGEMENTS

This book was the labour of a number of years, and an enormous number of people helped me along the way. I have the best family, friends, and colleagues anyone could ask for.

In particular, thanks to Alex Hunter, Kim Solga, and the Keyboard Scribblers (Beth Welsh, Sarah Makin, Emma Hall, Ava Leigh Fitzgerald, Julie Thompson) for concrit, first reading, brainstorming, and milkshake summits; to Sarah Makin, Kim Solga, and Beth Welsh for invaluable first-draft workshopping of specific scenes; to my beta readers, Roberta Barker, Anne Marie Corrigan, Tawnie Olson, Luisa Petroianu, Jeannie Scarfe, and Stephanie Sedgwick; and to my crack team of Latinistas – Kristen Chew, Patricia Larash, John Chew, and Michael Appleby – for very necessary Latin help. (All linguistic and other errors that remain are, of course, my own.)

Patricia Bray, Joshua Palmatier, and the Scribblers helped me write an effective query letter; Roberta Barker, Joshua Palmatier, Kim Solga, and Beth Welsh made my synopsis better. Thanks to Carleton Wilson, my website guy, and Nicole Hilton, who kindly took my author photos. The beautiful maps are the work of Cortney Skinner.

And thanks to my amazing agent, Eddie Schneider, and the rest of the team at JABberwocky Literary Agency; to my excellent editor, Jessica Wade, at Penguin/Ace and her able assistant, Isabel Farhi; to Amy J. Schneider for sharp-eyed copy-editing; to Christina Griffiths for the stunning cover; and to Michelle Kasper, Julia Quinlan, Erica Martirano, and the Ace/Roc publicity team for shepherding the book the rest of the way into your hands. Many thanks, also, to the team at Allison & Busby for bringing the books to UK readers.

Finally, gigantosaurus thanks to my far-flung and amazing family, who always believed I could do this even when I totally didn't, and especially to Alex and Shaina Hunter, who put up with my hogging the computer, keeping a plush skull on the desk, and muttering incessantly about my characters' inexplicable behaviour.